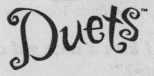

"So, do I kiss a nice girl on a first date?"

"I suppose it depends on whether she likes you." As if anyone in her right mind wouldn't like Cole, she thought.

"Come on, Tess. Teach me some nice-girl rules."

"Don't get smashed on the first date?"

"Good point, but if I were stone-cold sober, would you let me practice?"

"Cole, please..." Her heart was racing so hard she was afraid he'd hear it.

"I'll take that as a yes."

Once she would have done anything for a good-night kiss from him. Now she had a chance to see if he lived up to her fantasies.

The flesh around her mouth tingled as he gently touched it with his lips. His tongue slid between her teeth as he covered her mouth, drawing her into the best kiss of her whole dating career.

For more, turn to page 9

"You're safe with me."

Zack flashed Megan a devilish grin. "I won't even hit on you."

"We've established there's absolutely no attraction between us," she said in a severe voice that wavered slightly when he stepped toward her.

"Ultimately your goal is to settle down with a domestic type and raise kids," he said softly. "I'm not a candidate for that. Besides, we have a business arrangement. I don't have time for pleasure, otherwise..."

"Otherwise?"

"Otherwise I might be tempted to do this."

He leaned forward and brushed her lips with his.

"I wouldn't want you to be tempted," she said, but she wanted the wonderful tingling to go on and on.

"Don't worry, I'm not."

He moved a full step closer and lowered his head to hers.

For more, turn to page 197

HARLEQUIN DUETS

ISBN 0-373-44125-8

ONE BRIDE TOO MANY
Copyright © 2001 by Pamela Hanson and Barbara Andrews

ONE GROOM TO GO
Copyright © 2001 by Pamela Hanson and Barbara Andrews

One Bride Too Many

Jennifer Drew

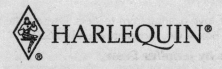

HARLEQUIN®

TORONTO • NEW YORK • LONDON
AMSTERDAM • PARIS • SYDNEY • HAMBURG
STOCKHOLM • ATHENS • TOKYO • MILAN • MADRID
PRAGUE • WARSAW • BUDAPEST • AUCKLAND

Dear Reader,

What could be better than one sexy, hunky hard-hat hero who wants like heck to avoid marriage? How about two?

Bad-boy twin brothers Cole and Zack Bailey are about to lose their bachelor status. They need to find nice-girl brides or risk their marriage-minded grandfather's wrath. It will take two special women to convince these reluctant grooms to head for the altar, and Tess Morgan and Megan Danbury are up to the task!

Cole's Ms. Right is a face from his past. He makes a deal with Tess for some matchmaking, but his real interest is in the matchmaker! Being reunited with a high school crush is an intriguing fantasy for us (Jennifer Drew is the pseudonym of mother and daughter Barbara Andrews and Pam Hanson) and provided inspiration for Cole's story.

Then there's Zack.... From the minute he creates chaos on the set of Megan's home-repair cable TV show, she's bothered and bewildered. They, too, strike a bargain...and then the sparks start to fly!

We hope you enjoy the results!

Jennifer Drew

P.S. We love hearing from readers. Please write to us at P.O. Box 4084, Morgantown, WV 26504.

Books by Jennifer Drew

HARLEQUIN DUETS
   7—TAMING LUKE
  18—BABY LESSONS
  45—MR. RIGHT UNDER HER NOSE

For Laura Huff Herring, Jody Myers Berry
and Sue Rozman Delia (1960–1998).
Nothing finer ever came out of the Motor City.

1

HE'D EAT SOME CAKE, kiss the bride and look for a virgin, maybe not in that order.

Cole Bailey pulled into a spot as far away from the sprawling Tudor-style building as possible. As an uninvited guest, he didn't want to make his pickup look conspicuous by using the Detroit country club's valet service.

This wasn't where he wanted to be. He'd been crazy to let a coin toss decide whether he or his twin brother, Zack, would be first to buckle under to their grandfather's unreasonable demand of marriage.

His immediate problem was to figure out a smooth way to crash the wedding reception of his mother's friend's niece. He drew a blank on her name, not surprising considering how mad he was at Marsh Bailey, his maternal grandfather and more recently evil nemesis.

The parking lot was crowded with enough high-ticket wheels to stock a ritzy dealership, but that was fine for him. Big receptions meant a lot of the bride's friends would be looking for a good time. There was nothing like a wedding to make shy girls bold and nice girls naughty. Unfortunately, the last thing he wanted right now was a fling. He wasn't here for a good time.

Darn! How could the old codger do this to the family? He and Zack had to marry nice girls and settle down, or their grandfather would sell his shares in the family business. That would leave controlling interest in Bailey Baby

Products in the hands of strangers on the board of directors. It didn't really matter to Zack and Cole, because they had great hopes for their construction firm, but their mother would be devastated. The company was her life now, and she ran it as well as her father ever had.

Only an autocrat like Marsh Bailey could believe the company would be better off with a male at the helm. He was deluding himself if he thought marriage would turn any of his three grandsons—the twins and their half brother, Nick—into management material.

Worse, how could Marsh do this to his daughter, his only child? Since their stepfather's death two years ago, Cole's mom lived for her job as CEO of Bailey Baby Products. To retain control of the business when her father was out of the picture, she needed votes from the stock that at least two of her sons stood to inherit. Nick was the lucky one. He was still in college, and Marsh hadn't started pressuring him to get married yet.

Cole rubbed his chin, which was smooth for a change because he'd taken the trouble to shave after work. He shrugged his shoulders, feeling confined by the jacket of his seldom-worn charcoal gray suit. Maybe all the hard manual labor he did trying to make a go of his and Zack's company had beefed up his shoulders. He ran his finger under the collar of his white dress shirt and loosened his conservative wine-colored tie a little.

He was twenty-eight years old and had spent his whole life trying to prove to his grandfather that he wasn't like his father, Stan Hayward—not that Cole had ever set eyes on the guy. Marsh had made sure of that. He'd sent Stan packing, threatening him with jail if he came near his pregnant seventeen-year-old daughter again. The Bailey surname was the one listed on the birth certificates.

Cole snorted derisively, but walked toward the clubhouse. He'd lost the flip to Zack with his own coin. He had to be the first to go wife-hunting, and he couldn't let his mother down—not that she even knew about this marital blackmail.

Marsh insisted his grandsons marry soon, and their brides had to be nice girls, his code word for virgins. Just because Grandad's own brother had messed up his life by marrying "a henna-haired hooker," the old man was paranoid about letting a bad girl—or in his daughter's case, a bad boy—into the family.

Cole stopped to admire one of the finest domestic sports cars ever to roll off the line in the Motor City, but he knew he was only procrastinating. He wanted to go to this reception like he wanted a case of poison ivy. Everything about weddings soured his disposition, especially the necessity of having one himself in the not-distant-enough future.

"Hey, will you help me?" a female voice called.

He heard the distress call before he saw the damsel.

"Please! It will only take a minute."

He hurried down the row of cars, spotting a pink dress with big puffy sleeves and enough skirt for a circus tent. Only a bridesmaid would wear a Halloween costume in June. He spotted her problem as soon as he got close enough—her taffeta tail was caught in the trunk.

"My bow is stuck," the voice said from behind a gift-wrapped box the size of a washing machine, "and I dropped my keys under the car."

"Let me take that."

He put the bulky but not heavy package on the ground.

The bridesmaid made a stab at twirling and trying to retrieve her keys with the toe of one pink satin shoe, but only succeeded in kicking them farther under the blue compact.

Cole bent to look under the car and felt around until he found her keys on one of those stretchy wrist things that she obviously hadn't bothered to use. Retrieving her keys took a few seconds longer than necessary because he found the view from that angle pretty spectacular. If the rest of the woman's legs matched her shapely ankles, it was criminal to dress her like a wad of cotton candy. Back in the days when he'd semiwillingly wasted half his weekends every summer going to weddings, he'd developed a theory about bridesmaids—their only real function was to look really bad so the bride looked better.

"Thanks, I really appreciate… You're one of the Bailey twins!" she said, sounding more astonished than the situation merited.

He stood, trying to get a look at her face under a hat that was more awning than headgear.

"Cole Bailey?"

"Yes," he agreed, wondering how she knew him and coming up blank.

"We went to high school together. Remember British lit?"

"My worst subject. I shouldn't have taken it, but I needed one more English class to graduate."

"I remember that."

She whipped off the hat, revealing a mass of reddish brown hair tortured into sausage curls.

He still drew a blank.

"No wonder you don't recognize me. This hairdo Lucinda dreamed up for her bridesmaids belongs in a nursery rhyme. I'm Tess Morgan. I helped you with Shakespeare."

"Tess Morgan? No way!" He remembered pudgy little Tess. He and Zack used to tease her just to see her blush. Her cheeks would get flaming red.

"I guess I've changed some."

"I guess!"

One thing hadn't changed. Her cheeks reddened in embarrassment at the comment he'd intended as a compliment. He remembered one of their nicknames for her— Miss Prim and Proper.

"I only tutored you because you promised never to tease me again if you passed the class."

"Did I keep my promise?" He honestly didn't remember.

"You graduated a year before I did, so I guess you more or less did. Anyway, would you please open the trunk? I feel like an idiot trapped by my own car."

"Oh, sure." He unlocked it and lifted out the wide ribbon of cloth.

"Thanks. I appreciate it."

He caught himself staring and had to remind himself that this was Tess Morgan, clueless Tess. In high school she'd been so naive and wholesome, the guys had called her Soapy.

"Let me tie it for you." He surprised himself by offering.

"Oh, would you? I don't know why they had to be long enough to go around a hippo."

He felt clumsy trying to make a bow out of the slippery streamers, especially since the one that had been caught in the trunk had a black smear.

"Can you do it?" she asked, looking over her shoulder.

"Sure, no problem."

He fumbled with the thing, managing to turn the grease spot so it didn't show. No need to make her self-conscious by mentioning it. The big bow did her slender waist a grave disservice, in his opinion.

"Is Lucinda a good friend of yours?" he asked. He

now knew the bride's name, but he had serious doubts about her character. What kind of woman made a friend show up in public looking like Little Bo Peep?

"We go way back." She didn't elaborate. "I've done this bit so many times, people are starting to think I'm a professional bridesmaid."

"Can I carry that for you?" He nodded at the gift-wrapped box. Chivalry aside, the bulky package looked as if it could be a good ticket into the reception. Who would question a guy who came in with a bridesmaid and a really big present?

"Would you mind? It's not heavy, but it's bulky. Lucinda is into wicker, so I got her a chair at the import store. Unfortunately they don't deliver."

Not so unfortunate for him. "I'd be glad to."

He hefted the box and walked beside her toward the clubhouse. How could one person change so much and so little at the same time? She had the same tentative smile, but he didn't remember her lips being so lush, no thanks to the metallic pink lipstick that was probably supposed to match the dress. Her eyes were bluer than he recalled, but maybe ten years ago she hadn't looked at him so directly. She had apple cheeks, part of the reason he and Zack had enjoyed making her blush, but there was nothing plump about any part of her now, including her face. She had golden-tan skin, a cute nose and arched brows, altogether a pretty package.

"I didn't see you at the church," she commented.

"I'm not big on weddings. It's a bachelor phobia."

"Oh, you're still single?"

"You sound surprised."

"A little. Girls liked you a lot in high school—more than Zack even, but I shouldn't tell you that."

"It's my brother you shouldn't tell. He thought he was quite a ladies' man back then."

Since winning the coin toss, Zack was the happy twin, free to continue playing the field. He was also the one who could get a date with a complete stranger anytime just by saying, "How about it?"

Cole wasn't at all eager to begin wife-hunting, but he hoped to get a date or two at this reception. Zack would have too much fun trying to give him advice on how to get a woman if he struck out.

"Is Zack married?"

"No, we're both lonely bachelors. What about you? Are you married?"

"No—and don't pretend you're surprised."

He protested weakly, but he wasn't at all surprised. As far as he knew, she hadn't had a boyfriend in high school and probably still put men off with her wholesomeness. It had had nothing to do with looks. She'd always been too reserved, too self-contained—maybe too shy.

"Meeting the right person isn't easy," he said glumly, thinking of his grandfather's unrealistic expectations. Maybe in Marsh's day virgins panting for husbands were plentiful, but the old man needed a wake-up call. This was the twenty-first century! It was a lot easier to find a playmate than a longtime partner.

They climbed the steps at the main entrance of the imposing pseudo-Elizabethan clubhouse, its stucco walls gleaming white and the timbers freshly stained a deep mahogany brown. He'd lucked out in connecting with Tess and her big box. Private security was hovering like dark-suited ghosts, and when he saw the gift room off the foyer, it was pretty clear why. Besides wicker, the bride was obviously into silver and other pricey stuff. He didn't need Tess's prompting to carry her gift in with the others and put it in a corner.

TESS WAITED while Cole discreetly made her gift disappear in the treasure trove of Lucinda's loot. He'd been a hunk in high school—she'd sighed over his picture in the yearbook for an embarrassingly long time—but he'd matured and lost his boyish cuteness. Now he was drop-dead gorgeous. His face was sun-bronzed, and a light crease line in his forehead made his dark brows and eyes even sexier.

A few minutes ago she'd been furious with Danny-the-creep Wilson for breaking his promise to go to the wedding with her. Now she was glad he was off sailing with his boss and some clients. She was tired of men like him, male friends who cadged meals, borrowed money and called her "good buddy." It would be a small, if short-lived, triumph to walk into the grand ballroom with Cole. He was just another pal from her past, but no one here knew that.

Why did she have so many male friends and no real boyfriend? Guys called her when they wanted to whine about work or the women who did them wrong. They never seemed to notice she was ripe and ready, not even after she slimmed down to a size eight and learned to lose at everything from tennis and video games to battles of wit.

Cole smiled broadly when he returned from disposing of her present.

"Thanks for carrying it," she said, smiling. "From now on, I give nothing but towels."

"Towels are nice," he said in a tone that labeled them boring, "but I'm glad we got together. Big receptions are a drag when you don't know anyone."

"Except the happy couple, of course, but they only have eyes for each other."

He offered his arm. She took it, more than a little impressed by the way his bicep strained against the sleek, dark sleeve of his suitcoat.

They walked into a ballroom that reeked of old money—a blend of greenhouse flowers, high-priced liquor and expensive perfumes.

He dropped his arm, and she felt let down. Of course, she couldn't expect him to hang with her all evening just because they'd once taken the same class.

"Fancy affair." He sounded vaguely disapproving.

"Yeah, I guess."

She knew he was much more likely to feel comfortable at a society wedding than she was. His grandfather was wealthy and important, and the twins had grown up in the lap of luxury, so to speak. Not that Tess wasn't inordinately proud of her family. Dad was a high-school coach who thought it was more important to teach values than win games, and her mom taught reading skills to kids who would otherwise wash out of the system. Her older sister, Karen, was a third-grade teacher with a peach of a husband and two adorable girls, Erika, five, and Erin, seven.

Tess was the family maverick, but thankfully she had a natural flair for business. She'd built up a successful baby store on her own and had recently moved to a high-rent location, the Rockstone Mall. So far the store was thriving, mainly because she stayed current on all the latest gadgets, gimmicks and gizmos made for little people.

"I prefer receptions at a lodge hall or in the back room of a restaurant," Cole said, scanning the enormous room.

"Where the girls are more fun because they're tipsy?" she teased, wondering why she felt free to say whatever came to mind with him.

He laughed. "There is that."

It was a huge reception, but the majority of the guests were north of forty. Lucinda's parents had lots of friends, but Tess's weren't among them. It was only an alphabetical accident that she and Lucinda were old friends. Since grade school, L. Montrose and T. Morgan had been paired up. They'd renewed their friendship when Lucinda's dad had called in a favor with the mall management corporation and gotten his daughter a job doing publicity for Rockstone, where Tess had her store. For the first time in her life, Lucinda had been out of her depth, possessing little flair for promotions. No surprise, she'd come to rely on Tess for sympathy and suggestions.

Tess glanced at the sturdy little wristwatch she'd managed to slip past the bride's last-minute inspection. She was genuinely fond of her longtime friend, but this wedding had brought out the worst in Lucinda, turning her into a control freak. A slightly plump blonde, she'd dressed the seven bridesmaids in nursery-rhyme costumes that made them look like pink pumpkins. She said it gave the wedding a quaint ambience.

Tess came to the reception with one thought—how soon could she sneak away without being missed? She was enjoying her moment in the sun with Cole, but no doubt he'd soon be snatched away by one of the many predatory, but not necessarily single, women who were looking for a way to milk a little fun out of an otherwise dull affair.

Fortunately the dinner was a buffet, and Lucinda wasn't going to share the limelight by having her quaint maidens on display at a head table. Unfortunately there were still little rituals that demanded Tess's presence—single girls diving for the bouquet as though they believed the prize was a wedding of their own, bachelors tussling manfully over the garter, the bride and groom smearing cake on each other's lips so they could do the giggle-and-smooch bit. Why had she agreed to yet another stint as a bridesmaid? Tomorrow she'd take this silly dress to her sister and let Karen make kids' costumes from the yards and yards of material in the skirt. Her nieces would love having pink taffeta Halloween costumes, if they didn't wear them out before then playing dress up.

A waiter came toward them with a tray of champagne in glass goblets, not the plastic throwaways that smelled like nail polish.

"Drink or dance?" Cole asked, snagging one for both of them with a casual thanks.

"Hard choice." She wondered if he actually wanted to dance with her or was only being polite.

"Both, then." He lifted his glass and clinked it against hers. "To the happy couple."

"To Mr. and Mrs. Menton." She took a tiny sip, then a more substantial one. It tasted a lot better than the usual bubbly vinegar served at receptions. "You didn't say whether you're a friend of the bride or the groom."

"I'm equally fond of both," he said. "Good champagne. I usually hate it," he said, draining the goblet determinedly.

"A friend of the couple? I'm surprised Lucinda never mentioned you."

She finished her champagne and looked around for a place to put the glass. Cole took it and put both on a passing tray.

"I'm more a friend of what's-his-name," he said. "Menton."

"Doug. His name is Doug."

"Guess I don't actually know him," he admitted sheepishly.

"So Lucinda invited you?" He was up to something, and she was intrigued.

"Not exactly. My mother is a friend of her aunt."

"Then why..."

"You've caught me!" He touched his finger to her lips. "I'm crashing the party. Will you keep it a secret?"

She nodded, and he took his finger away, leaving her lips with an oddly tingling sensation.

"But why?"

"Just for kicks. Want to dance?"

"Sure, why not?"

She didn't kid herself. He hadn't crashed the reception just to glide across the waxy hardwood floor with an old school acquaintance, but he really could dance. Responding to the firm pressure of his fingers on her satin-armored waist, she followed his lead with exhilaration.

"You're making me look good," she said a trifle breathlessly.

"You are good."

He sounded surprised, but she didn't care. Dancing with Cole was incredibly...stimulating. Her dress rustled, Cole hummed, and her ears buzzed. Could it be she was feeling tipsy on one glass of champagne?

"What do you do?" he asked, his lips so close to her forehead she could feel a warm whisper of air when he spoke.

"Do?"

He pressed the hand he was holding against his chest and twirled her around a flat-footed couple who were shuffling across the floor without much regard for the music.

"Job, career, work?"

His sarcasm got through to her.

"I have a store at Rockstone Mall."

"Let me guess. Flower shop?"

"No."

"Pet supplies—doggie sweaters and gourmet treats for pampered cats?"

"No, I'm into pampering babies. My store is Baby Mart."

The song ended, and the band members stood up for their break. Did they have to take one now?

"As a matter of fact, Bailey Baby Products is my main supplier. Your company's high chairs outsell all competitors five to one," she said enthusiastically, groping for common ground to keep him with her a little longer.

"My grandfather's company," he said dryly. "Zack and I have a construction business."

"That's nice."

This conversation was going nowhere, and he obviously wasn't focused on her anymore. Well, he wasn't her date, however pleasant it was to have a gorgeous man in tow.

"Thanks for the dance," she said as casually as possible. "I need to speak to a friend over there."

The friend was imaginary, but the technique was all hers. When a guy started looking through her, beyond her or over her head, she liked to be the one who walked away.

She headed toward the universal haven of unescorted women, wishing she'd had room for a hair pick in the tiny satin drawstring bag that came with the dress. Staring at herself in the mirror, she wished she could wet down the sausage curls and loosen the stiff nylon petticoat, but it would take more than that to get Cole Bailey to go home with her.

Dang, where did that thought come from? She was swearing off champagne forever!

After touching up her lipstick, she went back to the

reception, killed an hour gossiping with Lucinda's younger sister, then filled a plate at the buffet and sat at a table with the bride's great-aunt, who was allergic to every food from grapefruit to garlic and liked to talk about it. Tess murmured sympathetically and picked at the smoked salmon, but she couldn't help tracking Cole. It wasn't hard. For an uninvited guest, he certainly wasn't trying to be inconspicuous. In fact, he zeroed in on the most eye-catching women and was never without a dance partner.

Lucinda had assigned little jobs to all her attendants, and Tess had the task of organizing the bouquet toss. The clubhouse had once been a millionaire's mansion, and the front hallway had a curving staircase wide enough for a 1930s musical comedy number. Naturally Lucinda wanted to stand above the rabble when she tossed her artfully arranged bunch of orchids.

"Use the mike," Lucinda commanded when she swished by to give Tess her marching orders.

"Can't I just…"

"It's the only way everyone will hear you in this huge room."

Lucinda's way was always the only way. Tess had an urge to mutiny, but after the honeymoon, Lucinda would be back at the mall, her lunch buddy and walking partner. Most brides became real people again after their big day.

"I hate mikes."

Lucinda was impervious to pouting unless she was doing it. Tess went to the head table and located the dreaded instrument, which the groom's father was kind enough to test by blowing into it. The result was a whining whistle.

"Here you are, little lady."

Next he'd pat her head!

"Eh, ladies...girls...women..." The mike made her too nervous to remember what was politically correct.

The band was taking their forty-third break, and conversation prevailed.

"Can I have your attention? Please!"

"Talk up a bit, little lady," her coach prompted.

"The bride is going to toss her bouquet!"

That got them. Tess wiggled her tongue trying to get enough saliva to finish the announcement.

"Eligible women go to the grand stairway," she directed, surprised when the groom's dad took the microphone away from her.

"Come on, gals. Who'll be the lucky little lady to snag the bouquet?"

Tess crept away before he thought of doing an interview on why she wanted to be the winner. In fact, she didn't. She'd caught the bride's bouquet at four previous weddings, mainly because she could be trusted to return it to the newlyweds. Obviously the magic didn't work on a skeptic like her.

Judging by the stampede, Lucinda had invited an army of unwed women, although some of the throng gathering at the foot of the stairs had to be women looking for love the second or third time around.

The foyer was large with striking black-and-white checkerboard tiles on the floor. The walls were loaded with cloudy old oil paintings in heavy gold frames. Lucinda had gone to the top of the stairs so she could descend dramatically, her train hooked up to avoid a tumble. Her dress was ivory silk with an overskirt of antique Belgian lace from her grandmother's wedding gown. Tess had never seen a bride who didn't look beautiful, and Lucinda was no exception. It was the glow, not the trappings.

It was her job to announce, "Here she comes!" and whip the crowd into a frenzy. She intended to stand to the side and avoid the crush, but women jockeying for position outflanked her. She found herself squeezed in on all sides, threatened by a tall girl's bony elbow to her right and a pair of spike heels backing into her. Tess's silly bow had come untied again, but she was too squashed to reach behind and redo it.

She caught a glimpse of Lucinda nodding at her from the top of the stairs, her signal to make the big announcement.

"Here comes the bride!" she called, not that everyone couldn't see that.

A woman with jet-black hair gave her a hard hip thrust on the left, but Tess couldn't escape the press. They'd boxed her in on all sides.

Lucinda was descending with much-practiced stateliness. She threw from the halfway point, putting enough oomph into the toss to give the bouquet some spin.

Tess put out her hands defensively with no thought of catching it, but the flowers were coming directly at her. Hands were everywhere, reaching, grabbing and snatching. She heard an ominous rip and was nearly knocked off her spike heels as two contenders got their hands on the delicate arrangement of exotic blooms.

Neither woman would let go. They pulled until they split the prize, tearing the orchids away from the wiring. Tess heard another tearing noise and knew she was in trouble.

The crowd thinned with a mix of disappointed grumbles and good-humored laughter. Tess found herself standing alone with her skirt hanging limply on the tiles behind her. The wretched satin streamers had been torn loose, taking the back of the skirt with them. She knew the semitransparent petticoat wasn't enough to conceal a view of her pink bikini panties, and a couple of the groomsmen were strolling her way. She knew they'd noticed when they stopped and pretended to study one of the dark old oil paintings on the wall in front of her. Freddy, a pale blond, freckle-faced guy pretending to be an art lover, had already tried to corner her in a Sunday-school room at the church. He had breath like a sewer and at least seven arms. She'd rather get sucked into quicksand than let him get his hands on the part of her anatomy that was now hanging out of the ruined dress.

Reaching behind and grabbing a handful of satin, she tried to bunch it together enough for modesty's sake while she edged her way out the door. This reception was over for her.

She felt the jacket descend on her shoulders before she saw her rescuer.

"Let's go," Cole said, putting his arm around her shoulders to hold his suitcoat in place.

"Gladly!"

"Crazy ritual. I'd rather take on a wolf pack than get in the middle of a scramble for the bride's bouquet."

"I wasn't trying for it," she said. "I was in charge of getting the women together."

"You certainly did an admirable job," he teased, pushing open the door with his free hand.

Spotlights lit up the front entrance, and lightposts illuminated the whole of the parking area. A few smokers lounged on the steps enjoying the wonderful June evening, and a tipsy couple were doing something that resembled dancing on the asphalt drive.

He guided her toward the car, keeping his jacket firmly in place with his arm. She was happy to see her little compact, which was as out of place between a Mercedes and a Lincoln as she was at this reception.

"I owe you," she said. "This makes twice you've rescued me."

"No thanks necessary. Do you have your car keys?"

"Yes, and I can actually reach them this time." She dug into the little purse and extracted them, rather pleased when Cole took them and unlocked the door for her.

"About owing me," he said as she slid out of his jacket and onto the car seat. "There is one little thing you could do for me."

"What?" She was genuinely surprised that Cole Bailey could need anything from her. If truth be told, she was hopeful that the favor involved spending more time with him.

"You've always had a lot of girlfriends, if I remember right. Do you still?"

"I guess. I've never given it much thought."

"Are some of them...I mean, do you still have some sweet unattached friends who've never been married?"

"I don't exactly run a club for old maids." She was liking this less and less.

"Sorry, I didn't mean to sound..."

"Weird?"

"My intentions are honorable." He smiled ruefully. "I'd really like to meet some nice women."

"Is that why you crashed the reception?"

Surely this man could get a date in a convent if he put his charm to work! She was far more puzzled than pleased by the prospect of playing matchmaker for him.

"Weddings are usually a good place to meet...people."

"You seemed to be doing well enough." She bit her tongue, angry at herself for letting him know she'd noticed.

He shrugged. In shirtsleeves, his shoulders were broad and muscular. Her fingers itched to touch them.

"I'd like to meet someone our age."

"I'm a whole year younger than you are!"

"Point taken. But do you have any nice friends?"

"All my friends are nice—at least most of the time." She was thinking of Lucinda. "But I'm not good at setting up blind dates. It's the best way I know to lose friends."

She suspected he was too much man for most of the single women she knew. But oddly enough he didn't intimidate her anymore. She knew he'd never be interested in her—she was just his pal—but at least he didn't make her stammer, stutter and shake anymore.

"How about this." He took a coin from his pocket. "Heads, you introduce me to some of your friends. Tails, I give you a tour of the baby plant and a sneak preview of some new products that will be available soon."

She was tempted, but didn't entirely trust him.

"I'm not much on games of chance," she said.

"What is your game?"

"Tennis, but I wouldn't stand a chance against an athlete like you. I do play pool occasionally."

She didn't mention that she'd grown up practicing on her dad's table in the basement, or that she played in a weekly league in the winter.

"Pool it is. Same stakes. Do you like one game, sudden death or two out of three?"

"Two out of three." Her second game was usually better than her first. She needed warm-up time.

"I'll follow you. Where do you want to play?"

"You forget I did the Cinderella bit—ball gown to rags. Maybe a rain check?"

Which would give her time to wiggle out of the bet,

she thought, realizing how little she wanted to fix him up with someone else.

"If you're afraid you can't beat me…"

"No way!"

"I'll follow you home. You can change, and we'll go to the closest bar with a table."

"It's late, Cole."

"Not even eleven."

"I've had a long day."

"No disadvantage. I was on the work site at six a.m."

"Do you always get your own way?"

His grin was all the answer she needed.

She gave in, but darned if she'd let him win!

2

THERE WAS NOTHING Cole liked less than waiting for a woman to get dressed—except, of course, looking for a wife he didn't want.

He told Tess he'd wait in the truck while she changed her torn dress, but he was too restless to sit. He got out of the driver's seat and started pacing in a broad circuit in the parking area as soon as she went inside her ground-floor apartment.

She lived in one of a hundred or so small units in the brick complex, all with individual entrances either on the ground level or off a second-floor balcony that ran the length of each building with stairs at both ends. He approved. He liked a floor plan that allowed tenants their own private entrances and didn't waste space on a lobby.

The apartments were thirty or forty years old, built when buildings were still laid out in rectangular patterns with straight service roads. Today builders, including Zack and him, favored curving roads and cul-de-sacs for an illusion of spaciousness and privacy, but the place was well maintained and still looked good. Much of the vast sprawl in Wayne County was a conglomerate of enclaves linked by expressways and major roads. He knew it like the back of his hand, but never tired of the architectural diversity.

He'd rate Tess's place as ho-hum, a haven for singles and young couples with a smattering of seniors who'd given up their homes in favor of easy maintenance and social-security living. At least she didn't live with her parents.

Stopping to look at his watch, Cole thought about the evening so far.

The wedding reception had been about what he'd expected—a bunch of casual acquaintances and a few strangers pretending they lived the high life all the time. At least no one had challenged his presence.

He even got propositioned. Mrs. Donaldson wanted to give him a tour of the clubhouse, promising she knew some hidden niches where no one ever went. She'd conveniently forgotten he'd played soccer with her son in middle school. He politely declined!

As for the younger women, he'd had a hard time separating college girls from jailbait. Except for seeing Tess again, the evening had been a bust, but it forced him to be realistic. He wasn't going to find the girl of his grandfather's dreams at a party or a bar, which pretty much eliminated his usual stomping grounds.

Maybe Tess would open some doors for him, not that he deserved her help after the rough time he gave her in high school. But they were both adults now, right? Fortunately, she didn't seem to hold a grudge. She was the kind of woman who could be a good friend without all the game-playing that went with relationships. And she was the only person he knew who could help him meet some nice girls.

First he had to beat her at pool. He'd be sporting, though, and not win by too much. He couldn't expect her to help solve his problem if he humiliated her.

"Bailey, where are you?" she called, managing to startle him, because he'd expected to wait the typical half hour most females required for a simple change.

"Here."

He walked toward her from a row of cars parked south of his truck.

"Are you ready for a..." He nearly said lesson, then saw what she was carrying—a case that could only contain one thing. "You have your own pool stick?"

"I play in a league in the winter. If you want to call off the bet..."

"No way."

He had a hard time seeing Tess as a pool hustler, but she'd suckered him into a challenge he really needed to win. At least it would be more fun—and easier on his conscience—if she could give him a good game.

"Get in." He opened the door of his truck for her.

"I thought I'd drive my car, and you can follow. That way you won't have to bring me home."

"Get in. I don't mind bringing you back."

In the light from the cab she looked more like her old self, only better, much better. Jeans and a form-hugging white tank top did a lot more for her than the bridesmaid getup. She'd pulled all the sausage curls into a ponytail that bounced as she scampered into the pickup.

One of the nice things about taking a date in the truck was checking out her back view without being obvious as she climbed to the seat. Tess had a round, firm bottom, but of course she was no date prospect and never would be. Being with her was more like taking a ride with his sister—if he had one—or maybe a first cousin, which he also didn't have as far as he knew. No telling what his biological daddy had in the way of relatives, since Cole had never heard boo from the man. Apparently he'd taken Marsh Bailey's threats seriously way back when. Cole's deceased stepfather was the man who'd been a true father to him, and Zack felt the same way.

"I know a place not too far from here where we should be able to get a table without a long wait," she said.

He shrugged and let her give him directions.

"It's not a tie-and-jacket kind of place," she warned.

"All the better. Where did you learn to play pool?"

"My dad loves it. Has a table in his basement."

"Now I'm getting worried," he teased.

"Yeah, sure. How many times have you lost at anything?"

"Well, I'm still single. I certainly haven't won the girl of my dreams yet." And he wouldn't be looking for her if he hadn't lost the toss to Zack with his own coin.

"About what you want me to do—not that I plan to lose," Tess said, "you actually expect me to fix you up with a blind date?"

"Maybe several."

"You're serious? I mean, you're not going to break any of my friends' hearts just for fun, are you?"

"I'm serious." His answer came out sounding grim.

"Why now?

"You have a mother. You know how they get when grandkids fever hits," he said, giving her the first plausible reason that came to mind. The truth was too bizarre to lay on someone he hadn't seen for ten years.

"I guess, but my sister has two kids. I'm more or less off the hook for now. So you want to meet a nice girl to make your mother happy?" She sounded puzzled but not disapproving.

"I promised to give it a try, but working in construction I don't meet many girls I'd want to take home to Mom."

He didn't like this conversation, and the pool place wasn't as close as he'd like it to be.

"Well, I'd hate to disappoint your mom." She patted the case resting on her thigh. "But I'm looking forward to a sneak preview of Bailey's new line. My shop is getting a reputation for handling the latest baby products.''

He urged her to tell him more about her store without paying much attention to what she said. His interest in baby monitors and infant seats was nonexistent, especially since anything baby related reminded him of his grandfather's high-handed manipulations.

They got to the pool hall. Buck's wasn't the kind of place he would've expected Tess to like. It was a workingman's tavern with thick black glass windows and a neon beer sign over the door. He left his jacket and tie in the truck and followed Tess into a murky interior that reeked of smoke and boilermakers.

"Hi, Tess! How's my sweetie?" a bearded little man who'd never see seventy again called as she walked in.

"Doing great, Barney."

"Gotcha self a live one?" another grizzled old man asked from the brass-railed bar.

"Ready for plucking."

Bar regulars were territorial, and the stools belonged to old-timers, mostly men and a few women with faces that didn't match their vivid hair colors. What Cole saw at the tables helped explain why Tess felt comfortable here. They'd largely been taken over by twenty-somethings, young professionals trying to dress down and still look cool in designer jeans. The two groups seemed to tolerate each other well enough, with the possible exception of a few tough-looking young guys probably looking to prove something by hitting on classy girls.

Tess waved at a few younger people but headed directly toward the rear of the building. The pool tables were behind swinging Dutch doors in a back room with an old-fashioned metal ceiling. She'd chosen well. She scrawled her name on a chalkboard, but they were the only ones on the waiting list for a table.

"What can I get you to drink?" he asked

"A light beer, please. Playing pool is thirsty work."

He'd expected her to order a soda or possibly white wine, but then, he didn't know much about the Tess of today. He fetched a couple of brews and stood with her watching the action. Finally a couple of giggling girls abandoned their table and left with some guys in motorcycle boots and belts so heavily studded they probably pinched their bellies when they leaned over.

"You're the challenger," she said.

He racked the balls and tested the weight of the stick he'd chosen. The shaft had been sanded and the tip replaced recently. This place took their pool seriously.

Tess broke the rack and sank a striped ball. He liked the way she leaned over the table and studied her options. She had a loose, casual style, but once she committed to a shot, she went for it like a pro.

She impressed the hell out of him. This bet wasn't the sure thing he'd expected.

"Nice shot," he said as she sank another ball.

In fact, it was too nice. Beating her was going to take some off-table strategy. He stepped behind her and leaned when she leaned, reaching over her to take her wrist as she lined up her next shot.

"Maybe if you straighten your wrist just a little..." He began coaching.

"Cole Bailey!" She used her hips like a pair of cannon balls and knocked him away from the table. "I do not need lessons!" she said, confronting him like a raging rhino. "If you touch me again, the match is off."

"Understood," he said, feeling like a jerk. "Some girls appreciate a few pointers." And a little touchy-feely to go with the sport, he thought, vowing not to forget Tess was different from most women.

He walked to the other side of the table so he wouldn't have to watch the little tail twitch she used unconsciously when she was ready to take her shot. She might play killer pool, but she was still at square one in the boy-girl game. Men challenged each other for the competition, but it was a whole different contest to play with a woman.

I'm a chauvinistic jerk, he thought when she missed her next shot. He could win this bet without rubbing against her backside or distracting her with thinly disguised hugs. After all, this was Tess. He still owed her for getting him through English lit.

"Sorry," he mumbled as he stepped up to take his first shot. "I was only trying to be helpful."

"Yeah, sure." She frowned in disbelief.

He called his shot, knowing he deserved to flub it for trying to use sex to distract a friend. But Tess would keep her word if she lost the match, and he didn't have any better ideas for meeting nice women. He couldn't get help from Zack. His brother wouldn't recognize a nice girl if she came wrapped in tissue and ribbons.

He cleared the table and won the first game handily. Fortunately, guilt didn't blunt his skill.

"That makes me one up," he said cordially. "Want to concede now?"

"No way! The bet is two out of three. I'm always a slow starter."

"Nice stick you have," he said, because he found silence between them awkward, not that balls crashing and people talking and laughing at the other eleven tables didn't fill the room with noise.

"Seventeen ounces. My dad gave it to me when our team won the league championship last winter."

"I'm impressed." He actually was. He'd never played league pool, but he knew it attracted good players.

It was his turn to break, and he found himself wanting badly to win without giving her a turn to shoot. Maybe he needed to prove to himself he was the better player. No question his dirty trick had distracted her in the last game. Hell, it was hard for him to concentrate just thinking about it. He could still feel her snug against his front, her bottom wiggling just enough to make him wish she was a date, someone he could take home with him.

"Idiot!" he muttered under his breath. This was Tess. She'd lost the baby fat, but that didn't make her fair game. He felt uncomfortable enough using her to meet other women without toying with her. A friend didn't treat a friend that way.

He made a couple of mediocre shots, but his heart wasn't in them. He'd basically stolen the first game. When his third shot bounced an inch away from the hole, he was happy enough to relinquish the table to Tess. He hadn't exactly thrown the game, but his sloppy playing gave him what he deserved—a loss.

"Even up," she said with satisfaction. "Now let's see some real pool."

As the winner of the previous game, it was her turn to break the rack. Cole narrowed his eyes, concentrating on the balls and trying not to see the way her breasts filled out her tank top when she leaned over the table. Women always had the power of distraction on their side, but he had more riding on this game than an opportunity for cheap thrills.

He squeezed the pool cue until his knuckles were white. He wanted out. He didn't want to get married, especially not on his grandfather's timetable. But he knew darn well his mother would be ousted as CEO unless the stock stayed in the family. A young hotshot MBA would come in and take Mom's place. Even assuming Nick, his half brother, would get his share, he and Zack had to come through for her.

Balls moved on the bright green table, but his gaze was unfocused. His whole future could depend on Tess Morgan's ability to push balls with a stick. If she introduced him to someone he decided to marry...

Or if she won and refused to help...

Cole forced himself to pay attention. He was in trouble. Two more shots, and she'd be the winner. He'd lose the game and the bet without getting another shot.

"Oh, no!" She sounded genuinely distressed.

She'd missed her shot. He'd been sure she was going to beat him, and it took a minute to realize he still had a chance.

He bit his lower lip, telling himself not to get cocky. He could still blow it. Wiping first one palm, then the other, on the sides of his pants, he tried to psych himself up to win.

"Number seven in the side pocket." He called his shot as a courtesy of the game even though it was obviously his only option.

The cue ball banged the seven ball in with a satisfying thud.

"I knew you couldn't miss that," Tess said in a tone of disgust.

As the shooter, he could still miss the next shot and lose the bet. He didn't like the angle between the eight ball and the cup. He'd made harder shots, but he'd missed easier.

Holding his breath, he went for it.

The thud of the eight ball going down the hole was music to his ears.

"Well, I guess you're the winner," Tess conceded.

She put out her hand to congratulate him. It was soft against his work-hardened palm, and he didn't feel particularly elated at beating her.

"You shot a great game," he said.

"Oh, sure, I lost two out of three, and I was trying hard to win," she said with a look of disgust. "Getting a blind date for you of all people seems ludicrous. Tell me you were only kidding."

"Not kidding."

"Do you have a list?"

"List?" He reluctantly dropped her hand, but still felt a vague need to comfort her for losing.

"Shopping list, wish list, list of likes and dislikes."

"No, nothing like that." He laughed self-consciously.

"Everyone has some likes or dislikes. Give me a clue of what kind of person you have in mind." She sounded grumpy.

"Well, I'd rather she didn't pick her teeth in public."

"Be serious!"

"I am. I went with a girl—briefly—who had a teeth fetish. The minute she finished eating, out came the floss."

"None of my friends would be that gross."

"That's why I need your help. You know things about them. I trust your judgment."

She was putting her stick in the case when two women walked up to the table.

"Are you through for the night?" A platinum blonde batted lashes heavy with mascara.

"The table is all yours," Tess said. "I'm leaving."

"How about a challenge match?" the other woman said to Cole.

He checked out her breasts—it would be hard not to

notice them since they stuck out in all the glory silicone could produce—and backed away a step.

"Thanks, but I'm calling it a night," he said.

"Pool isn't the only game we play." The blonde was wearing a skirt so short it looked like black leather underpants. She sidled up to Cole, took his arm and rubbed her hip against his.

"I'm leaving," he insisted.

On his other side, the well-endowed friend wrapped her arm around his waist with the subtlety of a boa constrictor closing in on its prey. He tightened his buttocks when her hand crept downward.

"He's with me." Tess faced down the two predators, cue in hand.

Cole didn't know whether to laugh or be embarrassed. "Too bad."

One of them—he didn't know or care which—patted his butt. Any annoyance he might have felt was tempered by the fact that he'd tried to win a pool game by snuggling up to Tess's backside.

"Let's go," he said, taking her cue and her arm.

Women, he'd learned early on, could be just as obnoxious as men when they were on the make. He had to credit Marsh for trying to protect him from the dregs of the female gender, but the old man should give him credit for some sense, not to mention taste in women.

"Well, that was fun," Tess muttered as he followed her out to the parking area. "Where were those two when they could've done my game some good?"

"By taking my mind off mine? I don't think so." He didn't tell her she was distraction enough. "How about stopping for something to eat?" He was reluctant to let the evening end although he didn't know why.

"No, thanks. I've had enough excitement for one evening.'' She wasn't exactly sarcastic, but she made her point.

''Coffee then?'' He knew he was a glutton for punishment.

''I don't think so.''

''I'm pretty busy at work,'' he said, slightly miffed by her refusal, ''but I can be free next Saturday.''

''Free?'' She seemed distracted as she got into the truck.

''To meet someone. You know, a date to pay off your wager,'' he said, after climbing in on his side.

''I'm surprised the barflies back there didn't interest you.''

''You think bimbos are my type?'' She'd scored a point there.

''No, I guess not, but in high school you did—''

''That was ten years ago. Even the Bailey boys have to grow up eventually.'' He wasn't so sure about Zack, though.

''Sorry. I didn't mean to insult you.''

''That's okay.'' He was still disgruntled, but he wanted to close the deal on the blind dates. ''Maybe one date Saturday and another Sunday.''

''How many friends do you expect me to serve up?''

He didn't miss the distaste in her voice, and he felt like squirming on the seat of the truck. But she'd lost the pool match, and he wasn't going to let her welch on the bet.

''Even though I won, I'll be more than happy to give you a tour of the factory,'' he offered, hoping to soften her resistance.

''And a sneak preview of the new product line?''

If seeing a bunch of baby stuff would make her less reluctant to help him, it was a small price to pay—even though it meant deluding his grandfather into thinking he cared a rat's ass about the business. He couldn't show the new line without going to his mother, and she was sure to mention it to the almighty chairman of the board, Marsh Bailey. Damn, life was complicated for a guy who only wanted to build houses.

"Yes, a sneak preview," he promised. "I've heard about a baby-wipe warmer that plays a lullaby. And remember how happy my mom will be if I finally meet some nice girls."

"I suppose anyone you'd go out with has to be good-looking," Tess said.

He'd only managed to mollify her for a minute.

"Not conventionally pretty. I can appreciate an interesting face." He felt challenged not to sound shallow.

"Tall, short, blond, brunette?"

"Personality is more important." She was making him sound like the blurbs on women's magazines by the checkout counter at the supermarket.

"How do you define nice?" she pressed.

"Be reasonable, Tess. It's not about defining anything. It would be nice if she doesn't sleep around. Is that nice enough for you?"

"I've never really thought about it."

She sounded so prim he wanted to shock her pants off by planting a good, hard, lip-smacking kiss on her disapproving lips. Wouldn't that be a good way to scuttle the whole plan? Just make his little matchmaker so mad she'd get him the blind date from hell.

"I'm sure any friend of yours is a good person," he assured her.

"Except maybe Lucinda," she said thoughtfully. "That was the worst bridesmaid's dress in the history of weddings."

He laughed in agreement. ''But you did look cute with those curls.''

She slapped his thigh. A little gasp told him she'd acted on impulse and surprised herself.

''One of the deadly duo in the bar slapped my butt as we were leaving,'' he said, wanting her to know women stepped out of line as often as men, herself included.

The high moral ground was a sweet perch, he discovered. He wasn't sure whether his comment would help or hurt his cause, but even in the dark he could tell Tess's cheeks had flushed apple red.

3

WHEN SHE'D HAD the chance to play pool with Cole Bailey, why didn't she play for stakes that were fun? She thought of male pool players' favorite come-on, a bet to see who made coffee the next morning, not that she still had a thing for one of the bad-boy Bailey twins.

Tess continued glumly rearranging the display of Kozy Kountry bedding and accessories, not one of the best merchandising decisions she'd ever made. Baby Mart customers hadn't snatched up the comforters quite the way she'd hoped, not surprising since the cow looked more comatose than cute. One thing she'd learned early on—it didn't really matter that infants could see black and white better than pastels. The product had to appeal to grandparents and other gift-givers. That meant adorable designs and clever gimmicks.

She really wanted a jump on Bailey's new line so she could stock the most promising items ahead of her competition. But she was having a hard time convincing herself it was worth finding a date—or maybe even several dates—for Cole. A little winged cupid would make a cute quilt design, but she couldn't see herself in the role.

The big question was, who, who, who? Even her friend Mandy, who was practically paranoid about blind dates, might be tempted to go out with Cole, but Tess had even less enthusiasm for matchmaking than she did for dopey-looking cows that weren't selling. And she hadn't even had the presence of mind to put a limit on the number of dates she was willing to arrange. Her choice would have been zero, but as her sister, Karen, had pointed out when she talked it over with her on the phone, at least Tess would get to see Cole again herself.

Did she want to stay in contact with him at any price? Her saner self said forget it, but she'd had such a wild crush on him in high school, she didn't want him to disappear again without giving her a chance to see how wrong she'd been to idolize him. Face it, she'd been using him as a standard ever since, and it was time to get him out of her system for good. Certainly this matchmaking scheme would do the job. She hated it already.

She slapped another red label with a reduced price over a cow's lolling tongue and thought about the way Cole had plagued her in high school. He'd been a stinker but so cute she'd welcomed any attention from him, even his devilish teasing. She'd had a tremendous crush on him but had never deluded herself into believing they'd ever be a couple. Cole dated cheerleaders and party girls who, if not exactly brainless, were definitely dedicated to having a good time.

Imagine, Cole Bailey wanted *her* to find a woman for *him*. He had a pretty vague idea of what made a girl nice, though. Thank heavens she'd fully recovered from her girlish infatuation! Cole had walked away from the women in the bar, but she was still convinced boys like Cole grew into men who were heartbreakers. Reformed or not, he wasn't going to make her suffer the pangs of unrequited love again.

Already he had her thinking like the heroine in a Victorian romance novel. So he was gorgeous, lean, hard-bodied and darkly handsome. She could see men like that any day for the price of a movie ticket. The person she'd like to meet had to be sweet and reliable, a good companion for the long haul. She wasn't a love-struck adolescent easily impressed by a good-looking exterior.

Oh, he'd be easy to fix up, she thought crossly as she finished marking down the slow sellers in the baby-bedding display, but she didn't want to set up any of her friends for a big disappointment. Cole might think he wanted a nice girl, but how may hearts would he break before he found the right one—if such a person existed? He'd gone this far without committing himself to anyone. She'd expect a cow to wander off one of the quilts before a bad boy like Cole settled down with a nice girl.

Unfortunately, she'd lost the bet. Cole had distracted her in the first game—had he ever! But she'd blown the third and decisive one on her own. It was too late to complain about his underhanded tactics. Anyway, she'd never admit to him that having his arms around her had ruined her concentration.

She owed him, but she hated to put any of her friends at risk. Should she issue a medicine-bottle warning with every offer of a date? Beware—this hunk may be dangerous if taken seriously. If she did, who would accept?

If she flashed a picture of Cole, every single friend she had would beg for the opportunity to go out with him. Maybe she could lay a high-school yearbook on the coffee table and casually point out his senior class picture. He'd only improved with maturity.

Much as she hated to admit it, her big sister had been right about one other thing. Not only did she owe Cole for losing an admittedly foolish bet on pool, but he'd gotten her out of an embarrassing situation with Freddy at the wedding. He probably would've moved in on her like a snake after a mouse—her least favorite scenario.

Her clerk, Heather, was busy showing car seats to a

customer, so Tess stayed out front. She spotted a petite blond woman flipping through a rack of infant outfits and hurried over to offer assistance.

"Tess, how are you?" the woman asked when she turned and recognized her.

"Jillian, hello." Tess smiled automatically as she did with any customer. "Can I help you with something?"

"I hope so. I'm so excited! My sister is having twins, two girls if the doctor is right. Naturally I need something special for her baby shower."

Jillian Davis was in kickboxing class with Tess and was so good she could easily have been the instructor, except she already had a supergood job as a bank loan officer. She was one of those adorable women who made other women feel as if they had spinach stuck in their teeth and a run in their panty hose. In her spare time, Jillian volunteered for community causes and usually ended up as chairperson.

"We have some darling stretch jammies, almost like aerobics outfits for infants," Tess suggested.

"No, something more feminine, I think. By the way, I've almost decided to drop kickboxing." Jillian gave a cursory glance at the outfits Tess pointed out. "I'm absolutely fascinated by yoga. It enriches the total person, and the yoga academy looks like a wonderful place to meet Mr. Right."

When Jillian started moaning about how difficult it was to meet the perfect man, it usually meant she'd had a bad date the night before.

"How about quilts? I have a really good sale on them today."

Jillian took a quick look at the cutesy cows and shook her head.

Darn, thought Tess, all those attributes and good taste, too. Did the woman have no flaws?

She looked up to offer another suggestion and saw Cole striding through the mall entrance to the store. Someone could make a fortune by devising a calendar with no Mondays if they were all as bad as they were today.

He was wearing jeans so threadbare she was afraid to look closely for fear of learning the color of his underwear. His ensemble included dusty tan work boots and a faded blue T-shirt with a Detroit Lions football logo. Jillian perked up so much she looked two inches taller and a shade blonder.

"Hi, Tess," Cole said offhandedly, eyeballing Jillian with slightly narrowed eyes. "Don't let me interrupt with a customer."

"Oh, I'm a friend of Tess's, not a customer." Jillian was quick with the smile.

Wrong on the first count, Tess thought, ready to write off any sale she might have made to her non friend.

"Nice to meet you." Cole was quick with the handshake.

They both had good people-meeting skills—glad hands, big smiles, eye contact.

"I'm Jillian Davis."

"Cole Bailey." Still pressing her hand.

"Actually I'm a customer today, too. I need two baby gifts because my sister is expecting twins."

"No kidding? I'm a twin myself."

"What a good omen! I'm sure to find perfect gifts here."

"Looks like Tess has anything you might want for babies. What's this?" He picked up a Kozy Kountry crib sheet. "Cows. Cute."

"It is, isn't it?" Jillian looked at them again. "Look at

all the things that match it—a quilt, a bib, even a wall hanging! I couldn't be more excited about twins if I were having them myself. Of course, I'm not married...not even involved with anyone right now."

"Hey, you're in luck," Cole said. "Tess only has a few quilts left, and they're marked way down."

One word from Cole, and Jillian was grabbing up cows without even checking the prices.

"I think this will do it," she said a little breathlessly. "I can just see the little darlings cuddling up with these adorable cows."

Jillian wiggled her shoulders under a champagne silk blouse that matched her skimpy skirt, and it occurred to Tess that banks were open by now.

"I'll write them up fast," she promised. "You must be expected at work."

"Oh, my boss is so understanding," Jillian assured her. "The shower is tonight, and this is absolutely the only time I have to shop today."

Cole caught Tess's eye as Jillian carried her selections to the counter.

"Her?" He mouthed the question.

"No way." She spoke in haste, then wondered if this could be a way out for her. It would almost certainly save one or more of her friends from the pain of being dumped by a Bailey.

"Her!" he said in an emphatic whisper, nodding.

Convenient or not, Tess didn't like it. If he could come into a baby store and find a woman he wanted to date, why bother involving her at all?

He chatted up Jillian while Tess tallied the purchases. She should have been delighted to get rid of the cows, but the inane conversation at the counter was so distracting she had to check the total twice.

"Actually, I came here today because Tess promised to do me a small favor," Cole said.

"What's that?" Jillian's tone questioned whether there could possibly be anything a hunk like Cole needed from a drab shop girl like Tess. Or maybe Tess only wanted her to have nasty thoughts. Perfect people should have noble, uplifting thoughts. If Jillian's were unpleasant, then she didn't qualify as perfect.

"She promised to fix me up for Friday."

Jillian's jaw dropped. She recovered quickly, but Tess had seen what she'd seen.

"I thought you said Saturday." She didn't want any part of this pickup.

"Change of plans. You will vouch for me, won't you?" he asked.

"I vouch," she said, disgruntled by how pointless it had been to worry about finding him a date.

"I didn't know Tess had such a beautiful friend." Cole focused those dark smoky gray eyes on Jillian's pert little face. She giggled.

"Do you want a date Friday?" Tess asked Jillian.

"Well, I don't know. I never accept blind dates, but I have seen you, haven't I? And Tess vouches for you."

Whatever that meant, Tess groused to herself.

"I had in mind a late dinner, maybe pick you up at eight," Cole suggested.

"That would be very nice."

Tess had to give her credit for not showing too much eagerness. Jillian scooped up two big plastic bags and power walked to the exit, feet perfectly straight so there was no suggestion of a duckwalk. In a fair world, she would at least have had thick ankles or saddlebags on her hips

"I guess you're not here to buy a baby gift," she said

to Cole when they were alone. "Jillian is probably planning to have a set of twins with you as the daddy after that come-on."

"Doubt that, but thanks for…"

"I know, vouching for you." Whatever that meant. "She's perfect. I don't know why she's still single except she has a dynamite career. I hope you have a good time."

"Thanks, I probably will, but I doubt she's perfect."

Oh, come on, Tess wanted to say.

"She's a petite blonde with a perfect haircut." There was that word again—*perfect.* "Plus she has porcelain skin with a flawless complexion, sky-blue eyes, a really tasteful wardrobe…"

"Whoa, I meant it when I said it's what's inside that counts."

"Oh." This was a new side of Cole Bailey. "Well, she works with a lot of volunteer groups including the Humane Society, so she must care about animals and people."

"Well, you've helped me without even picking up the phone. Thanks, Tess. But I came here about the new products. I have to go to a builders' supply place east of here, so I stopped on the way to tell you I'll set up a sneak peek as soon as possible."

"And to check whether I'd arranged a date for you yet?"

"That, too." He grinned broadly. "But I knew I could trust you to keep your word. I'll let you know how it goes with…" He hesitated.

"Jillian. Jillian Davis. You can call her at Industrial Savings and Loan."

She watched him leave, surprised that his long, sexy stride still seemed so familiar. She didn't know how the date would go, but at least some of the comatose cows were gone.

COLE QUIT WORK early, which for him still meant putting in a twelve-hour shift to take advantage of the long summer day, and pulled up to the brick building that housed the research department and administrative offices of Bailey Baby Products. He'd called ahead to make sure his mother would be there, not that she ever left her office at a normal quitting time. If workaholism was inherited, everyone in the family but little brother Nick, Junior, had gotten it from Marsh, although with the twins it was more a matter of survival for their fledgling company than a compulsion.

He took the elevator to his mother's third-floor office suite, hoping Marsh wasn't in the building. How many kids were expected to call their grandfather by his first name as soon as they started talking?

It didn't much matter what Cole called him after the big blowup they'd had when he and Zack started their construction business. It'd been nearly a year since either twin had been at the plant, although for their mother's sake, they were civil to their grandfather during occasional dinners at her house. Still, Cole didn't want to bump into the old man. If he saw Cole, he'd harp on wanting him to take an interest in the family business.

The outer office was deserted. Sue Bailey worked long hours because she loved it, but didn't expect her employees to sacrifice their home lives for the company.

"Mom?"

The door to her inner office was slightly ajar, and Cole stepped into the cool interior. Somehow his mother had managed to make an efficient working office seem warm and inviting. She loved aqua, and the deep pile of the carpeting was a vibrant, dark shade of her favorite color. The tinted windows of the corner office were flanked by lighter aqua drapes. White walls and sleekly modern white metal furnishings left no doubt that this was a place of business, but one side of the room had a low round conference table surrounded by comfortable chairs with seats upholstered in a geometric pattern of black, white and aqua.

"I've got a date with a nice girl Friday night," he said without preamble.

His mother always looked happy in her work environment, but when she looked up at him she was positively glowing. He and Zack were doing the right thing—or rather, he was. His twin's turn would come soon enough. Their mom had been rocked by the death of Nick, Senior, her husband, a good man who gave his stepsons as much attention as his own son, Nick. She put all her energy into running the business to forget her sorrow, and it helped her immensely. After two years of widowhood, she was like her old self again, Cole thought. But if she lost control of the plant because of her father's high-handed manipulations, she'd be devastated.

"That's wonderful, Cole!" She gave him a hug and walked to a table where a big pitcher, damp with condensation, was on a tray with two tall glasses. "Would you like some iced tea?"

It wasn't his favorite beverage, but he was thirsty enough to drink Detroit River water.

"What's this thing?"

Cole examined a gizmo on her desk while she poured tea for both of them. He wasn't sure whether it was supposed to entertain babies or make them want to crawl back into the womb. He played with the weird spiral-shaped labyrinth wondering if maybe he'd accidentally hit on the truth when he told Tess his mom wanted grandchildren. Maybe part of her enthusiasm for her job came from loving babies. She had a lot to offer as a grandmother, so long as she kept the more bizarre Bailey toys away from them.

"It's a toy. It must be a winner because you're playing with it," she teased.

He dropped it like a hot rivet. She'd gotten him on that one, and he grinned sheepishly.

"Tell me about your date." She handed him the iced tea and daintily sipped hers.

"She's a friend of an old acquaintance. Remember Tess Morgan?"

"Isn't she the sweet girl who tutored you in British lit?"

"That's her. She owns Baby Mart in the Rockstone Mall. She's doing me a favor by introducing me to friends of hers. I promised her a sneak peek at the new product line."

He walked around the office, noting without enthusiasm that she still had tons of pictures of him, Zack and Nicky on the walls. The cutesy photos used in early catalog ads embarrassed him. Poses of curly-haired twins with Bailey toys made him remember how bored he'd been as a child model—bored but successful. To her credit, his mother had refused to let them work for any of the agencies that besieged them with lucrative offers. She even stood up to Marsh in limiting how much work they did for the annual Bailey catalogs. It was one of the rare disputes his mother had actually won when it came to showdowns with Marsh. She did much better these days, but as chairman of the board, he was still a tyrant.

"I guess there's no problem at this late date," Sue said thoughtfully. "The new catalog will be ready next month for wholesale Christmas orders. A leak now wouldn't be serious."

"Tess isn't an industrial spy," he said dryly.

"Of course not. Actually, this is a good time to give her a preview. We have a display set up in one of the design labs for some potential investors."

"Investors? Is Marsh going to go back on his word and agree to a buyout before he retires? Does he want to go public?"

"He's always playing around with the possibility. It's his way of keeping everyone on edge."

His mother didn't sound concerned. Cole was. It wasn't his employees Marsh wanted to unnerve. Cole's grandfather was holding the threat of a sellout over his head and Zack's. He'd better find Ms. Right soon and insure that his mother wouldn't lose control of the business.

"Why don't you and Tess join your grandfather and the investors tomorrow? Their tour is scheduled for 9 a.m."

He'd rather eat nails!

"I had in mind a private sneak preview. You know, give her a chance to look it over without the pressure of having Marsh there."

"A private showing with Tess. I see."

His mother smiled—slyly, he thought.

"She's only a friend. I owe her. Tess and me? No, no way. Not my type at all, and she remembers me less than fondly from high school."

"If you say so. Why did you persuade her to help you get dates?"

When his mother put it that way, it did sound ludicrous. When had he ever needed help meeting women? The only blind date he'd ever had was Zack's fault. Some girl wouldn't go out with him unless he found a date for her friend.

"She's not getting me dates, Mom." Maybe he sounded juvenile, but he wanted his mother to be perfectly clear on this. "She's only putting me in the loop with some nice women. I don't meet any when I spend all my time on the job."

"She's doing this just so she can see our new line?" She sounded skeptical.

"No, I'm showing it just to be nice."

"Then why?"

He hadn't been grilled like this since he drove without a license when he was fifteen.

"She lost a bet."

He was getting The Look. His mother was a head shorter than he was, and slender to the point of being too thin, but when she raked him with her smoky gray eyes, he still squirmed.

"Two out of three games of pool."

"This was a fair contest?" she asked, accusing him.

"Tess plays in a pool league. I nearly lost to her. Anyway, I can't leave the site of the condos we're building during the workday. I was thinking of bringing her around nine in the evening."

"Okay. The after-hours codes have changed, so I'd better write them down for you."

She took a legal pad and wrote a neat series of numbers and letters.

"Your grandfather has been tinkering with the new security system again. He's obsessed with catching industrial spies."

"He's not happy unless he can meddle," Cole said with undisguised bitterness. He wished Marsh would be content fiddling with mechanical things and leave people—especially his family—alone.

"The important part is punching in these numbers at exactly twenty-minute intervals. There's a panel in the lab as well as in the hallway." She pointed with one neatly polished, but not long, fingernail. "Best to set the timer on your watch. There's only a thirty-second margin for error."

"Got it. Thanks a lot, Mom." He bent his head and kissed her soft, smooth cheek.

"Don't let the security alarm go off. It would put your grandfather in a dither."

He patted her shoulder, then bolted for the door.

"Trust me, Mom."

He wasn't sure he trusted himself when it came to picking a wife, but he did have a date Friday night. She was a friend of Tess's, so she had to be a nice girl. Didn't she?

4

"WHY ARE WE sneaking in?" Tess asked in a breathy whisper.

"We're not sneaking." Cole answered a little louder than necessary to make his point.

"This feels sneaky. It's dark and creepy in here."

"The corridor lights dim automatically at night, that's all. My mother has no objection at all to having you see the new products. The catalog will be out pretty soon anyway."

"I still feel like a yuppie cat burglar. Why are you wearing all black?"

"These are the only clean jeans I could find, and I have a lot of black T-shirts. Do you see me wearing a ski mask?"

"I still feel funny."

"I cleared it with the head honcho, who also happens to be my mother."

"Not your grandfather?"

"Kicked upstairs to chairman of the board." He didn't want to talk about the old man. "Here we are. I have to punch in the after-hours code." He pulled out the slip of paper his mother had given him and entered the sequence of numbers on the panel beside the door.

"Just like in spy movies." She giggled nervously. "Are you going to eat the code when you're done?"

"Can't. I have to enter another sequence of numbers at twenty-minute intervals."

He opened the door and snapped on the bright overhead lights, gesturing for her to go ahead of him. He stepped into the big room behind her and took a couple of seconds to set his watch.

"What happens if you don't?"

She seemed more interested in the security system than the products she'd come to see. Darn, he'd forgotten about her raging curiosity. How long would it take for her to ferret out his real reason for wanting to meet her friends?

"The lab self-destructs, and we fall through a trapdoor in the floor to a chamber of horrors. We'll be strapped into giant high chairs, forced to eat mushy beets and spinach and subjected to talking toys until we're both raving lunatics."

"Imaginative. I've never seen a lab with a wall border of lambs, kitties and ducks."

She glanced around at the large lab, white and sterile-looking except for the wall decorations. The products were displayed on long, waist-high worktables with specifications printed on neat cardboard signs. Cole followed her gaze until it rested on a huge photo of Zack and him as kids. They were floating on an inflated water ship, one of Bailey's colossal failures thanks to a tendency to sink when the passengers weighed more than forty pounds.

"That must be you and Zack!" Tess walked over to the glossy framed blowup. "You were adorable! Oh, and look at this one!"

She walked over to a shot of a gap-toothed Zack crawling out of an inflated imitation of a sewer pipe while Cole sat astride the top.

Either his mother or his grandfather had hung the damn twins photos everywhere. Tess walked around the room pointing out advertising poses he'd erased from his consciousness long ago. His masculinity did a nosedive as she cooed over each and every cutesy curly-haired image.

"Did you get to keep every toy you posed with?" she asked.

"Not after we sliced up the inflated giant beach ball with a dagger from Marsh's World War II collection. Seems as though all our toys were metal after that. I thought you wanted to see the new products."

He liked babies but hated their equipment. Just being around all the baby stuff made him nervous, even though he could shingle a roof three stories up without a qualm. The world of bottle liners and diaper bags gave him the willies. His grandfather had tried for years to snare him into the family business, but both he and Zack were adamantly opposed to having any part of it. It was a measure of Cole's indifference that he'd never been in this lab.

"There are handouts for every product," he told Tess. "You can take one of each with you."

He was actually enjoying her interest in the stuff, following her and taking in her reactions. She commented on everything she saw without a single cloying *oh* or *ah*.

"Here's a winner," he said skeptically.

She slowly wandered over to see what he was pointing at.

"An inflatable potty for traveling. It's ingenious." She took a sample disposable liner and one of the handouts. "Where's the baby-wipes warmer that plays lullabies?"

"I wouldn't know one if it came up and bit me on the butt," he said, grousing.

"You're really not interested in any of this, are you?"

"Nope."

She lingered beside a Swedish-designed stroller that sold for more than his first car in high school, then exclaimed over a state-of-the-art high chair in screaming neon lime green. He was bored out of his socks by the displays but found himself enjoying the way she moved around the room. Her khaki walking shorts showed enough leg for him to see hers were sleek and smooth-skinned. Her waist was tiny, not much larger than the span of his hands. It had been criminal to bulk it up with yards of pink material at the wedding reception. Tonight she was wearing a blue knit T-shirt. With eyes like hers, she shouldn't wear any other color—they shone like a pair of pricey sapphires.

Easy as she was to watch, he couldn't share her enthusiasm for the products. He knew Bailey Baby Products was a highly lucrative business, but he didn't want to be lured by the prospect of easy money. He wanted to build his own designs, well-constructed, pleasant, affordable homes for people who'd never see the inside of a pretentious mansion like Marsh Bailey's. Cole and Zack had hopes of winning some commercial bids that would put their business on a firmer footing.

"Here's the baby-wipes warmer!" she said enthusiastically, her voice amplified and made lyrical by the silent vastness of the lab.

He walked over and watched her pick it up. A little beeping sound went off and didn't stop when she put it down.

"What's that?" she asked.

"The timer on my watch. Time to enter the code. It will just take a sec."

He had thirty seconds. No sweat. He went to the wall panel in the lab, trying to recall the code—three-seven-five-eight-nine, or was it six? Marsh had deliberately made it as random as possible. Why couldn't he use some significant sequence like family birth dates? The system was supposed to keep out thieves, not grandsons. He reached into the back pocket of his jeans and took out his billfold, where he'd stashed the code, counting seconds and pretty sure he was running out of time.

The dull thud he heard wasn't reassuring.

"What was that?" Tess asked.

"The locks engaged."

He punched in the code his mother had given him, but nothing happened. The door wouldn't open. He tried again in case he'd made a mistake. Still no results.

"Can't you open the door?"

"No." He tried a third time, but it was futile. He should have set his watch to allow extra time, but thirty seconds had seemed plenty long enough to punch in the code even if he had to look at the paper. Why did Marsh have such an elaborate system? Any thief who knew enough technology to get into the building could probably figure out a way to get out, but here they were, trapped in the lab. Unfortunately he wasn't a professional burglar and anything he might try could result in costly damage to the system.

"There has to be a way out," she said.

"Not if Marsh's damn anti-spy gadgetry works. I wish his James Bond DVD collection would self-destruct!"

"Do industrial spies really steal plans for baby stuff?" She sounded more curious than panicked.

"How would I know? I haven't had anything to do with the business since Zack and I gave each other haircuts to get out of posing for the catalog."

"What do we do now?"

"Wait for the baby police, I guess."

She laughed. He glowered at her.

"I don't suppose you have a cell phone in your purse?" he asked.

She shook her head. "No, but isn't that a phone over there?"

He walked over, annoyed because he'd been too rattled to notice it. It was dead.

"The phone service must cut off when the doors lock," he said.

"Why?"

If this were a spy thriller on the big screen, the heroine would be clinging to him like spandex. He could imagine Tess in a role like that, unlikely as it seemed.

"Probably so anyone trying to steal the butt warmer can't call a cohort to pass on the secret design," he said in a husky whisper. He had an odd notion he wanted to hear her laugh again.

"What do we do now?" she asked.

"Good question. Let me see if I can short out the system." Nuts to Marsh. If he ruined something, it wasn't his fault.

This was a lab. There had to be tools. He opened one of the cupboards under every workstation and found a screwdriver and a pair of pliers.

"Isn't there a night watchman or something?" she asked, hovering behind him as he removed the casing from the control panel on the wall.

"There's a whole crew of security people, but I'd rather get out of here before anyone comes."

"You said we weren't sneaking in."

"We weren't." He didn't want to look like a dope for getting the code sequence wrong, but the jumble of bunched wires was a puzzle with no solution.

"Look at all the colored wires. Just like a movie where the right one will deactivate a bomb and the wrong one will—"

"It's not a bomb," he grumbled.

"Can I pick the color?"

"Why not?"

"Yellow, pull out a yellow."

"Yellow as in no parking, no passing and crime-scene tape."

"Good point. So do you want to try the green as in go?"

He caught a green wire snaking through a bunch of other colors and yanked with the tip of the pliers. A shrill alarm sounded on the other side of the door.

"Wrong wire."

She shrugged with a nonchalance he didn't feel. He didn't relish being known as the idiot grandson.

"Try the blue," she suggested. "We're locked in with all that racket in the hall. What else can happen?"

"The walls could move in and crush us."

"Like Poe's 'Pit and the Pendulum.' You remember that story," she said enthusiastically.

He'd never read it, but then, he hadn't had Tess as a tutor that year. She'd read *Macbeth* aloud, scene by endless scene, then made him admit some of it was exciting.

He ripped out the blue wire. Nothing happened as far as he could tell. The door was still bolted shut.

"Cole, does it seem a little chilly in here?"

She hugged her arms across her chest.

"Yeah, it does."

She wasn't exaggerating. He looked around but couldn't find a thermostat to regulate the air-conditioning.

"Maybe when you pulled the blue wire..." she said, her lips turning blue.

The whole lab was one bizarre booby trap, he realized. Marsh had gone from designing clever toys in his early days to this diabolical trap. Cole tossed the pliers on the counter. No way was he pulling another wire. The red one would probably turn the floor into a giant griddle.

"Wonder if the wiper thing works as a hand warmer," he mused.

Tess was shivering too much to answer. The vents were sending out Arctic blasts, making a mockery of energy conservation.

"The SWAT team should be on their way. Until then, we'd better share body heat," he said.

He stepped behind her and wrapped his arms around her. The heat generated between her back and his chest was nothing compared to the inferno where her bottom snuggled against his lap.

"I'm warm now." She tried to squirm away.

"I'm not."

"Well, too bad! You got us into this."

"You wanted to preview the new line."

"Not if it meant being freeze-dried!"

"My grandfather likes to tinker."

"Your grandfather should be committed!"

Her teeth chattered like a pair of windup joke teeth, and he could feel a shiver ripple down her spine.

The door flew open with a bang, and they both whirled around, arms half raised in anticipation of some really tough cops.

"That's a pretty harsh judgment, young lady."

"Grandfather." Cole forgot about calling him Marsh.

"I'm glad you're taking an interest in the business, Cole."

Marsh Bailey radiated intimidation from his razor-sharp features and cold blue eyes to the immaculate press of his silvery gray Italian suit. He was the only person Cole knew who'd never owned a pair of jeans. The man didn't even loosen his tie on the rare occasions when he watched a public affairs program on TV. Cole instinctively put his arm around Tess's shoulders, surprised at how square and rigid they felt.

"This isn't a very nice way to treat one of your best customers, Mr. Bailey. The Baby Mart, which I own and operate, sold thirty-two of your inflatable play tents for Christmas last year."

"Thirty-two. I'm impressed. That's more than the Toy Warehouse in any of their north side stores. But that doesn't explain why you and my grandson set off the security system. If I hadn't been checking the surveillance screen for reception problems, you'd be looking down the barrels of some high-power firearms."

"The timing to enter the code the second time is off." His grandfather always made Cole feel belligerent.

"I can vouch for that," Tess said. "I saw Cole set his watch."

"Then it seems I owe you an apology, Miss..."

"Tess Morgan."

Marsh never apologized. He believed the rich didn't have to be sorry for anything. Cole had braced himself for a verbal flogging, and the old man was making nice with Tess.

"Now that you've seen the new line, Miss Morgan, what do you think of it?"

"The lime-green high chair won't sell. The design is wonderful, but the color will clash with almost everyone's kitchen. The portable potty is a stroke of genius, though."

Marsh ran his finger over the pencil-thin mustache he'd worn for as long as Cole could remember. His iron-gray hair was clipped to within a quarter inch of his skull. It was more than coincidence that both Cole and Zack wore their thick hair semilong and their faces clean-shaven when beards would have been more convenient.

"The potty is one of my designs." The old man actually puffed up. "The high chair also comes in sandy white for the American market."

Cole took Tess's hand. He'd had more than enough baby business for one night.

"About the yellow wire," she said as he pulled her to the corridor.

"Activates the sprinkler system." Marsh followed them through the doorway. "This has been a very satisfactory test of my new system."

TESS SPENT the rest of the week thinking about the new Bailey line—the one Cole had handed her, not the baby stuff.

Why ask her to become involved in his love life? Either he'd had too much champagne at the reception or a Bailey built brick wall had bounced on his head. She wished he'd remained nothing but a glossy memory in the yearbook.

Or did she?

Certainly he made life more interesting. She'd been trapped by a mad inventor—well, a quirky one, anyway—and suspected of industrial espionage. Even better, she'd told Marsh Bailey what was right and wrong with his new products. Would that she could do the same for Kozy Kountry cows!

As she lolled in her oversize yellow sleep shirt, munched microwave popcorn and watched *Bride of Frankenstein,* Cole was wining and dining Jillian Davis, of all people. If Tess had ever had any aspiration to be a matchmaker, this would have killed it. Jillian wasn't even on her Z list of possible dates for Cole, although, with brilliant hindsight, she had to admit her fellow kickboxer was probably his type. He thought so, anyway.

Darn, why had Marsh tried to turn the lab into the house

from *Dr. Zhivago*? She'd been blissfully ignorant of how it felt to have Cole's strong arms wrapped around her for real, not as a tactic to beat her at pool. She was going to remember the moment long after portable potties were forgotten in the mental haze of advanced old age.

The door buzzer aroused her from speculation about whether Cole had curly black hair on his tummy. Not that it mattered to her. Someday she'd find a man who was right for her, one who'd make analytical comments about *Bride of Frankenstein* while he nuzzled her throat and did other nice things.

She checked her spy hole, as she liked to call it. Cole's face was distorted like the image in a fun-house mirror, but there was still no mistaking how cute he was. Darn again! She didn't want him to see her in a nightshirt, and she especially didn't want to hear about his wonderful date.

Opening the door as far as she could without taking off the chain, she peeked out at him.

"Hi. Can I come in?"

"I'm not exactly dressed."

"You look decent to me. I really need to talk to you."

"Your grandfather's not going to have us arrested for trespassing, is he?"

She took off the chain and let him step into her snug little living room.

"Nice place."

He looked at the gray and pink striped satin couch—impractical, maybe, but she loved it—and the two deep rose velvet armchairs. The rest of her furniture was salvage from relatives or thrift-shop bargains, but she liked the touch of class her good furniture gave the light beige carpeting and white walls of the bland apartment.

"Are we in trouble for sneaking into the lab?"

"We didn't sneak."

"Of course not, but I'll pass up any more tours of Bailey Baby Products, not to sound ungrateful."

She didn't want to hear about his date, but eventually she'd run out of inane chatter.

"Next time you set me up," he said, plopping down on the couch, "I'd prefer it's with someone you know better."

He dipped into the metal mixing bowl of popcorn without invitation.

"Help yourself."

"Oh, do you mind?"

She didn't mind sharing her popcorn. She strenuously objected to arranging dates for him.

"You may remember, I didn't set you up with Jillian. You engineered that."

"Yeah, you're right."

"So, didn't you have fun?"

She couldn't pretend to be sorry. There was something about Jillian that was too perfect.

"I don't want to talk about it. What are you watching?"

"Bride of Frankenstein."

"That about sums up my evening."

"That bad?" She had this terrible guilt-producing reaction—glee.

"Have some more popcorn," she offered.

"No, thanks. We had a big dinner, surf and turf at Trocadero's."

"You do a first date right. Didn't she like it?"

"I guess she did. That's not the problem."

"What is?"

She stopped the VCR. She owned the tape and could watch it anytime. Truth to tell, he looked so glum the date had to have been interesting…to her.

"We went back to her apartment afterward."

"Horrors," she said dryly, not at all sure she wanted the intimate details.

"For coffee and lemon bars."

"Exactly what I thought," she lied.

He was dressed in tan pants and a black knit shirt that highlighted rippling muscles and dark, broody eyes. If Jillian had blown the date with Cole, her head had to be stuffed with sawdust.

"She slipped into something more comfortable—a fuzzy white robe shorter than my undershirts and fur-ball slippers that went plop, plop, plop."

"A girl has to relax sometime. So you had coffee and dessert. She can't make drinkable coffee? Her lemon bars were sour and soggy?"

"No, they both were perfect."

"Of course, perfect. Why are you here, Cole? Do you have something to complain about?"

"You've never been to her place, right?"

"Right, she's only an acquaintance. I hardly know her at all."

"She has wall-to-wall…" He took a deep breath. "Stuffed animals."

"Stuffed as in taxidermy?"

"No, the kind kids play with—plush bears and giraffes all over the furniture, dogs and kittens in wicker chairs, a duck, a whale, even a fuzzy turtle. There wasn't any place to sit without an avalanche of toy animals plummeting down on my head."

"You're exaggerating."

"No." He shook his head solemnly. His hair tumbled in spikes over his forehead, and she wanted to comb them back with her fingers. Maybe that was the point of the styling.

"When we got to her door, she warned me to be quiet so we wouldn't wake the babies."

"I didn't know she was a single mother."

"She isn't. She's a loony who talks baby talk to in-animate objects. Baby talk!"

Tess laughed…and laughed some more. Even when her ribs started to ache, she couldn't stop laughing at the expression on his face.

"I knew nobody could be as perfect as she seems," she said by way of explanation when his glum expression finally dulled her mirth.

"I didn't come here for sympathy," he said caustically. "I'm calling in your marker. You still owe me some introductions."

"Some! I understood one before we played, and you met Jillian in my store. She counts."

"I didn't get any help from you."

"I vouched for you."

"Whatever that means. You still owe me."

"If you're serious about this…"

"Dead serious."

"Then you have to give me some idea of the kind of person you'd like to meet. And why!"

"I'm not into lists."

"Or explanations?"

"Object—matrimony. Isn't that enough? I'd just like to meet some nice women."

"Nice meaning pure, untouched, unsullied, sweet, virtuous, kind, generous…"

"You talk too much!"

He moved so fast she didn't have time to protest…or time to enjoy the quick kiss he planted on her parted lips.

"Just serve me up a smorgasbord of eligible women. I'll do the rest."

Sure, she should sell him to her friends so he could break their hearts Bailey style.

5

HE COMPILED the list. Actually, he cheated a little by picking Zack's brain. They agreed on the basics—a sense of humor, pleasant personality and appealing looks. Truth to tell, they both favored lush breasts and a backside that didn't sag or spread, but what man didn't? Cole could have included lips like Tess Morgan's on his wish list, but he prudently decided to omit physical attributes.

He shouldn't have kissed her. Friends didn't smooch, especially not when the male friend wanted the female friend to find dates for him, a chore not to her liking. That was strange. Women he knew were usually so eager to play matchmaker, he'd assumed it was genetic.

He hadn't planned to drive all the way to the Rockstone Mall on Monday when he had a full crew to supervise at the site, but he needed to make a trip to a home and garden superstore. He decided to run into the mall first, ask Tess to lunch, pick out what his crew needed, then eat and give her the list she insisted was necessary. What could be more efficient? He wouldn't be making a special trip through heavy workweek-morning traffic just to see Tess.

This time he surveyed the situation before he barged into the Baby Mart. A blue-haired grandmotherly type was paying for some clothes at the counter, much better choices than the silly cow stuff. He should've been warned off Jillian when she took his caustic comment seriously and actually bought those dumb-looking quilts. Come to think of it, Tess owed him for helping her get rid of them.

The clerk looked about seventeen, round-faced with blunt-cut dark hair. No doubt Tess survived by using less expensive part-time help when she could. It was the only way a small business could make it today. He had the financial head in the partnership with Zack, and he was in awe of Tess's success. Just keeping the door open in a retail store was a major accomplishment, and the Baby Mart seemed to be thriving.

"Can I help you, sir?"

The employee was prettier than the sum of her parts, too young for him, but...

"Cole, I didn't expect to see you today. He's not a customer, Dawn." Tess shooed the young girl away.

"Have to make another trip to Builder's Supply." Not that he hadn't bypassed a dozen sources closer to their construction site. "I thought maybe we could grab lunch. I have *the list*."

"Okay, I guess."

He'd expect the same degree of enthusiasm if he asked her to bait a hook with a live worm.

"Let's go." He stepped halfway behind the counter, took her hand and started to lead her out of the store.

"Wait, I need my purse."

"No, you don't. I'll buy."

"My comb..."

"Be serious, you look great."

It was true. If he didn't know her from way back as prim and proper Tess, he'd be fooled by the way her glossy reddish-brown hair fell forward on her shoulders and her lips formed a sultry pout. She looked like a good time waiting to happen.

He'd be glad when this wife hunt was over. He didn't much like the way it made him feel to assess women as if they were beauty pageant contestants.

"I'll be right back after lunch, Dawn," she called as he steered her out of the store.

He drove from the mall parking lot to another equally crowded one at Builder's Supply. Cole was impatient with traffic and in a hurry to get back to work.

"Just as I remembered." He nodded at a little lunch wagon with a red-striped awning that sold spicy Italian sausages on hard rolls. "We can shop, eat and talk about the dates you're arranging for me."

To her credit, she waited patiently while he matched some trim for the twelve-unit condo he and Zack were building. After he loaded it on his truck, they walked to the lunch wagon, then carried paper sacks and disposable drink containers to the patio tables adjacent to the store's garden center.

"Just like Trocadero's—their parking lot, that is," she teased.

"Wait until you taste the lemon-pepper mustard. This is more fun than fancy food with Jillian."

His face suddenly felt hot. Why shouldn't it? They were picnicking beside a couple of acres of asphalt paving that simmered under the intense heat of the noonday sun.

"I'll test it." She peeled the paper wrapping on the sourdough bun and dipped the end into a little cup of sandwich spread.

He watched, fascinated by her technique. Her tongue curled out and touched the yellowy mustard, then she savored the little dab with slow relish.

"You're right!" She smiled impishly. "I can feel the buzz all the way to my toes."

She bit into the sausage and roll with so much gusto

he forgot about eating his sandwich until she finished and was sipping daintily at a cola.

"Aren't you going to eat?"

"Do you want mine?" he asked.

"No, thank you. I just wondered why you're not eating."

He wondered himself. It'd been six hours since he grabbed a bowl of cereal for breakfast, and he was usually famished by noon.

"I'll show you my list first," he said.

He had to stand up to extract the folded yellow legal-pad paper from the left pocket of his jeans. Frowning skeptically, she watched him so closely he almost checked to see if he was unzipped.

"This is pretty silly," he grumbled, sitting back on the flimsy plastic chair. He took a huge bite of sausage and roll, vigorously chewing it to mask his discomfort.

"Not at all. I have some people in mind. In fact, I have the list in my purse, but you didn't give me time to get it."

"Why bring your list to work? You weren't expecting me."

Her cheeks heated up, and he remembered how much he used to enjoy baiting her. He didn't quite manage to hide a grin when she picked up one of the paper napkins and scrubbed at her mouth, removing the last trace of lipstick.

"Did I get all the mustard?" she asked.

"All but a tiny dab here." He tweaked the end of her nose with his finger.

"I didn't get any on my nose!"

"Are you absolutely sure of that?"

"Not without a mirror," she grudgingly admitted,

"and, of course, I don't have one because I don't have my purse. Okay, let's see it."

She reached toward the sheet of paper he still held in his left hand.

"Don't laugh," he cautioned, not that she could be intimidated.

"I lost my sense of humor when you dazzled me with your pool hall prowess," she complained.

He handed over the list, not sure whether to be embarrassed by the characteristics written in a dark scrawl with a thick-leaded carpenter's pencil.

"Am I reading right?" she asked. "Number four is *inexperienced?*"

"Maybe a bad word." He felt six inches high.

"No, I get your meaning. You want to be able to teach her a thing or two."

"Not exactly!" He choked.

"Chew your food."

She didn't want to do this, so she was making him suffer, another thing Tess did very, very well.

"Are you sure you didn't copy this from a medieval handbook for husbands?"

"Let's just say, if her little black book has fewer pages than mine, I'll be happy."

"Like that wouldn't apply to every unmarried woman I know."

Was it possible sweet little Tess was nurturing a grudge for all the times he'd provoked her in high school? She was certainly stomping on his list with hobnail boots. He wasn't going to give her any more ammo by revealing his grandfather's horror of tainted women.

"You're not making this easy for me," he mumbled.

"Sorry. We both want this to be over. I like requirement number nine—family oriented. I adore mine, especially Erika and Erin.''

"Your nieces, right?''

"Yeah.'' When she smiled without the snide expression, her face lit up. "Here's a practical one. You like to be outdoors, so naturally you would enjoy a woman who shares your interest.''

"I'm glad you approve," he said dryly, wrapping the uneaten portion of his bun so she wouldn't notice. Anyone could lose his appetite once in a while.

"Several of the names on my list qualify so far," she said.

"Who?''

"Let me compare your list with mine and decide who's perfect for you. Then I'll see if any of my friends are interested in meeting you.''

"I don't want a perfect woman. Someone like you would be fine.''

"Thanks a lot…I think.''

Whether from the heat of the day or internal combustion, her cheeks were glowing sunburn-red.

"I didn't mean it as an insult." Dang, had he made her squirm this much in high school? He chugged the rest of his root beer, which he didn't like and didn't remember ordering. "By someone like you, I meant a nice, attractive woman with interests of her own and not a whole lot of dating experience.''

"How do you know I haven't dated multitudes of men since you knew me in school?''

"I don't know. Sorry." *A guy does know,* he thought, trying not to let her see his smugness. "Why are you making this so complicated?''

"I have too many possibilities on my list—friends, sisters of friends, cousins of friends, friends of friends, customers, friends of customers, relatives of…''

He laughed defensively. ''That narrows it down to all the eligible women in the greater Detroit area.''

''Not quite, but I have at least a dozen good prospects. I'll mull it over, then negotiate.''

She stood and brushed crumbs from the lap of her short, swingy, flowered skirt, forcing him to notice those spectacular legs again.

''Negotiate, as in union contract?''

''You have to realize, some of my friends may not be interested in meeting you.''

He did the wrong thing—he laughed.

''I have to get back to work,'' she said forcefully. ''By the way, I do want to thank you again for letting me preview the new product line. It was quite an experience.''

''One I'm trying to forget,'' Cole muttered.

TESS WENT BACK to work seriously considering signing up for a yoga class. Nothing she'd learned in the self-assertive discipline of kickboxing had helped when Cole showed up at the store without warning for the second time. She was embarrassed to remember her pounding heart and racing pulse.

He'd startled her. That could be the only possible explanation for her purely involuntary adrenaline rush.

Instead of working on the next week's work schedule, she laid Cole's list and hers side by side on her desk in the back room. The numbered lineup of unattached friends spilled over onto the back of her page, even though she'd printed their names in ant-size letters. She flipped the paper and put her own name at the bottom of the list in tiny, barely legible script. She belonged in this anthill, too.

Cole would get his fill of the eager and the eligible.

Meeting Mr. Right was the Mount Olympus of dating, and the older a woman got, the harder it was to scale up to where the Greek gods were hiding.

She stabbed at the paper with the pen point, obliterating her name. What had she gotten herself into?

Anyway, she said she would set him up, and she would, and why had Cole wrapped his sausage and bun instead of eating it? Did being with her zap his appetite, or was it the prospect of an endless string of blind dates? More puzzling, why was he gung ho to have her help him meet women when he didn't have the slightest bit of trouble getting acquainted with them wherever he went? She didn't buy his excuse about not finding *nice* women on his own.

She could keep him supplied with a new date every night of the week and double book him for lunch and dinner on the weekend. She'd begin with friends from high school. They'd at least know him by reputation—the Bailey twins' legacy had endured at least until Tess's class graduated, if not longer.

Lucinda deserved to sit on a jellyfish on her tropical paradise honeymoon. If it weren't for that ludicrous dress, Tess's bow wouldn't have been caught in the trunk and Cole wouldn't have paid the least bit of attention to her. Now she was really stuck—matchmaker to a man of many conquests.

She flipped the sheet, wrote her name above contestant number one, then blacked it out letter by letter.

The phone interrupted her as she turned the *n* in Morgan into an inky square.

"Baby Mart, how may I help you?" she automatically answered.

"Ms. Tess Morgan?" The woman spoke with diligently cultivated culture.

"This is she." She couldn't say, "Yeah, it's me," to this voice.

"This is Dorothea Danzig, Mr. Marsh Bailey's personal assistant. Mr. Bailey would be honored if you would attend a reception to launch the new catalog this Saturday evening."

"Me?" So much for outclassing the classy voice on the other end of the line.

"You are the owner of Baby Mart?"

"Yes, I am." She said that satisfactorily, hardly a gasp of astonishment in her businesslike response.

"Cocktails from seven to nine in the Windsor Room of the Sherman Arms Hotel, then dinner at nine. May I add your name to the guest list, Ms. Morgan? Mr. Bailey will provide transportation, of course."

"I'd be very pleased to attend." Did that sound all right, or was there a little wheeze in *pleased?*

"Splendid. Your limo will be there at 6:30 p.m., if you'll be so kind as to give me your home address."

Home address? Yes, she had one! She gave it triumphantly.

She was going to ride in a limo, a limo as in prom night, wedding…funeral procession!

"You may, of course, bring an escort if you like. I believe you're a friend of Mr. Bailey's grandson, but it's completely optional whether you choose to invite someone. The event is black tie."

Tess repeated the date and time, scribbling them on the margin of her list as the call ended.

Was it because she'd liked the portable potty? Or because lime green reminded her of lizards, pond scum and diet lime soda? More likely, Cole's grandfather was trying to use her to entice his grandson into taking an interest in the business. The Bailey men were leading her on a flimsy rope bridge over very sticky quicksand. She could only hope her common sense was an adequate safety net.

GETTING DATES for Cole proved as easy as locating a free cat. Friday night was a snap. Tess had gotten reacquainted with a classmate, Jordan Collins, who'd recently moved back to the area. She was on the thin side, but Cole hadn't made a point about size or shape.

"I had a huge crush on Cole in high school," Jordan admitted when Tess called her that evening after work. "But didn't everyone? He was so adorable in a naughty sort of way."

"Certainly not me," Tess lied.

Saturday was even easier to book. A real friend, Margo Hendricks, volunteered when Tess groused to her over lunch on Tuesday. She'd never met Cole, but a longtime relationship with a live-in boyfriend had fizzled a few weeks earlier.

"I hate all men, and I hate blind dates even more," Margo said. "But if I do this for you, we'll be even for all the time you spent listening to me sob about Rick."

"You'll be perfect," Tess declared.

She didn't have a free minute to tackle a really serious problem until Friday. What should she wear to a reception at the Sherman Arms? She took a long lunch break and covered the stores in the mall, deciding she really couldn't afford five hundred dollars for a midnight-blue evening gown shimmering with a touch of deep violet even though it made her look thin and feel like glamour personified.

After work she resorted to desperate measures—she went to her sister. Karen agreed to loan anything she owned in exchange for Tess keeping Erika and Erin overnight sometime soon so she and Duke could relive their wedding night at Martino's Resort and Spa.

"You don't know what pleasure is until you bask in one of their heart-shaped hot tubs," Karen enthused.

"I can't decide which dress to wear," Tess said, trying not to imagine Cole rising up in a cloud of mist and leading her to a bed covered in black satin sheets. "I'll have to take some home."

"Come back tomorrow. It isn't as if Royal Oak is as far away as the moon."

"Can't. Have to work in the morning. Then get my hair done."

"A French twist, have it piled up in a French twist."

"Maybe." It was a good idea, but if she gave her big sister any encouragement, Karen would want to choose everything from eye shadow to toenail polish.

By Friday evening, Tess still hadn't decided. Five of Karen's best dresses were spread out on her bed, and she'd just taken off a sixth when the door buzzer summoned her. She slipped into a short pink robe and hoped she didn't have a visitor who expected to come inside.

Why was she not surprised to see Cole's image in her spy hole? Was this part of his blind-date ritual, reporting to her on the state of the date?

She opened the door a crack.

"I'm not dressed."

"I don't mind." He sounded sheepish but adamant.

"Good or bad date?"

"Maybe a few suggestions so you can do better next week."

"I didn't enlist for the duration of the war!"

"You didn't enlist at all. You were drafted. Got any popcorn?"

"I'm not dressed for company." How could she resist his pathetic smile? "Oh, come in."

"I'll pretend you're at the beach. Guess you'd have to

take off more for that. Would you be more comfortable if I took my shirt off?''

''Don't!''

''Just kidding, not that I have much sense of humor left after that date. I thought she was going to attack me with a steak knife.''

''Oh, dear. Let me put some popcorn in the microwave. You're kidding about the knife, right?''

''I took her to a place that specializes in steaks. She doesn't eat meat.''

''That's not unusual.'' She set the timer, conscious of Cole hovering near the sleeve of her robe.

''She doesn't wear leather, she doesn't step on bugs and she only eats salad made with produce that comes with six different labels guaranteeing no chemicals were used in producing it. She made the waiter bring an empty bag from the kitchen. The lettuce flunked.''

''It's smart to be careful about what you put in your body.''

Tess felt defensive. After all, he was the one insisting she find dates for him. Could she help it if there were no perfect women on the dating circuit?

''I have no problem with vegetarians, but when I order a twenty-five-dollar porterhouse, I don't want it seasoned with sarcastic remarks.''

''She lectured, huh? No need to be testy about it with me.''

The popcorn bag inflated, and she tried to guess the moment when the kernels were through exploding but not yet scorched.

''Why do you want popcorn if you're stuffed with prime beef?''

''I didn't eat most of it. There's more.''

''It gets worse?''

"Jordan likes to purify her mind through abstinence—no drugs, alcohol, cigarettes, chocolate…"

"Good for her. She sounds like a great marital candidate."

"No sex."

"Oh. Are you sure… I mean, you want someone who doesn't sleep around."

"No sex, period." He looked grim.

"Come on, you're making that up."

"Except, of course, we do have to consider the future of the human race, so a weekend schedule is acceptable—after marriage, of course." He started pacing, hands hooked in his pockets.

"Jordan was pretty intense in high school, now that I think about it. Made straight As, worked as a candy striper at the hospital. Now she has a good job in the insurance industry."

"She probably spends her days denying payment for doctor-ordered treatment. I won't go into her health care theories except to say they involve a lot of yogurt. She has naturally curly hair and…" She followed his pacing into the kitchen, then put out her arms like a crossing guard to stop him.

"And she weighs ninety pounds with her pockets full of nails." He slumped over a kitchen chair.

"Maybe you're making snap judgments because you really don't want any blind dates." She stood over him feeling like a prosecutor with a guilty defendant.

"Untrue. And I'm not being picky. I can't have a long-term relationship with a woman who calls me a Jack the Ripper of sweet-faced bovines."

"Speaking of that, did I thank you for helping me unload the comatose-cow quilts?"

"No, and don't change the subject. She really did call

me a serial cattle killer, and she was pointing a steak knife at me when she said it.'' He pointed at her little wooden rack of knives on the counter.

"Sorry. She just moved back here."

"Not your fault. I'm not good at blind dates, I guess."

"Everyone hates them."

"Women, too?"

"I'd rather have my eyelashes removed."

She took the popcorn out of the microwave and yelped when hot steam singed her fingers as she opened the bag.

"Let me. There is one more small point for future reference. Maybe you could find me a more—let's say substantial woman."

"As in well-endowed?"

"Sort of."

"I thought appearance didn't matter," she said, putting her hands on her hips.

"I want to get married, possibly to someone who doesn't look embalmed."

"You're not being nice. Jordan had a tremendous crush on you in high school."

"Lots of girls did—on Zack or me." He nonchalantly stuffed a handful of popcorn in his mouth.

"You are such a—"

"Male?"

There was that.

"That's why I liked you," he said as he munched. "You didn't. It was fun having a girl as a friend."

She snorted, but he was too busy chomping to notice.

She wandered into her living room, belatedly wishing she'd closed the bedroom door. The bed was easily visible and so loaded with clothes it looked like a rummage sale.

"Packing to go somewhere?" He followed her, glancing curiously through the open door.

"No, trying to decide what to wear."

"Another wedding?" He licked his buttery fingers.

"Thankfully, no. Just a party. It's at the Sherwood Arms, so I probably should dress up."

"Who are you going with?"

"Feel free to ask me anything."

"If you're ashamed of him…"

"There is no him. It's just a party. I can invite someone if I like, but when have I had time to concentrate on my love life? Yours is a full-time job. Now, if you've had enough snack food…"

The phone rang just as she was gearing up to tell him what she really thought about his hunt for a woman.

She picked it up and listened while her real friend, Margo, happily explained how she and Rick had reconciled. Tess carried the cordless as far from Cole as she could, short of barricading herself in the bathroom.

"Sure, I understand," she said into the phone. "I'm delighted for you, but I have someone here. I'll talk to you tomorrow."

She dropped the receiver on the charger.

"Your date canceled."

"For tomorrow night?"

"Of course for tomorrow night! You may be booked until Christmas for all I know, but Margo is the only one who would call *me* to cancel."

"I know that." He licked his upper lip. Even his tongue was sexy. "That means…"

"Cole, I cannot find someone else for you by tomorrow."

"No need. I have something else in mind."

"In that case…" She took his arm, hoping to propel him toward the door.

"Now I'm free to go to your shindig tomorrow night." Cole had a teasing glint in his eyes.

"You don't mean…"

"You said you need a date."

"I said could bring, not need!"

"It's the least I can do after all the trouble you've gone to for me."

"You don't need to pay me back, Cole."

"How could I ever pay you back for a stuffed animal fanatic?"

"She was your choice!"

"Or an armed and dangerous vegetarian?"

"Not my fault," she grumbled, counting the reasons matchmaking was a thoroughly thankless job.

"What time should I pick you up?"

She had a revelation. She could see the cartoon image of an angel on her right shoulder and a devil on the left. After a very brief struggle, the guy in red won.

"It will work better if you meet me at the Sherman Arms Hotel. Be in the lobby at six-thirty," she said.

No way was she going to let him see the limo his grandfather was sending for her!

"Okay. By the way, black isn't your color." He glanced toward the bedroom, where half the dresses on the bed were black.

"No, but it's yours. The party is black tie. That won't be a problem, will it?"

Underneath his golden-brown tan lay the blanched visage of a man who'd just been trapped into wearing a tux.

"See you tomorrow evening," she said, purring.

6

THE MOST stunning woman Cole had ever seen was standing beside a giant flower arrangement in the center of the vast hotel lobby. She was wearing a long shimmering blue dress, sleeveless and slit well above her knee. With her upswept hairdo she resembled a princess.

His mouth went dry as he wondered what his chances were of meeting her. He glanced around and didn't see Tess. What was this mysterious business about meeting her here?

He walked toward the lovely vision, half expecting her to vanish like a mirage. Instead she turned slightly and looked directly at him with a mischievous little smile.

"Tess." He hadn't felt so winded since the last time his midsection had connected with a football helmet.

"Did you have trouble parking?" she asked with suspicious sweetness.

"I managed to get into the parking garage after I maneuvered around all the stretch limos. The street is clogged with them."

"Must be some fancy affair going on. You cleaned up well—the tux looks good."

"You, too." He was trying not to stare, but his eyeballs had a will of their own.

"It was nice of you to come," she said serenely.

"It's the least I could do after all you've done to help me." He felt a sudden rush of gratitude that tonight's blind date had canceled. "Why didn't you let me pick you up? I borrowed Zack's vintage Mustang."

"Oh, meeting here worked better." She smiled so slyly he was even more mystified.

"Glad you didn't wear black," he said softly.

"Glad you did."

Enough of this small talk, he thought. He wanted to tell her she looked gorgeous, stunning, fantastic, but this was Tess. He couldn't tell a friend she was so beautiful he felt as if he'd fallen on his head and was seeing stars.

"Shall we?" He offered his arm. "What's this party for, anyway?"

"It's in the Windsor Room," she said, which didn't answer his question.

The hotel worked hard to create old-world ambience. The staff spoke in hushed voices, and no litter would dare appear on the faux Oriental carpeting. They passed a cluster of massive burgundy leather chairs, and Cole thought how much fun it would be to pull Tess down on his lap and...

"Hey, how did you get here?" he asked, increasingly curious about her metamorphosis from shop girl to elegant partygoer.

"Here we are." She smiled brightly and ignored his question.

The lobby was shabby compared to the grandeur of the ballroom. He took in the gold-flecked marble walls and a chandelier big enough to light Toledo. Tables were arranged in a large T and covered with place settings on white linen. It was the centerpieces that really caught his eye. Huge arrangements of orchids, exotic lilies and other florists' fancies were festooned with baby rattles and clusters of pink and blue pacifiers.

"A baby shower? Let me guess. It's for the governor's daughter, or maybe there's a new Ford in the future."

He wanted to erase her Mona Lisa smile, shake her composure, make her tell him what was going on. Mostly he didn't want this to be what he knew it was.

"I didn't know you had such a vivid imagination."

She squeezed his bicep. Any other time he would've liked the tingling sensation.

"Why didn't you tell me?"

"You never asked. It's just a reception to kick off the new winter catalog."

"Why are we here?"

"Your grandfather asked me."

"He asked you to lure me here?"

"Certainly not! I didn't even speak to him personally, but I was told I could bring an escort. You were supposed to have a date tonight."

"Are you doing this to me because I put a frog in your backpack? Because I got Harold What's-his-name to follow you around?"

"You did that?" Surprise registered on her face. "Cole Bailey, that was so low!"

"Just matchmaking."

She might look like every man's dream, but she could still make him feel like a school-yard bully.

"Anyway, if you remember, you asked to come with me," she said.

"As a favor because you didn't have a date."

"Oh, please! Have I ever, ever, ever asked you to fix *me* up?"

"You could've warned me where we were going."

"Would you have backed out?"

"No, I asked you. I'd still be here." He said it with more conviction than he felt.

"You don't have to sound so stoic. This should be fun."

"Fun." He snorted. "The old man wants me involved in the family business. This is just another of his ploys."

A waiter ambled by with a silver tray of champagne goblets filled to the brim. Cole snagged two and handed one to Tess.

"I hate this stuff," he said, taking a big swig to lubricate his throat and a couple more to polish off the bubbly. "It gives me a headache."

"No wonder, if you gulp it down like it's a sports drink."

"Well, we're here. Let's party."

He put his arm around her and rested his hand on her shapely, near-bare shoulder. Her hip brushed his, and he began to see some potential in the evening, except she was still Tess. A guy couldn't screw up a friendship for a few cheap thrills.

"Tess, I'm so pleased you could come." Marsh broke away from a group of what were probably major distributors and gave Tess one of his two-handed grips, a handshake that involved her arm all the way to the elbow. "Cole, I'm surprised to see you."

"I bet you are, Grandpa."

There was nothing the old silver fox liked less than being called Grandpa. He was still holding Tess's hand in one of his and patting it with the other.

"May I steal this lovely lady for a few minutes?" Marsh asked.

He asked Cole but kept his eyes locked on Tess. Could the old man...did he think he could...

No! Preposterous! Tess had too much common sense to...

But Marsh was a longtime widower and a damned persuasive salesman. Cole had never given a thought to the possibility of his grandfather having affairs, and he didn't want to now.

"Five minutes is all I can spare her," he warned.

"It was nice of you to present yourself in a tux," Marsh said.

He made the compliment sound like a pat on the head for a schoolboy. With a sour taste in his mouth, Cole watched as his grandfather walked toward a cluster of people with his hand on Tess's waist.

Cole got cornered by an old friend who was a Tigers fan with lots of ideas to improve the ball club. He sipped champagne and tried to inch away, but the baseball fanatic stuck. He grabbed another glass of champagne, hoping the second one would taste better and looked around for Tess. She'd disappeared in the crowd.

An eternity and several champagnes later, he was ready to ditch the party and go home. Unfortunately, he couldn't. Tess wasn't exactly a date, but he did have to consider how she'd get home.

"Cole, I'm so glad you came." Sue Bailey appeared and hugged her son.

"Hi, Mom. You look great."

It was true. She was wearing a beaded beige jacket and dress, and he hadn't seen her so happy and animated in a long time. The business was really good for her.

"Tess is the one who looks absolutely lovely. She's really blossomed since she tutored you in English."

"Yeah, blossomed." Cacti did the same thing, but they didn't lose their spines.

"It was so nice of you to be Tess's date. You're even wearing a tux."

"Yeah, Mom." He had the tux, but no girl. "Where is she, anyway?"

"I think your grandfather wanted her to talk to a Japanese supplier."

He talked to his mother until she deserted him, too, but the waiters with their little short jackets and loaded trays of bubbly were always an arm's length away. Finally, about the time every taste bud in the room was anesthetized by alcohol, dinner was served.

Cole tried to find Tess, but the whole scene was getting a little blurry. He took one of the last empty seats at the banquet table, half expecting to see his date enthroned at the head table with the baby business Baileys. She wasn't.

He didn't spot her until the beef medallions and wild rice with wine sauce—or something like that—had disappeared and the after-dinner wits were standing up to make toasts. She'd been hidden beside a massive blond German who stood and made some remarks in an accent too thick for Cole's equally thick brain to decipher. Tess laughed so hard, he thought she'd shake the sleek coils off her unfortunately gorgeous head.

Good thing they weren't on a real date. He'd be feeling pretty testy by now.

He finished the last of the excellent wine—something red—in his glass as his stuffed-shirt grandfather brought the house down with a joke about little baby boys and little baby girls. And the old man wondered why Cole and Zack would rather join the Foreign Legion than work in the family business.

Was there still a Foreign Legion? There should be. Someone had to smooth out all those sand dunes. Was he making a total ass of himself? His face felt stiff from the fake smile he'd plastered in place. Still there. Good thing he didn't have a real date. She'd dump him for sure.

He had to get away to clear his head. If he remembered right—and he asked a girl dressed like an old-fashioned parlor maid to be sure—there was an elevator to a bar on the roof. If his grandfather wanted him on the Bailey team, this was a hell of a way to recruit him.

TESS SAW COLE sneak out. She'd wanted to sit with him at dinner, but Marsh practically threw her at Johann. She couldn't blame the senior Bailey for wanting to keep an important customer entertained, but he was too accustomed to getting his own way.

If Cole were a real date, she might feel guilty. Instead, she just wanted to talk to him, get his opinion on the reception, see if he enjoyed his dinner.

Who was she kidding? When she was with him, she saw life through a rosy haze. Finding dates for him was like sticking pins in her heart. Of course, they'd never be a couple, but she didn't want anyone else to have him. If he got married, it would break up the set—the wild Bailey boys would be history. She'd have to accept her own realistic expectations and settle for a nice guy who wanted a home and family.

She found Cole with a little help from a waitress who naturally remembered seeing him get on an express elevator to the top of the building. No woman ever forgot an encounter with Cole.

The Roof Garden was a bar with a view, although Tess had never understood people's fascination with watching pinpricks of light from cars moving on the freeways. It also felt as if it was a place for clandestine lovers, bored traveling salesmen and serious drinkers. The bartender was the only one with enough wattage to see beyond his own nose.

Thankfully Tess was spared the embarrassment of searching from table to table. Cole was lounging on a bar stool, one foot on a brass rail. He didn't see her coming.

She couldn't say the devil made her do it, but the little rascal perched on her left shoulder must have applauded when she came up behind Cole and tickled his ribs on either side.

He yelped and jumped off the stool. Served him right for sitting like that, one cute, round bun hanging off his seat.

"That's for the frog!"

"What would you do if it'd been a snake?"

"You don't want to know."

"Can I buy you a drink?" He spoke with the exaggerated precision of someone who'd already had quite a few.

"Ginger ale, please." After champagne and dinner followed by a sinfully rich chocolate mousse, she was stuffed.

"Is the party over?" he asked.

"No, the band was warming up when I left."

"Won't Hans expect to dance with you?" He sounded petulant.

"Your grandfather made me sit with him. And his name is Johann."

"Whatever. It's all right if you do. I just came along to help you out. It's not as if I'm your date."

"Of course not."

"You've been working so hard finding dates for me, I wanted to do something for you."

"Maybe I make it sound harder than it is. Several of my friends would love to meet you."

Unfortunately this was true, and she couldn't imagine anything worse than being a bridesmaid when Cole got married.

Her ginger ale came. She sipped as Cole watched her with hooded eyes.

"We can leave now, if you like," she said.

She didn't want the evening to end. This was her one chance to be Cinderella, and she'd hardly spent any time at all with Prince Charming.

He drained the tall, damp beer stein and laid some bills on the bar.

"Let's go."

She left half of her soda, disappointed he hadn't insisted she finish it. He must really want to get rid of her.

He pushed the elevator button for the ground floor, and she remembered the limo. They wouldn't even be riding home together.

When they got off, he took her arm and steered her toward the ballroom.

"I thought you wanted to leave," she said.

"What kind of escort would I be if I made you miss the dance?"

"You don't have to stay, Cole. I did trick you into coming. I know it's the last place you'd choose to be."

"Kind of makes up for Harold, doesn't it? I told him you had a major crush on him."

"I thought Zack was the troublemaker!"

"Him, too, but I'm more creative."

A dance band was playing a mellow Motown hit as Cole led her toward the polished floor at the far end of the room.

She'd dreamed of dancing with him so often this didn't seem real. She felt the warmth of his hand on her waist and closed her eyes, letting him lead her in a pattern of steps that didn't register on her conscious mind. She could feel his starchy white shirtfront and black satin lapels against her cheek.

"You're good," he whispered, his breath warm and ticklish on her ear.

"Only because you lead so well."

He laughed softly. "Flattery isn't your style."

"Isn't it possible I'm just being honest?"

He rested his cheek against her forehead and moved with the fluid grace that had first made her admire him. He'd been the star at her first track meet in high school. She took third in girls' broad jump, and he collected a slew of blue ribbons. He'd excelled in all sports, but his athletic prowess never seemed to go to his head.

She had a new passion—slow dancing. What could be more dreamy than moving when Cole moved, surrendering herself to his rhythmic moves? Every time he twirled or dipped, she seemed to end up closer to him. Her breasts flattened against his broad, hard chest, and his hand strayed lower, his fingers resting lightly on her hip. If this were anyone but Cole, she'd think he was coming on big-time.

"May I cut in?" Johann, Nordic-blond and gorgeous, hovered expectantly between numbers.

"Sorry, we don't allow cuts in Detroit. Local custom," Cole said, not relinquishing his hold on her.

He whirled her away before the music resumed.

"That wasn't very nice," she said.

"I'm not trying to be nice," he murmured.

No one else tried to separate them.

You'd think we were lovers, Tess thought wistfully when the band took their break.

"I wish," he said, keeping his arm around her waist, "I hadn't tried to run up Grandpa's champagne bill."

"If you want to leave now…"

No matter how many times Cinderella's big scene played out, the ball always ended badly.

"Think I'd better call a cab. No way should I drive."

"I agree, but I can drop you off in my limo."

"Your what?"

"Limo. Your grandfather sent it for me."

"That's why you had me meet you here."

"Would you have come if you'd known it was a Bailey Baby Products reception?"

"I am a man of my word," he said with mock indignation.

She couldn't quite believe it, but the long, sleek vehicle was waiting exactly as the driver had promised. Imagine, the man had done nothing all evening but await her bidding. She felt decadent and giddy and pampered, all at the same time, but mostly she wanted Cole to leave his arm across her shoulders.

The business of giving the driver instructions was a letdown. He insisted it was much more convenient to drop her off first, and he'd be on overtime in approximately twenty minutes. Tess couldn't waste Marsh's money even though he probably wouldn't notice or care if they went the longer route to take Cole home first.

The back seat was far too wide. She sat by one window. Cole sat by the other. There was space for a pair of Great Danes between them, and Cole gave no indication he wanted to continue their dance-floor intimacy. In fact, she wasn't even sure he was awake.

The trip from the city to her Madison Heights apartment took a good forty minutes in daytime traffic. The limo made it in the speed of light.

Cole roused himself when they stopped in front of her place.

"I'll walk you to the door," he offered.

"You don't need to. It's not as if this was a date."

He slid over to her side and came out behind her when the driver opened the door. The walk to her door was maybe twenty feet. She wished it were twenty miles.

"Tell me," he said, grabbing her hand and laying it on his bent arm. "Should I kiss a nice girl on a first date?"

"That's up to you and your date."

"Give me some help here, Tess. How would a nice girl react to a kiss on the first date?"

"I suppose it depends on whether she likes you." As if anyone in her right mind would not like him.

They reached her door, where a small light glowed all night, triggered automatically by a master switch she knew not where. Before, it had been a comfort when she got home after dark. Now she wanted darkness to swallow up the two of them.

"I don't have a clue, Tess. Teach me some nice-girl rules."

"Don't get smashed on a first date?"

"Good point, but if I were stone-cold sober, would you let me practice, just so I don't blow a good thing if one comes along?

"Cole, this is champagne talk!" Her heart was racing so hard she was afraid he'd hear it.

"No, I really need to relearn the basics before I tackle more blind dates. Any guy in his right mind would try to kiss beautiful lips like yours, but would a nice girl like you let him?"

"The driver is watching—you're embarrassing me."

"He drives on prom nights. A little good-night kiss won't shock him."

"Cole, please..."

"I'll take that as a yes."

His lips came closer, and she told herself to shut up. Once she would've done anything—anything at all—for a good-night kiss from him. Now she had a chance to see if he lived up to her fantasies.

His lips parted when they met hers, and she quivered

with anticipation, afraid she'd betray how much this kiss meant to her. He put both hands behind her head, his fingers stabbing into her elaborate hairdo.

"Are you ready?" he murmured.

What a silly thing to ask, she dreamily mused. She'd been ready for him forever.

The flesh around her mouth tingled as he gently touched it with his lips. She didn't know how long she could stand his leisurely teasing, but she wrapped her arms around his torso to steady herself.

Oh, my!

His tongue slid between her teeth as he covered her mouth and kissed her so forcefully her ears rang. He kissed her again, drawing her into the best kiss of her whole dating career.

"Was the tongue too much?" he asked, nibbling her earlobe and tickling her ear with his warm breath.

"Yes, too much." She meant it was too good to waste on a blind date.

"Tess, I have to tell you something."

"Tell me."

"I'm dizzy."

She felt the same way.

"Champagne does not agree with me."

"Time to go home," she sighed, returning to earth. She tried to slip free of his arms, but he wasn't having it. "The driver is waiting."

"I'm too tired to walk all the way to the limo."

"Cole, you have to go home. Now."

"Let me lie down on your couch," he mumbled. "Just a few minutes."

"*No!*"

He nuzzled her neck, his hands dropping so low she could sit on them.

"Cole Bailey, this isn't the way to behave on a first date—not that this is a date."

"I could sack out on your doorstep."

"Oh..." Her resistance was crumbling. "Move your hands."

"Just a little nap on your couch, and I'll leave."

"The driver can't wait while you sleep."

She could feel his long, lean length buckling. If he went down, she'd never be able to get him on his feet again.

She waved at the limo driver, who was still standing dutifully by the open car door.

"You can go," she called, waving him to leave.

He didn't take any persuading.

Cole didn't have any trouble steadying himself enough to take her key out of her hand and open the door.

"You asked for the couch. You get it."

"Tess..."

She ignored him and beat a hasty retreat to her room, pushing the door shut with a thud.

This wasn't the way fairy tales ended.

7

"GOOD MORNING, party animal."

Cole looked up through a haze of pain and tried unsuccessfully to straighten his legs. He was wearing so many clothes he felt like a mummy.

"Was my couch comfortable?" Tess beamed at him.

"Like sleeping on a rack."

The starched shirt was a wrinkled mess but still scratched his neck. He couldn't remember what he'd done with the studs that held it shut, but the suspenders were hanging down like stirrups on a horse. His modesty was intact, but he couldn't say the same for his dignity.

To make matters worse, Tess looked even more kissable in the morning than she had as belle of the ball. He was a pushover for the reddish-brown hair that bounced on the shoulders of her little pink top.

"What can I get for you? Coffee, juice, aspirin?"

"All of them, please. I haven't felt like this since I was a sophomore at Michigan State."

He pressed the sides of his head, and sparks bounced in front of his eyeballs.

"I think I'm allergic to champagne."

"One sip and you break out in hives?"

She sounded so perky and brisk, he wanted to bring her down to his level—somewhere between swampy morass and bottomless pit. At least she was wearing short white shorts. Not only were her legs spectacular, she had cute kneecaps.

"Are you tormenting me just for fun?" He cautiously sat up and inched his feet to the floor. He didn't know which looked sillier, the bare toes on the right or the black silk sock at half-mast on the left.

"I'm sorry." She didn't sound it. "It may help if you massage your temples right here." She demonstrated on herself. "If you have a headache, that is."

"Have you ever seen a hangover without one?"

"Well, actually…"

She shrugged, and he had her number. She was trying to pretend that having a man on her couch in the morning was no big deal. He'd bet it was a first. *Good try, sweetheart,* he thought, wondering if she'd let him take a little nap on her bed.

Now there was a really bad idea. Next he'd think about snuggling up to her and maybe…

"I'll make coffee," she said, disappearing into her kitchen. "You'll find a bottle of aspirin in the bathroom cabinet."

He found his other rumpled sock and pulled it on, then yanked up the suspenders. She'd tricked him into a rented tux. She'd outfoxed him on the party. He couldn't remember a worse evening…or a better one when they'd danced.

In the bathroom he splashed cold water on his face until he felt waterlogged, but he couldn't wash away his guilt. Champagne didn't agree with him, but he'd exaggerated his state of intoxication as an excuse to kiss Tess. His theory was, her lips seemed especially desirable because they were forbidden fruit. A guy didn't kiss a friend, especially not one who was helping him find a wife, but a little sample would prove her lips were nothing special.

Boy, had he been wrong! He deserved the jackhammer

that was assaulting his brain. He found the aspirin and chugged down four.

The one thing he could not do was have a casual fling with Tess. It would ruin something precious—their friendship.

Damn, when would he learn not to toss a coin with Zack? How could he expect to beat blind, dumb luck? Worse, he hadn't seen his mother so happy in ages. She loved being part of Bailey Baby Products. He couldn't get off the hook. He had to make sure his grandfather didn't sell out to strangers.

Thinking of his lucky brother, Cole groaned. They'd promised to give an estimate on a kitchen renovation. The auto exec's wife had insisted both the Bailey twins come for brunch. He felt as though he were part of a circus act, but the condos would be finished before fall. He and Zack had to line up winter jobs to keep their crew employed.

The smell of Tess's coffee was soothing as he padded into the kitchen. He drank a huge glass of orange juice, then sipped the hot brew at her table while she pretended to be busy.

"Thanks," he said.

"For the coffee? You're welcome."

"For taking me in last night."

"What are couches for?"

"Oh, man, I have to get Zack's car." He'd just remembered abandoning it.

"I'd be glad to drive you downtown, but I'm due for a family day, big noon dinner and all."

"No problem. I have to call Zack anyway. We're supposed to give an estimate on a job."

"On Sunday?"

"In our business, the client calls the shots." Especially

when the lady in question could drop a hundred thousand on a kitchen without blinking an eye.

"Well, if Zack can pick you up..." Her cheeriness sounded a bit forced. "I guess I should thank you for going to the party. It couldn't have been much fun for you."

"It wasn't all bad." He gave her a frog-in-the-backpack grin that sent a fierce stab of pain across his forehead.

Once Cole got on the phone, Zack blistered his ear for leaving his vintage car in a downtown parking garage, but when had Cole ever paid any attention to his twin?

At least knowing his Mustang was at the mercy of parking attendants got his brother moving. Zack broke a cross-suburb record getting to Tess's from their apartment in Livonia, which he and his brother temporarily shared until the business paid enough to build separate places.

Good thing Zack was quick. Cole ran out of small talk with Tess, and he didn't want to tell her she danced like an angel and kissed like a sex goddess. She might read something into it if he started giving her compliments like that.

When he saw the bright red of his truck pull into the parking area outside her place, he beat a quick retreat. Almost.

"Cole, you forgot your tie." Tess came out the door waving the little strangler like a battle trophy.

He backtracked and grabbed it with a hurried thanks, feeling like a kid who'd forgotten his lunch while the school bus waited.

"That's Tess Morgan, the Tess Morgan we used to know?" Zack asked as he pulled away from the curb. "You spent the night with her? Wow!"

"I drank too much champagne. I spent the night on her couch. No wow!"

"She grew up nicely."

"I guess."

"She might be *the one?*"

He knew what Zack was suggesting. They hadn't had a good rough-and-tumble fight in a long time, but maybe they were due. Or maybe he was just hungover and disgusted with the whole business—blind dates, bride hunt, Tess as matchmaker.

"No way," he mumbled.

"You could do worse." Zack started whistling what they used to call their girl-hunting song.

"She has too much sense to take me on," Cole mumbled.

"Maybe she thinks you've reformed. She's trying to set you up with her friends, isn't she? She can't think you're too bad."

This business of twins sharing everything was getting old.

"I'm just not interested in her that way, okay?"

"Why not? She took my breath away. Who knew blushing Tess would grow up to be that sexy?"

"She's still too nice for her own good."

"Well, I'll keep her in mind when it's my turn to bite the bullet."

Zack could be damned annoying sometimes.

TESS TRIED to reach Cole Monday evening, then again on Tuesday and Wednesday. He didn't return her calls. Was he angry about the Bailey reception or uncomfortable because they'd gotten a little too close for platonic friends? Either way, she was steamed. She had another prospect lined up for him Friday night.

She was tempted to cancel this blind date and forget about getting any others. Her debt was paid. If Cole couldn't be bothered to call her, why should she get her friends excited about a no-show?

This time she'd done her best. Melissa Van Cortland was Lucinda's cousin, not exactly a friend, but a sweet girl with no black marks on her record as far as Tess knew. She certainly was pretty—dark-haired, tall and willowy, except for being on the top-heavy side, as if any man would object to that. Better still, according to Cole's list, she met the requirements of being outgoing, friendly and athletic. She'd won some amateur golf tournaments and had just gotten her degree in biology. She was younger than Cole, of course, but she seemed normal and nice. Lucinda seemed a little jealous of her, which could be another plus.

Tess hated to cancel the date with Melissa after making Cole sound like a cross between a superhero and a cuddly new puppy. He wasn't going to get away with ignoring her calls. She had a very good reason of her own for wanting this date to happen, and she knew where to find him.

She left the store hoping to get back in an hour or so, but the condo site was farther west than she'd expected. At least the gravel-voiced woman who ran the office for Bailey Construction had given her good directions. When Tess got there, she liked the look of it. Venerable old trees had been left in place along the curved white concrete drive circling to a row of units with spacious second-floor balconies. A play area with swings, slide and climbing gym was ready to be used. The buff brick complex was so appealing, she had to remind herself she wasn't here to house-hunt.

She found him in the third unit she checked, down on his knees installing a handle on a kitchen cupboard. His dusty jeans were riding so low on his lean hips she could see the white elastic and navy knit of his briefs. He was shirtless, the skin on his back bronzed and glistening with sweat. She watched for a minute, pretty sure she'd never been within touching distance of a better body. Considering how he'd jumped off the bar stool when she tickled him, wouldn't it be fun to…

"What do you need?" he asked without looking at her.

"You."

She succeeded in startling him.

"I thought you were Zack," he said.

He stood, hitched up his jeans and frowned at her as he hooked his thumbs in his side belt loops.

"I'm not Zack."

"Yeah, I always could tell you apart."

She'd driven all this way to read him the riot act, but his chocolate-drop nipples and adorable little belly button made her flush self-consciously. Why were men allowed to strip naked to the waist? As if women didn't get turned on by a gorgeous torso.

"You're nothing like Zack."

How could she be mad at a man who made words feel like caresses? She'd been an idiot to track him down when he didn't return her calls.

"Nice condos," she said, looking around as an excuse not to look at him. "I love the curved fronts and big windows."

"Thanks. What brings you out here? In the market for a condo?"

"Not yet. I'm still plowing everything back into the business."

"I know the feeling."

"Did you get my message?"

"All eight."

"Cole, blind dates were your idea. This time I've done

it right—Melissa Van Cortland. She's beautiful, smart, likable. She wins golf tournaments—I remembered the outdoor requirement on your list. She just graduated from college with a degree in biology.''

"Sounds young."

"Not that young. You haven't hit thirty yet."

"Close."

"Well, stop pick-nitting." He was so fussy she wanted to shake him.

"Nit-picking. Maybe this wasn't such a good idea, having you fix me up."

"Now you tell me! I had to persuade this girl to go out with you. She's anything but desperate to meet men!" *Unlike some of my friends,* Tess thought sadly.

"You know, coming here in that dress wasn't such a good idea."

Her jaw dropped, and she stared at the naked expanse of his chest.

"What's wrong with my dress?" She self-consciously smoothed the sides of her bright orange T-shirt dress. "I think it's cheerful."

"Sure, it looks great, but I can see the ribbon on your panties and the hook on the front of your bra."

"It hooks in back!"

"Just a guess." He smiled broadly. "But we have some rough types working for us. I don't want to put down a riot."

He'd done it again—made her blush hot and red. Just the thing to set off the orange of her dress.

"This is it, Cole Bailey! If I have to cancel Friday, I'll never, ever fix you up again."

"I'll go," he said mildly.

"You'll go?" All her righteous indignation fizzled like a damp firecracker. "Why didn't you answer my calls?"

"Busy."

He took her arm and helped her over a pile of scrap lumber, steering her toward the open door where she'd come in.

"Busy? Is that your excuse for being so rude and making me drive all the way out here for your answer? I work for a living, too, you know."

"I'm sorry."

"I hate it when people who aren't sorry say they're sorry so I'll feel sorry for them."

"Run that by me again."

"You're impossible!"

"I have been busy. We're having the first open house right after Labor Day. There's a lot to finish."

"Well, I'm too busy to run a dating service for a man who never in his life had the slightest bit of trouble getting women to go out with him."

"I trust your judgment more than mine."

He followed her outside and started herding her toward her car, or at least that's how it felt.

"There's another reason I didn't call you."

Cole sounded sheepish. Something was wrong here.

"Besides being inconsiderate?"

"I really am sorry about the way I behaved—you know, last Saturday. I was out of line."

"You're sorry about kissing me?" What a kick in the ribs!

"No, it was terrific. I maybe enjoyed it a little too much. I was afraid you'd take it wrong."

She wanted to give him a good wake-up punch. Instead she laughed, forced at first, but building until she felt giddy.

"You must think I'm a porcelain doll that's never been out of the box. It wasn't my first kiss, Cole."

"I never thought it was."

"I've been kissed thousands of times, millions, zillions. A kiss doesn't mean anything."

"You probably have a lurid past I know nothing about."

Then he did the unforgivable. He grinned.

She got down to business.

"I wrote everything down—her name and number, the restaurant where I made reservations, time we're meeting you…"

"You're picking up my date?"

"No, of course not. You are. Her address is on the paper."

"A list?" He frowned and reached for it.

"No, just the information. We'll meet you there at seven."

"We?"

"We're double-dating."

"You're chaperoning? Is this girl too nice to be alone with me?" He opened the car door but blocked her way.

"Of course not. I just happened to have a date…. Well, it seemed like a good idea at the time."

"Okay, I'll pick up my date and meet you. Why don't I pick everyone up?"

"Zack thought it would save time if we all meet at the restaurant. I could only get an early reservation."

"Zack? You know some guy named Zack?"

"So do you."

"Not my brother?"

"He called me, unlike his twin for whom I have gone to great trouble to arrange a meeting with a lovely woman."

"Great, just great." He clenched his fists and stuck them in his pockets.

"We won't cramp your style, I promise. If you're upset, we can go somewhere else."

"No, it's fine, just fine. I'll see you and my brother Friday evening."

He stalked away without a goodbye.

"Have a nice day," she called after him in a tone usually reserved for customers who abused her merchandise, then returned it.

8

COLE WAS CALLING the shots on this date, and it wasn't going quite the way Tess expected.

He did pick up his date.

He did drive to the restaurant with her.

And yes, Tess seemed to have done well by him this time. Melissa was supermodel material with a full complement of brain cells and a natural breeziness that only occasionally showed a hint of snobbery, which could be her way of covering first-date nervousness. Cole was willing to cut her some slack for now.

What he couldn't condone was letting his lecherous brother broadside Tess. Zack wasn't interested in marriage or any other long-term relationship. He was hoping to get off the hook with their grandfather, and he might succeed. Marsh would be placated if Cole produced some great-grandchildren, and there was always the chance Nick might want to get married, thus sewing up two-thirds of the stock shares, enough to fend off a sellout without Zack's help. After all, little bro was in college, a happy hunting ground for armies of marriage-minded coeds. He wouldn't be the first to get a BA and an MRS the same year.

"Here we are," Cole said, opening the door of the truck for Melissa.

She'd even passed his stringent climb-in-the-truck test with flying colors. How could she not when her yellow leather miniskirt clung like a second skin? Maybe he was getting old, though, because he wished she weren't braless under the silky white tank top. He didn't want to know the size of her nipples, not with Tess sitting at the table monitoring the date.

Melissa was still talking about golf. His grandfather had made such a big deal about lessons and practice rounds that neither Cole nor Zack had played in years. He didn't tell his date that.

"Oh, there's Tess. Her date must not be here yet," Melissa said.

Cole gave an evil grin but said nothing.

"Hi." Tess was waiting outside the solid wooden door with fake iron fittings, which suited the restaurant's nautical theme. "I must be early. Zack isn't here yet."

"About Zack…"

This is for your own good, he thought with a twinge of guilt.

"Where is he?"

"He had to handle an emergency."

"What kind of emergency?" Tess asked.

"A tile emergency." He winced.

He should have come up with something better, but it was too late now.

"What is a *tile* emergency?" She sounded like a teacher who'd just caught a little boy writing dirty words on the chalkboard.

"We promised to grout some shower tiles for the woman who wants to renovate her kitchen. I hate piddly jobs like that. Well, I guess we forgot about it, and she's having some big-deal guests tomorrow. One of us had to get over there and do the job. Zack lost the coin toss."

He didn't mention he'd hidden the work order until it was too late to send one of their guys. Or that he'd had to dig deep in an old box of junk to find the two-headed coin from a magic set he got when he was about seven. Zack's luck had run out this time.

His backup plan had been to lock his brother in the supply room at the office. One way or another, he wasn't going to let Tess get involved with Zack. No good could come of it for her. She was no match for a really determined seducer like his twin, and Cole didn't want to see her hurt.

"Why didn't Zack call me?"

"Maybe you'd already left."

"Or maybe I didn't notice the light blinking on my answering machine. I was in a hurry."

"Zack's not good about leaving messages," he said, improvising.

"Well, you two have a good time." She started to leave.

"Wait! The three of us can have dinner."

"No, I don't think so," Tess said. "Three's a crowd."

"Definitely," Melissa agreed, putting her hand on his arm.

"But Zack is planning to meet us here if the job doesn't take too long. He said to order, and he'll be here as soon as he can."

He was lying. Zack couldn't do the job in under three hours, longer if the client hovered as she most likely would. Cole was supposed to apologize for him and say he'd call Tess tomorrow.

It was dumb, deceiving Tess so she'd stay for dinner, and not part of his original plan to save her from Zack. Maybe his conscience had belatedly kicked in, but he couldn't stand to see her go home alone when she was all dressed up for a big date. She was wearing a short blue linen dress that was perfect with her sparkly eyes.

"This doesn't seem right." Tess hung back.

Cole opened the heavy door, held it with his knee, steered Melissa into the restaurant with one hand and prodded Tess into moving by nudging her waist with the other. Handling two women at once was a snap, right? He imagined playing underwater tag with two sharks and blamed it on the aggressively nautical decor, an assemblage of ropes, anchors, nets, brass fittings and mummified sea creatures.

Dinner could have been worse. Melissa ordered sirloin medium rare and ate all but the obligatory last bite that was supposed to prove she wasn't a big eater.

Tess had baked trout and asked the waiter to remove the head before he served it, which only meant she didn't like dinner staring at her. Cole felt like the poor fish at this meal.

He and Tess only entered the conversation when Melissa allowed a momentary lull for chewing, which wasn't often. She kept wondering where Zack was.

"Are all your condos sold?" Melissa asked, not waiting for an answer. "I have a friend who bought a condo by a golf course in Florida. She never has to buy a ball. They just plummet over the fence, good brands hardly used at all. Of course, it makes for hazardous sunbathing, but she's a natural redhead—can't tolerate more than fifteen minutes of sun or she turns lobster-red. Does your tan last all year, Cole?"

She tossed off questions like an investigative reporter, but never paused to hear an answer. He caught Tess's eye and raised his brows, but she looked away as if it were his fault there were three people at the table but only one talking.

"Are you sure Zack is coming?" Tess asked.

"He'll make it if he can. You never know with tile emergencies."

She narrowed her eyes, her lips puckered in a skeptical pout.

"I'm beginning to feel stood up. Maybe I'll skip dessert."

"You've already ordered." Cole nodded at the waiter, who'd just arrived with fresh berries and whipped topping for the women, pecan pie for him. "Here it is."

Melissa continued her barrage of words as they ate dessert. Her voice was beginning to grate. She was so lovely, yet so loquacious. Maybe it was partly his fault for insisting on a threesome, but he couldn't send Tess home alone feeling rejected.

"Excuse me," Tess said, standing.

"You're not leaving so soon? Zack could still show up," Cole said.

"I'm only going to the rest room," she explained.

"Oh."

At least she didn't say little girls' room or some other silly euphemism.

He watched her walk away, feeling more and more like a jerk as the evening wore on with no possibility of Zack making an appearance.

"Have you ever been abroad?"

Melissa had asked a question and was actually waiting for an answer. He'd started to tell her about Marsh's fishing camp in Canada when he felt her foot creeping up his thigh.

She knew what she was doing. Her toes wiggled against him triggering a wholly involuntary response. He grabbed her ankle to remove her foot, but she misinterpreted, giggling seductively while he tried to stop her teasing.

Was that waiter smirking? No, Cole was being paranoid. What were long tablecloths for? He felt her probing toe. Oh, yeah, she knew exactly what she was doing.

He stood abruptly, nearly knocking over his chair and putting her off balance on hers. She kept her seat like an experienced rider.

"Excuse me," he said.

For the first time Cole saw some merit in massive potted plants. He discreetly positioned himself behind one of the jungle giants and waited for Tess to come out of the women's room.

"Come here," he whispered, grabbing her arm as the door closed behind her.

"What on earth are you doing?"

"Hiding from your friend."

"Oh, no!" She groaned dramatically. "So she talks a bit excessively. Maybe she's nervous. Maybe this isn't her idea of a double date. I really tried this time, Cole."

"And I appreciate it, but as soon as you left the table she started feeling me up."

"Oh, be serious! In a crowded restaurant? On a first date?"

"She stuck her bare foot between my legs."

"She wouldn't do something like that!"

"No? Want to check out what she did to me?"

"No, certainly not!" She stole a quick peek but tried to pretend she hadn't. "You probably liked it." She didn't sound convinced.

"No, I did not like it! I can't help an involuntary physical reaction."

If he hadn't been worried about the tile emergency he'd concocted, something important might have registered earlier. There was no panty line when Melissa climbed into his truck. She was trouble personified, the hottie every man hoped to meet—when he was seventeen.

"Why are you telling me? I'm going home," Tess said.

"You can't!"

"Zack isn't coming. I don't know why you wanted me to chaperone, but I resign. You're a big boy. You handle it."

"Don't you feel an iota of responsibility for fixing me up with an amateur hooker?"

He wanted Tess to stay. It was that simple, and it had absolutely nothing to do with What's-her-name. When Tess was around, the sun was shining and all was right with the world. He just didn't know how to backtrack on their dumb deal and all that had happened since he'd asked her to be his nice-girl connection.

"I hope you mean one who hooks shots in golf."

"You've got to get rid of her."

What he wanted to say was, *Please stay because I want to be with you.* But this was Tess, and he didn't know where he wanted to go from there.

"Me? She's your date. You brought her here."

"She's trouble."

"So be a troubleshooter."

"You can handle a situation like this much better than me," he insisted.

"What am I supposed to do? Tell her there's a tile emergency, and she has to let me drive her home so you can go save another shower?" She glared at him.

"You shouldn't have left me alone with her."

He wanted to take it back. This wasn't him talking. He didn't whine and try to weasel out of situations, but he wanted to keep talking to Tess even if she thought he was a jerk.

"My apologies for going to the women's room."

"Well, don't do it again!" He managed to say it with a smile.

"I won't. It's time for all of us to go home. I have to open the store in the morning. My assistant manager went to Cleveland for a wedding."

"Someone has to take Melissa home." He wondered how long she would go along with his game.

"You do!" she insisted.

"No way! You found her, you take her back."

"She's your date, a date you insisted I find for you. I tried, Cole. She's gorgeous, friendly, sharp...."

"Aggressive, pushy, threatening..."

She burst out laughing.

"Don't tell me Cole Bailey, conqueror of cheerleaders and every parent's nightmare, is afraid of a woman."

"All right, I'm not afraid, but I like to be the one to make the first move. I'm sure she's not my type, but I don't want to hurt her feelings."

"She used to be your type, right?"

"Tastes change."

"You don't like beautiful, sexy, eager women anymore?"

"I want someone more like you." When all else fails, try honesty.

"How can I argue with that?" She pouted, but reluctantly asked, "What do you want me to do?"

She sighed deeply and, he thought, a little sadly, no doubt regretting all the time she'd wasted trying to help him.

"Go out and pretend your car won't start. Then come back inside, and I'll offer to give you a ride home. That way, I won't be alone with Melissa."

"Isn't this getting ridiculous? Every time I'm with you, we abandon a vehicle."

"I'll drive you back to get it as soon as we drop off the siren of the golf links."

"That won't take any time at all. Just a couple of hours of fighting Friday-night traffic."

"You're a good sport, Tess."

Her face told him that wasn't what she wanted to hear. Truth to tell, it wasn't what he wanted to say, but he was groping his way through a fog when it came to the way he felt about her.

"Melissa is your date. She'll expect you to take me home first."

"I'll drop her off, then come back with you to help with your car."

"Yeah, like Melissa will buy that!"

They went back to the table separately, Tess first. Cole hurried after her, not allowing the women any time to get chatty, then Tess left.

For a few anxious moments he was afraid she wouldn't come back. Melissa had slipped onto Tess's abandoned chair, the better to fondle his thigh and ask increasingly personal questions. What was it about Tess that made him indifferent to the prospect of a good time with anyone else?

Cole flinched when Melissa started caressing his thigh. Where had Tess found her? And why? Nowhere on his list had he put sexual predator.

"Bad news, guys," Tess said, returning to the table.

She looked glum enough to have real car trouble.

"Oh, Tess, I thought you'd left," his date said with barely concealed annoyance.

Melissa was single-minded. He pushed her hand away—again.

"My car won't start. I've heard excessive heat can be as hard on batteries as extreme cold. Now that I think of it, I probably do need a new one."

She was overdoing the stranded motorist bit. Cole glanced at Melissa to see if she was buying it.

"Have you called your towing service?" Melissa asked icily, pinching his thigh to send him a message—let the pros handle this.

"Tess mentioned just yesterday she forgot to mail her auto club renewal." He spoke quickly, having no great faith in Tess's ability to lie.

Of course, she had gotten him to go to his grandfather's reception—in a tux—but he couldn't remember her lying to do it.

"I guess we can give you a ride home." Melissa was playing queen, condescending to grant a small favor to a peasant.

Not only did Cole dislike her poking and pawing, he didn't much care for her snide attitude. How could she be nasty to the person who'd arranged this dream date turned nightmare?

"I'll drop you off first, Melissa, and come back to see what I can do about the car," he said resolutely, wondering which woman would have to ride in the tool compartment behind the seats in his truck.

He solved the problem by insisting Tess drive and sitting there himself, safely out of Melissa's reach. He gave Tess a quick lesson while his date fumed in the passenger seat.

Tess not only drove the pickup as though she owned one herself, she tactfully soothed Melissa's ruffled feathers and let him know he was on her list of losers and louses.

His plan worked well except for Melissa insisting he walk her to her door, which was inside a ritzy gated complex. She rubbed against him like a cat with an itch, but he broke free.

Back at the truck, Tess wasn't pleased. She insisted on driving his pickup to the restaurant.

After she retrieved her car, he tailed her home and headed her off at the door.

"You didn't need to follow me."

"I wanted to make sure your car was working okay."

"There was never anything wrong with it!"

"Actually, I was hoping to come in for—"

"You're stone-cold sober, and my couch is not available tonight. You can hop in your truck and go home or wherever. I'm going to bed."

"I just need to talk to you for a minute."

"I know, your blind date was a dud or whatever. You don't need to make a report. I was there, Cole. I'm sorry, but how could I know she's so aggressive? She's Lucinda's cousin, and I've only been around her a few times."

"You fixed me up with Lucinda's cousin? Have you never heard of gene pools?"

"They're nothing alike. Anyway, Lucinda has her good points. She's fun when she's not getting married."

She stabbed her key into the keyhole.

"Give me five minutes," he pleaded.

He wanted to take Tess in his arms so she couldn't get away. Or maybe he was still reacting to Melissa's fondling.

"Three minutes."

"Okay."

He followed her inside. There was no ceiling light in the living room, so she turned on the brass table lamp beside her couch.

"If you're going to complain about Melissa, forget it. She didn't deserve me chaperoning."

"She wasn't all bad." Once he would've thought she was hot stuff. "About Zack..."

"What about Zack?"

"There was no tile emergency."

"Surprise, surprise," she said dryly.

"Don't get me wrong! He didn't want to break your date." Boy, he didn't!

"He just preferred to spend the evening with shower tiles."

"No, I arranged that. I hid the work order until it was too late to send one of our crew. The woman insisted they had to be grouted before tomorrow. She's on the verge of signing a big renovation contract with us." He shrugged, distracted by the way Tess's brows arched like the wings of an angry angel.

"Why?"

"We flipped a coin to see who had to do the job. Zack lost. I used a two-headed coin from an old magic kit I had when I was a kid."

"I meant, why did you sabotage our date?"

"I know Zack." This wasn't going well.

"That's lame, Cole, really lame. He's not a big bad wolf, and it's been a long time since I needed rescuing."

"Zack is just the way he's always been. I didn't want you to get hurt."

"Like it doesn't hurt my feelings to be stood up, not to mention roped into a threesome?"

"I meant well." He shrugged and, grinned trying to look pathetic.

"Very admirable."

He was getting schoolmarm Tess again, and he very much wanted to shake her composure.

"I went to a lot of trouble—"

"Cole, I'm a big girl now. I can take care of myself. I always could, even in high school when the Bailey twins bugged me every time they saw me."

"If you let yourself get interested in Zack, you'll be sorry. There's no chance he'll settle into a cozy one-on-one with you or anyone else."

"Aren't you rushing things? All I signed up for was dinner. But tell me one thing. Between you and Zack, you went out with practically every girl in the school—every good-looking girl."

"Not all," he denied.

"You were just as, let's say, active as Zack. Why this rush to settle down now?"

What could he tell her? How would she take it if he said he only wanted to be sure to get his share of the baby business? Would she buy the part about his mother? Or would she think he was a money-grubbing phony?

She had him cornered, but she was going to be very disappointed if she learned the truth. She'd either be angry because he hadn't told her sooner or she wouldn't believe him.

He stepped close and put his hands on her shoulders.

"I don't understand—" she began.

He kissed her hard.

She wiggled. Was she angry or just plain agitated or...

He kissed her again. A lot of hokey words flashed through his mind—searing, burning, pulsating.

She tasted so good he had visions of kissing her until dawn.

"What was that for?" she asked, coming up for air.

He was bluntly honest. "To get you to stop talking."

"Your three minutes are up!"

She gave him a shove that caught him off balance and nearly knocked him on his butt.

So she was kicking him out. He'd go, cheerfully even. The evening hadn't been a total loss. Zack grouted tile, and he kissed Tess.

9

HER LIST of potential dates was crisscrossed with lines where she'd scratched off Cole's rejects. In the month since she'd been a third wheel on that really fun date with Melissa, Tess had grudgingly set him up with at least a woman a week.

It wasn't hard. Word of his quest for the perfect woman had spread through her circle of friends, and all the singles wanted to try on the glass slipper.

He was giving new meaning to the word *picky*. Last night he took Brandy, a very cute redhead, to dinner and a show. He called Tess afterward, of course.

Brandy cut her meat into tiny pieces and took forever to eat. Brandy didn't know when to laugh in the movie. Sure, she was cute, but looks weren't everything.

Did he have any idea how she felt about all these blind dates? It was high school all over again, watching him pursue one girl after another when he belonged with her.

Zack called once to ask her to a motorcycle race, but she had to work. He looked like Cole, more or less, and sounded like Cole, but her heart knew the difference. She wasn't crushed when he didn't call again.

She'd made one whopping big mistake when she'd agreed to help Cole—not setting a time limit on her dating service. She'd already paid a high price for losing that ridiculous bet, but it had to stop. She couldn't concentrate at work, and her social life was going to pot while she moped over a bad-boy Bailey twin.

It was time to give him an ultimatum. He hadn't come to her apartment since the fiasco with Melissa, and she didn't want to have a showdown on the phone. Sunday afternoon seemed as good a time as any to let him know this had to stop.

She drove to his place in Livonia rehearsing what she'd say and anticipating possible arguments from him. If she cut him some slack, he'd have to admit how reasonable she was. Since she had friends lining up for the chance to meet him, she'd give him one more month with no more than one date per week arranged by her. After that he could call 1-900-DATE for all she cared.

She'd never been to Cole's house, but she had a Metro Detroit map and knew her way around Livonia. Driving there was easier than getting up enough nerve to knock on his door.

If the address in the phone book was correct, he lived in half of a brick duplex on a tree-lined street where people washed their cars on Sunday afternoon. She didn't see the pickup or Zack's Mustang, but the garage door was closed.

This was a bad idea. She didn't want to talk to him almost as much as she did want to see him.

She pushed the door buzzer but didn't hear it through the cherry-red door. Was Bailey Construction Company too busy to fix the owners' doorbell? She knocked softly, then louder. Darn, she didn't want to leave without telling Cole what was on her mind.

Using her bunched fist, she tried again, wincing as her knuckles connected with the wood.

"Come on in," a distant voice called.

Feeling like an intruder, she turned the knob and was surprised to find the door unlocked.

"Hello?" She stepped inside with some trepidation, hoping she was at the right place.

Again the muffled voice spoke. "Be out in a second."

The living room was casually male and sparsely furnished, just an oversize black-leather couch placed for TV viewing, a coffee table with newspapers spilling over it, a couple of boxy end tables and a yellow tweed recliner no charity store would accept as a donation.

Nothing here to tempt an intruder. Good thing. If Cole caught a burglar, he'd probably want a date with the thief's sister.

She was losing her nerve. Coming here was a very bad idea. Not seeing Cole for a month made it doubly hard to face him. She thought of retreating before he saw her, but then he'd keep expecting her to line up dates.

No noise was coming from what she took to be the bathroom. It was now or never. She moved toward the closed door.

"I need to talk to you now!" she shouted.

The door opened a crack. She couldn't see Cole.

"Can I get dressed first?"

"Oh, uh, sure. Cole, is that you?" She moved away from the door.

"Nope, Zack. Cole's not home yet. Will I do?"

The wrong Bailey twin came toward her with a towel wrapped around his waist. He was wet, water trickling from his hair onto broad tanned shoulders. The wet whorls on his spectacular chest trailed down to the white terry-cloth towel wrapped around his waist.

She backed up and collided with another tall, broad Bailey. Cole had come in silently behind her.

"No, you won't do," Cole answered his brother.

Tess got one more glimpse of a beautiful Bailey body before Cole whisked her through the doorway to his pickup, which was parked beside the curb.

"How do you know I didn't come to see Zack?" she asked, annoyed by his high-handedness. "I'm not your girlfriend!"

"Are you Zack's?"

"No, but…"

"Do you make a habit of dropping in on naked men?"

"I thought you were the one in the shower."

She realized what she'd said and felt her cheeks burn. For once he didn't seem to notice.

"Get in my truck."

"No."

What she had to say didn't require a cozy one-on-one in the cab of his pickup.

He lifted her by the waist and shoved on her bottom to get her onto the seat.

"Don't do that!"

"It's done. Don't get huffy."

"Me get huffy?" she blustered as he walked around to the other side and slipped behind the wheel.

"It's none of your business if I want to jump into the shower with Zack! You have no right to drag me—"

"I didn't drag you."

"And shove me."

"I invited you to sit in my truck and talk."

"Ha!"

"You're not Zack's type."

"Like you're the matchmaking expert!"

She was mad enough to do desperate things, like go back inside and…what?

"I couldn't do much worse than you have," he accused.

"How can you say that? I've set you up with beautiful women, smart ones, nice ones—"

"Melissa and her wandering toes?"

"There was no way I could know she was—she was…"

"Oversexed?"

"You weren't so picky in high school! In fact, Melissa is exactly the kind of girl you liked then."

"That was then. This is now." He halfheartedly defended himself. "Why are you here?"

"If I say I came to see Zack…"

"You saw quite a bit of him, I'd say."

"Not intentionally."

"That doesn't explain the way you were gawking at him."

"I know why none of your dates work out! You're insufferable! You wouldn't recognize a nice girl if she had angel's wings."

"It's not easy to find a special person," he grumbled.

He was telling her! And sometimes when the right person did show up, he was too blind and dumb to know who was perfect for him, namely her.

"The reason I came here," she said in what she hoped was a cool, reserved voice, "is to tell you we have to put a time limit on this dating service."

"That wasn't part of the bet."

"Cole, finding dates for you is a second full-time job! Do you know how many hours I spend on the phone? There's the initial call, then whoever I ask has to be coy, not seem too eager. She'll call back. When she does, I reassure her. I call you to confirm the date, then I call her back and tell her again what a great guy you are. And that doesn't include the what-to-wear and what's-he-really-like calls. Or the ones I hate the most—after the date. What did I do wrong? Why doesn't he call me? What did he say about me? Then, of course, you check in with your commentary, regardless of what time it is.''

''Sorry, I didn't know it was that much trouble for you.'' He tried to look contrite, but she refused to be swayed.

''Not to mention my own social life has become non-existent since I became your personal matchmaker.''

''Maybe I'm doing something wrong on the dates.''

He was trying to distract her, but she had his number.

''Try going someplace more romantic than a steak house. A French restaurant is good, or an Italian one with a violin playing at the tables. But that's not the point. I refuse to keep doing this forever.''

''You lost the bet.''

''Show me the contract. Bring on your witnesses.''

He groaned.

''One more month, Cole. Thirty days from today.''

''After Labor Day I'll have more time. You'll be deserting me when I need you most.''

''One date per week, and only because I know a few women who are still interested in meeting you. It will be a miracle if I have any friends left after they meet the one-date wonder.''

''How about two months?'' he pleaded.

''Two weeks would suit me fine.''

''I'll take the month,'' he said quickly. ''One more thing. I don't think you should go out with my brother. Seriously, he's really not your type.''

''Why not?''

''He's only interested in having a good time.''

''I can remember fun. I used to have a lot of fun before you made me responsible for your social life.''

''Not Zack's kind of fun, you didn't.''

"Are you trying to tell me who I can go out with?"

"You tell me."

"Yes, but you want me to!"

How could she be falling in love with this maddening man? No, erase that thought! What she felt for him couldn't be love. There were no warm fuzzy feelings, no mooning over his picture or hanging out by the phone hoping he'd call. He was just driving her crazy.

"Please, take my word for it. Zack's not for you," he insisted.

"Are you trying to protect him or me?"

"You! My brother can take care of himself."

"And I can't?"

"You can in most situations," he admitted reluctantly. "But, please, take it from me—"

"Oh, never mind! I don't have a date with Zack, and I know better than to get involved with one of the Bailey twins. But you have to stop being so picky. You don't give your dates a chance."

"From now on, they can eat with their fingers, and I won't hold it against them."

"Oh, give me a break."

She slid from the seat of the pickup, still feeling branded by his hands lifting her and shoving her bottom. He was making her nuts!

COLE WATCHED HER drive away. She had no idea how hard it was coming up with reasons not to call any of her friends for a second date. Ordinarily he was easy to please. He wasn't picky by nature, but this marriage hunt had him spooked. The dates he'd been having were more like job interviews. He hadn't met anyone he liked as much as Tess, let alone a woman he could imagine as a wife.

When he went inside, Zack was dressed in khaki slacks and a new red polo shirt.

"Big date?" Cole asked, scowling at the wet footprints on the carpet that reminded him of his brother's performance.

"Hope you don't mind if I borrow your shirt. I don't have any good ones clean." Zack was loading his pockets with keys and stuff.

"I mind, but go ahead anyway."

"If you have a date…" He started to take it off.

"No, wear it."

"I was surprised to see Tess here. You see a lot of her these days?"

"No."

"Maybe you'd like to?"

"No."

"Then why warn me off? She's a cute kid," Zack said.

"I thought you were going somewhere."

"I'm early. Anyway, she'll wait. What's really bugging you?" Zack sat beside him.

"This whole marriage thing. You try shopping for a wife. It's not fun."

"My turn will come. Meanwhile, there's a hot little number right under your nose. If you're not interested, I'll keep Tess in mind when Marsh puts the screws on me again."

"Are you serious?"

"Nah. She looked right through me. Any woman who can resist me in a towel has eyes for someone else."

"Not for me! If she did, why would she spend so much time helping me meet other women?"

"Don't be dense! She's picking all your dates, and they're all duds."

"No, some are pretty foxy." He gave his brother a brief rundown on Melissa and her wandering toes.

"You still owe me for the tile job," Zack said. "I can't believe you ended up with two women, and I had to grout tile with Mrs. Henry Des Plaines watching my butt."

"You lost the toss." A two-sided coin only worked because Zack always called heads.

"Seriously…" Zack always used that word when Cole wasn't going to like what he said.

"Aren't you supposed to be somewhere?"

"Listen to your older brother," Zack said.

"I don't think seven minutes makes you the wise sibling."

"You don't want me to see Tess. I got that message loud and clear. So why not spend more time with her yourself? You could do a lot worse."

"No, it wouldn't work, and I don't want to screw up the best friendship I've ever had with a woman. If she finds out why I have this sudden interest in settling down…"

"You didn't tell her?"

"She doesn't need to know."

"I gotta get going. I think you're going at this the wrong way." Zack stood and patted his back pocket to check whether his billfold was there and jangled the keys to his car.

"It's not your problem," Cole grumbled, wondering why he'd agreed to share temporary housing with his brother. He needed some space of his own—a life of his own. The twin act had worn thin years ago.

He was stopped from telling Zack to mind his own business by a knock on the door.

"Got to fix the doorbell," Zack said. "I wouldn't have heard Tess if I hadn't turned the water off."

Cole went to the front door as Zack left through the kitchen exit to the garage.

"Hi." Tess was pink-cheeked and breathless as if she'd been running.

"Did you come back to see me or Zack?" He sounded churlish and wasn't proud of it.

"You, of course. Can I come in?"

"Please do."

She stepped past him into what he just realized was a cluttered living room.

"I started to drive home when I had a really good idea." She blurted her words like a rehearsed speech.

"You've decided to give me two months?"

"No, absolutely not! But I know a way for you to meet women on your own without me deciding who's nice—"

"And who's naughty?"

"Let me tell you."

"You look a little hot and bothered. Can I get you something?" he asked.

"No, thanks. I won't be here long enough to drink anything. I was thinking about everything I have to do this next week."

Better than thinking about Zack's shower-soaked bod, Cole thought.

"Then it came to me," she went on. "Next Sunday afternoon I'm invited to a baby shower for couples. You can come with me."

"A baby shower?"

She wanted him to suffer. This was revenge for getting her to arrange all those dates.

"Not everyone there will be with someone. It's a great opportunity for you to meet nice women. Nothing puts a girl in a marrying mood more than a baby shower."

"Women cooing over baby stuff." He'd rather have a root canal.

"I know it's not your idea of fun, but it's a great opportunity. Several of the women on my list will be there. Think of all the time you'll save if you do your nit-picking before I set you up."

"No. I don't want to go to a baby shower." He was whining and didn't care.

"Are you serious about settling down?"

She sounded so stern he wanted to smile, but he didn't have one in him with the ominous threat of the shower hanging over his head.

"Yeah, I'm serious," he grudgingly admitted.

"Then you should take my suggestion seriously."

"I'm not going to a baby shower. No way!" It was time to be assertive.

"Have you ever been to one?"

"Of course not."

"It's just a party with pink icing and baby presents. You might enjoy yourself."

"Not bloody likely," he said under his breath.

"You won't need to buy a present. I'll pick out something and sign both our names."

"Will the women there be oohing and aahing over stuff made by Bailey Baby Products?"

"Very likely."

"Then I'll hate it."

"Tough! Do you want to pick me up or meet me there?"

"I'll pick you up." No way was he walking into this disaster by himself.

Just when he thought he knew her, she'd managed to surprise him. She'd been emphatic about the time limit and downright tough about the shower. He had to admire her for laying down the law. He'd found fault with every date she'd arranged. She had to be ready to write him off like a bad debt.

What she didn't know was how much he enjoyed her annoyance and everything else about her. His life would be a lot less complicated if he stopped thinking of her as a very desirable woman.

"Good, it's a date," she said, then got flustered. "I didn't mean date...."

"No, of course not," he agreed with exaggerated seriousness.

She flushed, and he felt better—a little better. He was committed to going to a baby shower. Okay, he'd rather be home watching a baseball game on TV and drinking a cold beer, but what normal American male wouldn't?

"It's a girl."

"What?"

She caught him off guard yet again.

"They're expecting a girl."

"Oh, yeah, you did mention pink icing." He let her know he'd been paying attention.

"I'll see you next Sunday. Be at my place at two-thirty. This counts as next week's date."

She left without giving him a chance to object.

Through the front window he could see Tess drive away. He stood there a long time wondering how she'd managed to trap him into a baby shower. As if he really needed to hear women rhapsodizing over the kind of stuff he'd tried to avoid his whole life.

10

"WHERE ARE the men?" Cole whispered, keeping his arm securely locked around Tess's shoulders so she couldn't slip back into the house he'd just dragged her out of.

"You met Patty's husband." She gestured toward where the guests were gathering in the family room on the other side of the sliding glass door.

"He lives here!"

"Well, yes, but we're early. I doubt if half the guests are here."

"They're probably lost in this maze of brick pillboxes. Whoever laid out this subdivision will have to answer to the Great Builder in the Sky."

"It's a starter home. Don't be such a snob! Patty and Gil have only been married a year."

He flushed, embarrassed to have her think he judged people by where they lived.

"I'm not a snob! I was commenting on the developer, not the home owners. It's a professional opinion. Let's leave."

"We just got here."

"You duped me into coming! Couples shower, my behind!"

"Don't be so impatient. I can think of half a dozen people who should be here soon. This is your golden opportunity. If you're not willing to take my advice, you can go sit on a bar stool at Buck's Tavern and wait for the bimbos to swarm.''

She sounded madder than he'd ever heard her. Of the guests so far, all he'd met was a foxy octogenarian, but this didn't seem the time to mention it to Tess.

"Okay, I'll stay a little while." He reluctantly capitulated.

"When we were in high school, I never dreamed I'd someday drag Mr. Heartthrob of the Valentine's Day dance to a baby shower to meet women. I thought by now you'd be married two or three times.''

When she was on a roll, she had one sharp tongue.

"Okay, I exaggerate,'' she went on, "but do you have any idea how uncomfortable it is for me fending off questions from your disappointed dates? I've been telling all your rejects to call you themselves if they want a second date. This is the twenty-first century. Matchmakers are obsolete!''

He dropped his arm from her shoulders, much as he liked having it there. What could he say in his defense that wouldn't rile her even more? He shrugged and grinned sheepishly.

"I think you're super picky because you aren't ready to settle down,'' she accused him, her blue eyes flashing.

"Not true.''

"Well, take a good look while you're here, because I can't do better than this.''

She stormed into the party, her cheeks almost as red as the patio bricks where he was still standing. He hadn't felt so dejected in years. What was wrong with him? He didn't give a rat's ass about meeting women here or anywhere else. Tess's anger made him feel rotten—and ashamed of himself. She stuck her neck out when she arranged dates for him, and all he did was grouse about them. He was ready to tell Marsh what he could do with his shares of Bailey stock.

But he couldn't. His mother would be devastated if a hostile board of directors voted her out as CEO.

He gritted his teeth and went inside.

Eventually more people did come, but they didn't make the shower less of an ordeal. He tried to hang with Dilbert—Gilbert—some name like that, but Patty's husband was on kitchen duty refilling the punch bowl, bringing out little squares of bread that looked more like decorations than food and dumping pink heart-shaped mints in candy dishes.

He tried to sort out the politics of the party. Two friends were hosting it, but their apartment was too small, so they had it at the house of the parents-to-be. A bevy of aunts had brought food, and someone else had been responsible for making the dining area a spider's nest of pink streamers.

He wasn't ignored. Every woman there made chitchat with him, even Patty's great-aunt with auburn hair and vampire-white skin. Everyone except Tess. He followed her with his eyes, but she was giving him the silent treatment.

A few more guys showed up. The kitchen got crowded as they tried to distance themselves from the feminine festivities. Cole didn't dare hang out there. Tess would probably drive him back to the horde of women with a wooden cooking spoon if he tried.

He was glad when the guest of honor sat on the floor to open gifts, even though he didn't see how she'd get back up in her swollen condition. Maybe that was why guys had been invited—to hoist her up.

Tess, too, had an important job. She had to kneel beside Patty and hand her the gifts. Her hair bounced on her shoulders, and she bubbled over with enthusiasm. She still wouldn't give him a glance.

The doorbell rang, and Dilbert or Gilbert raced to answer. It saved him from having to ooze appreciation as his wife opened a bottle warmer with giraffes dancing on it.

A royal couple had arrived. At least this pair made an entry worthy of crowned heads. Cole wasn't sorry to see another guy until he recognized him. Ron Howser, evil nemesis of his football days, the one guy who could be counted on to trip his own teammate to make himself look good, stood at the door, smirking.

The blonde with Ron knocked Cole's socks off. She joined the women, but she was dressed for the men. He didn't know what to call the thing she was wearing. It was sort of a black jumpsuit without arms, legs or superfluous cloth anywhere else.

The present unwrapping continued. He'd have to tell his mother how popular Bailey baby monitors were. Patty got three.

Ron found him lurking in the kitchen doorway trying to be inconspicuous. Most of the guys had wandered out to the patio.

"Bailey... Which twin are you?" Ron thumped his shoulder.

"Harry."

"Ha, ha. What are you doing here, buddy?"

There was no answer to that, and none was needed.

"Probably the same thing I am, you rascal. Showers are great places to meet women." Ron flashed a toothy grin. He looked to be in pretty good shape, fit except for beefy jowls and slightly thinning blond hair.

"Who's the lil' darlin' next to Patty?" Ron asked after a short pause to comb his hair with his fingers.

"She's with me," Cole said.

"Sure she is, like Candy's with me. Candy's my cousin."

"You date your cousin?" This was interesting.

"Naw, she just asked me to drive her over." He lowered his voice to a whisper. "You want to connect with a beautiful babe, you're halfway home being seen with one."

Some people never change. Cole wondered how it would feel to knock the smirk off Ron's face with a stack of the baby wipes Patty had just opened.

Patty finished with the presents and managed to get on her feet by clutching the edge of the couch.

"They're going to cut the cake now." Tess slipped beside him with Ron's cousin in tow. "This is Candy Allen. You're going out with her next Saturday."

What happened to letting him meet women on his own? Wasn't that why she'd dragged him to the shower?

Next to him Howser was salivating, sticking out his hand at Tess until she didn't have any choice but to take it.

"My name is Ron. Will you marry me?"

She laughed.

Damn it, Tess laughed, and Howser was almost as funny as a heel blister. Worse, she let herself be led away by the jerk, leaving Cole to talk about this date thing with Candy.

He tried to track the two of them, but Candy said she was crazy about cake. She got him to grab a piece for both of them, then nibbled at tiny chunks she speared on a plastic fork. He found himself watching her lips and wondering how she could move them so much just chewing cake.

"You missed most of the shower," Cole said, not critical but envious.

"I've been to dozens. They always open one present as slowly as possible, gush, open another. You know there's not going to be anything the least bit interesting in any of them."

Tess had disappeared, hard to do in a two-bedroom house filled with talking women.

Candy left him to find what she called the little girls' room.

The handful of men, even Dilbert or Gilbert, were on the back lawn tossing a Frisbee. Heavy gray clouds threatened to break up their game. Or maybe it was their plan to get wet—soaked clothes and muddy shoes would break up the party in a hurry. None of them seemed inclined to go inside when it started sprinkling. Ron wasn't one of the fugitives in the backyard.

There was nowhere else to look but the basement. It was only a single concrete-block room with the usual furnace, water heater and leftover moving boxes—except for the pool table. Tess and Ron were playing. The skirt of the blue dress he liked so much was taut over her bottom, showing enough thigh to make him weak-kneed.

"I'm challenging Tess for a dinner date," Ron boasted with satisfaction. "If she can beat me, I'll spring for Chez Henri. She tells me I'll love the frog legs."

"No kidding? Let me give you some pointers, Tess."

He stepped up behind her before she could wrap the cue stick around his neck.

"Go away, Cole."

He'd never heard her sound so hostile.

He slid his knee between her legs and leaned forward, sure she'd be too distracted to make the final shot and win the dinner. He felt her tense and wanted to squeeze her tighter, but she jerked back and came down on his foot with a spike heel.

He yelped and backed up.

Howser laughed uproariously.

Tess took her shot, and the dull thud of a ball in the side pocket said it all. She'd won a meal at Chez Henri's with Ron. Cole would rather win a truckload of garbage on his front lawn.

"This is great, Ron," he said, resisting the urge to take off his shoe and clutch his crushed toe. "Since I have a date with your cousin, we can double-date."

"Oh, no, we can't. We are not double-dating," Tess said.

She held the stick like a Samurai sword. He didn't for a moment doubt what her target would be.

Ron looked puzzled. He didn't have a clue why sweet little Tess was playing gladiator with a pool cue.

"Okay." Cole backed up a few steps. "No double date. It was only a thought."

He went to find Candy. They had a date to arrange.

TESS WANTED to go home. She wanted to put on her pajamas, watch *Bride of Frankenstein* and figure out why she'd agreed to another silly bet.

Until Cole showed up, she'd planned to throw the pool game. She would've missed her last shot, let Ron win and gotten out of going to Chez Henri's with him. He wouldn't have been too unhappy. Henri's had a reputation for charging more per ounce for food than any other restaurant in the Detroit area. Tess would have wiggled out of a date with Ron without the rejection thing.

Ron didn't remember her from high school, and she saw no reason to refresh his memory.

Now, thanks to Cole's interference, she had a date she

didn't want and no way to get out of it. After he deliberately tried to make her miss her shot, she had no choice but to win the game.

Double date indeed! She started looking for someone who could drive her home without going too far out of his or her way. She didn't want to owe anyone favors. Cole had used up her whole store of good deeds for some time to come. Unfortunately, no one seemed to live within dropping-off distance.

"Ready to go?" Cole asked.

She should have known he would be hovering near the door. Candy had already left with Ron because she had a date that evening.

"More than ready," she muttered.

It was pouring. He offered to move the pickup closer, since he'd had to park down the block, but she didn't want any favors from him.

"It's only half a block," she said, stepping outside and trying to ignore the torrents of water raining down on her head.

"Well, wear my jacket."

He took off his lightweight navy blazer and draped it over her shoulders. She wanted to shrug it off, but Patty was standing in the open doorway with swollen legs to say goodbye. Tess gave her a weak wave and plunged into the storm.

She splashed through puddles that had formed wherever the sidewalk dipped a little. Her hair was dripping wet, and she'd be lucky to salvage her shoes. She'd also been one of three people at the shower to give the mother-to-be a baby monitor. The day just couldn't get any better.

Cole stood behind her as she climbed into the awkwardly high passenger seat of the truck. There was no shoving today. If he even thought of touching her, she'd probably bawl like a baby. How could one man be so obtuse?

How could she be so downright dumb? She'd never really gotten over her big crush on him, she realized that now, and it was too late to change anything. She was infatuated again—no, that wasn't true. She was head over heels with the big lug, and he was looking everywhere but in the right direction for love.

Candy was no nice girl! Cole didn't want a nice girl. If he fell for Candy, it would prove he'd been fooling himself all along.

This love business hurt more than having her tonsils out and missing a debate that would have made her undisputed champion of the school team.

Cole got in beside her, his wet shirt sticking to his muscular torso. He looked invincible, but he had mush for brains if he couldn't see love waiting right under his nose.

"I can't believe you're going out with Ron Howser," he said crossly.

"A bet's a bet." How well she knew.

"You didn't have to win."

"I didn't plan to until you got cute and tried to make me lose."

"That doesn't make sense."

"You've got that right."

"What's wrong with a double date?"

He drove slowly on the narrow suburban street, his windshield obscured by the driving rain and the back-and-forth movement of the wiper blades.

"Like the last one you were on was a blast."

"Ron isn't a nice guy."

"He probably isn't."

"Zack and I dated girls. He used them."

"Probably still does."

"You're pretty calm about it."

"I can take care of myself. What can happen at Chez Henri's? Anyway, Ron is cute."

"Cute?" He snorted. "I just don't want you to get hurt."

It's too late for that, she wanted to say.

Cole wasn't interested in her, but he didn't think she had enough sense to find someone for herself. Did he think no nice guy would want her just because he didn't?

"You don't need to worry about me." She felt petulant and wanted to have the last word.

They rode without talking while rain beat on the roof of the pickup and made her window blurry. She felt as if the sky was crying for her.

She didn't pay any attention to where they were going. They could've ended up in Ohio for all she cared. When Cole finally pulled into her apartment complex, she slipped out of his jacket and botched the job of folding it neatly.

"Wear it inside," he said.

"No, thank you." She didn't want a visit from him to pick it up, and she never intended to go near his place again.

"You'll get soaked."

"Doesn't matter."

"Thanks for taking me to the shower."

She hadn't expected him to say that.

"It was a good idea except for Ron," he added.

"Just because you don't like him…"

"I don't trust him." He cut the motor and turned to face her.

"I can handle him."

"Can you? What if he tries something?"

"Like what?"

Common sense was urging her to go inside, but she wanted to prolong her time with Cole, even though it didn't mean anything to him.

"Like this."

He leaned over and scooped her into his arms, kissing her before she saw it coming.

"What will you do if he does this?"

He let his lips wander over hers, the touch of them so tingly and light she felt electrified.

"Or this?" he murmured.

His mouth closed over hers, and she knew a real kiss when she felt one. She didn't consciously part her lips, but oh, how delicious it was to feel his tongue teasing the top of hers while his lips puckered in a kiss that made her light-headed.

"What will you do if Ron kisses you like that?" he asked softly.

"This."

She kissed him back with all the oomph she could put into it.

Then it didn't matter who was kissing whom. He ran his fingers through the damp strands of her hair and held her head immobile while he created havoc with his lips. He gently caressed her eyelids with kisses and nuzzled her cheek and the sensitive spot under her ear.

She braced herself, sure he would kiss her again, and when he did her bones melted. She'd waited forever for a kiss like this. She was giddy, swooning, transported into her own fantasy.

If only this meant something to Cole...but it didn't. Reality intruded and brought her down like a grand piano tumbling off a skyscraper.

Without saying anything, he got out of the pickup and ran to her side. She had the door open by the time he got there, and she tumbled into his arms in her haste to get out.

They ran side by side to her door, the wind plastering her skirt against her thighs as the rain lashed at both of them.

"You're soaked." Cole pulled her into his arms under the low overhang that sheltered her door.

"So are you." She held her key and twisted out of his arms to open the door.

When she got it open, she tried to slip inside, but he held her back, his arm circling her waist.

"You didn't tell me how you'll handle Ron."

He kissed her as if he meant it, and then he wanted to talk about Ron, dopey Ron?

She jerked free and darted through the doorway.

"Like this!" she shouted over the drumming of the rain and her own pounding heart.

She resolutely shut the door in his face and secured the chain, not letting herself hear the persistent knocking that went on for endless minutes.

She learned something that evening—*Bride of Frankenstein* wasn't much fun viewed through tears.

11

TESS STARED at the artfully arranged slivers of veal on the silver-rimmed dinner plate. The three tiny boiled potatoes were so perfectly shaped they reminded her of Ping-Pong balls, each sprinkled with bits of dried parsley and swimming in butter. The asparagus spears were arranged like soldiers on full-dress parade—heaven forbid one bright green head should list to the side.

She wouldn't be surprised if an enraged French chef charged her with a carving knife if she dared disturb his work of art by eating it.

But then, a fancy French restaurant was a good place to go when you weren't particularly hungry. She had a strong suspicion the customers were there to admire, not to eat.

"Do you want your bun?" Ron asked, most of a buttery cloverleaf roll still tucked in his cheek.

"Take it, please."

She pushed her bread plate across the brilliant white tablecloth. Maybe with both cheeks full of dough, he'd stop talking about his favorite person for a minute. Already he'd covered every event in his life from birth to buying his first sports car in tedious, mind-dulling detail.

She cut the asparagus into small bites, rejecting the French way of sucking in the whole stalk. Okay, so she looked provincial, unlike Ron, who not only inhaled the vegetable, but explained why he was doing it as he slurped.

If she ever bet on pool again, she was going to shave her head and tattoo the word *Idiot* across her forehead.

Oh, sure, Ron was superficially a good date—tall, blond and relatively handsome, but *superficial* was the key word for his personality. He knew everything about matters no one cared about and nothing about how to connect with another human being.

The sad thing was, she couldn't even be bothered with disliking him. Any man who sat across from her would fall far short of Cole, but she was feeling anything but cordial toward him at the moment. She listened to Ron with one ear and fantasized about Cole, not the ideal dating mode. She wanted to shanghai the troublesome Bailey twin and send him through the St. Lawrence Seaway in a canoe with earphones glued to his head playing the "Wedding March."

She picked at her meal—actually it only took a couple of picks and it was gone—and decided the evening couldn't get much worse. Then it did. Cole walked in with Candy.

The word she said made Ron stop talking and look at her.

"What's wrong?" He dropped the fork he'd been using to scrape up the last drops of what looked like a delicious sauce from his plate.

"Oh, nothing, just a twinge in my tooth." She fibbed, afraid if he saw his cousin with Cole he'd want to share a table with them, not that the tiny tops were big enough for two, let alone four. They were designed for ankle rubbing and knee bumping, maybe so the diners would forget they were being robbed blind by the minuscule portions.

In the touchy-feely department, Ron was either easily

discouraged or he was going to make his big pitch later. One little knee squeeze, and he'd given up.

"The dessert cart looks interesting." He watched the waiter push a number of sweet treats to a nearby table. Fortunately they provided enough distraction that he didn't see Cole and Candy sitting on the other side of the room.

"I'm much too full for anything but coffee," Tess said, "but you can indulge for both of us. You don't look like a man who has to watch his waistline."

How low could she stoop? Not only did she flatter Ron to keep him there, she did it so she could spy on Cole and his date.

What were they talking about? Why was Cole laughing? Candy wasn't funny! Even worse, why did he have that silly grin? She knew what it meant when men had a certain goofy look—love at first sight...or maybe lust at first sight.

"Smallest coffee cups I've ever seen," Ron grumbled.

"Sure are."

She couldn't help smiling at the way his thick fingers clutched the delicate little cup. Ron didn't score very high as a date, but she wasn't much of one herself. The guy was spending next week's paycheck on dinner. The least she could do was be cheerful—and show Cole Bailey she was having a great time.

Ron was getting restless, but she ordered refill after refill of the coffee, dreading the moment when they would stand up to leave. Not that Cole didn't know she was there! She'd caught him looking over the top of a menu in her direction. She couldn't catch his eye, but she knew he'd heard about Chez Henri's at the shower and deliberately come to the restaurant where she was having a date. What she didn't know was why.

This business of Cole involving her in his social life was making her crazy, but she couldn't sit there torturing herself any longer. Nor could she consume another drop of coffee without a comfort call, which meant passing close to Cole and Candy's table.

She chose to make a dash for it when the waiter was serving their salads, giving her a few seconds to move by unseen.

Darn, that waiter was quick! Didn't he know enough to fawn or chat or do something entertaining to earn a bigger tip when he served salads? She'd heard of a French restaurant where the waiters wore roller skates. She needed a pair herself to streak past Cole, but it was too late. He spotted her.

"Tess! What a surprise seeing you here." Cole flashed that wicked Bailey grin.

"You knew Ron and I were coming here," she accused him. "Hi, Candy. Having fun?"

"Cole is a stitch!" Her blond hair bobbed like a doll's wig. "Have you heard the joke about the mayor's masseuse?"

"Tess wouldn't like that one," Cole interrupted. "Don't want to make her blush."

His salad was smothered in thick orange dressing. Tess's purse was hanging from her shoulder on a long strap. Not for nothing could she make a pool shot with the best in her league. All she'd have to do was turn sharply, knock the purse with her hip and...

No, Candy didn't deserve to have her evening ruined. All she'd done was agree to go out with Cole. Tess couldn't go through life hating other women just because they were with him. She mumbled a hurried goodbye and didn't look back.

Five minutes later she was out of there. Ron drove her

home and made a halfhearted attempt to get some reward for the pricey meal. The stud's code of honor probably demanded it, but he was good-natured about her refusal. They parted on civil terms, and he was as sincere about calling her again as she was about wanting him to.

Cole didn't call to report on his date that evening or all the next week. Tess put her dating service on hold, not that she was all that happy to be done with matchmaking if it meant Cole had found someone. Maybe he thought Candy was the woman for him, but how could she be? Just because she was gorgeous, blond and sexy didn't mean she was right for him.

Tess started working even longer hours at the store, catching up on work and preparing for the Christmas season, the make-or-break time of year for retail stores. It was hard to plan displays of Santa's elf pajamas and red caps and mittens when the weather was hot and muggy in the last throes of summer. It was much harder to pretend she wasn't dying inside, her heart shriveling up like a dried apple when she thought of Cole with anyone but her.

Lucinda didn't come back to her job at the mall. She wanted to have a baby right away while she was still young enough to enjoy it. On Thursday, though, she did drop in to see Tess at the Baby Mart and drag her to lunch.

"You should start thinking about your future, Tess. After all, you're two months older than me. Doug has a friend at work," Lucinda said as they ate in the mall's food court.

"No! Oh, please, no. No blind dates. I'm perfectly happy with my life the way it is."

Before a Bailey bad boy made everything complicated, she'd believed that. Now she was reduced to lying to a friend, not that Lucinda could be discouraged once she had an idea.

"Well, I'll sound him out anyway in case you change your mind."

Or in case you can badger me into going, Tess thought, but who was she to complain? She'd set up her friends with Cole even though she'd been skeptical about his desire to meet a nice woman and get married.

Lucinda's honeymoon report was mildly interesting, but Tess forgot about her friend's dream trip as soon as she got back to the Baby Mart. It was hard to concentrate on anything when Cole's image was hovering in her mind like the ghost of a high school crush.

Life took a turn for the worse that afternoon. Anyone could turn up at the mall, but Tess was downright disoriented when she saw Candy walk into the store.

"Tess, I'm glad you're here. I need another stupid shower gift, but I wanted to thank you, too. I owe you big time! My date with Cole was fabulous! We're going out again Saturday."

"Well, that's nice." Her Chinese stir-fry lunch turned to battery acid in her stomach, and she forgot how to smile.

"I think he's the one for me," Candy gushed. "He is so funny and cute and sexy. I haven't had so much fun in ages! Best of all, I think he feels the same way about me. I know we're made for each other."

Professional women didn't burst into tears in their place of business. They didn't scream or strangle customers, either.

"You know all this after one date?" Tess asked woodenly.

Mr. Picky was smitten after a single evening with

Candy? It was harder to believe than a politician's campaign speech.

"Well, maybe I'm rushing things just a little, but since he has to get married..."

"Wait a minute. He has to get married?"

Candy giggled happily. "Turns out his grandfather is going to sell the business if his grandsons don't settle down with nice women. Not that Cole cares anything at all about making baby stuff, but he and his brother flipped a coin to see who has to get married first."

"He told you this, and you still want to go out with him again?" Tess's head was reeling, but she didn't have any reason not to believe Candy.

"He didn't exactly tell me—"

"You're making it up?"

"No, absolutely not!"

"Then how?"

"I really shouldn't have mentioned it, but I'm so excited..."

"How, Candy?" She was going to find out if she had to badger, bribe or blackmail the woman!

"Oh, I guess it doesn't matter whether you know. We had such a wonderful date, I thought I'd just drop in on his construction site. You know, see him when his muscles are rippling and—"

"Yes, I get the picture."

"Well, they have this trailer they use as an office, I guess. I didn't see Cole, so I went up to the screen door. I could hear him talking to someone, had to be to his brother. I have three brothers, and they have a way of talking to one another, a kind of secret language...."

"So he was talking to Zack? What did they say?"

"Just what I said. They were arguing about Cole losing the coin toss and having to get married."

"They actually said that? And you'd let yourself be part of it?"

"Hey, his grandfather is a little weird, but how many men do you know who actually want to get married as soon as possible?"

Candy was turning surly, but Tess needed to hear more.

"I wasn't criticizing you," Tess was quick to say. "But you always have lots of boyfriends. I just wondered if Cole's ulterior motive puts you off."

"Well, it's kinda strange." Candy pouted but wasn't one to hold back any thought she might have. "But do you know how hard it is to meet men as good-looking as Cole Bailey? Not to mention he'll be rich some day if he stays on his grandfather's good side and gets married."

Tess felt as though she'd been kicked in the midsection. It didn't even help that Candy bought the last comatose-cow crib sheet.

COLE SAT on a table in the emergency room staring morosely at his stitched and bandaged finger. Now all he needed was a shot in the butt, and he could leave.

Pain throbbed all the way to his elbow, but his stupidity bothered him more than nearly losing the index finger of his left hand. Where was his head? Rank amateurs knew enough not to saw their own fingers. Zack was in the waiting room, and Cole didn't know how to explain to him why he'd been so careless.

The brunette nurse looked good even in hospital cottons, but he was too depressed to speculate on how she'd look without the shapeless smock.

"Lie on your tummy and slide your pants down, please," she said in a professionally cheery voice that made him feel five years old.

He hated shots, especially in places he couldn't see. She

swabbed his backside with cold alcohol, pinched up some flesh and nailed him hard enough to make him forget the finger for a few seconds.

Zack was there when he limped to the waiting area. Cole expected to be roasted, grilled and ridiculed by his twin, but Zack took one look at him and said nothing. He didn't need to. Cole was so mad at himself, any other criticism was superfluous.

Worse, he knew why he'd been so distracted all week. He felt something for Tess that he didn't understand. Sure, she'd grown up gorgeous, and any sane man would be turned on by her sensational body and subtle sexuality. Every time he saw her it was harder to be good buddies. If she hadn't shut the door in his face after the baby shower...

But she had. There was nothing subtle about that message.

He'd tried to get interested in Candy, even agreeing to another date with her for Saturday. Maybe he could use his accident as an excuse to cancel it.

"Did they give you something for pain?" Zack asked.

"A prescription, but I don't want to be doped up." He crumpled the paper and tossed it into a trash receptacle outside the building.

"You may want it later." Zack retrieved it. "I'll hang on to it just in case."

He must look awful. His brother was being nice when what he deserved was a good swift kick for being such an idiot. Rule number one in the building trades was keep your mind on what you're doing. His had been on sparkling blue eyes, waves of reddish brown hair and full, kissable lips.

What the hell was he going to do about Tess?

Zack picked up a pizza, and they watched a game on

the tube. It didn't take his mind off the missing tip of his finger or the way he felt about Tess. Zack went to bed after the game, but Cole's chances of sleeping were nil.

He punched out a number he'd conveniently memorized and wondered if Tess had gone to bed.

She answered. He didn't have to leave a message on the brittle tape of her machine.

"I just wondered how you're doing," he said, trying to sound casual.

"It's eleven-thirty. I'm ready for bed."

He wanted to ask what she was wearing, but Tess wasn't a phone-sex kind of girl.

"I'd like to see you."

He hadn't meant to say that even though it'd been the only thought in his head through nine tedious innings of baseball.

"It's too late for you to come over," she said.

"I wouldn't stay long."

Only as long as she'd let him. Maybe his bandaged finger and sore butt would buy him some sympathy time, not that he was sure what he'd do with it.

"No." She sounded adamant, not what he hoped for when he called her. "I saw Candy today."

"Oh?"

"She had a wonderful time on your date."

"It was okay, I guess."

"You actually asked her for a second date."

"She sort of cornered me—concert tickets—no reason to refuse."

"Oh."

Her response was anything but revealing.

"I really want to see you," he insisted.

"I don't think it would be a good idea for you to come here."

He thought it was the best idea he'd had in a long time.

"Meet me somewhere." His body said no, no, no, but he wanted to see her so badly he nearly forgot how much he was hurting.

She paused so long he expected her to refuse.

"Maybe one quick beer," he coaxed.

"All right. I'll meet you at Buck's Tavern."

"I can get there in half an hour at this time of night." If he could drag himself out to his truck, that was.

"Okay." The phone went dead.

He was still wearing bloodstained jeans and a sweaty black T-shirt, but he couldn't waste two minutes changing. Something in her voice told him she wouldn't wait if he was late. He hobbled to his truck, still not sure why it seemed so urgent to see her right away.

Buck's wasn't crowded on a Thursday night. A few regulars had their elbows on the bar, but only one couple occupied a table. The way they were leaning into each other and whispering, they probably weren't supposed to be together, unlike Tess and him. He was beginning to believe they belonged with each other, but he wasn't sure what to say to her.

She wasn't there yet. He even checked the pool room.

He bought two light beers at the bar and carried them to a corner table, hoping hers wouldn't get warm before she got there, hoping she really would come.

She didn't make him wait long. The door swung open, letting in a momentary flow of fresh air and the most beautiful woman he'd ever seen. Tess's hair was windblown, and she brushed a strand away from her lips before she walked to his table.

"Hi," he said.

She didn't give him time to stand and pull out her chair, something he wanted to do for her.

"Candy seems to think you're meant for each other," she said abruptly. "What happened to your hand?"

"Just a little accident at work." He wanted a lot more from Tess than sympathy.

"It doesn't look little. Your bandage is bloody."

He put his bandaged hand on his lap. Having her there made the pain irrelevant.

"My own fault," he admitted truthfully. "What have you been doing all week?"

"Working. What about your date with Candy?"

There was a conversation killer if he'd ever heard one.

"Nothing. She's nice."

Tess wasn't buying his lukewarm evaluation. "That doesn't tell me much."

"I had frog legs. Not bad. Sort of like chicken, but not filling. I picked up a drive-through burger on the way home."

"Candy came to the Baby Mart to buy another shower present. She told me all about your date."

"Tess, there wasn't much to tell."

"She's expecting a proposal any time now."

"A marriage proposal? That's crazy! I hardly know her."

"I know the truth, Cole." She was turning the damp beer stein around and around, not looking at him.

"The truth?" He felt cold but didn't think it was because the evening had turned cool.

"About your big woman hunt, the reason for all the blind dates."

"You knew from the beginning I'm looking for someone."

"A nice person to marry."

"Possibly." He hadn't expected a conversation like this and didn't like where it was heading.

"You only want to get married so your grandfather won't cut you out of the baby business. You flipped a coin with your brother to see which one of you had to get married first." Her voice was tight, controlled, but he heard deep disappointment.

"Did Zack tell you that?" If he couldn't trust his twin brother...

"No, Candy did. She came to the store to let me know you're practically engaged."

"Only in her imagination."

"How could you? You used me in your cold-blooded scheme, and you didn't even have the decency to tell me what was going on."

"Tess, can we talk about this some other place?"

She wasn't soft-spoken when she was mad, and he wanted to explain without an audience. Even the sneaky-acting couple at the other table had stopped whispering to listen to them.

"There's nothing more to talk about. I quit as your matchmaker. No way will I ever help you get a date again—not that you'll need help if Candy gets her way."

"She won't."

She pushed the chair back so hard it fell over when she stood. By the time he achingly righted it, Tess was out the door.

He hobbled after her—that nurse had given him a poke he wouldn't be able to forget for a while. By the time he reached the parking area, she was pulling away.

Where would she go but home? He started the truck and awkwardly steered with one hand, trying to follow her taillights. He lost sight of them when she turned, but he'd been right about her destination. He managed to pull into her apartment complex right behind her.

"Talk to me," he called, wincing as he slid out of the truck.

At least she stopped by her car door so he could catch up.

"I've heard it all from Candy. She heard you and Zack talking in your trailer at the construction site. You have to get married to inherit the business from your grandfather. I suppose I'm lucky you didn't involve me in setting up a marriage of convenience for you."

"I wouldn't—"

"She bought the last cow sheet."

"What?"

"Candy. Just wanted you to know her taste runs to cows with their tongues hanging out."

She turned and sprinted toward her front door, but even hobbled by pain, he was desperate enough to catch up.

"You don't have any reason to be so mad." He tried to reason with her.

He didn't believe that himself. He did believe he'd never wanted to hold a woman in his arms as much as now.

"Are you mad because I let my grandfather bully Zack and me into—"

"It's not my business."

"Or is it because Candy made you think we'd really hit it off?"

He wanted to tell her how much he hated his grandfather's machinations. He wanted her to know he only went along with them for his mother's sake, but what he wanted didn't matter to Tess at the moment.

"I don't care if you marry Candy tomorrow!"

She wasn't a very good liar, but she was furious.

"You went out with that dope Ron, and I trust him like a rattlesnake. Why do you think I went to Chez Henri's?"

"Ron is very nice. I don't care why you took Candy there."

"Nice!" He snorted in derision. "Did he tell you his star quarterback stories? Believe me, he scored more off the field than on, and he hasn't changed an iota since high school."

"People can change, and he's not the one who lied to me!"

She was at the door, key out, no doubt planning to slam it in his face again.

"Tess, I didn't lie—"

"You certainly never mentioned your grandfather was pressuring you to get married. Not telling me the truth is the same as lying. You haven't changed at all since I first knew you. All you cared about then was having fun and getting your own way."

"Is that what you really believe?"

"I think you had no right to make me your matchmaker. And I can beat you at pool any day of the week. You cheated!"

"How?"

"Your phony lesson! You tried to pull the same thing when I was playing with Ron. I wouldn't have had to go out with him if you hadn't interfered."

"I apologize for that, but not for trying hard to get you to help me. I had a good reason—"

"I don't want to hear it."

She had the door open. He looked inside longingly, more than willing to give up his stock shares in Bailey Baby Products for the chance to lie beside Tess on her bed.

"Go away! Just go away!" She backed inside.

Short of forcing his way in, which he would never do to Tess, he couldn't do anything but let her shut him out.

She closed the door. His pain had nothing to do with saws and needles.

She was right about one thing—people could change, and he'd changed for the worse. He'd shelved his integrity to buckle under to his grandfather's unrealistic demands.

No more! If he ever did get married, it would be for love.

12

HE WAS LATE, but she was waiting. Cole slid into the booth across from his mother and mumbled an apology.

"I had to finish a few things before the next open house," he explained. "Two more condos to sell, and we'll actually end up in the black this year."

"I'm proud of you." Sue gave him a warm smile.

"Thanks. Where's Zack? He left the site before I did."

Every couple of weeks the three of them met on Friday at Washburn's, a no-frills restaurant where they could keep in touch without the protocol of a family dinner with Marsh.

"He's not coming. I think he's avoiding you," his mother said.

"Why?"

Cole knew the answer. He was so grumpy he'd like to hide from himself.

"He says you've been a real bear the last couple of weeks."

"He always was a big mouth."

"He told me you've met a girl."

Cole glanced at the laminated menu he practically knew by heart, not much liking this conversation.

"Renewed a friendship with an old acquaintance is how he put it." She sipped at a tall glass of iced tea, and he knew she was trying to pretend she wasn't avidly interested in his love life—or lack thereof.

"He has a way with words," he said sarcastically.

Cole loved his mother, but he would hate to work for her. She was a pit bull with a bone when she was onto something.

"You look nice tonight." He tried to redirect the conversation.

"I wore this to East Lansing when you and Zack graduated, and I've had to cancel three hair appointments because work keeps me so busy. So don't try to distract me. What about Tess?"

"I haven't seen her for a couple of weeks."

He wasn't going to mention the thirty or forty times he'd gotten in his truck and thought of driving to the Baby Mart or her apartment. But the door-in-the-face thing had sent a pretty clear message.

"Um." His mother pretended to study a menu even though she would undoubtedly order the vegetable plate for the two-hundredth time. "That's about how long Zack says you've been sulking around like a lovesick puppy."

"Zack said that?" His jaw clenched automatically.

"The lovesick-puppy part is my interpretation."

She was teasing, but he was not in the mood to banter with her or anyone else.

"Let's order."

He beckoned to a young red-haired waitress with the best come-hither smile he could muster. She ignored him.

"Seriously, Cole…"

"Mom, when have you ever seen me—or Zack, either, for that matter—moping over a girl?"

"Never, I guess, but the two of you trampled on a lot of hearts in your younger years. I can't feel too sorry for you now."

The waitress finally ambled over to their table. "Can I take your order now?"

"Are you sure you have time?" Cole grumbled, surprised when his mother tapped his ankle with the toe of her shoe. He ordered the vegetable plate for her and the pork chop special for himself.

"When did you start kicking people under the table?" he complained when the server had left their table.

"When one of my sons started being rude to waitresses."

"She kept us waiting while she flirted with a busboy," he told her, knowing his foul mood had nothing to do with ordering dinner.

He wanted to eat fast and escape his mother's interrogation. At least the waitress served the meal quicker than she'd taken their order. He concentrated on his food and kept his mother talking about Nick and the baby business.

"Tell me," she said, after they ran out of routine chitchat. "Who did you take to your high-school senior prom?"

"Who did I take or who did I take home?"

He hadn't been this surly with his mother since she'd confiscated his car keys for two weeks after his seventeenth birthday party—and he had definitely deserved that punishment. If she'd known the whole story, he still wouldn't have them back.

"You're not funny," she said with a chill in her voice.

He probably wasn't, but she was making him feel like a ten year old about to be banished to his room. She rarely meddled in his life and never tried to pull rank anymore. What was she up to?

"I took a girl who'd just moved here from South Carolina. Beth Ann something…Beth Ann Hardy. Why dredge up ancient history?"

"I always thought you might ask Tess."

"She was my tutor, not my girlfriend."

He'd never had to justify his choice of dates before, and he didn't like it.

"She did you a big favor just to be nice. I offered to pay her, but she adamantly refused. Somehow she pulled off a miracle and actually got you interested in Shakespeare. Good thing. You needed the British lit credit to graduate."

"She did make it interesting," he admitted.

He couldn't help wondering if even then he'd had a soft spot for her. She certainly wasn't like the hot little numbers he usually dated, but maybe if he hadn't tried so hard to keep up with Zack in the stud department...

"I suppose you never noticed she had a terrible crush on you."

"Tess? No, I don't believe that."

"Just because she didn't have enough confidence to show you how she felt doesn't mean she didn't care. She spent a lot of time drumming *Macbeth* into your head."

"Did Tess tell you this? Did she say she wanted to go out with me? Did she want to go to the prom with me?"

"She didn't need to tell me. I could read it on her face every time she looked at you."

"I gotta go, Mom."

He bussed her cheek and rushed out, not realizing until he got to his pickup that he'd stuck his mother with the check.

TESS HAD NEVER been a clock-watcher, but her Saturday stint at the store seemed to drag on forever. Ordinarily she didn't work Saturday evenings, but she was training one of her more capable clerks to close up. Madge, her assistant manager, would've done it, but Tess had given her the night off to baby-sit her grandchildren.

Working was better than moping about Cole, she

thought as she watched Wanda shut down the register. All that remained to be done was set the burglar alarm, dim the lights and lower the steel gate across the mall entrance to the store.

"Hey, Tess, I was supposed to deliver this just before you closed."

Russ, the florist who ran the shop at the south end of the mall, hurried into the Baby Mart just as she switched on the nighttime security lighting. He handed her a box with his logo embossed in gold.

"This is a corsage box," she said, puzzled by his delivery.

"Take a look. I made it myself."

She carefully lifted the lid and stared at a lovely corsage of yellow roses, baby's breath and delicate greenery.

"It's lovely." There was no card.

"Big date?" Russ asked.

"No, no date at all."

"Well, enjoy." He started to leave.

"Wait, who sent this?"

"Customer confidentiality," he teased as he walked away.

When the store was secure for the evening, Wanda hurried off to meet her boyfriend by the fountain in the central concourse. Tess said good-night automatically, still bemused by the flowers she was juggling along with her purse and raincoat.

"Do you like it?" A man stepped from the bookstore entrance across the way.

"Oh!"

She could only stare at Cole and wonder whether he was a mirage she'd conjured up because she so badly wanted to see him. He looked more handsome than ever, his dark hair brushed to the side of his forehead and his height emphasized by a smartly tailored charcoal suit and gleaming white shirt. He was wearing highly polished black wing tips and a striped gray and gold tie.

"I seem to remember you like yellow," he said.

"Yes, but…" She stared from him to the corsage box. "You sent this?"

He nodded, his expression unreadable.

"But why?"

"Come for a ride with me, and you'll find out."

"I have my car here."

"Just another abandoned car in our checkered relationship. It'll be fine."

"We don't have a relationship!"

He took the corsage out of the box and slid his hand under the V-neck of her moss-green cotton knit jumper, his fingers resting on top of her white turtleneck as he pinned on the flowers. The gesture was so intimate she could practically feel his fingers searing her skin through layers of cloth.

"What is this?" she asked.

"A corsage."

He was gorgeous when he grinned, but she wanted answers, not charm.

"I know that, but…"

He stepped so close she thought he was going to sniff the tiny rosebuds.

"Are you ready to go?"

He helped her into her rainy weather navy trench coat, careful to keep it from crushing the corsage, then put his arm around her shoulders and propelled her toward the exit.

All this chivalry was terribly confusing. What was he up to?

"Thank you for the corsage," she belatedly said, "but I don't understand why you sent it."

"You will."

He squeezed her against his side, momentarily distracting her.

The rain had stopped, but the pavement on the dark, nearly deserted lot glistened under the pinkish safety lights. It had been unseasonably cool all day. She inhaled a deep breath of fresh, damp air, and her nose tingled from the intoxicating scent of Cole's spicy aftershave.

She looked around for his truck, but spotted Zack's vintage Mustang instead.

"You borrowed your brother's car. Why?"

"To take you to a dance."

"How do you know I don't have something better to do? I could have a date or—"

"Do you?"

"No, but—"

"Please, will you let me surprise you?"

"I'm not dressed to go anyplace."

"You look like a doll in that jumper, but you're always gorgeous to me. It doesn't matter what you're wearing."

She couldn't glow with happiness and be surly and suspicious at the same time. The choice was a no-brainer.

"All right, you can surprise me, but I still don't understand."

She looked at the arrangement of flowers on her left breast. Touching the velvety softness of one tiny bud with the tip of her little finger reminded her of the bandage Cole was still wearing.

"How's your hand?" she asked when they were inside the small car.

"Not a pretty sight, but it's healing." He held up the freshly bandaged digit. "Thank you for asking."

She couldn't read his expression in the dark interior of the car, but his tone was even more puzzling than his gift of the corsage. She'd never heard his voice so mellow, so soothing, so—truth to tell—downright sensual.

"If this trip involves Candy," she said, still afraid to let herself believe that Cole was focusing on her like a man who really cared.

"Absolutely not. Our second date was not wildly successful."

"Oh, didn't you have fun?" She tried to hide her elation.

"She wasn't thrilled by my main topic of conversation—you."

"Me?" Her voice squeaked in disbelief.

He didn't answer, instead torturing her with silence, a sneaky grin on his face. Or so it seemed from what she could see of his profile in the dark.

He drove through neighborhoods of neat brick homes, weaving his way across town in a shortcut she was too agitated to follow.

"Where are we going?"

"You'll see."

Soon she did see familiar landmarks—a church with a white steeple, the entrance to a medical clinic, a sign for the hospital.

By the time he pulled into the school's staff parking area, she knew there they were, but not why.

"Our old high school?" she quizzed him. "Why on earth come here?"

"Did you know it's been converted to a middle school? Zack and I did some work on the science labs when we were just starting out in business."

Cole Bailey could write a manual on how to avoid answering questions. He got out of the car and came around to help her out.

"What are we doing here?"

"Just a little breaking and entering."

"You can't be serious!"

"No, the custodian will let us in."

"Why?"

"He has to be here when the gym is rented for the evening. It's our lucky night—nothing else on the schedule."

"You rented the old gym?"

"Yeah, and I'm pretty proud of it. Had to rouse out school-board members and get my grandfather to call in favors to arrange this in twenty-four hours."

He walked to a side entrance that led directly to the wing with the gym and knocked on the small glass panel in the door.

"This must be how it felt to go to a speakeasy in the old days," she quipped to cover her nervousness.

Just when she thought this was all a joke, a burly man with gray bristles on his square face opened the door.

"Cole Bailey. I have the use of the gym tonight."

"Yes, sir. I'll go ahead and switch on the lights."

"No overheads, thanks. Just put the footlights on the stage on dim."

"Whatever you say."

They followed his shambling form down a familiar corridor lined on either side with military-green lockers. The students might be younger these days, but nothing else seemed to have changed. The place smelled the same as it always had, a nostalgic and not unpleasant blend coming from lockers crammed with everything from sweaty gym shorts and socks to wadded paper. She could even conjure up the aroma of hot lunches served in the cafeteria. How she'd loved the macaroni and cheese, always served with carrot sticks and Jell-O.

It wasn't much of a stretch to imagine a group of her friends in a circle by the lockers exchanging lipsticks and gossiping about every girl's favorite subject—boys. She had a tiny tinge of regret that they couldn't see her come in with Cole Bailey now.

''Cole, this is crazy!'' she whispered as they watched the custodian walk to the far end of the darkened gym. He mounted steps to the stage, now devoid of a curtain, and in a moment the footlights glowed upward, giving off just enough light to make the cavernous room seem spooky and romantic. Cole squeezed her hand, and she didn't want to let go of his.

In the center of the room a rectangular cafeteria table was draped with a white cloth and festooned with yellow and green streamers and a centerpiece of bright yellow mums. A punch bowl was surrounded by plastic cups, fancy cocktail napkins and a platter of petits fours. Cole had even thought of little paper cups with mints and nuts.

She scarcely noticed when he helped her out of her coat and walked to the edge of the stage. He started a tape player that was sitting there waiting to be turned on, and soft, dreamy music drifted through the gym.

''What on earth...'' Her eyes were misting, and she didn't recognize her own voice.

''We should have done this ten years ago, sweetheart.''

Before she could digest his term of endearment, she was in his arms, moving to music that gave an illusion of a real band playing just for the two of them.

''Cole...''

''We've lost a lot of time because I couldn't recognize the right woman for me when she was right under my nose.''

He held her close, taking steps so small they were scarcely moving.

She was genuinely speechless for the first time in her life.

"I missed my chance at the senior prom," he said in a voice that radiated warmth. "This is our prom night together."

"Cole, I can't believe we're doing this."

She'd never danced with anyone who made her feel this special. She was wholly aware of his body, so close they melded together. When his lips brushed her forehead she started hoping this was the most important night of her life in spite of lingering puzzlement and doubts. Could this really be happening to her? Was Cole doing this because he...

She didn't dare let herself hope that all her dreams might be realized.

Then he was holding her, not pretending to dance. She heard him breathe deeply, then their lips met, gently and sweetly, in a kiss that was incredibly intense.

"Will you forgive me?" he murmured.

She couldn't remember anything to forgive, not with his hands locked below her waist and his lips wandering over her face, brushing her brow, her eyelids, her cheek and chin, teasing the tip of her nose.

"I guess," she gasped, meaning yes, definitely yes! '

His knee parted her knees until she was practically riding his thigh, riveted by the materialization of all her most secret dreams.

This couldn't be happening! Cole was seducing her in the very building where she'd longed for him with all her heart so many years ago.

"I don't want to crush your corsage," he said, putting the thickness of a rosebud between them.

Crush the flowers, crush me, she wanted to cry. She reached up to caress his lips with the tip of her finger. He drew it between his teeth and gently suckled, making her feel all shivery and strange.

"What made you think of a prom?" she asked, afraid of what was happening to her in his arms. After this, she'd never again be able to deny her feelings for him, especially not to herself.

"It doesn't matter, as long as you like it," he said.

"I love it."

He was right—it didn't matter. Nothing did but what was happening between them.

He kissed her long and hard, his fingers stroking her hair as his lips made hers swell with passion.

The music stopped, and so did their pretense of dancing. She pressed against him, feeling what she'd only imagined before—the firmness of his chest, the concave fitness of his tummy, the erotic swell at his groin. She'd known him so long and yet so little. She wanted him so badly her fear of disappointment was like the specter of her teenage hopeless yearnings.

"Let me get you some punch," he said in a voice so husky she barely recognized it.

She was already drunk on sheer elation, but she drank the punch he handed her.

"This is delicious. Did you make it?"

"I had a little help. And I didn't need to spike it to feel high tonight."

A sheepish Cole was a man she didn't know but very much liked.

"Aren't you going to have any?"

She put down her cup and dipped a serving for him in another, holding it to his lips.

They sipped and smiled, and words seemed superfluous.

"We've hardly begun to dance," he said in a softly enticing voice.

She didn't need any coaxing to put the cup down and hold out her hands.

"Don't you want music?" he asked with a bemused smile.

She was already hearing an enchanted melody, bewitched by the love pouring through her. She didn't need real notes but was glad when he started a tape of the world's most wonderful dancing music, or so it seemed to her.

He whirled her around the gym, and she never once missed overhead streamers, the press of other dancers or the chattering of spectators. He gave new meaning to the word *prom*.

Tess didn't know if they danced for minutes or hours. She scarcely noticed the custodian watching them from the doorway when it was time to go. She was only vaguely aware when Cole spoke to the man and handed him a wad of bills for his trouble in cleaning up.

She left the nearly deserted building with the glow of a real prom in her heart.

"Did you enjoy yourself?" he asked needlessly when they were in the car.

"It was lovely. Thank you, Cole. I still can't believe you did all that for me."

"I only did what I should have done ten years ago—taken the one woman in the world for me to the prom."

He leaned over and kissed her again...and again and again.

"I keep expecting Principal Royce to knock on the window and make us stop,'' he admitted with a soft, shivery laugh.

''Me, too.'' Not that he'd ever had to knock on a car window with her inside.

''I guess it's time we act like grown-ups again,'' he said in a teasing tone.

''How do grown-ups act?''

''Let's find out.''

Cole drove without talking, and his silence made her crazy. Was this some kind of compensation he thought he owed her for not telling her about his grandfather's manipulations? Or something he'd concocted to thank her for the matchmaking? Her mind worried, but her heart was rejoicing. He was everything she'd ever imagined and more. When he really tried, he could make her insides melt.

She had an unsettling flashback of Cole hanging out by a blond girl's locker and making her squeal with excitement because a Bailey twin was paying attention to her. Tess quickly tried to suppress it.

That was a memory from ten years ago. Tonight, instead of sighing over him from the sidelines, she'd been the girl in his arms. Her lips were still tingling from his kisses. She fairly ached to have him hold her again.

She loved him, but her doubts would not go away. Gradually a cold sensation crept up her back as if her spine were changing into a steel rod. She was in love with Cole, but she'd rather never see him again than be a conquest, a one-night stand, another notch on his infamous bedpost.

They stopped at a red light, and he reached over and stroked her thigh. It was a long light. He slid his hand under the skirt of her jumper. His nails rasped on the taut nylon of her panty hose. She couldn't seem to take a deep breath.

"The light is green," she whispered, not liking the husky tremor in her voice.

Why didn't he say something? She wasn't totally naive: She knew what he might want when they got to her apartment. But why with her? Why set up a pretend prom just for the two of them? Was he so desperate to find someone—anyone—that he was ready to settle for good old Tess?

She sniffed and had to find a tissue. She was gloriously happy and miserable at the same time. She wanted Cole with all her heart and soul, but not if he was doing this for stock shares and his grandfather's approval.

Fog was thickening, hovering in the low spots and making the streets a misty maze.

"We're socked in," Cole said when he finally reached the parking area in front of her apartment. "Much too dangerous for me to drive home tonight."

"You never know what's out there in the fog," she murmured.

"Ghosts and ghoulies and things that go bump in the night." He laughed softly, and the sound sent shivers down her spine.

She hugged herself to stop trembling while he walked around the front of the car to open the door for her.

This isn't good…this isn't right. If I do this, I am not bright, a singsong voice repeated over and over in her head. But she wasn't going to let the evil little demon perched on her shoulder spoil this night for her. She tucked her hand in the crook of Cole's arm and smiled at him.

"Give me your key." He held out his hand when they reached her door.

"I can open it."

"I'm not risking a door in my face. This time I'm going in first."

She handed over the ring with shaking fingers.

He was the one who switched on the table lamp beside her couch. He slid the raincoat off her shoulders, pushing aside her hair and kissing the back of her neck as he did.

She wiggled around and faced him.

"Cole, I don't think—"

"Don't think."

His mouth was sweet, and his hands were hard on her shoulders. All his other kisses had only been practice for the way his mouth covered hers now. She couldn't respond...she couldn't not.

"Will you please stop!" she pleaded.

"Why?"

He nuzzled her ear and spread his fingers on her bottom, which was incredibly cheeky and too exciting to ask him to stop.

"Why is *my* question! Why are you doing this?" she asked in a hoarse voice.

"Because I love you. I'm in love with you. All I think about is you."

She was so stunned she stammered. "In love...with me...but..."

"I know. I'm an idiot. I tried to get interested in other women even after I knew you were the only one for me."

"But—but..."

"I can make you happy, Tess. I can make you love me."

"I already do. I love you, Cole." She said it matter-of-factly, not at all the way she'd always imagined her confession of undying love.

"I'm only sorry it took me so long to realize it." He

kissed her lips so softly it tickled. "Let me make love to you."

"Now? That is, I mean, I'm not, I haven't…"

"I understand. You've never done this before, and you're scared."

"I am not scared! And I have—well, only with… And I'm not even sure that counts."

How could she explain anything if he kept kissing her? He stroked her breast, the one without the corsage, which felt hot-wired in place.

Why did anything matter but the way he was holding her and whispering her name like a magic spell and caressing her back and shoulders and nuzzling her ear?

He held her tighter, pressing her head against his chest where his heart hammered like a crazy drumbeat.

He touched her, slipping his hand between her legs, and her hands clenched the firm swell of his bottom. She dug in her nails when he moaned with pleasure.

Slowly she realized she would have to lead him to the place where they both wanted to be. He wanted her as much as she wanted him to want her and as much as she wanted him, but this slow, sensual torture might go on forever if she didn't give him a sign, a signal of acceptance.

She removed one hard palm from the place he was pleasuring and led him to her bedroom.

There was no more hesitation. He tossed his suit coat on the rocker beside her dresser and emptied his pants pockets on her bedside stand. She couldn't help noticing the long foil-wrapped strip of packets.

"You planned the evening to end this way!"

She backed away, wondering how many times he'd played this scene with other women in other places. She wanted to believe he loved her, only her. Was she fooling herself?

"I planned to tell you I love you, Tess. I've never, ever said that to anyone else. If you want me to leave, I will. It won't affect the way I love you…won't stop me loving you more than I ever believed possible."

Her heart leaped. Her spirits soared. She believed him, really, really believed him.

She bounded into his arms and threw him off balance. He buckled backward onto the bed with her on top.

He kissed her—deeply. She tried to unbutton his shirt, but the slippery little rascals resisted leaving their holes. He lifted her skirt and tugged on the sides of her panty hose, but they went nowhere. She wanted to see all of him, be naked with him, feel his skin against hers, but they weren't getting anywhere because their lips were out of control, locked together with their tongues entwined.

"Tess, bashful Tess, beautiful Tess."

His voice was so hoarse she scarcely recognized it, but she stood on quivering legs and tossed aside her clothes as quickly as possible.

He was even faster, stripping off his shirt and reaching toward her nightstand. She no sooner registered the rasp of his zipper than he was standing beside her fumbling at the snaps on her bra and tossing it aside, then kneeling and rolling silky panties down her legs.

She thought she'd dissolve when he parted her legs and kissed where no man had kissed before.

His hair was soft under her hands, and she combed it with her fingers, holding tight when the shudders began. She collapsed on the bed, her feet still on the floor and her knees spread wide. Rising from his knees, Cole lifted her hips and filled her.

"Oh!"

Who knew anything could feel so good?

She sighed, came back to planet earth and soared into Cole's outstretched arms.

He pushed aside her wildly inappropriate pink bedspread adorned with faded red, purple and blue carousel horses. She made a mental note to check out jungle prints as they snuggled together under a pastel sheet. "I love you," he said.

Could she ever hear those words enough?

"I love you, too."

What else could she say?

"Every inch of you is gorgeous."

He pushed the sheet back and hovered over her, kissing wherever his fancy took him, and it took him practically everywhere.

She moaned happily when he took her nipple in his mouth and trailed his fingers down her thigh.

The ceiling light was on. Which of them had turned it on? Did it matter? Not when he was trying so hard not to neglect any square inch of her!

He fumbled on the nightstand again, but had to get off the bed to look for his foil packets, which had fallen on the floor. She sat up and admired the view.

"Cute butt," she teased in the understatement of the century.

"You are incorrigible," he growled, picking up the packets and tumbling her onto her back.

The second time was even sweeter. It was her first time with her eyes open, and watching Cole's handsome face glisten and his eyes cloud with passion, she vowed never to close her eyes again.

"Happy?" he asked later, cradling her on his chest, his own drooping with sleepiness.

"Are you kidding? Of course."

"When I think of how I nearly blew it with you..."

"Scary," she agreed.

"Will you marry me, Tess?"

Even on a night full of surprises, this threw her for a loop.

"Marry you?"

"You know, preacher, ring, the happily-ever-after part. Whatever you want, although I see no need for the bridesmaids to wear ugly dresses. You're the most beautiful woman in any room, anywhere, anytime."

She'd lived to hear these words, but doubt reared its ugly head in spite of the euphoria she felt lying in Cole's arms.

"You need to get married to appease your grandfather." If she didn't say it, it would prey on her mind.

"No! Absolutely not!"

He rose on one elbow and looked at her with dark smoky gray eyes that made her throat ache with longing. She so wanted his denial to be true.

"But the baby business—"

"I don't want any part of it."

"Then why—"

He sighed deeply.

"I should have told you the truth right away before I used you to get dates for me."

"I still don't understand why you did."

"It seemed like a good idea at first," he said bleakly. "I guess I was ashamed of myself for agreeing to go along with the bet, and I started seeing it the way it would look to you—pretty lame. You're nice, so genuinely nice you seemed like my only chance to meet other nice women. Marsh has a phobia about loose women since his brother made a spectacularly bad marriage. Of course, his idea of nice is a naive little virgin."

"Pretty hard to find one of those over the age of sixteen," she said, cynical because she didn't want to be the solution to his problems with his grandfather.

"I tried," he said, sounding desolate. "With your help, of course. But the more I saw other women, the more I realized it wasn't going to work. Guess I'm a little dense, but I finally figured out I can only marry if I'm crazy in love."

"I still don't understand. Were you afraid of losing your grandfather's money?"

"No, that isn't the issue. He was trying to force us to take an interest in the business. If we buckle under to his dictates, he thinks we'll assume some responsibilities at the plant, at least by serving on the board of directors. Nick might someday, but Zack and I have plans of our own."

"Then why go along with what Marsh wants?"

"He's threatening to sell the shares we're set to inherit. That means control of the company would go to outsiders, and Mom would most likely be out as CEO. The business is the only thing that kept her going after my stepdad died."

He sat and pulled his knees up, resting his chin on them.

"So you still need to get married."

"No, Zack and Nick can insure Mom's job by getting married themselves. I'm through playing Marsh's game. Who the hell does he think he is? He sent my real dad packing—gave him a choice of jail or leaving."

"Oh, Cole, I'm so sorry." She sat up and put her arm around his back.

"We've learned to live with it. Zack and I had a great mom. We lucked out on our stepdad, too, so I'm not complaining. I've just had it with Marsh's machinations. I could've married someone else just to placate him and never met up with you again.''

"I'm awfully glad you did." She pressed her cheek against his arm, feeling all was finally right in her world.

"Does that mean you'll marry me?"

He lay back and cuddled her against him.

"I have a confession to make."

"Go ahead. I love it when you blush."

"I had a terrible crush on you in high school."

"No kidding?"

He leaned over and kissed the tip of her nose.

"You knew! That's why you did the prom date."

"Not then, I didn't. I'm a little slow sometimes."

"I'm not the perfect woman, you know."

"Don't tell me your closet is full of stuffed animals."

"Only one. A ratty brown poodle is living in a shoe box on the closet shelf."

"If it's yours, it can even sleep on the bed…but not between us."

"Not a chance!"

"Good, this bed is only big enough for two. Those carousel horses will have to go."

"I had in mind a jungle motif with tigers lurking behind the trees."

"No cows?"

Her answer was lost as he gathered her close and lowered his lips to hers.

Epilogue

COLE KNEW he was grinning like an idiot, but he couldn't stop. Who knew a wedding could be this much fun?

Of course, it was Tess's and his wedding. That made all the difference.

She smiled at him as they danced, love and promise shining in her eyes.

"My dad is crazy about you. He was afraid I'd never get married," she teased.

"What did he expect when he raised his daughter to be a pool shark?"

He hugged her closer and brushed her forehead with his lips.

"It was nice of you to let Lucinda be a bridesmaid." He laughed when he said it.

"She did bring us together. When I asked her, I didn't know she'd be swollen like a blimp before Christmas."

Tess was grinning, too, but not maliciously, even though the deep red velvet gown made Lucinda look like Mrs. Santa Claus.

"Have we done all the little rituals?" he asked.

"Let's see. We cut the cake…"

"And you stuffed frosting up my nose."

"You exaggerate!"

"Moi?"

"You tossed my garter. And I'll get you for that!"

Maybe his hand had strayed a bit high, but he hadn't been able to resist making her cheeks flush apple-red one more time. Judging by all the fun they'd been having in bed, there wasn't much that embarrassed his bride anymore.

"Everyone's having a good time," he said, an understatement if he'd ever made one.

"You were right. Buck's Tavern is perfect for our reception," she said.

"Yeah, plenty of room to dance once a few tables were pushed against the walls."

"We're the only ones dancing!"

He knew that. Guests of all ages were gathered around the tables, and the clank of balls competed with her cousin's little band. He suspected it was the first gig for the high-school group, but they were giving it their all.

"May I cut in?" Marsh was grinning, too.

"My pleasure," Tess said.

The old boy whirled her around a few times, giving Cole a chance to see her silk floor-length gown hugging her spectacular form. She didn't need lace or frills to be the most beautiful bride he'd ever seen, and she'd wisely avoided them.

Marsh brought her back to him.

"I have to admit," his grandfather said, "I was disappointed when you kids wouldn't let me spring for a reception at the country club, but this is more fun than I've ever had at a wedding."

"Thanks, Grandpa." Tess used the forbidden name, but the old boy beamed when she leaned over and kissed his cheek.

"Pool is fun even if Nick did beat me three games running." Cole's mother came up to them looking flushed. She'd shed the prim little aqua jacket that went with her mother-of-the-groom dress. "I'm sorry we didn't have a table when you boys were growing up. Now that Nick is nearly through college, I guess it's too late to bother."

"That's okay, Mom. Gave us an excuse to hang out at bars," her handsome son Nick said, coming up behind her.

She playfully punched his arm.

"Time to throw your bouquet, Tess."

Sue handed over the little bunch of white rosebuds and carnations she'd been keeping safe.

"Time out, everybody!" Marsh bellowed as only Marsh could. "Let's have all the single girls line up by the doorway to the bar where there's some open space."

It would only stay open until more of the bar's patrons decided to wander in and join the festivities, Cole thought, still grinning.

Tess's mother, her sister and his mother flanked the bride like referees about to start a game. Cole watched the single women flock together, bemused by the thought that Tess had tried to help him find a wife from among this bevy of nice girls. He felt so fortunate his grin broadened.

"Okay, I'm going to cover my eyes and toss," Tess called. "No favoritism."

She put one hand over her eyes, twirled around twice and heaved the bouquet with a hard overhand pitch.

It soared over the women's heads.

It landed right in the arms of the tuxedo-clad best man, coming through the entryway from the bar.

Zack caught the wedding bouquet.

His face said it all. It was the last thing he ever wanted to land in his arms.

Cole claimed his bride amid howls of laughter.

One Groom To Go

Jennifer Drew

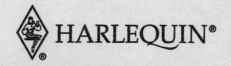

HARLEQUIN®

TORONTO • NEW YORK • LONDON
AMSTERDAM • PARIS • SYDNEY • HAMBURG
STOCKHOLM • ATHENS • TOKYO • MILAN • MADRID
PRAGUE • WARSAW • BUDAPEST • AUCKLAND

1

THE YOUNG WOMAN in the pink smock smacked Zack's face with a powder puff, oblivious to the low growl rumbling in his throat.

"Mr. Bailey, we have to talk about the script." Megan Danbury, the host of "Do It Herself," appeared at his side and waved a sheaf of papers in front of him.

"What script?" He stood and ripped off the lavender sheet the makeup woman had fastened around his neck. Lavender with little flowers!

"I know my show looks spontaneous, but every segment is planned ahead. You won't have to memorize the exact words, but..."

"Stop right there. All I agreed to do was refinish an old kitchen cupboard."

His brother was going to pay for getting him into this! Cole was the one who'd agreed to be a guest on the local cable program. It was supposed to be good free publicity for their construction firm, but Cole had ducked out of doing it. He was in Wyandotte that day preparing a bid on some school renovations. The financial end of the business was his twin's responsibility, but Zack would rather shovel dirt all day than do this TV bit.

He'd had enough of showbiz already, but the Danbury woman was too fired up to notice his lack of enthusiasm.

"I have all the steps worked out," Megan said. "If you'll just scan this..."

"What do you mean, all the steps worked out?"

"I've assembled all the materials and planned the procedures."

"Then why do you need me?"

He was hoping she'd tell him to get lost. He had enough trouble without making an idiot of himself on television. Baily Construction could always use a publicity boost, and his grandfather was holding Zack's shares in Bailey Baby Products over his head to pressure him into getting married. Zack wanted nothing to do with the company, but keeping the shares in the family meant his CEO mom would keep her job.

"It's just good programming to have guests," she said lamely.

He raised one eyebrow, a little trick he could do but his fraternal twin couldn't.

"Actually it was my producer's idea," Megan admitted.

"Oh, yeah, your brother-in-law, Ed Garrison. He sent some business our way last year." Which was why Zack felt obligated to be there, as powdery as a sugar doughnut and awkwardly out of place.

Zack looked her over and liked what he saw better than what he'd heard. She was a generic TV type, definitely a photogenic performer with long ash-blond hair and intense blue eyes. A tiny scar above one eyebrow was her only imperfection.

"We're on a tight schedule here," she said, as they walked toward the main set. "Normally we tape live before a studio audience and the edited show airs the next day, but the set was being remodeled earlier this week, and we're behind schedule."

"You're gorgeous." He said it matter-of-factly so she wouldn't misinterpret. "You don't need me."

"My show is geared to women, and Ed thinks the audience will respond well to a male expert."

"If I'm the expert, why do I need a script?"

"Please." It was an order, not an appeal.

"Okay, I'll take a look at it."

"Let me go over it with you."

"Ms. Danbury, I can read."

"Yes, yes, I'm sorry. I get a little hyper before a show. Be sure to call me Megan. We try for an informal atmosphere. If you have any questions…"

"I'll raise my hand."

She was wearing jeans—designer jeans too nice to mess up doing a refinishing job—and a pale blue shirt with the sleeves rolled up. She'd left enough buttons open for her cleavage to tease without being blatant. When she turned away to give him a moment's peace with the script, he wondered whether she could bend over in her tight pants. If she did, he wouldn't mind watching the view.

He skimmed a few pages and swore softly to himself. She must have done her research in a thirty-year-old home handicraft book. If he followed her cumbersome directions, he really would look inept.

The studio was a barnlike room with lights and cables everywhere. The audience was clustered together on metal folding chairs, and he wondered if they got paid to watch the show.

Megan was standing at the side of the room hissing at a man with a dog.

"One bark out of that canine show stealer…"

"Prince won't make a sound," the handler assured her. "I have to get him used to the lights and people before my show starts."

She was fuming when she came up to Zack, and he was happy for the distraction. For no logical reason at all, his palms were sweating and his stomach felt funny. True, he'd been dreading his TV debut, but he hadn't expected to suffer pregame jitters.

He couldn't bolt now without looking ridiculous. He dug his nails into his palms and tensed every muscle in his body, then forced himself to relax. He wasn't going to be stripped naked and tortured with hot pokers. He could walk a steel beam ten stories up, so he certainly could bluff his way through this, no matter that he couldn't remember a single word from her script.

Ed scurried around waving a clipboard but not consulting it. He gave Zack a pat on the shoulder and a jumble of instructions that boiled down to pay attention and take your cues from me.

The cupboard Zack was supposed to transform was a shabby section ripped from the wall of a kitchen that was being remodeled on the show. Most builders would scrap it. He had a few questions but didn't get a chance to ask them. Ed hustled him behind a chalk line to keep him out of camera range until his time came.

"Make your entrance when Megan says, 'Let's welcome our guest to "Do It Herself."'" Timing is everything in TV. Move briskly. Smile like you're glad to be here."

That hit close to home. The last time he'd been this reluctant to do a job was when he flushed a skunk out of a garage he and Cole were building.

Ed told a few stale jokes to warm up the guests, who were already squirming on the metal seats, then had them practice applauding. Lukewarm didn't cut it with the producer. He wanted thirty pairs of hands to resound.

The timing was tricky. Megan strolled onto the set just as Ed finally got some volume out of the hand clappers. She was smooth. He had to give her that. Her smile came across as genuine, and she managed to sound enthusiastic without phony perkiness.

Zack resented Ed's nudge in the small of his back, then realized Megan was waiting for him.

"Our guest is a little shy. Let's give him a big welcoming hand," she said.

He walked into the glare of the lights, conscious of a trickle of sweat between his shoulder blades. Already his blue plaid flannel shirt was sticking to his back. He couldn't remember a word of the script, and his mouth was so dry his tongue was sticking to the roof of his mouth. What in blazes was wrong with him? He hadn't felt this whipped when Shanghai flu knocked him off his feet for a week last winter.

"Tell us, Zack, what's the first thing you'd do?" She waited expectantly.

"Haul this piece of junk to the dump." He hadn't intended to be so blunt, but the rickety old cupboard was no antique.

She laughed. "That's not what we're about, Zack. Our viewers enjoy turning castoffs into treasures. Now if you'll show us how to begin stripping off this unsightly green paint..." She poured paint stripper from the can into a metal mixing bowl, expecting him to take it.

"There's a lot to do before we begin stripping, Megan," he said, glad his well-stocked toolbox was on the floor beside the cupboard. "First we take off the doors and remove the hardware."

"I'm sure that isn't necessary, Zack." Obviously that step wasn't in the script.

A few people in the audience must have thought their difference of opinion was funny. Or maybe they were laughing at her tone of voice. She was definitely not pleased.

He started to remember the script. He was supposed to smear on some stripper so it would cut through the paint during the commercial break, not that it would work that fast.

He flipped open his big box and took out a battery-powered tool to remove the screws holding on the hinges.

"I'll have one of these doors off in a minute. You can get a table ready for stripping, Megan." He was starting to get into the swing of it. Giving her orders helped. "If you do this at home, folks, always remove the metal hardware before using any kind of paint remover. And remember, wear rubber gloves. You're dealing with some powerful chemicals."

Zack resisted an impulse to glance at his watch. He didn't need to look at the beautiful blonde to know she was seething with disapproval. She didn't like last-minute script changes, but she was pretending to go along, hovering beside him with the bowl of stripper.

"We'll be right back to show you the easy way to remove old paint," she said in her professionally chipper voice.

Ed called out that they were off.

"You're ruining my show!" she said angrily, forgetting the audience leaning forward on their chairs, maybe hoping for a brawl. "I gave you a script!"

"You invited me here to show how an expert would do the job."

"So you know more than the people who write books?"

"Assuming I'd do a stupid project like this—and I wouldn't—my time is money. It takes less time to do a job right."

Ed hustled a couple of guys to set up a folding table and cover it with newspaper and a sheet of plastic. Megan whispered to the producer but didn't seem to get the answer she wanted.

Zack wanted to walk away, but when the program credits rolled, their company name would be listed. He had to get through the rest of the show. He put a cupboard door on the table and steeled himself for round two.

When they were on again, she was still holding the bowl of stripper as though she'd forgotten she had it. He did give her acting credit for turning on the charm. She gave him a two-hundred-watt smile and launched him into the next segment of the program.

"Do this in a well-ventilated place," she said, as Zack stood over the battered old door on the table. "You'll need an inexpensive brush and a...ugh!"

The big shaggy dog streaked toward them just as Megan was handing Zach the stripper. Prince wanted to play, and he picked her as his playmate. He bounded into her and sent the bowl flying.

Megan shrieked, the trainer scolded and lunged for the dog, and Zack took a direct hit. The thickened chemicals spilled across the front of his shirt.

He reacted instantly and ripped off all the buttons in his haste to shed the shirt before the stripper soaked through to his skin.

"Oh, oh, my!" Megan said.

"I guess we'll need more stripper," he said mildly, feeling more in control now that he'd handled a situation that definitely wasn't in her script.

He was sure of one thing—this was his first, last and only appearance as a guest expert!

"Of course, there's no reason to waste all this." He picked up the ruined shirt and applied it directly to the cupboard door.

"Oh," Megan said again.

The dog was led away, Megan rallied and launched into mostly accurate directions on removing paint, and Zack stood bare to the waist trying to pretend he cared a rat's rear about stripping wood that was pitted and scarred by hard usage.

The lights were hot, his chest itched, and he wanted out. Too bad the stripper hadn't landed on her. The show would be a lot livelier if she'd had to rip off her shirt.

"Don't you think so, Zack?"

"What?" He'd missed most of her lecture, probably straight from the script.

"There's no reason a woman can't renovate her home without help from a male," she repeated.

"No reason at all, Megan. Just hire someone for the tricky stuff and go to it. But any man in his right mind should take cover if he sees a woman with stripper."

The audience laughed. She didn't take it lying down.

"The only stripper most men care about is one who takes her clothes off," she said wryly, getting a laugh of her own.

"If you mean no sensible man wants to waste time on a beat-up old board…"

The audience roared. He looked at his watch.

"Our guest has been Zack Bailey of Bailey Construction. Thank you for being with us today, Zack," she said with a noticeable lack of enthusiasm. "We'll be right back with hints on staining stripped wood."

He bolted, grabbing his toolbox and leaving the TV studio, indifferent to the cool spring rain pelting his bare shoulders. He never again wanted any part of a fiasco like that. At least none of his friends would watch that home-handicraft-for-girls show. He certainly never would, not even to see its easy-on-the-eyes host.

LEFT ALONE in the little closet she liked to call her dressing room, Megan didn't know whether to cry, scream or leave town. The show was a disaster. She was humiliated. The station owner would give her spot to "Pets on Parade," and she'd never work in TV again.

It was all Ed's fault! Guest expert? Why not hire a clown with a dog act? She was ruined, her hope of someday taking her show to a national cable network crushed.

She loathed Zack Bailey! If he'd intentionally set out to spoil her show, he couldn't have done it more effectively. Maybe he was a ringer working for "Pets on Parade."

It was bad enough that he got cold feet and had to be pushed onto the set. Then he refused to start the stripping process without taking the cupboard apart. Women weren't going to run out and buy an electric screwdriver just to remove hardware that could be covered with masking tape.

She shuddered when she replayed his big scene in her mind—ripping off his shirt and revealing the brawny bare chest. He'd popped off the buttons, then made a joke of the whole segment by using the shirt to spread the paint remover. For the first time since Broadcasting 101 in college, she'd lost it in front of the camera. How could she remember her script when she had to stand there looking at sexy dark nipples and silky chest hair on a torso that was like a Greek god's?

She'd gone to half a dozen salvage yards to find an old cupboard with character, and he'd belittled her treasure and her plan to restore it. Where did Ed get him? She could drag someone off the street at random and have a more satisfactory guest expert.

All she could do now was go home and wait for the phone call. Her show would be moved to the 6 a.m. slot, if it wasn't canceled outright. With eight months to go on her contract, she might even have to be the next stooge on the Bulgarian chef's show.

She'd had such high hopes. There was a real need to teach women ways to make their surroundings more functional and beautiful without great cost—or reliance on men. Her mother had made a wonderful home for her two daughters after Megan's father deserted the family when she was seven and Georgia was nine. Mom eventually married a kind, friendly man, but before she did, she worked full-time and turned their small, aging house into a place that radiated love and good taste.

Until she learned the worst about her show's future, all Megan wanted to do was sneak home and forget her woes with a good book. Her sister swore by a good cry followed by chocolate-marshmallow cookies, but Megan turned to a happily-ever-after fantasy every time. She was nearly twenty-nine, and she couldn't afford the luxury of gaining weight, not in a business where looking good was essential.

"Megan!" Her dressing-room door flew open, and Ed barged in, his handsome but jowly face flushed bright pink.

"You could knock."

"Sorry. I've been going crazy. The phones are ringing off the hook, and e-mail is pouring in."

"That bad?"

"Bad? Are you kidding? Mr. G. himself had me on the line sixty seconds after the wrap."

"Mr. Gunderdorf?"

Now she did feel sick. The owner was an old-money big shot, but he pretty much had a hands-off policy at the station, one of his many investments. If the television profits were enough to buy him a couple of pricey antique cars for his collection every year, he didn't trouble himself with program content. If he made a personal call to pull the plug, her career was history.

"He caught your show today."

"I assumed."

"He said it was more entertaining than he dreamed possible on our humble little endeavor."

"Say again?"

"He loved it! Called his wife away from a museum board luncheon at their home to watch the shirtless segment. He automatically tapes everything but watches less than one percent and likes about one percent of what he does see."

"Oh, give me a break, Ed. You're making this up so I won't climb down your throat and pull out your tonsils with my bare hands. Zack Bailey is totally your fault."

"Remember that when you sign a new two-year contract with a healthy raise."

She sat down hard on the piano stool she'd refinished for her dressing table.

"I can't believe it. There has to be a catch."

"One tiny one, maybe. Bailey has to sign for a certain number of appearances in the next twelve months."

"That man will be a regular on my show?" She couldn't have been more stunned if Ed had sprouted bunny ears.

"Not every week. Mr. G. wants to keep the format of guest experts. Maybe attract an auto buff on touching up cars, an auctioneer on spotting good buys in antiques. You know, add some class. Good guests will line up for a chance to be on the show if we triple the audience. After today it's practically a sure thing."

"Ed, you're insane! Gunderdorf is insane! I cannot work with that man."

"For way more money and a chance to go national? Don't kid with me!"

"Maybe you can hire an actor instead. One who will stick to the script." Megan kept her fingers crossed but knew what Ed's answer would be.

"Not an option. Mr. G. loved the sparks between you and Bailey. You don't have to like him. The show will be better if you can't stand each other."

"He'll never do it. I've seen camera shy before, and he was sweating blood before he came on. He hated being there and he wasn't too keen on me, either."

"He settled down. Ripped off that shirt like Brando in his prime."

"He's a builder, not an actor."

"Bailey Construction is in a competitive market. There's a well-heeled grandfather in the picture, but he won't advance the twins a dime to promote a business that isn't his."

"Twins? There are two like him?" She groaned from the heart. "How did you learn all that?"

"From Mr. G. He knows all the money people in Detroit. Bailey needs free publicity. It's not easy to keep a small construction company afloat in this city."

"You'll never sign him. I won't let myself get excited."

"I don't have to. You'll have to sign him yourself."

"Me? No way! The station has a business manager, lawyers, people with clout."

"They also have you, Megan." He had the grace to look uncomfortable.

Oh, she didn't like this. She didn't like this at all.

"You're good, honey," he said in his best brother-in-law voice. "But if J. R. Gunderdorf blackballs you, you won't be able to get a job in Nowhere, North Dakota."

"He wouldn't do that." She tried unsuccessfully to re-assure herself.

"He wants to make you a star, and he loved the vibes between you and Zack."

"Bailey won't do the show again, especially not if I ask."

"Ask anyway. Beg, cajole, cry. Sleep with him if you have to."

"I will not!"

"Beg or sleep with him?"

"Both—neither. I'll resign first."

"And do what?"

She put her elbows on the obsessively ordered surface of her dressing table and buried her face in her hands.

"Listen to me, Megan. Your concept for 'Do It Herself' is a great one. This is your chance to make it fly. You're no newcomer to this business. There's always a price to pay, and you know it."

"Why do I have to be the one to recruit him? It's not fair." For once in her life, she didn't care if she whined.

"It's your show, your future. Mr. G. is pretty astute. He saw something to make him think you're the only one who can wrap up a deal with Bailey. Are you going to be a quitter?"

"My sister told you to say that."

"What?" he asked, keeping his voice bland.

"The one thing I can't stand to be called is a quitter."

"Then call Bailey."

"He'll say no."

"Call again."

"Make an absolute fool of myself? Maybe kiss his boots?"

"Have two dozen roses delivered to him at a construction site. Wine and dine him. Whatever it takes. The station will pick up the tab.''

''I can't do it.''

''Sure you can. You're a hammer-totin', crowbar-swingin' kind of gal. You're not scared of Bailey, are you?''

''No!'' She denied it, but she would rather walk on hot coals than try to sign Zack Bailey as a regular on her show.

2

"ANOTHER delivery for you, Zack."

Gus Graham, the construction foreman and an old
buddy of Zack's, stuck his head through the door of the
on-site trailer and held out a bud vase with three long-
stemmed pink roses. A card with little cupids dangled
from a pink ribbon tied to one of the stems.

"What is this, the fourth this week? You must have
some secret admirer." Gus roared with laughter, put the
vase on the corner of Zack's cluttered desk and got the
hell out of there. He knew darn well what his boss thought
of little pink posies.

Zack wanted to make him eat the flowers, never mind
that Gus topped his own six foot two inches and was as
broad as a bear. He was sick of being embarrassed by
Megan Danbury's cutesy flower deliveries. Did she really
think she could manipulate him by making him look ridiculous in front of Cole, his brother and business partner,
and their crew?

He yanked the card off the ribbon and tossed the roses,
vase and all, into a plastic-lined trash can. He was mad
at himself for even bothering to read her message, not that
it was different from Monday's, Tuesday's or Wednesday's.

Please let me take you to dinner to discuss a business
proposition. Megan Danbury.

Somebody should clue her in. This was the twenty-first century. She could deliver a message via answering machine. Pink roses!

As he crumpled the card and tossed it on top of the discarded flowers, he remembered the several hang-ups he'd had on his machine at home. Was she the pest who never identified herself? What was so important that she had to tell him in person?

The "Do It Herself" host didn't know it, but she was poking a stick in a hornet's nest when she made him look like an idiot in front of his men—and his smugly happy married brother. What he ought to do was make an unscheduled personal appearance at the TV station and see how *she* liked being embarrassed at her workplace.

But that would mean he'd have to run a gauntlet of oddballs who thought TV was real life—the powder-puff fanatic, sly former client Ed Garrison, the dog trainer who didn't know enough to hang on to a leash, not to mention Megan herself.

"Hey, bro, I told Tess about your mystery girlfriend and the roses," Cole said, sticking his head through the doorway without coming into the trailer. "She said you should bring her to dinner Saturday."

Zack gave him the lantern-jaw look, his lips compressed and eyes glaring. It intimidated most people but never his twin. Cole was so darn happy being married to Tess, he didn't even notice he was treading on dangerous ground.

"She's not my girlfriend," he said with intentional hostility. "She's the dip who dumped paint stripper on me on the TV show you were supposed to do."

"What's with the flower deliveries if she's not hot for you?"

Cole stepped into the trailer. He wasn't the mirror image of Zack, but they were enough alike so no one ever doubted they were twins. Zack always conceded his brother was the pretty one. They had the same dark gray eyes and thick black hair, but Zack wore his longer. Cole's nose was straight, not slightly off-kilter as Zack's had been since he'd broken it playing flag football a long time ago. Zack was a few minutes older and an inch taller, which, he jokingly insisted, made him the dominant twin.

"The woman has a screw loose," he complained.

Not true, but he didn't want to talk about Megan the-fix-it-chick Danbury with his brother or anyone else. He didn't have a clue why she was sending him flowers and making him the joke of the day four days running.

He and Cole spent the next hour going over some specs for the bank branch they were building. His brother, who was in a big hurry to clean up and fire up the grill before his wife got home from work, left after him.

Zack hung around the trailer until the crew was gone. He could take their ribbing but he was getting tired of wolf whistles and off-color remarks. If Megan Danbury was trying to make him look ridiculous, she was better at it than she was at home handicraft for girls.

He picked up the denim jacket he'd worn to work because the mornings were still cool for May and wished tomorrow was Saturday.

Damn! He loved the construction business. He hadn't dreaded going to work since he spent a summer break from college holding a stop sign on a state highway crew. This flower bombardment had to stop.

Pink roses!

He picked up the phone.

Five minutes later it was set. His nemesis agreed to

meet him for dinner at seven the next evening at Rondo's Grill.

ON FRIDAY no purple florist's van came to the site, not that Zack's mood improved much in the absence of another floral humiliation. His men were still having so much fun with her stunt, he should dock them for all the time wasted.

After work he showered under the cold-water hookup in the trailer, but there was no way he would shave in icy water for Danbury. She was lucky he washed off the day's dust and sweat considering the dumb way she'd gotten him to talk to her. He already regretted setting up a dinner meeting. He should've made her come to the site for a quick bawling out.

He padded naked through the ancient Airstream trailer, which served as their on-site command center, and found the clean Jockey shorts and jeans in the gym bag he'd brought along. He slid bare feet into a pair of old loafers and put on his worn denim jacket without a shirt, snapping it halfway up his chest. Where he was meeting her, this was formal wear.

He got to the roadhouse at seven sharp even though it was way out beyond the airport. They made legendary ribs, which partly accounted for the crowded parking lot, but Rondo's Grill was mostly famous for serving a last meal to a crooked contractor who disappeared without a trace more than fifteen years ago. Rumor had it he was wearing cement overshoes at the bottom of the Detroit River or buried under the forty-yard line of a college football field somewhere in the hinterland of Ohio.

Danbury was late, which gave Zack time to get a booth, sip a beer and wonder what she wanted. He stared at yellowing newspaper clippings about the ancient disappearance framed on the walls:

Colarie Last Seen at Rondo's
Alleged Mobster Connection
Colarie Disappears after Plate of Rondo's Ribs

The whole place was plastered with lurid headlines. Zack wondered if Rondo had had most of them printed himself. The missing man was a slimeball contractor, not Jimmy Hoffa.

Where the devil was that woman? He had two inches of beer and half a bowl of popcorn left. When they were gone, so was he.

He had problems of his own without dealing with hers. Now that Cole was happily domesticated, his grandfather, Marsh Bailey, was dead set on marrying off Zack, too, and Marsh was carrying one big stick—shares in Bailey Baby Products. Mom ran the family business now, but Gramps, as he hated to be called, was threatening to sell out to strangers if his grandsons didn't settle down with nice women. Cole's one-third of the business was safe now, Marsh adored Tess. But they had to keep two-thirds in the family to keep Mom as CEO.

With their thirtieth birthday looming like doomsday, Marsh insisted it was time his twin grandsons grew up and got serious about the business—the business of making baby stuff or babies. Their half brother, Nick, was still in college and safe from the old man's machinations for now, so Zack was next in line to take the fall.

He bit down so hard on a jaw full of popcorn his teeth hurt. He wasn't the marrying kind, and he sure as hell wasn't interested in anyone Marsh thought was a nice girl. Zack wondered if he took after his birth father, a man he'd never met. Gramps had scared him off with the threat of jail or worse when he learned his only child was pregnant at seventeen. In nearly thirty years he'd never tried to see his twin sons. The man didn't have it in him to be a father, and neither did Zach. Maybe it was bad blood, but the single life suited him just fine.

Luckily for Cole and him, their stepfather had been an okay guy, but Mom had taken his death hard. Only her job as CEO of Bailey Baby Products had kept her going. Now the old bastard was threatening to sell out, knowing damn well Mom would probably be ousted if outsiders took control.

Cole had secured his share of the business by marrying Tess, but Cole was lucky. Who could've guessed the pudgy kid they used to tease in high school would blossom into such a gorgeous woman? Now either Zack or Nick had to secure a second third of the shares, and his half brother was too busy scoring with sorority girls at Michigan State to think about marriage.

Double damn! Here he was waiting for uptight Danbury when he should be finding a way for Mom to keep control of the business without his help—in this case that ball and chain called matrimony.

He swallowed the last of the beer, felt like having another but didn't. He'd waited long enough. Where was his waitress so he could pay for the beer? A leggy woman in Rondo's standard attire, cowboy hat, boots, and shorts so skimpy the crease of her butt showed when she leaned over, was serving the next table, but he seemed to remember his server had a long blond braid.

He dropped a couple of bills on the black tabletop and started to slide out of the booth when he spotted a gorgeous blonde by the podium where the hostess took names. She was wearing a little red dress almost as skimpy as the waitresses' shorts, but no one in the crowded restaurant could fill it the way she did.

In spite of looking red-hot sexy and ready for anything,

Megan Danbury managed a lost-waif expression that brought Rondo himself, resplendent in a Western dude outfit with snakeskin boots and a ten-pound silver and turquoise necklace, rushing over to help her.

Zack had picked this place because Danbury was a linen tablecloth and four forks kind of woman, but his plan to make her uncomfortable had been plain silly. She glided toward his booth with Rondo hovering in her wake like a pet boxer, the canine kind.

"Here he is. Thank you so much, Mr. Rondo. I'll be sure to look at all your clippings before I leave."

No one called the pudgy little restaurateur mister, and he lapped it up like a pit bull with a platter of steak.

"You're late," Zack said as she slid onto the seat across from him. There wasn't enough dress to keep her bare thighs from making little squishy noises on the vinyl upholstery.

"How could I not be? This place is halfway to Kalamazoo!"

"Nice to see you, too." He tried for droll, but it came out mad. He should have given her ten minutes, not half an hour.

"We could have done this at the studio."

She shouldn't pout. With her lips puckered like that, no man was going to think of anything but wiggling his tongue between them.

He barked at her to cover his wholly involuntary and unwanted reaction. "Why not at my job site? Maybe with violin accompaniment and a collar of flowers like the kind winning racehorses wear. You could make me look like a complete fool in front of my men."

"Didn't you like my flowers?"

If she batted her eyelids, he was out of there no matter how far she'd had to drive to get there.

"Don't ask unless you want me to tell you what you can do with them."

"Mr. Bailey, I'm so surprised you didn't appreciate them. I love roses, any color, pink, white, red, yellow…"

She batted! Her long spiky lashes fanned the air as her lids rose and fell in several quick movements.

What the devil was this woman trying to pull? He felt a stirring of curiosity in spite of his deep misgivings about anything and everything involving Megan Danbury.

"I do want to thank you for agreeing to meet me," she said in a voice dripping with honey.

"You could have just asked me. I don't need a truck-load of flowers cluttering up my job site."

"That would look great on my expense account," she said, dropping her sweetie-sweet tone. "Shall we order? This is my treat, of course."

On her expense account? He was liking this less and less.

"First tell me why you sent flowers four days running."

No more Mr. Nice Guy. This woman was pure poison, however attractively she was packaged.

"To get your attention."

"All you'd have to do is show up on the site in that skirt, and you'd have more attention then you'd know what to do with."

She had enough grace to look uncomfortable, but the elusive waitress with the braid saved her from the censure she deserved.

They ordered—grilled salmon for her and a porterhouse for him.

He wanted to know what was behind the game she was playing, but she was coy, pretending she loved Rondo's because it was quaint and folksy. He caught her wiping her fork on a napkin.

Did he follow the Lions, the Tigers, the Red Wings? What else had Bailey Construction built? Did he grow up in the Detroit area?

Was she interviewing him or just stalling until she hit him with something he wasn't going to like?

"What is it like to be a twin?" she asked as she nibbled at her salad with lemon, no dressing.

"What is it like not to be one?"

It was his standard response to a question both he and Cole thought was too dumb to deserve an answer. If she asked whether he flossed once or twice a day, he was going to ask what color her hair really was, even though he suspected the pale ash-blond mane was the most genuine thing about her.

He had to hand it to her. She was a master at small talk. No wonder she made her living with her mouth—with a little help from a spectacular body. The way her cleavage filled the low-cut neckline, he had a hard time remembering to chew his steak.

But he did remember pink roses.

She avoided getting down to business until the waitress brought after-dinner coffee, which was too hot to drink right away.

"You were a sensation on the show."

She gritted her teeth when she said it, or so it seemed to him.

"We got triple the number of hits on our Web page as 'Pets on Parade' did."

"Always nice to best a show with cats, dogs and gerbils."

"No, I'm serious! Our audience loved the show. We'd like you to come back again."

Her body language sold her out. She wanted him back like she wanted a zit on her delicate chin.

"Who wants me back?"

"Ed, my producer."

"Your brother-in-law sent you after me?"

He narrowed his eyes, pretty sure she was holding back something.

"Actually, it was Mr. Gunderdorf's idea."

Zack knew the name—one of Marsh's golfing cronies—but how did he come into this?

"Why should he care who does the parlor tricks on a chick show?"

He struck home with "chick show." Her eyes blazed with blue fire, and she shifted on the seat, her bare thighs separating from the tacky vinyl with a sucking sound.

"Ratings," she said without parting her lips. "He likes big ratings. He owns the station."

"So I'm supposed to come back so you can zap me with a hot glue gun? That would go over big with viewers who never miss major surgery on the tube."

"I'll give it to you straight."

She leaned forward, thighs smacking on the vinyl again. By now they must be as pink as her roses.

"My show is near cancellation," she went on. "'Pets on Parade' is waiting in the wings with a hot idea on dog grooming, panting to glom on to my spot."

"Yeah, I met the star of that show."

When was an accident not an accident? Maybe when a dog handler didn't have enough sense to hang on to a leash. This didn't mean he felt any obligation to give Danbury another shot at him.

"*My* show on stripping turned things around."

He noticed she didn't actually give him the credit.

"I've been offered a wonderful new contract that guarantees my time slot, plus a good raise. If you knew how poorly local shows pay…''

"Congratulations." He drank his coffee and eyed her warily.

"There is a condition. Mr. Gunderdorf himself wants you to be a regular guest. You wouldn't have to do every segment—"

"I don't have to do any segment."

"No, of course not, but you'll be well paid, and it's marvelous publicity for your construction company."

Sure it was. Women who watched daytime TV would clamor to have his brother and him build doggie digs and fancy mailboxes.

"Well, what do you think?"

She was breathless, but he doubted it was from the exciting prospect of sharing her show with him.

Was she insane? Why would he go along with such a ridiculous idea? Hot lights, heavy makeup, silly projects? He was an outdoor man, and the business needed his full attention, especially since Cole was still basking in marital bliss, improbable as that had once seemed.

"No."

"It wouldn't be a full-time job by any means. I'd work out all the content. You'd just have to show up for an hour or two, and only on a certain number of segments. There's lots of potential for your business—our sponsors, contacts in the television business."

"No."

"I could tell you were a little uneasy being in front of the camera, but a lot of performers get stage fright at first. I still get a little uptight before every show."

A little? If she could, she'd script the number of slaps with the powder puff the makeup girl gave guests.

"No."

"Please, don't be hasty."

Did this woman grasp the meaning of the simple two-letter word?"

"You don't want to work with me."

He had her there.

"We could work it out. Granted, you're more spontaneous than I am. I like to do things by the book. Afraid I'm addicted to lists and schedules, but I can change."

"Miss Danbury." He forgot she'd told him to call her Megan. "Thanks, but no thanks."

"But—"

"Don't make me go into all the reasons I'd rather pump out septic tanks than make a fool of myself on another of your shows."

"You haven't given this any thought."

"I think it's a lousy idea. Find someone else to do your pratfalls. I've never wanted to be a clown."

He couldn't put it any plainer than that—not in mixed company in a public place.

"Thanks for the dinner," he added. "If you send me any more flowers, you'll get a surprise package at your workplace, and it won't smell like roses."

She'd reduced him to threats and sarcasm. He left her fuming impotently, her anger following him out the door like invisible death rays in an old sci-fi flick.

Watching a game on the tube was as close to the wacky world of TV as he ever planned to come.

Did she really think he'd sign on as her personal stooge?

3

MONDAY MORNING Megan sat in her sensible compact car in slot number twenty-seven at the far end of the parking lot. Larry, the dog man, had slot six a few steps from the entrance, a pretty good indication of their relative status at Channel 98.

She'd had her chance to improve her standing at the station, but she'd blown it. Why did she go along with Ed on the flowers? Instead of intriguing Bailey, they made him furious. He turned down the offer without even listening to the details.

Wearing her red dress without panty hose had been another mistake. Sure, she'd wowed the funny little man dressed like a cartoon cowboy, but her thighs kept sticking to that icky plastic seat, making vulgar noises every time she moved. Some impression she'd made on the shirtless stud!

That was another irritation, as long as she was cataloging complaints. If women couldn't go topless, not that she wanted to, why were men allowed in public places with bare chests? How could she concentrate on her lines when she was distracted by his admittedly awesome washboard stomach muscles?

His pecs were the problem. The last person she wanted to share her airtime with was a male stripper, but Ed was still getting rave reviews and pleas to see more of Zack Bailey on her show.

Her show—ha!

She wanted to scream in frustration, but she had to concentrate on a show that showed viewers how to replace a broken windowpane without the expense of calling a glass company. It was her idea to help women improve their homes on their own, and she'd always had faith that someday she'd win a spot on a home improvement network.

Getting out of the car, Megan tried to put her anxiety on a back burner. Bailey wasn't going to save her time slot or her show, and she hated feeling out of control. Her goals were straightforward—first to gain recognition for her show, then to meet and marry a fabulous man and have two adorable children.

When Megan walked into the studio, Ed was lying in wait in the little room that served as her office.

"I tried calling you all weekend. How did the meeting with Bailey go?" he asked.

"He said no. Did you remember to get a new putty knife?"

"Everything's on the set. Did you talk money? Was that the holdup?"

Megan liked her sister's husband, but sometimes she wished Georgia had married an ore-mining boat captain, a deep-sea diver, even a trash collector, anyone who wasn't the producer of her TV show. He tried to run it the same way he'd played lineman on the University of Michigan football team—hit, block, batter and annihilate the opposition. He laughed at her list making and was always trying to get her to wing the show instead of follow a script.

"I'll tell you all about it after taping," she said.

"Do It Herself" was not a rip-roaring success that morning except to viewers who liked a little gore with their entertainment. Megan sliced her finger on a shard of glass stuck in the old window frame and finished the project with a wad of tissues sopping up the blood.

"Good save," Ed said cheerfully. "You couldn't have planned a better safety lesson. Now where do we stand with Bailey?"

"Ed, I'm leaving a bloody trail."

"Do you need stitches?"

"No, I need a bandage."

He reluctantly ambled off to hunt for the first-aid box. Where was Mom when Megan needed her?

Megan got her goal-setting habit from her mother. When her husband ran off with another woman, Gretchen had coped by making a warm, loving home for Megan and Georgia, then seven and nine. She remarried after her daughters left home and was leading the life she deserved in sunny Florida, but "Do It Herself" was very much a tribute to Gretchen.

As kids, Georgia ate chocolate-marshmallow cookies and moped while Megan established a troop record for earning Little Daisy Girl badges. Other Little Daisies made shrunken apple-head dolls, but she used her grandfather's tools to build a hummingbird condominium that made the Badger Boys' projects look lame.

She took off her makeup and retreated to her cubbyhole of an office, which at least had a door she could shut. Ed would track her down eventually and demand a play-by-play on her conversation with Bailey, but maybe if she hurried through a few bits of business, she could leave before he showed up to grill her.

She found a bandage in her purse and stanched the trickle still beading on her right pinky, but a loud knock dashed her hopes of avoiding a strategy meeting with Ed.

"Come on in."

"How's my sweetie today?"

The one man she wanted to see less than Ed was her grandfather. Ed only wanted to manage her career. George Peters had plans for her whole life, and they started with finding her the right husband.

He was a doting grandparent, and she adored him. But lately he was on a crusade. He was polling all his golfing buddies to find eligible grandsons. Worse, he was playing matchmaker, getting a tremendous charge out of arranging blind dates for her. He'd cajoled her into going on two, one only boring, the other a total disaster. The jerk had started his touchy-feely tactics when he picked her up and gotten so obnoxious by the time dinner was over, she took a cab home.

She hadn't had the heart to tell her grandfather he'd set her up with a sex maniac, but she'd had enough of his friends' grandsons.

"Hi, Grandpa."

She gave him her best imitation of a warm, welcoming smile. He rarely came to the studio, and she couldn't help but be wary.

"Thought maybe we could have lunch together," he said.

"Oh, I'd love to, but let me check my schedule." She glanced at the desk calendar, as if she hadn't already memorized her day's appointments. "Darn, I have to interview a banker about home-improvement loans at one. It's for a segment next week. No time for lunch, I'm afraid. Aren't you playing golf today?"

"Supposed to rain again."

"I'll give you a rain check on lunch."

She walked around her desk and soundly kissed his cheek.

"You work too hard." He growled, but she knew he

was proud of her. "When am I going to get more grand-kids?"

"You have Jason."

"Little stinker snitched my car keys and hid them last time I went to Georgia's. Spoiled rotten. Needs a brother or sister to share the attention."

"He's just mischievous." And Attila the Hun just liked to travel.

"Genetics," George muttered. He wasn't Ed's biggest fan. "Important to pick a good man."

"Not on my list yet, Grandpa." She tried to kid but still suspected this was no social call.

"Your dang lists," he grumbled. "You do work too hard, honey."

"I just like to be organized like you and Mom."

"If I hadn't taken a little time off from work now and again, you wouldn't be here."

"I'm sort of in crisis right now," she said, letting a little of her job anxiety slip out.

"All the more reason you need some fun. One of my friends has a grandson…"

Didn't he know anyone but old cronies with bachelor grandsons?

"Haven't seen him in a while, but we talked before about introducing the two of you."

No, no, no! She smiled, but inside she was screaming.

At least her grandfather helped her evade Ed on the way out. Her brother-in-law wouldn't come within a hundred yards of the older man unless Georgia made him. Grandpa was always trying to get Ed to play golf—totally not Ed's sport—lose the spare tire around his waist or have more kids.

Other people's grandfathers lived in Florida condos or Arizona trailer parks. Hers hung around the used-car lot he once owned and gave pointers to the salesmen—and sometimes the customers. For all she knew, he was screening potential husbands there, too.

She left him standing in the parking lot with a cockeyed grin on his face that didn't bode well for her peace of mind.

SHE WENT to work the next day determined to let her producer worry about whether Zack would appear on the show again. There was nothing more she could do.

"Do It Herself" ran two times a week, alternating with the Bulgarian chef in the 11:00 a.m. slot. With that much airtime to fill, Megan did sometimes bring in guests, preferably women with skills such as tile laying, wallpapering or carpentry—role models for her audience. The one time she'd let Ed talk her into having a male guest on the set, it had led to the Bailey disaster.

Ed was lurking around her office when she got there.

"Megan, we have to talk."

Not for nothing had he blocked against Ohio State, Michigan State and Georgia, his headstrong wife. Megan tried her three best excuses to avoid talking to him—a phone call to make, a script to study, an appointment to keep.

"You don't have to worry about your show because there won't be one," he said, sounding madder than she'd ever heard him. "Come into my office."

He had three chairs to her two in his minuscule space, but she preferred not to dwell on her relative status at a station where the custodian's closet was bigger than her office. Keeping her show on the air was the first priority.

"I want the whole story on Bailey," Ed said, making the room seem claustrophobic when he closed the door behind him.

"The whole story is no story. He emphatically is not interested. The man builds buildings. He's not a performer and doesn't want to be one."

"How did he react to the flowers?"

"He hated them!"

Ed liked lounging in the oversize executive desk chair Georgia had given him on his birthday. Megan took it as a bad sign that he was on his feet, leaning forward with his palms flat on the desktop in a confrontational pose.

"He was embarrassed," she added, realizing she didn't much blame the man.

"What we have to do is pull out all the stops. Show him we'll do anything to convince him to do the show."

"He can't be convinced. I could dance naked at his construction site, and he wouldn't budge."

"That's it!" Ed bellowed so loudly he startled her.

"What?" She hadn't intended to ask. It just slipped out.

"A striptease! Bailey will realize how serious we are."

"That's a dumb idea!"

"No, it's not. No man can resist the lure of naked flesh—well, I don't mean me, of course. I'm happily married."

"We are not going to hire a stripper!"

"Well, no, I'd hate to itemize that on an expense sheet, but there must be some way to convince him."

"You're not being realistic. Zack Bailey is more likely to swear out a restraining order than sign a contract for my show if I bother him anymore."

"I hate to tell you," Ed said in such a somber voice she expected big phony tears to roll down his fleshy cheeks, "but the show is hanging by a thread. Gunderdorf wants more of what he saw last week. The chemistry between you two was electric—his words, not mine."

"He only imagined it. Forget Bailey. He's not doing my show again."

"There won't be a show if we don't sign him."

She didn't want to believe Ed, but he sounded seriously worried.

"The ratings aren't that bad! I can live with a worse slot."

"That's not the point, Megan. Gunderdorf wants a winner, and he thinks Bailey will be the ticket. If we can't sign him, the show gets the ax and you'll finish out your contract doing bits on other shows."

"I'll take my show somewhere else."

She tried to sound defiant, but it came out depressed. A canceled show was almost impossible to peddle in another market.

Ed didn't say anything for several long moments.

"It's not just about you, Megan. If the show is canceled, my job is history."

"Why? It's not your fault."

"You have a lot to learn about the real world. When Gunderdorf says do it, he assumes it's as good as done."

"That's not fair! There's no way to force Zack Bailey to make appearances, and our ratings have been sound without him. We don't deserve to be dumped!"

"It's not fair that my knees kept me out of the pros. I only took broadcasting in college because it looked fun, but I don't have the talent to be on-camera. If I lose this job, where do I go? Idaho, Iowa, North Dakota? Georgia doesn't want to live anywhere but here."

She stared at the walls Ed had turned into one big bulletin board with clippings and souvenirs of his college days playing football plastered all over them. She could walk away from her job, but his future looked really bleak if he lost his. Georgia's life was a paint-by-number scene.

She hated change, and Ed's chances of getting a job in the Detroit area were slim to none. Megan couldn't stand it that Gunderdorf, a man who never came near the studio, had the power to pull the plug on people's lives. It was so unfair she wanted to scream.

Then there was her nephew, Jason. He could be a little snot, like the time he deliberately smeared ice cream on her new raincoat, but raising kids cost a lot of money. Georgia was writing a cookbook using Ed as her taster, but at the rate she was going, it would be years before she was ready to submit it to a publisher—and then it might not sell. How many people would buy a cookbook featuring a hundred and one recipes using chocolate-marshmallow cookies?

Ed was morose but silent. He was a competent producer, but she couldn't rely on him to save the show. Creative ideas were her strength, and she badly needed one that would persuade Bailey to make more appearances.

"I hate this!" she said as she left Ed's office. "It's just not fair." There had to be something she could do to persuade Bailey.

ZACK WAS on the phone trying to nail down a date to pour the concrete for the sidewalk in front of the bank building. Cole was arguing with the electrical contractor about some substandard wiring that had to be corrected. Their jobs would be a snap if everyone else would do theirs right. It was only Wednesday morning, and already it felt like a long week.

At least it wasn't raining anymore. The site was a muddy mess, and the forecast was for more cool, wet days.

"Hey, boss," one of the carpenters yelled, opening the trailer door a crack to be heard. "You got a visitor."

"I'll be right out," Zack said absentmindedly as he jotted down the results of his call.

"Maybe you want to, you know, meet in private."

The door slammed shut before Zack could ask why. He was pretty sure he heard a muffled laugh through the partially open window. What was up now?

"Oh, no!" He had a bad feeling. If this was another delivery, any florist who dared come onto his work site would soon discover a new use for cutesy posies.

He slammed his chair into a file cabinet in his hurry to get outside.

Danbury was wearing black spiked heels and a tan trench coat and holding a brown paper grocery bag. He stepped on the temporary walkway of old wooden planks and gave her a stony-faced look.

"You'd better find a firmer place to stand or, better still, leave. You're sinking." He nodded at the heels sinking into soft ground.

She pulled one foot free and tried to step forward, but the second shoe stayed put, stuck in the mush. Her bare foot came down, causing mud to ooze between her toes.

"This place is a swamp."

"We like it," he said dryly, with no intention of retrieving her lost shoe.

She turned slowly, bent and got it herself, her tightly belted trench coat taut over her shapely backside. His men were inching toward her like zombies smelling raw meat.

"I need to see you in private."

She stuck her muddy toes into the ridiculously high-heeled shoe.

Did the woman never wear panty hose?

"I'm swamped with work." Not entirely a falsehood. "Anything you have to say, you can say right here."

She went to the end of the wooden walkway, smiled coyly, set the bag down beside her and fiddled with something inside.

Music suddenly began blaring. He hadn't heard anything like it since he'd snuck into a strip show on a high-school trip to San Francisco.

She yanked off the coat belt and started swinging it over her head, legs spread wide and hips gyrating like a pro. She was no cowgirl. The end of the belt slapped the side of her face and wrapped itself around her neck.

Barely managing not to choke herself, she untangled the belt and stuffed it in her pocket, still wiggling her hips and prancing at the end of the walkway.

She unbuttoned the coat, missing a few beats in the process, and slid it seductively down one arm—at least he guessed that was her intention. Her elbow got stuck, and she had to tug it free.

"You're going to get your coat muddy," he warned an instant too late.

The hem swept across the ground, and she mouthed a word he easily interpreted.

The men were edging closer. If she wanted an audience, she had one. The question was why?

She found the other sleeve and flapped the coat like a bullfighter's cape, giving him a fleeting glimpse of something pink and frilly.

"Wouldn't you like to go inside, big boy?" she asked in a mock whisper that brought a few laughs from the crew closing in behind her.

Gus caught her coat when she tossed it aside. The burly foreman tried to stuff it inconspicuously under his arm, but a couple of guys ribbed him.

Inside was a good idea—no, a bad one, a very bad one. The pink thing was a short nightgown, totally see-through, and there was a lot to see. All she was wearing under it was a skimpy red bikini, two scraps of cloth on a body too sensational to describe.

Blood pounded in his ears, almost blocking out the blatantly suggestive music.

She twirled around—yeah, give every malingering goof-off on his crew a good look—and flicked the hem of the nightie thing up and down.

"You're out of step," he said dryly, feigning indifference to the display of her charms.

For once in his life, he didn't have a clue what to do. If he rushed over and stopped her, he'd look like a jerk in front of his crew. If he stood there and enjoyed her act, he *was* a fool. If he asked her inside, he'd be playing her game, whatever that was.

"How about a private show, big guy?" she asked purring.

She was probably more eager to cut the act than he was to have her stop.

He shook his head and folded his arms across his chest, more interested to see what she'd do next than he'd admit to himself.

She was beating the air with the nightie, obviously hesitant to take her striptease a step further. He heard the rip over his men's heavy breathing. Or maybe it was his own.

"Oh." She stared at the long tear along the side seam, obviously not part of her act. If she expected him to rush to the rescue, she was in for a disappointment.

"Oh, what the heck!" She grabbed the torn gown with both hands and yanked hard, separating it all the way up the side and whipping it off in one gesture.

She tossed the nightie in Gus's direction and, no surprise, he rushed forward to grab it. Cole and the electrician were standing behind her grinning as if their brains had taken a leave of absence.

She had to stop now. Maybe a few more bars of wiggling and teasing, and she'd chicken out. This was the uptight tool girl who lived by the script. He was calling her bluff. She didn't dare go any further, he thought anxiously. If she didn't give up soon, she'd embarrass herself a lot more than him.

She had her audience panting. Zack was afraid the new kid would break his kneecap with the hammer he was unconsciously swinging in rhythm to her body bumps.

"Okay, everybody get back to work," he yelled ferociously. "I'm not paying you to stand around gawking."

It was like yelling at a brick wall. No one even seemed to hear him except Cole, who looked at him and grinned like a chimp.

"Wouldn't you like me to finish my show in your trailer?" Megan called. "We can talk about your personal appearances on my show."

She made *personal* sound like a dirty word.

"Forget it, Danbury!" So much for rescuing her from the leering jerks his crew had become.

"Isn't there *anything* I can do to change your mind?"

Hoots, hollers and wolf whistles drowned out his response, but she got the message—no.

He thought she'd give up. He was sure she wouldn't go any further. She had his answer about the show, and this didn't change it. She couldn't sway him with her crazy stunts, not even if she took up naked lap dancing.

"I'm sure we can reach some agreement," she called, still gyrating vaguely in time to the music.

He crossed his arms again and broadened his stance, hoping he looked as immovable as he felt.

"No way." He mouthed the words.

He was sweating. She wasn't giving up.

Her bumps and grinds got rowdier. She kicked her legs in an imitation cancan, hands on her hips and heels clanking on the muddy boardwalk.

The men were shouting, encouraging her with gusto. Next he'd have a riot on his hands, never mind that he had the best view.

He opened his mouth to order her off the site when one leg went up in a high kick and the other slid out from under her. She fell backward—luckily for her, because she landed on the soggy ground at the end of the hard wooden boards. She squealed as she hit the cold mud with a resounding plop. She'd totally embarrassed herself, and the men's good-natured snickers added to the humiliation. She looked so pathetic he had to do something.

He stripped off the plaid flannel shirt he was wearing over his T-shirt and hustled to her. He pulled her up and wrapped it around her, not bothering with armholes, and half pushed, half dragged her to the trailer.

His spine was tingling like a loose power line, and it took all he had not to tumble her onto the desk, muddy as she was. Why did such an annoying woman have to come in such a gorgeous body? But he wouldn't have anything to do with her if she were the last woman on earth. She was trouble personified.

"Can we talk now?" she asked weakly.

Her teeth were chattering, whether from nerves or the cold mud caking her legs and butt he neither knew nor cared.

"That is the dumbest stunt I've ever seen! What made you think I'd give in and be on your stupid show after your amateur bump and grind?"

"The plan was for you to invite me into the trailer

before the show began,'' she said with enough defiance to make him smile inwardly.

Her face was puckering, and he wasn't going to deal with a crying half-naked woman.

''One tear, and I'm tossing you back in the mud—without my shirt.''

Cole opened the door a crack. He was still grinning. ''Do you want her coat?''

''Yes, bring it in.''

Cole didn't look too keen on coming in, but he did, holding her coat at arm's length.

''Meet Megan Danbury,'' Zack said gruffly, grabbing the coat and tossing it at her. ''My brother, Cole.''

Cole was still hanging on to the see-through nightie. He dropped it on the seat of a chair.

She wiggled out of Zack's shirt and slipped into the coat, pulling the belt so tight her hips looked curvy and tempting fully covered. He could imagine how uncomfortable she was, but she'd asked for trouble pulling an act like that on a muddy construction site.

''There is nothing, absolutely nothing, you can do to get me on your show,'' he said emphatically. ''I would rather crawl through broken glass.''

''You really do have bad stage fright, don't you?'' she asked.

''I'm more afraid I'll strangle you if you ever do anything like this again.''

She did the worst possible thing then—she smiled, making it impossible to properly vent his opinion of showbiz silliness.

Cole slipped out the door, but not before Zack saw his grin. Zack didn't want to be left alone with this menace in muddy spike heels.

''Leave,'' he ordered.

"I'm not going to give up. The show is history, and so are Ed's job and mine if we can't sign you. Mr. Gunderdorf wants you. Myself, I'd rather have a performing baboon, but he's the boss."

He watched her saunter out the door, not bothering to close it behind her. Outside she picked up the grocery bag, striptease music still booming out of it, and hurried toward her car.

She'd forgotten the nightie.

If he happened to think of it, he'd mail it to her.

Could this day possibly get any worse?

A minute later he got his answer.

"Zack, I need to talk to you," Marsh Bailey said, poking his head through the door.

4

MEGAN DUG two fingers into some blue gel and finished smearing on the face mask. Gunderdorf was in Milan looking at a pasta plant he might buy and hadn't fired her yet. She was using her rigatoni reprieve to catch up on all the things a girl should do before job hunting in a field where twenty-eight was considered old.

She closed the lid and rinsed her fingers, but no amount of busywork could make her forget she'd made a complete idiot of herself. It was Saturday, and she still felt Wednesday's humiliation like a fresh wound.

She'd been so sure Bailey would ask her into the trailer and hear her out rather than let her disrupt work at the site. Instead he'd played her like a fish on a line, rattling her so much she'd made a total fool of herself.

The dance was bad enough. Thank heavens Miss Berry, the ballet teacher she'd adored when she was nine, hadn't seen it.

Thinking about the finale made her cringe. She never should have gone eyeball to eyeball with her evil nemesis. Bailey's smug, you-wouldn't-dare expression had flustered her so much she'd nearly chickened out. She'd momentarily forgotten the construction workers egging her on. It had been just Zack and her standing on opposite ends of the dirty boards—a shoot-out without bullets. One minute she was kicking her legs like a pro trying to ignore the mud squishing in her shoe. The next she plopped down in cold, icky muck that soaked through her bikini bottom and coated like wet cement.

Scratch one trench coat. At least it was the one with Jason's ice-cream stain. Also scratch one show—hers.

While she buffed her nails and waited for the timer to tell her when she could remove the gel mask, she couldn't stop thinking of her embarrassment. She couldn't even get consolation from her big sister and favorite confidante. She didn't want to be the one to tell Georgia about Ed's imminent unemployment.

The doorbell interrupted her miserable thoughts. A visitor was about as welcome as the chicken pox, and she wanted very much to ignore it. Unfortunately, it could be Ed bringing bad tidings he didn't want to deliver from his phone at home where Georgia might overhear. She was going to be mega-upset when Ed lost his job. Megan hoped her sister wouldn't go on a record chocolate-marshmallow cookie binge and gain back all the weight she'd worked two years to lose.

Megan yanked tight the belt of her robe and reluctantly went to the door. It was a measure of her glum mood that she didn't even bother to check the spy hole before opening the door.

"Danbury— That is you under the zombie makeup, isn't it? Can I come in for a minute?"

Her first thought was, Why had Zack tracked her down in her Southfield apartment?

She didn't have a second thought, only a moment of panic before the humiliation kicked in. He'd kept her out there dancing like a lunatic until she did her muddy pratfall. She'd rather face an invasion of killer termites than this clean-shaven version of her tormentor.

"Or we could talk here on the landing," he said dryly.

She glanced across the narrow space at the top of the

stairs that separated her door from the Woodruffs'. They were a dear couple, but unfortunately, the joy of their retirement years was keeping track of every other tenant in the cluster of two-story buildings around a central court. She didn't want Bailey's visit to be the topic of the day.

She motioned him inside and closed the door.

"Why are you here?"

"You do have an affinity for mud," he said, ignoring her question and staring at her face mask.

He walked into her living room and looked around, taking in the small kitchen off to the right with black marbleized countertops, stark white appliances and black-and-white checkerboard flooring.

Her apartment was small but uncluttered. The living room, bedroom and small combination guest room and office were carpeted in tweedy gray and white, which made it easy to pull together her small collection of furniture—a living room set upholstered in a black and mossy green geometric pattern, ebony-finish occasional tables and a blond bedroom set her mother left behind when she moved to Florida. The spare room had a wrought-iron daybed with a burgundy and pink quilted spread, a file cabinet and a metal and Formica desk she'd assembled herself. She'd also put together bookcases and a black tubular chair with fabric back and seat. It was neat and functional. It was her.

"Nice place," he said conversationally. "Good floor plan. The building is cheap construction, but it's livable if it's well maintained. No security, though."

He was right about that. The street door was always unlocked and led to a small hallway with mailboxes and doors to the first-floor apartments. The building was on a slight rise so there were two stories in front and three in back with a laundry room, basement apartments and open-fronted parking slots on the lowest level.

"Thank you for your professional appraisal," she said primly to cover her intense discomfort.

It was bad enough to answer the door with a blue face. She wasn't exactly dressed for company, either. She was swathed in a pink terry-cloth robe with enough material to cover two of her, but he made her feel undressed. Fresh from the shower, she hadn't bothered to put on underwear yet.

He walked to the sliding glass door of her balcony where she'd yet to plant summer flowers in a row of earthen pots.

When he didn't explain why he was there, she spoke again.

"How did you find out where I live?"

"It wasn't easy tracking down a local celebrity like you, but I have friends."

"I'm not a celebrity."

"But you'd like to be one, wouldn't you?"

"No, I'd just like to meet my career goals."

The timer sounded in her bathroom, the signal to rinse off her mask. She didn't know whether to ignore it and risk having her face pucker up like a prune or leave Zack alone in her living room without knowing why he was there. The desire to get rid of the clown face won out.

"I need to rinse my face."

"I'll vote for that," he said in a sardonic drawl that made her seethe.

"Have a seat," she said, wishing she could wave a magic wand and make him disappear.

She hurried into the bathroom, conveniently off her bedroom but out of sight of the living room, and pushed the door half-closed with her knee. She wanted to put on real clothes as much as she wanted to lose the blue hue, so she ducked her face in the basin in her haste to scrub it.

"What is that stuff supposed to do?"

Zack startled her so badly she shrieked.

"Allow me." He handed her a towel hanging on the rack.

"Get out of my bathroom!" She buried her face in the towel, so angry she was stuttering.

He didn't budge.

"Why? You're wrapped up like a mummy—unlike your dancing costume."

She automatically wrapped her arms across her chest, letting the towel fall to the floor.

He retrieved it with a grin she wanted to sand off his face.

"I made a terrible mistake expecting you to be a gentleman and invite me into your trailer. It will never happen again," she said emphatically. "Now go away!"

"Gladly, but first I have a proposition for you."

He backed out of the bathroom and sat himself down on the edge of her bed.

"In your own words, no, no, no."

"Proposition was a bad word choice. Let's say it's a business proposal."

"Out!"

He settled more comfortably on her heirloom bedspread embroidered with baskets of flowers and crossed one leg over the other like a man who planned to sit awhile.

"This is something you need to hear," he said stubbornly.

She was angry enough to scream but reasonable enough to know he could do something worse to pay her back for invading his work site—he could confront her at the station and let everyone know about her stupid performance.

"At least have the decency to wait in the living room while I get dressed."

"I can do that."

He gave her an evil grin and sauntered out of the room.

She couldn't decide what to wear. If she wore a nice outfit, he might think she'd dressed to impress him. If she wore old jeans and a baggy sweatshirt, he'd know she was deliberately trying to make him forget he'd seen her in a muddy bikini.

She locked her bedroom door and put on the designer jeans she'd worn for his disastrous appearance on her show. Just to be sure he didn't think she cared what he thought, she slipped into old clogs and a red plaid flannel shirt she used for dirty jobs and buttoned it up to her throat.

"This had better be good," she said, returning to the living room where he was staring through the balcony door at the mostly concrete courtyard.

He turned slowly and looked her up and down with an appraising stare.

"Well," she prompted, "what do you want?"

"The way I see it, we agree on one thing—we can't stand each other. Right?"

"Yes, we agree on that," she said cautiously.

If he wanted something, he had a peculiar way of leading up to it.

"Good." He sat on the edge of the couch and stared at her in that same appraising way. "Would you marry me?"

"What!"

"You want something from me. I want something from you."

"There's nothing on this earth that could persuade me to marry you!"

"Good. Let me lay this out for you."

He stood again. She took it as a sign he wasn't all that comfortable with what he was going to say.

"You want me to be on your damn home-handicraft-for-girls show."

"Home improvement for women," she said coldly.

"Whatever."

It was her least favorite expression, but he at least had made her curious.

"I'll make more guest appearances if you help me out with a small problem."

"Small?"

This conversation was too weird. Considering what she'd gone through to get his attention, she didn't want to deal with anything weird again.

"Small, in that it won't inconvenience you. Obviously it's a major problem to me, or I wouldn't consider making an idiot of myself again."

"You were a hit. I don't call that being an idiot," she argued.

"Which is why you're ideal for this. There's no possibility we'll ever be anything but opponents."

"I can agree with that, but get on with your prop— proposal."

She nearly said *proposition,* not a word she wanted to use with a hundred and eighty or so pounds of lean masculinity emitting pheromones like heat from a blast furnace. Not that she was the least bit attracted to Zack.

"I have this marriage-pushing grandfather...."

She snapped to attention.

"So do I! His mission in life is to turn me into his idea of a happy woman—a married one."

"I don't think Marsh cares a hoot whether I'm happy or not."

"Marsh?"

"He doesn't like to be called Grandpa. He wants his three grandsons married and on the board of Bailey Baby Products. Cole got his third of the shares when he married. Nick, our half brother, is still in college, so now it's my turn."

"If this is some bizarre marriage of convenience thing—"

"No! I'd pick someone I like if it was."

"Thank you," she said sarcastically.

"I hate the baby business, and I want a wife like I want jock itch—"

"Feel free to be blunt."

"Anyway, our mother is CEO of the company, but Marsh owns it and is chairman of the board. He's threatened to sell out to strangers if we don't toe the line. That means getting married. Mom lives for her job since Nick, Senior, Cole's and my stepdad, died a couple of years ago. Her chances of keeping it are slim to nothing if Marsh sells controlling interest to outsiders."

"He's making you get married to keep your mother's job. Is she his daughter-in-law?"

"No, his daughter."

She could tell he hated telling her about family problems, so didn't understand why he was.

"I still don't see where I come in."

"Cole and his wife, Tess, are eager to start a family. If they succeed, we hope to persuade Marsh to settle my share of the stock on the baby and forget about coercing me into marriage. I don't care anything about the business. I intend to make my own money, and I sure as hell don't want to be on the board of directors of Bailey Baby Products.''

"Then why pretend you're going to marry me? It *will* be pretending?''

"Absolutely." He snorted. "I can't imagine marrying you even if I wanted a wife. Which I do not.''

"We're agreed on that." She tried to snort, but sniffed instead.

"In fact, we don't even have to pretend to be engaged. I just need a serious girlfriend, one I can use to block the old boy's matchmaking mania. She has to be someone nice. Marsh's brother ruined his life by marrying a hussy—Granddad's word, not mine. I guess you'll do for the short time I need you.''

"Thanks," she said dryly. "How can you pass me off as a serious girlfriend if you don't even like me? You're no actor!''

"Granted, but I don't see all that much of Marsh. I just want a reason not to wine and dine the women my grandfather digs up. He came by the site just the other day to ask how the wife search was going. The only way to hold him off is to say I've already met the perfect woman.''

"Make someone up.''

"Ha! He's too sharp for make-believe. Probably check out anyone I invented. I need a live body. He can see you on TV and make up his own mind about you.''

"But no dating?''

"Be serious.''

"For this you'll sign a contract to do one guest appearance per week for twenty-six weeks?''

"Twenty-six! I don't have time for six, let alone twenty-six. All those men you so effectively distracted from their work with your act depend on Cole and me for paychecks. Summer is our busy season.''

"We take a break from taping later in the summer. The twenty-six episodes would run into next year."

"I'll do three."

"That won't save the show or Ed's and my jobs."

"I don't get it. Why don't you hire an actor who'll follow the damn script?"

"I wish! The boss wants you." Megan still had trouble believing it.

"Six episodes, and I can pick the times."

"Twenty, whenever you're scheduled."

"No way."

"Okay, you do the show as long as you want me to pretend to be your girlfriend. I'll let the legal department work out the details."

"Guess I can't fault that," he conceded.

She knew what he was thinking. He could bail out any time by dumping her—well, pretending to dump her, since you have to be involved with someone to do it for real.

"You'll come to the studio next week?"

"I'll try."

"I'll have Ed call you." Let him struggle with this tenuous arrangement.

He rose languidly and walked over to where she was standing.

"Okay, I guess this will work," he said without enthusiasm.

He offered his hand. The palm was hard and calloused, but his grip was gentle. This was a man who didn't resort to bone-crushing handshakes to show how strong he was.

He held her hand overly long as though debating whether to change his mind.

"If that's settled…" she said.

"Yeah, I have things to do." He turned and left abruptly.

Her hand stayed warm from his, and she felt jittery all over, the way she had when her show debuted.

Was this how it felt to make a deal with the Devil?

ZACK SHOWED UP at the studio on Monday morning to sign the contract, regretting every minute he had to be away from the job site. Sure, he could trust Cole to supervise things, but not for nothing did the men call Zack Benito. He wasn't Italian, and he didn't look like the World War II dictator, Mussolini, but Zack did run things on schedule. If that made him a tyrant, it wasn't a bad thing in the competitive construction business.

His skin was crawling just being under the unlit klieg lights in the studio. He hadn't connected with Ed yet, but Megan welcomed him as though she hadn't expected him to show. She hurriedly told him a few of the basics. The Tuesday show was taped on Monday, which explained her agitated behavior. The Thursday show was shot on Wednesday, a less inconvenient day for him to be away from work.

"Remember, we always tape in front of a live audience," she warned him.

"Better than a dead audience, I guess," he grumbled.

"Please, just go along with whatever I plan," she begged. "You're the guest, not a co-host."

"In other words, I'm your flunky."

"No, you'll be here to demonstrate a few simple techniques...."

"You're not going to create any more accidents just to get a laugh and boost ratings?"

"You're safe. I take my show very seriously," she said.

Megan flounced away, but Ed hurried over, perspiring even without the lights on.

"Bailey, glad to have you aboard."

"Yeah," Zack said noncommittally.

"So you're signing on for two shows a week."

Ed was pushing it. He had to know more than that about his deal with Megan.

"Once a week with time off for good behavior."

Ed's laugh was forced as he slapped him on the back with locker-room heartiness. Zack felt like decking him just because he hated being there, but the big guy had a hundred pounds on him. Anyway, it wasn't his fault. He'd made his own deal.

Megan dashed over to them. Apparently she tried to insure the success of the show by rushing around before the taping like a headless chicken on speed.

"I didn't realize this shirt shrank in the dryer," she said to Ed. "Maybe I should wear a jersey with the station logo."

She tried to yank on the pink knit top to make it cover her cute little belly button, but it was no go. A good two inches of flesh showed between the hem and the waistband of her black jeans.

"You look gorgeous—a lot different than you did in your robe," Zack said sweetly, watching Ed's neck do a hundred-and-eighty-degree turn.

The producer's face gave him away. He thought Megan had slept with him to get him on the show.

"Don't make it sound like—" Megan heatedly began to protest.

"What made you change your mind?" Ed interrupted suspiciously.

"A series of events did it," Zack said, "which had nothing to do with Ms. Danbury's silly stunts."

"I have to call Mr. Gunderdorf about a few details of your contract, then our business manager will have you sign the standard form." Ed hurried away.

"Don't you dare tell anyone about the mud!" Megan said to Zack.

Her eyes flashed with anger, which, unfortunately, only made them sparkle more appealingly. Good thing he knew she was pure poison, as wrong for him as any female could be. Not that he wanted a serious relationship with anyone. In spite of Cole's happy marriage, Zack was still convinced he was genetically unsuited for long-term commitments. After all, his birth father had cut and run before he was born.

"Has anyone ever told you how blue your eyes are?" he asked, maliciously playful, turning on the infamous Bailey boys' charm full force.

"Only about a hundred times, usually when some jerk with an overinflated ego wanted to get me horizontal. So unless that's your intention, how about a tour of the studio before you talk business with Joe Johnston, our business manager."

"I'm not in this for money," he reminded her. "Just remember our deal. You're supposed to be my main squeeze. No snarling at me, no heaping scorn on my hapless head, no scowling if I'm a less-than-perfect performer."

"I'll keep my end of the deal if you keep yours. You will get paid for every appearance, but I managed to talk Joe into an open-ended contract—no set number of appearances. He wasn't crazy about selling that to Gunderdorf, but I convinced them both that your one appearance could have been a fluke. Maybe we'll want to get rid of you without paying off a long-term contract."

"I should be so lucky."

"You're not going to change your mind and back out?"

"No."

For now he couldn't, not without a backup plan, and where could he find another woman this sanitized? It was a big plus that Marsh could check her out on TV. She'd wow the old boy, and that should be the end of his meddling.

"Well, you sound crabby," she accused him.

He was crabby. When she flashed those baby blues, the thought of doing the horizontal bop with her definitely passed through his mind. When it came to looks, she was one pleasing package, which, of course, would make Marsh willing to believe they had a thing going. If he didn't dislike her—well, maybe dislike wasn't exactly the right word—he wouldn't mind some up-close-and-personal fun with her.

Fortunately, since he was desperate to get Marsh off his back, all he wanted to do with Megan was buy time.

This had better work! As soon as his grandfather had stopped congratulating himself—for no good reason—on Cole's marriage, he'd turned the full force of his bombastic personality on Zack.

So here he was, the last place he wanted to be on a sunny May morning when he had a full crew on a site.

"Hey, Johnston wants to see you now," Ed called to him.

"I'll see you Wednesday morning when we tape the Thursday show," Megan said. "I'll arrange everything. All you have to do is show up and try not to ruin the segment you're in. We'll be building a wall shelf."

He watched her walk away, the undulating sway of her backside in tight black jeans almost too much for his libido.

If strains of the wedding march didn't make him paranoid, if tuxedos didn't make him break out in hives, if hearts and flowers didn't make him feel as if the walls were closing in on him, he sure as hell wouldn't be in this TV studio dreading his next session on the home-handicraft-for-girls show.

5

ZACK SHOWED UP at the studio Wednesday with a circular saw and a copy of the script in his toolbox. Danbury was about to learn lesson number one in the business world—always be involved in contract negotiations.

He'd had a big advantage hammering out a contract with the moneymen because he didn't care what they paid him. What did matter was he couldn't possibly tape on Mondays. He had to be on the job to handle any problems that had cropped up over the weekend. Also he insisted on getting a copy of the script at least twenty-four hours before the Wednesday tapings. He intended to be ready for anything Megan threw at him.

Unfortunately he'd had to give a little. Gunderdorf, participating by phone, had insisted he sign up for at least twelve appearances. Zack would have to live with that.

So far, production of a Bailey baby seemed to have stalled, but it wasn't because the job foreman wasn't willing and eager. It was all Zack could do to keep Cole at work until five o'clock every day. Until the happy day when there was another Bailey on the way, Zack needed Megan to masquerade as his significant other. He hoped it wasn't longer than twelve weeks, the duration of his contract.

Inside the cavernous room where the show was taped against an interior wall braced by two-by-fours so it could take a lot of pounding, Zack looked around for Megan.

She wasn't going to like his take on today's show. He grinned in anticipation of a battle.

The only one in sight was a harried young woman setting up chairs for the audience. He couldn't imagine why anyone would waste time watching all the takes, retakes and breaks that went into a half hour of television. If last time was any indication, taping would drag on for a couple of hours. What they shot today would be edited for the actual show.

"Where is everyone?" he asked, taking in her pierced eyebrow and short-cropped hair with burgundy tips.

"Don't ask me. I'm only slave labor—they call it being an intern. Here, set up that stack of chairs. Megan is having some hotshot guest, and half the women in town want to watch."

Zack was willing to oblige, but before he could put down his saw and toolbox, Ed came barreling toward them.

"He's the talent, Julie," he shouted at the intern.

Zack grimaced at the word *talent*.

"I don't mind setting up chairs," he said, as much to irk Ed as help the girl.

"No, we've got people for that. Brad, get your butt over here."

A sullen-looking kid with long, lank blond hair took his time ambling over.

"Megan wants to go over the script with you," Ed said to Zack. "And they want you in makeup."

"Tell Megan I'll be right there," Zack said.

Ed followed orders as well as gave them. He hurried off.

"Kids, I need you to go out to my truck in spot twenty-eight and unload a few things." He pulled out two five-dollar bills and gave the interns some instructions.

Saving the worst for last, Zack made his way to the makeup room and reluctantly let himself be swathed in lavender and coated with powder again.

Was he insane to do this? Probably, but Marsh's words were still fresh in his mind.

"Find the perfect girl yourself, or I'll send a veritable army of hopefuls to your doorstep. What's so hard about finding a wife?"

Well, Zack had found Ms. Perfect, and fortunately she couldn't stand him. All he had to do was keep up the charade until there was positive news about his impending unclehood. Marsh was sure to be amenable to giving Zack's shares to a new Bailey.

He ripped off the cape when the primping was finished and sneezed from the flurry of loose powder. It was time he tackled his new little sweetie pie.

He barged into her dressing room ready to do battle. Danbury wasn't going to make him look like an idiot this time, not that he expected more than a few dozen people to watch the show.

"Do you have any idea what the significance of a closed door is?" she asked, hurriedly buttoning a man-tailored blue pinstripe shirt, but not before he got a glimpse of creamy skin and a lacy bra.

"I've seen your act before, so what's the big deal?" He drawled the words in a way calculated to irritate her. He could see murder in her eyes, but she let it drop.

"Are you ready for the show?"

"I've read the script."

That gave her pause.

"How?"

"It's in my contract. I get them at least twenty-four hours before each taping."

"I told you, all you have to do is show up. It's my show."

"You're the TV personality. I'm the builder. Why have an expert if you're not interested in doing things the right way?"

"What's your point?"

She folded her arms across her chest, then dropped them, probably remembering not to wrinkle her shirt.

"There's a much easier way to install floating shelves."

He waved his copy of the script for emphasis.

"I did my research. There's nothing complicated about installing wall brackets."

"Where do you get your ideas? In a fifty-year-old high-school shop textbook?"

"I use a lot of sources, including my grandfather, who's extremely handy at building things."

He let that pass. She already looked ready to staple him to the wall.

"You don't need brackets or clunky hardware," he said.

"My viewers are used to working with brackets and other attractive hardware," she said in a voice so frigid he practically shivered.

"Did all three of them write in and tell you?"

He'd fired the first shot in a war and knew it, but he wasn't going to look like a fool—well, a bigger fool—in front of an audience. He had a professional image to protect. If he looked silly, so would Bailey Construction.

Ed knocked on the door even though Zack had left it partly ajar. Such a gentleman.

"Ten minutes, folks."

Zack walked out. This wasn't the moment to explain what he had in mind for the show today.

"I'll take you to the Green Room," Ed said. "That's

industry talk for the place where guests hang out before going on.''

He talked to Zack as if he were three years old. Ed was the one who didn't seem to remember he'd been a guest once before.

From the small lounge, which was painted a putrid shade of green, Zack could hear lukewarm applause greet Megan as Ed introduced her with a voice-over. She did some opening pitch about sponge painting, her tip of the day, then it was his turn to get out there.

Then the invisible Ed introduced him, too.

''Please give a warm welcome to Zack Baily of Baily Construction.''

There was loud applause and shrieks of approval, which did nothing for his clammy palms and jittery stomach. Damn, he hated stage fright! It was totally illogical and completely unlike him.

''Welcome back, Zack,'' Megan said, managing—just barely—to sound as though she wasn't sucking on a lemon.

Hell, he'd feel the same way if she came to the site and tried to tell his men how to put up drywall.

She launched into another spiel on how everyone could use extra shelves to display little treasures. Already sweat was trickling down his spine. He was wearing a tank top under his lightweight green plaid shirt, hoping he wouldn't soak through. These lights seemed hotter than high noon in hundred-degree weather, so why did Danbury look so cool?

''Today Zack is going to help us install a store-bought shelf kit for an easy, inexpensive addition to any room from the bathroom to the kitchen.''

''Actually, Megan,'' he said, forgetting what he'd planned to say and winging it, ''there is a way that's just as cheap and easy, but looks a whole lot better. Also you're saved the nuisance of sanding and painting.''

''You're supposed to follow the script!'' She hissed the words under her breath.

He narrowed his eyes, spotting the two young interns in the shadows just beyond the bright lights.

''Guys, bring in the stuff from my truck.''

''Apparently Zack has another surprise for us today,'' Megan said, pretending all this was really planned.

He gave her credit for managing a facsimile of a smile.

The two kids were grinning when they deposited his stuff on the set. Zack could hear Ed's voice ragging at him through the tiny earpiece clipped behind his ear, the producer's way of relaying instructions.

Zack was nervously aware of the overhead mikes and the three heavy cameras that swiveled on their bases to track every movement he made. Sweat was pouring out of every pore. He wondered if the wire that ran down his back from the earpiece to the little box hooked onto his back waistband would short out.

He had to move beyond his panic and get this job done. After all, he could build anything made of wood. If he forgot he was in front of cameras, maybe this stage fright would lessen its hold.

''I've built these a couple of times for friends and clients,'' he said, struggling to get to his high-confidence level. ''They're strong, have no visible signs of support and don't need to be finished in any way if you like the wood surface.''

He picked up Megan's shelf kit, walked to a trash bin against a back wall beyond the stage area and dumped it in.

She probably wanted to kill him, but, damn, she was good on comebacks.

"That's not very economical, Zack, throwing away a kit that cost twenty-nine ninety-five plus tax."

She got a laugh from the audience. No matter. He was willing to be the straight guy as long as he didn't look stupid.

"This is a wooden, hollow-core door," he said, warming to his project.

"In case you women don't know a door when you see one." She zinged him again.

"And this is a cleat." He held up a precut strip of wood used to support the shelf.

"Can we take a break here, Ed?" Megan asked, being serious.

The audience even thought that was funny.

"We have to start over," she insisted. "This isn't a segment about doors."

"I'm going to saw the door lengthwise and install the cleat. One door makes two prefinished floating shelves. The only trick is getting them straight."

"I told you to stop the cameras," Megan scolded. "We have to start over. Thank heaven, we're only taping."

"Let's get on with it," Ed ordered without bothering with the little ear mikes.

Apparently the show's producer did have some clout when they were shooting. Megan settled down, outwardly resigned to doing shelves Zack's way.

He began where he'd left off.

"You'll need a chisel, a hammer, carpenter's glue, a level, a stud finder..."

"We've already found a stud!" a woman yelled from the audience, setting off a spate of giggles and titters.

"Thank you, darlin'," Zack said, becoming more comfortable with his role as handyman hunk, especially since he could see Megan silently fuming. "What I had in mind was finding the boards behind the drywall so the shelf is well anchored.''

"Zack will show you how to do that,'' Megan said, obviously trying to regain control of the show.

He said he'd do this gig, but that didn't mean assembling idiot kits and looking like a dope. If she didn't understand that after this show, he'd find another way to make it clear to her.

Maybe it was her showbiz training, but she warmed to his project, asked some intelligent questions and helped install one door-turned-shelf on the backdrop wall of the set.

"We have time for a couple of questions,'' she said in response to Ed's prompting, which Zack could hear through his earpiece.

A dozen hands shot up.

"Yes,'' Megan said, pointing at a grandmotherly woman with a benign smile.

"Are you married, Handyman Zack?'' she asked loudly.

"Alas, no,'' he said, so relieved the show was nearly over he felt playful. "I'm looking for a girl who can handle a hammer.''

He got a bigger laugh than his response warranted. These women were easy to please.

"Do you have a girlfriend?'' A middle-aged redhead shouted her question without waiting for Megan to call on her.

"I do indeed,'' he drawled, remembering his grandfather might watch the show. There was a collective groan from the audience.

"That's all the time we have for questions,'' Megan said. "I hope you enjoyed today's 'Do It Herself.'''

"Cut.'' Ed's voice boomed into Zack's ear.

Julie, the intern, rushed to Zack, detached the speaker from his jeans and ran her hand under his shirt and up his back to pull down the earpiece he was wearing. "Can I do that?" he heard someone call.

"That was a great show!" Julie said enthusiastically.

He'd started to gather his saw and tools when the audience charged toward him.

"Will you sign my grocery receipt, Zack? It's all I have with me!"

"Does your company do little projects like shelves?" another asked.

"Not usually," he managed to say as he signed a dangling receipt using his knee as a writing surface.

He was bombarded by more questions and requests than he could sort out. These ladies weren't shy! Didn't they have lives? All he'd done was hang a shelf!

He tried to sidestep his fans, but short of hurting someone, he was trapped.

"Zack will do another show next Wednesday," Ed yelled in the voice that had once carried the length of a football field on game day. "Anyone who would like a ticket should go to the reception desk now. We only have a limited number left."

The announcement started a stampede away from Zack, who had a whole new respect for the ex-jock. Seeing his chance, he grabbed his saw, wholeheartedly thanked the two interns who'd put all his tools in his box and hurried to Megan's dressing room, hoping she wouldn't try to deck him.

Apparently he'd been a whiz-bang success, but he didn't feel good about it—not at all good.

MEGAN SAT in front of the brightly lit mirror in the dressing room trying not to think about the show they'd just taped. Unfortunately she couldn't erase it from her mind. Even with a good edit, the segment with Bailey would make her look inept. She didn't have a chance with the hunky handyman running roughshod over her scripts.

She creamed away the last of her stage makeup but didn't have enough energy to dab on fresh lipstick. Zack didn't know a wireless mike from a wad of bubble gum, but he was a natural when it came to pushing women's buttons. He was exactly the kind of man she'd avoided since she started wearing a training bra.

Her show worked without gimmicks because women needed to be more self-reliant. Bailey only muddied the concept by being the focus of attention.

Trouble was, he was a natural with women. If she didn't watch herself...

No, it couldn't happen. He was far too irritating to appeal to her. Anyway, her Mr. Right had to be a natural-born family man, and nothing about Bailey suggested he could ever fill the bill.

The door, firmly closed, vibrated from a heavy-handed knock.

"Go away!" she called.

She wasn't ready to rehash the show with Ed or anyone else.

Again the knock.

"I said go away—"

Zack barged in and closed the door loudly behind him.

"Do you ever do what you're told?" she challenged.

He frowned, appearing to give her question serious thought.

"Nope."

He pulled a folding chair up to the mirror, sat and looked at the assortment of cosmetics spread on the table.

"You do your own makeup?"

"Yes, of course."

"Good choice. The makeup girl wields a wicked powder puff."

"Woman," she said automatically.

"No one ever accused me of being politically correct."

He leaned back, tilting the chair on two legs.

"Those chairs have been known to collapse," she warned.

She brushed a wine-rose shade on her lips just to be doing something.

"Probably what I deserve," he said blandly.

"You made me look like a fool!"

She didn't want a confrontation with him, but everything about him provoked her, even the way he'd unbuttoned his shirt and let it hang loose over his lean hips.

"If I'd put together that trashy kit, I would've looked like an idiot. I know the company that made it. They forget to drill holes, package substandard materials and put in directions written by chimps."

"It's the kind of project my viewers are likely to do. And I checked for screw holes. Give me some credit!"

"Isn't your show about helping women do projects without a man to help?"

"Yes."

His criticism really hurt. She tried hard to put herself in the place of her viewers. She sniffed, holding back a highly uncharacteristic urge to vent her frustration with tears.

"Aww, don't cry," he said.

"I never cry."

"Then you need a plumber 'cause you're leaking."

"Is that your idea of a joke?"

"Made you cut off the waterworks, didn't it?"

"No one told me you had the script," she said, changing the subject.

Both Ed and Joe had a lot to answer for.

He shrugged. "I don't want a battle over every show. But even more, I don't want to look stupid—not to mention condescending—by doing lousy projects. Wouldn't you rather do things that turn out well? Your viewers will try a good idea and feel clever, like they can really do home improvements by themselves."

"I suppose you have a point," she grudgingly admitted.

"The show is a pretty good idea." He sounded even more grudging than she did. "Maybe you should toss the books and get out of the studio. Get more hands-on experience."

"I built a hummingbird condo when I was only eleven. I have experience."

"Did the birds move in?"

"I don't remember." She lied, knowing it was still in her grandfather's attic with other things he was storing for her.

She'd been too proud of it to put it outside to weather.

He plopped the chair down on all four legs and leaned close, arms resting on his knees.

"We weren't exactly cuddly-cozy on the show today," he said.

"Ha!"

"When the audience asked if I have a girlfriend..."

"I was there. My hearing is fine."

"The point is, if we were really dating, there would be some chemistry between us."

"Chemistry isn't my field, but I seem to remember oil and water don't mix."

He wanted something, and she wasn't going to like it.

Given his stage fright—she'd seen it before, and he had it bad—he'd agreed to do the show too easily.

"My grandfather is sure to watch tomorrow, and he'll pick up on your antagonism."

"Antagonism! What do you expect when you make a shambles of the show? It's fine with me if you never come near this station again."

"No choice. I signed a contract, so you're stuck with me. Now you owe me."

"I'm just your pretend girlfriend. You did say 'pretend'?"

"Of course, but it won't do me any good if Marsh thinks I'm faking."

"That's your problem."

She stood, her signal that there was nothing to discuss.

"Marsh is coming to the construction site after work Friday to see how the work's coming. He likes to play sidewalk superintendent every once in a while."

"He needs a hobby," she said dryly.

"It's a chance to prove we're really an item."

"We're not."

He ignored her protest. "I already told him we hooked up after the first show. So, if you show up while he's there, we'll pretend we're going on a date."

She knew it! She knew there was going to be more to this agreement than she bargained for.

"That is so juvenile! You can't really believe I'll ever again set foot anywhere near that place."

"Hey, you don't have to do your act again. Just show up, meet Marsh and—"

"And you'll tell Grandpa what a nice girl I am while your crew hoots and hollers for another performance!"

"They knock off at five on Friday. You're not in any danger if you come at six."

"What would my motivation be?"

"Your show," he said flatly.

"You said you signed a contract."

"I did."

He said it with so much satisfaction she began to feel threatened.

"You wouldn't—"

"Do every show exactly the way I want to? You bet I would!"

She had visions of havoc on the set, screaming fans, total chaos. The show might get good ratings that way, but everything she'd worked to accomplish would go down the drain. She'd end up as a straight man in a cartoon, the underdog clown in a circus of mayhem.

She groaned theatrically, but inside she was appalled at the power she'd blithely handed over to him.

"You hate being on TV."

"Oh, yeah, I do, but you have to admit today's show was lively."

"The second most lively I've ever done," she admitted unhappily.

"What was the first? Oh, yeah, the paint stripper."

"All right," she said, her jaw clenched so tightly her teeth ached. "What time should I make my very brief appearance?"

"Six will be fine. Cole can drive the company truck home, and I'll go with you."

"Great, I'll be stuck with taking you home."

"Be nice to Gramps," he warned.

"Why wouldn't I?"

"Oh, and wear clothes!"

He ducked out the door before she could sputter an answer.

That wasn't all she was going to wear.

6

"HE'S HERE!" Gus stuck his head into the trailer and delivered the bad tidings with glee.

"Marsh is here already?"

Zack checked his watch. It was only three o'clock, hours before his grandfather had said he'd be there.

"Yup, he's supervising the installation of the urinals. Mike isn't too keen on supervision."

Great. Now he had to calm down a prima-donna plumber and find something to keep his grandfather out of everyone's hair. Unlike the average sidewalk superintendent, Marsh felt completely free to share the benefits of his long experience with men trying to get their work done. What the chair of a baby products company could tell construction workers, Zack would never know.

Maybe it was Marsh's way of making amends for his vehement opposition to Bailey Construction when Zack and Cole first started it. Whatever his reason, the old boy could be a nuisance. Zack hurried to the building where workmen were finishing the inside.

"Marsh, good to see you," he said, tracking him down in an unfinished men's room.

And Megan thought he wasn't an actor!

"I thought you might have some ideas on traffic flow around the bank," Zack continued, offering to let his grandfather do what he liked best—give advice.

"Another time, maybe, Zack. I'm going to Palm

Springs for the weekend. Maybe get in a few decent rounds of golf. Never saw so much rain in May.''

''Megan's picking me up here at six. I thought you'd want to meet her.''

''I saw the television show. She didn't seem to like you much.''

''That's just show business. The audience likes it when we disagree.''

''Well, I have a plane to catch.''

Marsh Bailey was a silver fox, still handsome when most men his age had saggy chins and a road map of wrinkles. His hair wasn't visibly thinning, and he wore it cropped in a precise short cut. His idea of informality was wearing khaki slacks with his black wing tips.

''Another time then.'' What else could he say?

Marsh left for the airport, and Zack had another problem. Megan was coming to meet his grandfather. He had to stop her. No way did he want her to think she'd been lured there for a phony reason.

Cole returned to the site before Zack could call Megan, and by the time they talked about five or six pressing work-related problems, he couldn't reach Megan at the studio. The receptionist said she'd gone out to run some errands.

If she got mad about Marsh not being there, what could she do? Fire him? He'd be glad to have her try.

For the next couple of hours he lost himself in tedious desk work. He didn't realize what time it was until Cole stuck his head into the trailer.

''Your pizza is here,'' his brother said.

''What pizza? I didn't order a pizza. I'm just waiting for the queen of the airwaves to show.''

''Well, you've got one. I'm leaving. See you Monday.''

Zack stretched lazily and went to the door. Outside, a

frizzy-haired redhead in owlish shades was holding a giant pizza box. She was wearing a bulky dirty yellow leather jacket with navy wool sleeves that probably went to her knees.

"You've got the wrong place. I didn't order pizza."

She whipped off her sunglasses, and he recognized the baby blues.

"Megan, you didn't need to bring dinner."

"Okay." She tossed the box into the trash bin. "It's an empty box left from the crew's lunch."

"Why the delivery girl routine? Where'd you get the clown wig?" He had to suppress a laugh.

"I have my sources. You said to meet you here. You didn't say anything about coming as myself."

"A technicality. What are you wearing under that get-up?"

"You'll have to keep guessing. I'm done with construction-site performances."

"About my grandfather…"

"Where is he?"

"On a plane. He showed up a couple of hours ago. Couldn't wait for you. Sorry, I tried to call."

"Great, I psyched myself up for nothing."

"How about I spring for dinner? Not a date. Just compensation for wasting your time."

"Okay, but only because I'm starving. All I had for lunch was one piece of pizza."

"Let me change my shirt. Aren't you hot with that jacket on?"

"I'm not taking it off."

Why was she being so secretive? He was leery of taking her to a restaurant. She could be wearing something really bizarre under it—imagination failed him—or nothing at all.

He fantasized about the possibilities for a couple of seconds, then cleared his mind with a cold dose of reality. He wasn't attracted to Megan. That was the whole point in having her pose as his girlfriend. He didn't want to be involved with anyone for real, and she won hands down as the woman least likely to trip his trigger.

He did a quick wash in the trailer john and came out shirtless. In spite of his intention to stick to business with Megan, he enjoyed teasing her. He may have put his bad-boy days behind him, but he was still one of the Bailey twins. Getting a rise out of her was fun.

She didn't disappoint.

"You won't get fan mail from me by parading around half-naked."

The trailer seemed hot to him, but she hadn't unsnapped the jacket.

"You could've waited outside."

He found a navy knit shirt in his gym bag and slipped into it.

"What about the clown wig? Are you going to wear it all night?"

"You'll never know what I wear all night."

She didn't take it off.

He hadn't counted on taking her into a restaurant looking like a circus act. If he chose someplace nice, would she relent and ditch the Halloween costume? If she did, what surprise lay under the oversize jacket?

Maybe a fast-food joint was safer, but he had a better idea.

"Let's go, Red. You're my ride."

He opened the door and gave her a playful pat on the bottom, not that she could feel it through the crackly old leather of the jacket.

MEGAN SUPPOSED she should be mad. She'd dressed silly
to show Zack she wasn't taking this fake-couple business
seriously, but his grandfather was a no-show—if he'd ever
planned to be there at all. Still, she could cut Zack some
slack on this part of the deal. It was messing with her
show that really riled her.

She had no intention of going into a restaurant looking
so weird, but Zack deserved to stew for a while. He had
nerve, giving her a skin show, she thought as they walked
to her car. Not that it impressed her in the least. She'd
seen hundreds of better chests—well, dozens anyway—
well, maybe none up close that rivaled his. But that didn't
mean he should stroll in front of her, jeans hanging below
his navel, hair still clinging damply to the chest that had
created havoc on her show. She was immune to his
charms, totally impervious to whatever had excited the
women in her audience, but was it too much to expect
him to dress where she couldn't see him?

*He's no more to me than another piece of meat is to
the butcher,* she told herself, trying to inoculate herself
against the one thing he admittedly had—sex appeal to
spare.

Even though she chose to ignore it, she wouldn't forget
the pat on her bottom, either.

"Where are we going?" she asked, willing to settle for
a drive-through burger.

She shouldn't have agreed to dinner. Hunger was no
excuse.

"A surprise. Let me drive."

"You can tell me where to go."

Was she supposed to turn her keys over to him just
because he was a man?

"It'll be a whole lot easier if I do the driving. I doubt

you can see well enough to drive with that fake hair hanging over your eyes.''

He took the keys out of her hand, and there was nothing to gain by wrestling them back.

''I can't surprise you if I'm giving directions,'' he said.

He grinned and, unfortunately, he did have smile power.

Restaurants were not scarce in metro Detroit. Every United Nations delegate from Aden to Zimbabwe could feast on home cooking there, so why was he speeding down the freeway ignoring all the exits that led to food?

''Fast food would be fine,'' she told him. ''Hamburgers, chicken, burritos. I'm not fussy.''

''Don't tell me you maintain a bod like yours on junk food?''

''I work out,'' she said, not knowing whether to take his comment as a compliment or criticism of her eating habits.

He exited the freeway, and her frequently muddled sense of direction went bonkers.

''Where are we?''

''Livonia.''

''So what's the attraction here? Oriental buffet, Irish pub, Texas roadhouse?''

''You'll see.''

He made lots of turns, leaving behind the commercial strips. She was liking this less and less.

When he pulled into a driveway beside a brick duplex, she had an inkling of real trouble.

''What's this?'' As if she didn't know.

''Home.''

''Our deal was dinner *for* a ride home.''

''Do you like pasta?''

''Sure, everybody does.''

"This is the best place in eastern Michigan for spaghetti."

"You cook?"

"Sure, bachelors have to eat."

"I get it! You're embarrassed to be seen with me." The thought that her little plan worked thrilled her.

She yanked off the wig, letting her hair fall back in a ponytail.

"Naw."

"I wasn't going into a restaurant this way."

She wiggled out of the huge jacket she'd borrowed from Ed. She was overheated and glad to be free of the itchy woolen sleeves.

"Weren't you?" he mused, getting out of the car at the same time she did. "You look great." He gave a low whistle.

"For a clown."

She was wearing a pink dress with narrow shoulder straps, a princess waist and a skirt that flared to midcalf. It was her travel dress, and apparently not even Ed's old jacket had wrinkled it.

"One problem," he said, ushering her into the living room. "Cole took his couch when he got married. I've been too busy to worry about replacing it."

"You lived with your brother?"

"Until Tess."

"Did it bother you, having him get married?"

He grinned broadly. "Don't tell me you want to switch careers and be a call-in radio psychologist. No, it didn't bother me at all. I'm delighted he was the one to get married, not me. Make yourself at home."

The only places to sit were two fat green beanbags in front of the TV. They looked as if they would swallow her whole if she sank into the depths of one of them.

"At home," she repeated, at a loss what to do next.

If this were a date, it'd be an odd one. Fortunately it wasn't. They weren't friends, either, and she never felt this awkward with her co-workers. The pop psychology she enjoyed in women's magazines didn't have a neat category for show-stealing, conniving macho men who caused bedlam in your life.

For sure, she wasn't going to plop down in one of his swamp-colored beanbags.

"Ah, anything I can do to help?" she asked, not able to visualize Bailey cooking in a cozy little kitchen.

"Can you wash lettuce without a script?"

"Let's just forget dinner."

"Stay. You'll be doing me a favor. I can't cook spaghetti for one. I'd have to eat it for a week."

The heck of it was, she really wanted to see him cook dinner.

"Okay, but no more witticisms."

He rummaged in the fridge, which seemed to be well stocked compared to the few others she'd seen in bachelors' homes. Not that she'd dated many men who recognized the potential of refrigeration as something beyond a beer cooler.

"You look pretty in pink," he said, straightening. "Here, catch."

He tossed a head of lettuce in her direction, and she managed to catch it.

"Oh, it's not the kind in a bag."

"I like to do things the old-fashioned way, I guess."

She stood at the sink washing, patting dry and tearing lettuce leaves into a wooden salad bowl, then scrubbed big white button mushrooms for him. The kitchen was cozy with Zack bustling around, frying ground beef and onions, dumping spaghetti noodles into a big pot of boiling water, assembling spices in a neat row on the counter beside the stove and adding them to the sauce at different stages without measuring.

"You wing it on the seasoning," she said as she put ice cubes in water glasses.

"Not really. I know exactly how much of each I want. What would you like to drink? I have a good merlot. Otherwise the choice is beer, orange juice or milk. Sorry, no diet cola."

"What makes you think I drink diet cola?"

"Your figure."

"The camera does add ten pounds," she admitted, "but I'd love to try the wine."

He directed her to sit at the small round table in the kitchen. After setting heavy white stoneware plates on the plastic green and white checkered tablecloth, he served the pasta with tongs and spooned on rich tomato sauce with a ladle. At the last instant he pulled crusty bake-and-serve sourdough rolls from the oven.

"I'm impressed," she said after twisting a long saucy noodle around her fork and taking the first bite. "I didn't know spaghetti could taste this good."

"The secret is doing it a little different every time," he said with a sly smile. "Turns out better every time, so I never get tired of it."

"I could never cook that way."

She didn't cook at all, unless broiling a chicken breast counted, but when she contributed to a holiday meal at Georgia and Ed's, she studied cookbooks weeks ahead of time and followed recipes religiously.

"Tell me truthfully, is your whole life scripted like your show? No surprises, no highs or lows?"

She was mellowed by the delicious meal, but he was still getting too personal.

"I think it's important to set goals."

"Okay, so your show goes big time, you move on to Hollywood or New York or wherever the top market is. What happens in Act Three?"

"You're making fun of me."

"No, I really want to know. I've never met anyone quite like you. But you are a sloppy spaghetti eater."

She looked down, expecting to see sauce on the front of her dress, but he reached across the table and wiped a spot at the left corner of her mouth.

"It's all in the wrist action, winding the spaghetti on your fork."

"I'll take your word for it," she said dryly.

"Now tell me your secret plans."

"Just what most women want. Settle down with the right man someday, have babies. You probably think it's silly."

"Why should I?"

"You're so anti-marriage."

"Only for myself."

"A lot of men want a family."

"Not me."

"Why not?"

"Just not the marrying kind. Guess I come by it genetically. My birth father didn't even stick around to know he had twins. Not that I blame him. My mother was seventeen, and he wasn't much older. Marsh must have been pretty scary in those days. He even made sure we had his name."

"That's too bad."

"Not at all. I love the way my life is going."

He stood abruptly, leaving part of his second helping on his plate.

"Sorry, no dessert," he said. "Would you like more wine?"

"Thanks, no. I'm too full. It was a wonderful dinner."

She felt awkward, as she had before dinner. Did he resent her for leading him to talk about his personal life? He started it!

"I have to go," she said.

"I'm not sure I should let you."

He was clearing the table with an efficiency that impressed her.

"Why?"

"The wine. You don't have a designated driver, so you'd better crash here for the night. I'll use the camping cot in Cole's old room, and you can have my bed. One of these days I'm going to build a house for myself. Until then, I'm not much on accumulating things like furniture."

"No, thank you. I only had one glass of wine." Actually she'd found it a bit strong and had poured the remainder in the sink.

She wasn't sure why he'd asked her to stay. Certainly not because of a few sips of wine. Thanks to the long spring days, it wasn't even dark yet, so she would have no trouble finding her way home.

"You're safe with me." He flashed her a devilish grin. "I won't even hit on you."

"We've already established that there is absolutely no attraction between us," she said in a severe voice that wavered only slightly when he stepped close enough for her to see the faint shadow of bristles on his chin. "I don't know why, but—"

She clamped her mouth shut, horrified because she'd been about to ask why he didn't find her at least a little appealing. Why was she so much *not* his type that she really did feel completely safe sleeping over? Of course, she wasn't going to do it.

"Ultimately your goal is to settle down with a domestic type and raise kids," he said in a soft shivery voice. "I'm not a candidate for that. All I want to do is build a business that will make Bailey Baby Products look small-time."

"Being in my show can't hurt." He was making her defensive again. He had a knack for it.

"Probably not, much as I hate to admit it. But we have a business arrangement. I don't have time for pleasure. Otherwise…"

"Otherwise what?"

"Otherwise I might be tempted to do this."

He leaned forward and brushed her lips with his, a little nothing of a kiss that made her knees go weak.

"I wouldn't want you to be tempted," she said, but she parted her lips and wanted the wonderful tingling to go on and on.

"Don't worry, I'm not."

He moved a full step closer and lowered his head to hers again, this time putting his hands on her shoulders and nuzzling the sensitive spot below her earlobe.

"You can see how easy it would be for us to be distracted from our goals," he said softly.

"I wouldn't want that to happen," she murmured.

His lips caressed her lowered lids and moved down her cheek.

"It would be a terrible mistake," he mumbled just before his lips met hers again.

She didn't exactly see stars—at least, not real ones—but she learned quickly why women had mobbed him on the set. She couldn't define *it,* but he had it.

At least he moaned first.

"Dessert," he said.

She giggled nervously, and then his tongue parted her lips. She didn't bother to worry whether this was insane.

"I'd better go before it gets dark," she said after a very pleasant few minutes.

It took all her willpower to focus on the awful fact that she was still stuck with him on her show.

"Okay," he agreed amiably, dropping his arms and stepping back.

What was going on? Why didn't he ask her again to stay? She tried to pretend she wasn't totally confused.

"Thanks for dinner. You're a great cook. The Bulgarian chef is always looking for a new helper. He has a little temper problem. Maybe instead of doing my show…"

"Don't even think of it!" he warned. "I'll walk you to your car."

It was ten steps away in the driveway. She didn't need a goodbye kiss. Another kiss was the last thing she needed!

"Not necessary," she insisted. "See you next Wednesday."

"Next Wednesday," he grumbled, his romantic mood, if that was what it was, dissolving into surly remembrance of their deal.

Before she could change her mind, she was out the door, accidentally slamming it behind her without looking back.

Okay, Bailey had proved he was sexually exciting, but it had nothing to do with the chaos he created every time he came on her set.

They had a business deal, and the sooner she forgot that he kissed like a heartthrob-cowboy-prince-cop hero in a romance novel, the better for her show. And her heart.

7

ZACK HAD AN IDEA that was off the wall, but he called it self-defense. After all, he had to do eleven more episodes of "Do It Herself," and he didn't want to plunge in blindly another time. Either he'd look like a fool or Megan would be too mad on air for Zack to convince his grandfather they were involved in a relationship. His solution seemed reasonable to him—work out their differences ahead of time.

He knew where she lived but still didn't have her home phone number, and he figured Ed owed him for talking Cole into doing a guest spot in the first place.

Ed obliged.

Zack dialed Megan's number early Sunday afternoon, not without some trepidation. He knew their kiss—kisses—had only been a fluke, a momentary weakness because she was eminently kissable, but how did she feel about them? He'd never expected her to sleep over, but how had she interpreted his offer?

"Hello." Her voice was as mellow on the phone as it was on TV.

"Megan, this is Zack."

"Oh?"

"You probably didn't expect me to call."

Now there was a dumb way to begin a conversation.

"Are you calling to apologize?"

Her voice was sugary sweet, but a great actress she was not.

"Did I offend you in some way?"

"Let's say you overstepped the bounds of hospitality."

"Sorry."

He wasn't, not in the least, but he had to get past the kissing to sell her on his suggestion.

"Really?"

"No."

Enough was enough. He hadn't begged for a kiss since—well, ever—and she'd seemed plenty willing at the time. Not that it had been a good move on his part. Sure, she was gorgeous, tempting and theoretically available. She was also prickly and opinionated. He was tempted to hang up, but there would be more satisfaction in inconveniencing her.

"Well, why are you calling?" she asked.

"It's about next week's script." He tried to sound humble but doubted she was buying it.

"Do you have it already?" Surprise made her sound a little more friendly.

"No, but since we have such different takes on how things should be done—"

"Your way or chaos," she said dryly.

"Yeah, I guess I have given you a bad impression. That's why I thought we could rehearse ahead of time. Work out our differences before we go on camera."

"That's not a bad idea." She sounded pleasantly surprised. "I have a rough draft for your next appearance. Should I fax it to you?"

"You could, but maybe it would be better if we meet at the studio. We could go over it on the set."

"It might help you get over your stage fright if you were better prepared," she said.

There was a topic he didn't want to discuss.

"Are you free this evening? I didn't think anyone would be using your set tonight."

"Let me check."

Little faker! She knew whether she was busy. She probably had a schedule for brushing her teeth.

"Yes, I can meet you at seven at the studio. I'll bring what I have for Wednesday's taping."

"Great, see you then."

He stared moodily at the phone after they'd disconnected. This might solve their differences on the show, but how did he feel about another one-on-one with Megan, this time in a deserted studio?

He muttered a colorful cuss word and slammed down the receiver. His life was a whole lot more complicated than he wanted it to be, thanks to his grandfather and the home-handicraft girl.

Zack wasn't one to kid himself. He'd been hanging loose for quite a while, too darn busy for the dating game and uptight about Marsh's ultimatum. It wasn't like him not to have a main squeeze, but he couldn't seem to meet anyone who didn't have marriage on the brain. It was easier to avoid that kind of entanglement than to get out of it.

He knew precisely how he felt about Megan. She was stubborn, officious and bossy. What their relationship needed was a weekend in bed, but if he read her correctly—and he was sure he did—she wanted a forever kind of guy. A fling with her would probably involve guilt, recriminations and eventual ill will, none of which he needed.

He did allow himself a minute of pleasurable fantasy. He imagined sliding up the hem of the little pink dress she'd worn under that ratty jock jacket, peeling her panties over her hips and spectacular legs and…

"Forget it," he told himself crossly.

The day dragged. He ate leftover spaghetti around five, then remembered there was garlic in it. The way he rinsed with mouthwash and sucked breath mints, you'd think he was a guy with a big date.

Just to prove that Megan Danbury was no date, he didn't shave his bristly face. He put on a pair of old jeans well past their prime and a black T-shirt that had faded to charcoal.

The main entrance at the station was locked when he got there, but Megan had already arrived and opened it.

"There's usually someone here," she said, "but we keep it locked for security except during business hours."

"How are you?" he asked, a little miffed because she didn't even say hello before explaining station policy, which he could figure out for himself.

"Fine, thanks. Let's go to the set."

Did she sound a little breathless? Was that a pink flush on her cheeks? Was it possible she was uncomfortable because they'd enjoyed a few kisses at his place?

He docilely followed, allowing himself to enjoy the teasing wiggle of her bottom in white, very tight jeans. Her sandals made a soft slapping noise in the deserted corridor, and he tried not to imagine slipping his hands under her navy tank top to cup those round, firm breasts.

She flicked a switch, and overhead lights illuminated the big barnlike room, only a small part of it used for the set of "Do It Herself."

"What's on the docket for the next show?"

"Wallpapering."

"Not my specialty."

She frowned at him over her shoulder and led the way to the set.

"I thought you could give some hints on measuring, hanging it straight, things like that."

"I guess."

"Your enthusiasm is overwhelming."

Why the sarcasm? He was here to work on doing a decent show. Maybe she *was* upset about the lip exercises.

"I had a nice time Friday," he said to test her.

"Your dinner was very good."

The way she said it, he could've served sautéed slugs. He wasn't fooled. He guessed she was ticked because she'd liked kissing him. Now he was sure they couldn't sleep together and still have a friendly working relationship. Women got funny once they shared sheets with a guy, especially the marriage-minded ones.

Well, he wasn't going to risk ruining the ruse with his grandfather. Too bad, because she was a fine-looking lady, lean but shapely in all the right places.

She walked away from him, making a pretense of moving the long table she used for projects. When she turned and bent to pick up a scrap of paper on the floor, her breasts fell forward, making him wonder what she'd do if he strolled over causally and lightly stroked them, just a gentle bit of foreplay to see if she was as disinterested as she would like him to believe.

Maybe meeting her in a deserted television studio wasn't such a hot idea. He hadn't expected to be turned on just by being in the same room with her.

"I thought I'd feel more comfortable in front of the cameras if I spend some time on the set without a lot of people around," he said, deciding that talking about this unpleasant subject was better than letting her know what he was really thinking.

His statement sounded plausible to him even though he wasn't sure what triggered his on-camera jitters. Certainly it wasn't the audience or the crew. People never intimidated him, and that included Megan. Also he didn't worry about how he'd look on camera. Even when he forgot what he was supposed to say, he was always able to come up with something. So stage fright wasn't logical.

But then, neither was sex. Why were hard-to-get women like Megan always more tempting?

"You sounded pretty comfortable on the last show," she said, rustling a sheaf of papers she took from a briefcase beside the table. "I made you a copy of the rough script for Wednesday."

"Thanks."

He took it, wondering if the big empty studio seemed spooky to her. If so, she wasn't trying to stay close to him. In fact, she handed over the script and backed away as though he'd been munching raw garlic cloves.

Straddling a folding chair, he started scanning the pages.

"Your mother must be nice. You're going to so much trouble to make sure she keeps her job," Megan said. "My mom is the one who gave me the inspiration for the show. After my dad deserted us, she did all kinds of things to make our home nicer."

He recognized her monologue as nervous chatter, but she was making it hard to concentrate on all the stage directions in the script.

"My mother is great, loves her job. Doesn't pry into our personal lives," he said, talking by habit about himself and his twin. "I don't think she has a clue about Marsh pressuring us to get married."

She kept chattering, something about Georgia—that

must be her sister—and Ed not wanting to move. He was too unhappy with the script to pay much attention.

"This project is boring," he said factually, not intending to be unkind.

"What?"

"The script tanks."

"It's only the bare bones. I'll have sample papers to show and some clever ideas for borders and accent walls."

"Have you ever thought of taking the show out of the studio?"

"The logistics are too complicated. Besides, we tape in front of a studio audience."

"I'm sure the station has the equipment, and the audience would love it, since they'd be out of the studio. Definitely a way to liven things up."

"My show—"

"Our show," he interrupted mildly.

"Doesn't need livening. Anyway, you made a deal. You follow my scripts, and I pretend to be your—your..."

"Girlfriend. Tell you what. I'll do the wallpaper script your way. I'll bring my trusty tape measure, cut a strip or two of paper and slap it on that phony wall. But you ask Ed about taking the show to a real site."

"He'll hate it," she said grimly.

Not as much as I hate this show, Zack thought.

MEGAN TOOK JASON to the zoo Sunday afternoon so Georgia and Ed could have an afternoon to themselves. Blessedly, Jason seemed intimidated into good behavior by the snarling giant cats. It was one of their nicer outings, much better than his fifth birthday treat from her. She'd taken him to a pizza place specializing in kids' parties, and he promptly buried himself in a pit of plastic balls, forcing her to wade in after him.

Afterward she sat in Georgia's kitchen and indulged in a homemade chocolate mint wafer with peppermint tea while Jason ran to the back yard to help his father plant flowers.

"How do you like it?" her sister asked. "It's a new bottom for my choco-marsh specials."

"I like it without the marshmallow." She didn't share her sister's passion for chewy sugar-flavored blobs.

"Okay, tell me about him!" Georgia beamed at her from a rounder, softer version of her own face.

"I'm not seeing anyone special now." Megan crunched the last of the wafer and frowned in puzzlement.

"I mean the hunk on your show. Ed said he's a hot ticket."

"Just a guest. Jason was really good today."

There was no changing the subject when Georgia got her teeth into it.

"He's gorgeous. Rugged but sexy. Is he really a bachelor?"

"Confirmed bachelor."

"I watched the tape three times," her sister confessed.

"I thought you were busy working on a final draft of your cookbook."

"Would I like to have him on the cover! You don't think…"

"No."

MEGAN FELT BETTER about the show when she went to work Monday morning. Zack said he'd cooperate next time, and she thought he meant it. His suggestion of taping outside the studio was just a typical male power ploy. Why did men always want to be in control? Bailey knew as little about cable television as her grandfather knew about finding a husband for her, but that didn't stop either of them from meddling.

At least she could count on her brother-in-law to hate Zack's idea. Truth to tell, Ed had a lazy streak. If there were two ways to do a thing, he'd pick the one that made his job easier. He wouldn't go for the hassle of shooting outside the studio.

She found her producer in his office and casually tossed off Zack's idea, only because she'd said she would.

"I love it!" When Ed was excited, his voice boomed.

"You do? It will mean twice as much work for you," Megan said.

"Doesn't matter."

Doesn't matter? This from the man who shoveled tracks for his tires in his driveway instead of removing all the snow?

"You'll have to deal with making contacts, getting releases, checking on insurance liability, lighting problems..." She tried to make shooting in the field sound a lot harder than it was.

"Let's try it a week from Wednesday."

Her brother-in-law sprang up from the comfy chair that molded to the contour of his beefy backside and paced beside his desk without even glancing at the football photos of his younger but no less husky self on the wall.

Remember this man is your sister's husband, she told herself. *Do not hurt him!*

"The sponsors will love it. The audience will love it. Gunderdorf will love it," Ed raved.

He was like a windup toy—as annoying as he was repetitive. He was running out of pacing space but not enthusiasm.

"We'll make it one long commercial. Advertising dollars will roll in. No projects, just shopping. I'll set it up at the Home Stop. They'll double their advertising time on the network after we do the show in their store.''

''That's not what 'Do It Herself' is about.''

''Sure it is,'' Ed argued, as unstoppable as a freight train. ''Women don't know beans about shopping in a hardware store. Since female reporters started invading locker rooms, it's the last true male bastion. Your viewers will love it. Damn, I'll even love it!''

''And we all know how you feel about any TV show that doesn't star a pigskin,'' she said morosely, insulted by his comment about women and hardware stores.

Taping went well that day, really well, even without Bailey and his rippling muscles. She had a female expert demonstrate how to restore and reupholster a beat-up thrift-store couch at minimal cost. The audience was fascinated and asked really worthwhile questions. This was the way her show was supposed to go.

After the shoot Ed was still raving about taking ''Do It Herself'' to the Home Stop. By three o'clock he'd sold the idea to the store, the ad department and, worst of all, Gunderdorf.

''He loves it!'' Ed announced to Megan as she briefed the two interns about Wednesday's program.

If anyone else loved it, she was going to barf.

Bailey started this, she thought later, and it was worth a twenty-minute drive to the construction site to let him know how his meddlesome idea had evolved into an absolute fiasco.

She saw him from the road. He was standing outside the colonial-style redbrick bank building, which seemed to be nearly complete. He was so engrossed in conversation with a burly man in low-slung jeans and a muddy-red T-shirt he didn't notice her.

She walked up the newly paved and slightly tacky entrance drive, not keen on attracting the attention of his crew. Fortunately most of them seemed to be working inside. The only obvious outdoor work still to be done was landscaping, but she was there to talk about her business, not his.

Her soles felt sticky, and she scuffed them on the dusty walkway that led to the trailer, hoping they hadn't picked up tar from the driveway. She was itching to confront Bailey, but she contained her impatience. Construction workers were not her idea of a congenial audience, especially not when she'd come to vent her frustration on their boss.

Zack saw her and gave a wave she interpreted as saying, Stay there. She scraped her soles on the walkway another time and bristled while he took his own sweet time finishing the conversation and ambling over to her.

He was wearing a yellow hard hat and khaki T-shirt with work boots and, no surprise, low-slung jeans. Only his weren't the usual baggy work pants. They hugged his thighs, and the way he moved in them left no doubt he was in charge. He boss-walked over to her and scowled.

"What are you doing here?"

"Hello to you, too," she said, pointedly ignoring the deeply tanned, muscular arms he folded across his chest.

"I don't see a pizza box, and I'm hoping you won't dance. Any chance you're here to fire me from your show?"

"My fondest desire."

He was making it impossible to tell him the results of his brainy idea in a calm, rational way.

"Ed loved your idea of taking the show outside the studio."

"Really?"

He wouldn't look so smug when he heard the whole story.

"Gunderdorf loved it. Joe the business manager loved it, the salesmen loved it...."

"I get the picture."

"You should be proud. Thanks to you, we'll be doing the show at the Home Stop next week. You'll get to help me push a cart down the aisles while you enlighten me on weighty matters like nail sizes or picking the best paintbrush. Isn't that a wonderful take on your idea?"

"I hate it!"

He skirted around her and headed toward his office in the trailer.

"You can't hate it. It was your idea. I'm the one who gets to hate it!" she yelled after him.

He walked toward the trailer, and she scampered after him, one heel catching between the boards of the temporary walkway. In an instant she was on her hands and knees with him looking down at her.

"If you can't walk in heels, wear sensible shoes," he scolded without a trace of sympathy, squatting to extricate her foot and pull the heel of the shoe out of the crack.

She stood up gingerly and looked at her dirty knees and hands.

"Oh, a splinter!"

Cuts, burns, gouges, scrapes, even breaks she could handle, but she turned to a quivering mass of jelly when she had to dig out a splinter.

"Let me see." Zack took her right hand in his and brushed away loose dirt. "Yup, that's a splinter, all right."

He kept holding it.

"Maybe I should go to the emergency room."

He laughed. "You're kidding, right?"

Trouble was, she wasn't. She couldn't do it herself, not because she wasn't left-handed but because she was too squeamish. Her mother was the only one she trusted, but she was far away. Georgia could do it, but not without her don't-be-a-sissy lecture. Ed would do it, but with his locker-room technique, he'd probably poke holes in her bone trying to find it. She mentally sifted through her friends, co-workers and neighbors, but she'd be too embarrassed to have any of them see what a big chicken she was.

"It could get infected." She groaned.

"Doubtful, but I'll get it out for you."

"You?" She snatched her hand away. "No, no, no."

"Don't be silly. I've had a course in first aid, and there's a kit in the trailer. Come on."

He took her other dusty, smarting hand and pulled her toward the old trailer that served as his office, still carrying her shoe in his other hand.

"Stop! I'll get splinters in my foot!"

"The heel on this is nearly off," he said, dangling the ruined shoe. "Want me to snap it the rest of the way?"

"Oh, why not?"

She knew she was being as ungracious as Jason sometimes was—he'd bitten her once because he didn't like the birthday present she gave him—but Bailey was treating her splinter crisis like…like…

Her resistance collapsed. She was being a big baby, and she knew her splinter phobia wasn't rational.

"I'd appreciate it," she said meekly, wincing when the heel of her best white pump snapped like a twig.

He knelt and lifted her foot, sliding it into the mutilated shoe.

"Want the other to match?" he asked.

She looked at the white leather, badly scuffed when she fell, and nodded.

He broke the heel off the second shoe, so at least she could walk semi-normally.

Dang, her knees were smarting, too, but that was irrelevant. She had a giant splinter imbedded in the fleshy part of her palm. That meant a needle probing and piercing, sending white-hot stabs of pain coursing through her nervous system. Every muscle in her body would stiffen. Her eyes would water, and she'd shriek in agony. Okay, maybe she was exaggerating....

Zack was going to think she was totally psychotic! For some reason she didn't have time to analyze, she didn't want that to happen.

"I'm going home now," she said firmly.

"Are you left-handed?"

"No."

"Then you're going to have a hard time getting the splinter out of your right. Come on. It won't take two minutes, and I promise to be gentle."

He smiled, although she wasn't convinced of his sincerity. Inside he was probably laughing hysterically at her irrational fear of splinters.

"No, I'm leaving."

She looked around for her purse with the all-essential car keys, but he scooped it up before she could make a move.

"Let's get it over with, Megan. You know it has to come out."

"I'll just let it dissolve where it is."

"There's a plan if you're into gangrene."

Now who was exaggerating? "Give me my purse. Please."

"Nope. Get inside, or I'll carry you."

"You wouldn't!"

She took in his frame, six-two to her five-four, all of it steely hard except maybe his earlobes and the more vulnerable parts somewhat lower that she tried hard not to imagine.

With a sudden flash of insight, she realized why Zack made her uncomfortable. She never felt in control when he was around. Even Ed, who dwarfed her, never intimidated her in the least, but Bailey was too much his own person.

Well, this was one battle of wills she was going to win. She snatched at her purse—and came up empty-handed.

"Hey, this isn't funny!"

"Granted." He slipped her purse strap over his shoulder.

One instant he was facing her with a crooked little smile more teasing than menacing. The next he pounced.

Before she could scream or escape, he grabbed her thighs and heaved her over his shoulder.

"No!"

Suddenly, she was staring at his back, the blood rushing to her head, and her arms flailed at air. She was bottom up, her shoes dropping off as she tried to squirm free. This was worse than her silly performance! At least that had been voluntary. Zack was giving anyone who cared to look a splendid view of a caveman hauling his hapless female off to his lair.

He carried her up the two steps to the trailer, let the screen door swing out and bang the aluminum siding, then slammed it shut.

"There," he said, plunking her down in her stocking feet. "Now behave."

She was breathless, indignant and speechless. How could he! What would he...

He was getting something out of a drawer behind his cluttered desk. She glanced at the door and weighed her chance of making an escape against another humiliating ride over his shoulder as he put a first-aid box on the desk.

"You're making a big deal out of nothing," he said, coming around to her side of the desk.

"You manhandled me! That's sexual harassment," she cried, latching on to an accusation that made most men quake.

"It's not harassment," he countered, talking in a voice that reminded her of a kindergarten teacher. "And it's certainly not sexual."

"Why not?" It was the dumbest question of the day, but it popped out by accident.

"Because if I wanted to make a sexual move, you'd recognize it."

He moved so quickly she only had time to blink and open her mouth in a round O. He put his hands on either side of her neck and none too gently ran them through her hair as a single gasp welled from her throat.

His sunbaked face was hot against hers, and his lips seared when they covered hers.

No fair, no fair, she thought, frantically wondering why his kisses were so different from other men's, why she wanted him to kiss her harder and longer even when his tongue started to tango with hers.

He was too good at this! His hands, hotter even than his lips, slid under her shirt and up her back to release the hooks on her bra.

She knew he was going too far too fast and should be stopped, but she leaned toward him when his hands found her breasts. He caressed slowly, cupping them and holding their weight while his thumbs made lazy circles without touching the hardening tips.

"This, sweetheart, is sexual," he said in a soft, seductive voice.

He teased her nipples with his thumbs, all the while silencing her with a bombardment of little kisses on the corners of her mouth, her chin and her tender, swollen lips.

"Now let's get that splinter out," he said, abruptly releasing her.

"No!"

She'd forgotten the splinter, but it would be impossible to forget the way he'd kissed her. They didn't even like each other. Or did they? She was so confused, she hardly noticed when he pushed aside a stack of papers and boosted her onto his desk.

She sat, legs dangling, trying to decide whether to be mad, scared, embarrassed or terribly pleased.

"I'll clean it off with peroxide, sterilize the needle with rubbing alcohol..."

"You have a needle in a construction office?"

"In the first-aid kit. Carpenters get a lot of splinters. I'll have yours out before you know it."

"I'll know."

Dread was rearing its ugly head, almost making her forget the shivers of excitement his kisses had sent coursing through her.

Almost.

"I'd rather go home," she insisted, bunching both hands into fists.

"Hey, Zack, do you want—" A burly man she'd seen before stuck his head in the doorway.

"I'll be out in a couple of minutes," Zack said. "Doing a little first aid.

"Sure, first aid. No rush," the workman said, retreating.

"You have to get back to work," Megan said.

"I'm the boss, remember? Let's do this."

He pried open her fingers, but not as easily as he'd slung her over his shoulder.

"There it is."

He swabbed her palm clean with a cotton ball saturated with rubbing alcohol and picked up the needle.

"I can't do this!" She wasn't faking her panic.

"You don't have to do anything but relax."

He held her hand on his palm, preventing her from making a fist.

"This will only be a pinprick. You can't be that sensitive to pain."

"I'm not." This was true. "It's not the pain."

"You have a needle phobia? Just don't look."

"No! I have a splinter phobia! I know it's there whether I look or not."

"Hand me one of those gauze pads in the first-aid box, would you? It's right behind you."

She turned to oblige, but he held on to her right hand. Before she could find what he wanted, a sharp prick made her wince.

"There."

"There what?" She pulled on her hand, and this time he released it.

"Your splinter. Do you want it as a souvenir?"

"It's out?"

"Came out clean as could be with these."

He held up a pair of tweezers.

"But you had a needle."

"A little sleight of hand. I didn't need it. Here, slap on a bandage if you like. I have to get back to work."

He leaned forward, kissed the tip of her nose and left.

She stared at her palm. The splinter really was gone.

And she'd forgotten to say thanks.

8

MEGAN WAS AWAKE at five o'clock worrying about the show, so she went to the studio early. It was Home Stop day, and she couldn't be more depressed if they were shooting at a mortuary.

The cutesy shopping tour had absolutely nothing to do with her concept for the show, and it irked her that Ed had been right about the powers that be loving the idea. They were so enthusiastic the Bulgarian chef was in a snit and the dog man's nose was out of joint.

The only one as glum as Megan was Julie, but the intern was suffering from the throes of unrequited love, over a guy in her apartment building. She walked around in a haze of misery. Even when she was mildly cheerful, she dressed like the mother of all vampires. Lately she'd been downright scary.

Megan was checking a couple of things in her dressing room—where the higher-ups had not bothered to install a phone line—when Julie brought bad news.

"Zack can't do the show today," she said in what was becoming a habitually tragic tone. "He's sick."

"He isn't coming?"

"That's what someone named Gus said. I told him to hold until I found you."

Megan sprinted toward the phone in her office.

"This is Megan Danbury. Who is this, please?"

"Gus Graham, ma'am. Zack said to—"

"Let me talk to him."

"Uh, he's at home sick. Can't do your TV show today."

"He can't not do it!" Like it would do any good to rant and rave at one of his employees. "Never mind, I'm going to his house to see for myself."

"Nothing to see," the man quickly said. "He's just under the weather."

"Thanks for calling."

She hung up and checked her watch. Plenty of time to get to Livonia and convince Zack he wasn't too sick to honor his contract.

She found Brad, the less-than-efficient but more loquacious intern, and dispatched him to Ed. She didn't have time to take any flack from her producer.

"Tell him I'll meet him at Home Stop. Bailey is trying to bail on us, but unless he has bubonic plague, we'll both meet Ed and the crew at the store for the taping."

"Bailey has bubonic plague," Brad said with his mouth full of jelly doughnut, "and you'll meet him at the show."

She gave it to him once more, and the message seemed to penetrate. Better to risk a garbled message than try to explain to Ed in person. He was going to blow a gasket if *the* show was sabotaged by the golden boy's defection.

By the time she got to Livonia, her heart was pounding almost as loudly as her fists on the door of Zack's duplex. She was going to see for herself just how sick he was, then kill him!

He had to be home; a company truck was in the driveway. She rang the bell and pounded on the door. Maybe he was unconscious, in a coma, too sick to come to the door.

She tried the knob and was surprised when the door opened inward.

"Zack, where are you?"

"In here."

She followed a hoarse, feeble voice to the bedroom.

He was in bed, all right, with a green cotton blanket pulled up to his chin. He did look a little flushed under the deep bronze of his tan. He lifted his head a couple of inches off the pillow, then sank back.

"A man called and said you were sick."

"Gus, my foreman," he explained weakly.

"Why did he call for you?"

"I had to call the site to say I wasn't coming."

"What's wrong with you?"

She remembered the splinter and tried to sound sympathetic, but dang, she dreaded trying to do a shopping show alone. When it tanked—and it most likely would—she was the one who'd look bad even though she'd hated the idea from the beginning.

"Achy, queasy, coughing. My head hurts." He gave a little hack.

"This show is your bright idea. Take it out in the field, you said. Are you sure you can't take a couple of aspirin and get through it?"

She didn't try to hide her skepticism. He looked pretty good to her, unfortunately.

"I'm not a well man," he said crabbily.

"I'll take your temperature."

"No thermometer."

Still suspicious, she remembered what had happened in the trailer. She wasn't getting close enough to feel his forehead.

"I'll get you something to settle your stomach."

"Don't trouble yourself."

"Oh, no trouble." No trouble at all compared to whipping together a show that excluded him while everyone from the cameraman to the store manager waited. "Something to drink will help your cough, too."

Or maybe he'd already been drinking. Was he hungover? She sniffed delicately and rejected the possibility.

"I'll see what you have in the kitchen."

"Maybe a little warm milk, not too hot."

"Okay, I'll be right back."

She zapped a cup of skim milk in the microwave. A person had to be sick to drink something that yucky, but she was still suspicious. This debilitating illness was a little too convenient for him.

Carefully carrying the hot cup, she stepped into the bedroom.

He'd pulled the covers up an inch too far. She saw the ridged sole of his work boot.

"You're busted!"

"What?" He lifted his head.

"You're a despicable fraud! I can't believe you'd sink this low!"

He could have his warm milk—sans cup. She threw the contents at the mound under the covers.

"Yipe!" He bounded out of bed before most of the hot liquid could soak through to the strategic location she'd targeted. "Why did you do that?"

"Why are you in bed in your boots? You lied to me! You were probably standing right next to your flunky when he called! What did you do, race home when he told you I was coming here?" She glared at his jeans, belt and Tiger baseball T-shirt."

"Who made you bedroom monitor?" He sounded surly.

"I can't believe you lied after you agreed to do the show. You signed a contract!" she admonished, her hands on her hips.

"What is the point of having me stroll up and down the aisles of the Home Stop? You don't need me to toss stuff into a cart."

"I don't want you to toss anything anywhere, but thanks to your brilliant suggestion, I'm stuck with you. And you have to do it!"

"Have to?"

He raised one eyebrow, deepening the crease line on his forehead. She was much too mad to be intimidated by his dark scowl and smoldering gray eyes.

He moved toward her and, okay, she was leery of all those muscles, but she was more angry than cowed.

"You made your own deal. You agreed to be on my show twelve times."

"This isn't one of those times."

"Did you wake up intending to chicken out, or did you get scared when you thought of all those ferocious fans of yours mobbing you in a hardware store?"

"I'm over my stage fright, and you don't need a so-called expert. Anyone with half a brain can do the simpleton stuff on your show."

"Apparently you can't! Hiding in bed when you're supposed to honor your commitment is a schoolboy trick."

"Well, what happens next? Do I stand in a corner or do you whack me with a ruler?"

"Go ahead, joke! If you don't come with me now, Ed will look incompetent, the show will be a total dud—not that it won't be anyway—and I'd rather date a boa constrictor than pretend to be involved with a cowardly lion."

"Are you through expressing yourself?" He stepped so close she could see milk stains on his T-shirt.

"I guess so."

"Then let's go shopping."

He turned abruptly and stripped off his shirt.

"Pick out a shirt for me," he ordered.

"What?"

"It's your damn show. Get one out of the middle drawer."

He pointed at a heavy oak dresser.

Opening his drawer felt like an invasion of his privacy, but she grabbed the first thing she saw, a jet black T-shirt that looked new.

"Formal wear," he said, grabbing it and pulling it on. "Let's go before I begin to doubt my own sanity."

He drove his truck faster than she wanted to follow, and she didn't really believe he'd make an appearance at the Home Stop until she spotted his truck already parked near the back of the large lot.

She couldn't shake a panicky feeling. This was going to be her worst show ever.

"I GET TO have lunch with a TV star." Sue Bailey slid into the booth at Olivia's Garden Café and grinned at her son.

"Don't tell me you wasted your time watching TV." Zack sheepishly returned her smile. "Nice suit. Is it new?"

"It was a couple of years ago." She flicked an imaginary speck off the shoulder of her heather-gray suit. "You're just like your brother. If I bring up a sensitive subject, you mention my clothes."

Zack smiled for real. His mother was one of those rare women who looked good in anything, even when the mood struck her to play games with her hair color. Today, he noted with satisfaction, it was light brown worn short with straight bangs.

"Imagine, twins alike," he teased. "Maybe Cole has

watched me operate so long, he mimics my fine qualities.''

''I got a kick out of the women trying to rip your shirt off,'' she said, not one to be distracted from a subject for long.

''Give me a break, Mom! I'm trying to forget the whole fiasco.''

''I did like the shows in the studio better.''

''How did you happen to watch daytime programs?''

''Cole tells me when you're going to be on so I can tape them. Are you going to do more?''

''A few, maybe,'' he reluctantly admitted.

''Aren't they fun?''

''No, not really.''

About as much fun as having his butt tattooed, but his mother didn't know about the panther head on his left cheek.

''If you don't enjoy it, why do it?''

There was a question he had to evade. If his mother even suspected Marsh was using her job to maneuver him into marriage, she'd be horrified.

''I promised a girl I would,'' he said.

''Ah.''

He hated that ''ah,'' maybe because it always meant she'd caught him at something.

''Nothing serious,'' he quickly assured her. ''Cole is the marrying man in this family.''

''Thank heavens! But you know I want grandchildren before I'm too old to enjoy them.''

''You have a long way to go before then. Just don't use them as models for the baby ads when you do get some.''

Zack had hated posing for the company catalog even

more than Cole when they were young. Maybe that was why he loathed the television camera.

"Would you like to order?" a young brunette waitress asked.

"We're waiting for another person," his mother said.

"Cole's coming? He was busy at the site when I left."

"No, not Cole. Your grandfather heard I was meeting you—"

"You told him?"

"Well, he almost always has lunch with his old cronies. How would I know he'd ask to join us? It's a little weird, actually, but... Oh, here he is."

She slid over to make room for her father.

"Hi, Gramps." Might as well start off by annoying him, Zack thought, pretty sure Marsh's presence didn't bode well.

The old man knew his daughter was in the dark about his demands and wanted to keep it that way, the one thing all the men in the family agreed on. So why was he here?

He didn't even gripe about being called Gramps. Bad sign.

They ordered. That in itself was an experience, since his grandfather was on a strict heart diet but never seemed to have a clue which entrées were really bad for him. Zack kept out of it as his mother nixed one item after another. Marsh finally ordered a double bacon cheeseburger. Sue canceled it and requested the baked fish for him. Zack wondered which meal the waitress would deliver.

"So, you're a TV star now," his grandfather said with something he probably thought was jovial goodwill.

"He's only doing it for a young woman," Sue said.

"That so?"

"Sort of," Zack mumbled.

Lunch was passably good. Marsh behaved, which in his

case meant eating his fish and not giving any advice, business or personal, to either of them. His mother finished her salad and had to hurry off for a meeting.

"Good news, Zack," the old man said when she was gone. "I'm setting you up with my golf buddy's granddaughter."

"I'm seeing someone."

"Which I still find hard to believe. Besides, you're not married, *are* you?"

"Of course not, but—"

"I've been working on this a long time, and I'm getting tired of waiting for you to get married. At least Cole had initiative. Can't hurt you to have dinner with the girl." He smiled smugly, in itself suspicious.

"Marsh, I appreciate all your efforts—"

"Good, it's all set for tomorrow night. I'm not so sure that television woman is keen on you. She seems pretty cold on air."

Zack would've said *hot* was a better word for Megan's attitude, especially when she'd slammed the Home Stop cart into the backs of his ankles, which, fortunately, were protected by work boots. Not to mention when she tried to cook the family jewels in hot milk.

"I'm doing you a favor. You know, I'm a pretty good judge of character. I liked Tess right away. Your brother did well for himself. Anyway, plan to bring the TV girl to family dinner sometime soon."

He really wanted to parade Megan in front of his grandfather while she was still mad enough to spit nails. Maybe the blind date would give them both some breathing space. He didn't even want to think about the next show they'd have to do together.

"Okay, I'll go," he reluctantly agreed.

"Good. I have reservations for the two of you at a nice cozy restaurant. It's my treat."

Zack groaned inwardly. Life just kept getting better and better.

IT WAS Saturday night. Megan was in the shower when the phone rang, but she rushed out in a towel, dripping water on the floor, to check the answering machine. Hope sprang eternal! Maybe her blind date had called to say he was canceling.

"Hi, sweetheart. This is Grandpa. Just wanted to remind you to wear something pretty for your date. You're gonna have a good time tonight."

"Aah!"

Wasn't it enough her grandfather had coaxed and wheedled until she reluctantly agreed to meet his friend's hotshot grandson? Did he have to call to make sure she wouldn't back out? Men! With Jason, Ed and her granddad in her life, she didn't need more aggravation. If she did, there was Bailey waiting in the wings to drive her crazy. She still couldn't believe he'd raced home from work and tried to hide in bed to avoid doing the last show.

She was meeting this latest mystery man at the Kingston in Royal Oak. Her grandfather had even made the reservation. She'd never been there, but he made it sound like a trendy upscale restaurant.

She hadn't allowed much time to dress, on the theory that the last-minute rush would propel her out the door before cold feet paralyzed her.

What to wear? A sack over her head was choice number one, but she grabbed her never-wrinkle little black dress, austere enough for funerals with a boat neck, short cap sleeves and a modest hem only slightly above her knees.

With dangly silver earrings, it gave her an I-didn't-fuss look.

Why didn't her grandfather believe her when she'd told him she was dating someone already? He'd swept aside her objections and insisted she meet tonight's so-called perfect-for-her man. Her only consolation was that her date might be as reluctant as she was. If so, they'd have a quick dinner and go their separate ways.

She hoped!

What did she know about this guy? His grandfather was sort of a stuffed shirt, according to hers. They were golfing cronies because they'd been paired up by chance in a seniors' golf tournament several years ago and had finished in second place. Now they practiced together, hoping for a win some year.

She purposely got to the Kingston a little late, at a few minutes past six. Usually she thought it was rude, but she hoped to get a glimpse of her date while there was still time to run. They were supposed to meet at a table reserved in her grandfather's name. She was surprised they didn't have to wear red carnations or carry blue balloons. It was embarrassing to have a grandfather arranging things for her.

She shuddered when she tried to imagine whom her grandfather called perfect for her. Fat chance of that!

She peered past the maître d's podium, pretty sure she'd recognize her date. He'd be the two-headed, four-clawed, fire-breathing geek sitting alone in the darkest corner. She could depend on her loving grandfather to pick 'em.

There was one consolation. As the price of getting her to this date, Grandad had sworn never to set her up with anyone again.

As if she believed the former king of used car salesmen!

"I have a reservation," she told the officious host. "George Peters."

"Yes, miss." The way he smirked, he must be in on the joke.

He led her through an elegant dining room with white linens, subdued lighting, candles glowing on the tables and gilt mirrors in discreet locations. She glanced nervously in all directions, but the maître d' didn't stop.

Behind the main room, there was a maze of small, intimate rooms with three or four tables each. Most were empty at this unfashionably early hour, probably another part of the grandfather conspiracy—no distractions.

Great! She wouldn't even have the security of a crowded restaurant.

"Your table, miss."

She braced herself for the blind date from hell and saw the profile of a dark-haired man in a navy blazer at the rear of the cozy room.

Oh, no, oh, no…it couldn't be!

It was!

Zack stood and looked as surprised as she felt.

"What are you doing here?" she gasped.

"Your grandfather is the hotshot senior golfer?" he asked.

"Yours is the stuffed shirt?"

"Yep, fits the description," he admitted ruefully.

"What are we going to do?" And why did she feel so panicky?

"Eat dinner," he suggested mildly. "What else?"

She slid onto the chair across from him.

"I'm actually relieved. If you're the prize Marsh has been raving about, it will be easier to get him off my back. He's been pretty skeptical about us. Judging by the shows, he didn't think we were too thrilled with each other."

"Very perceptive of him," she said dryly.

"So, we'll have dinner, give glowing reports on the date and make the old boys happy—for a while."

"The old meddlers! My grandfather sounded too sure of himself when he said you were perfect for me. I should have known—this is his kind of trick."

"It'd serve them right if we left now."

"Maybe we should be cagey about it. Let them think their scheme was brilliant so they'll back off."

"I guess you're right," she reluctantly admitted.

"Of course, we need some ground rules for this so-called date," he said. "Not a word about the fiasco at the Home Stop."

"Amen to that! But it did have a cute finale."

Some women had tried to rip off his T-shirt as she and Zack were leaving the store.

"I especially don't want to hear a word about my *fans*," he said scowling.

"Not from me, you won't." She batted her eyes with fake coquettishness. "But I don't want any more suggestions from you on how the show should be done. Not now, not ever!"

"You had to get in a dig about that. I had in mind going to a real renovation site and doing some actual work."

He looked as annoyed as she felt.

"So this is what we aren't going to discuss. By the way, I'll buy my own dinner."

She hadn't seen the menu, but the trappings shouted big check.

"No need to."

"Yes, I insist."

"Then call your grandfather. The conspirators took care of it in advance."

"That's awful! They are so manipulative, so…"

"Yeah, all that and more. How about we order, enjoy the food, then get out of here?" He turned his attention to the menu.

"Fine."

Her opinion of blind dates dropped a few more notches.

What made her grandfather think she wanted to see Zack socially? He was one cupid who was going to have his wings clipped the next time she saw him.

They started by talking about the weather and ordering shrimp cocktails.

Zack told anecdotes about being a child model, and she had him in stitches telling some of her Little Daisy Girls mishaps.

Her salmon in orange sauce was sinfully delicious, and he ate his stuffed pork chop with relish. He moved on to college exploits, and she made him laugh at Jason's little ploys to get his own way.

"Thanks for not asking any dumb questions," he said.

"Like what?"

Several other couples had been ushered into the small dining room, but it was still a cozy room that encouraged confidences—a great place for a real date. They were waiting for coffee after passing on dessert.

"You know, some women aren't happy unless they're messing with your mind. The twin thing, my father and stepfather, growing up with a tyrant like Marsh—I've come to terms with all of it and don't want to spread it out for anyone's entertainment. I love my life now except for Marsh pressing me to get married."

"That's nice." She was so full she was sleepy.

"Guys hate that psychobabble stuff."

"Women hate replays of football games."

He grinned. "Did I do that?"

"Only in passing."

Their coffee came, and he waited until the server left to reach over and lay his hand on top of hers.

"I have to admit, this wasn't such a bad blind date."

"Best my grandfather has done. You don't even drool."

She lifted her cup and sipped the scalding coffee cautiously as his mellow expression radically changed. His face was easy to read, his brows mobile. His eyes seemed to change color with his mood, and she saw a flash of anger.

"What's wrong?"

"Don't look toward the door," he warned.

"What—"

"Play along with me, okay? The over-the-hill cupids are spying on us. Couldn't be content with meddling from a distance. They had to see the results firsthand."

"They're out there? Both of them?"

"That's my guess. I recognize mine. The other one is wearing a bow tie."

She groaned but concealed it with a fake smile. No one but her grandfather still wore little bow ties he tied himself.

Zack stood, keeping his back to the arched opening.

"Come here," he said in a sexy way that was anything but subtle.

Her eyes darted around the room, but none of the other diners were paying any attention to them.

Against her better judgment she slowly stood and put her hand in his outstretched one. She saw it coming, but his kiss nearly knocked her off her feet. She clutched him to keep her balance and found herself in the circle of his arms, being kissed with tornado force.

Wow! She swallowed hard before he did it again, this

time giving her a chance to kiss him back—well, maybe a little.

"Peek around me and see if they're getting an eyeful."

She did. There were two gray heads standing sentinel like matching gargoyles on either edge of the door.

"Still there." She giggled.

"Let's shock the socks off them," he whispered close to her ear.

"Okay."

He wrapped his arms around her and slid his hands provocatively low, coming to rest at the end of her spine. She tensed, tingled and flushed with embarrassment.

"It's a public place," she mumbled. "They've seen enough."

"Have they?" He was grinning. "Let's give them something to talk about the next time they hit the links. They'll be so busy patting themselves on the back they'll set a club record for hitting the ball out of bounds."

Her ear tickled from his amused whispers.

"You have to fake it!" she insisted. "No more of that—that…"

"Like this?" His lips brushed hers.

"Yes— No—"

How could tiny little kisses make the back of her neck vibrate?

She should stop him, but he was sapping her will to resist. He nibbled her lower lip and pulled her closer.

"No," she moaned, but there wasn't enough conviction in her voice to slow him down.

"You taste better than dessert," he teased, trailing the hard tips of his fingers over her throat.

"Let me see if they're still watching."

Seeing around Zack took some cooperation from him.

"They are." So were a couple of curious diners.

"Sure they are," he said.

He lowered his head and really kissed her—really, really kissed her.

"Enough," she said, trying to catch her breath.

"One more for the road."

As if he knew what button to push, he started rubbing her shoulders and back in a slow, sensual rhythm. She loved a man's hands on her shoulders, and she shuddered with pleasure even before his mouth covered hers. He teased her lips apart with his tongue and kissed her until she saw pinpricks of light inside her closed lids.

"That's really enough!" she said breathlessly.

"Okay, you can finish your coffee now."

"I should think so!"

She had a hard time sounding indignant when every nerve ending in her body was humming with contentment.

They sat again, eyes not meeting, with not much to say.

Zack tried to give their server a gratuity when the man returned, but he adamantly refused.

"It's all taken care of, sir."

"I can afford to buy you dinner," Zack grumbled when the accommodating waiter left. "The business was touch and go for a while, but we have all the work we can handle now. I don't like my grandfather's charity."

She couldn't shake the feeling that this wasn't really happening. Bailey, the bane of her existence, was looking more handsome than he ever had—and on a bad day he was a candidate for hunk of the month on anyone's calendar. It was definitely time to break up the party.

"That should convince them their services are no longer needed," he said.

"I hope they're through matchmaking," she said, standing to leave. "Thank you for the nice dinner."

"Thank you," he said without his habitual irony. "It was my pleasure."

He walked her to the parking lot along a walkway with strings of lights hanging overhead. Her little compact looked like a lost orphan lined up with all the expensive cars and sport utility vehicles, but she never let chrome intimidate her.

"Well, guess I'll see you Wednesday," she said, then instantly regretted ending the evening on a sour note.

"I'll follow you home, make sure you get there okay."

"You don't need to bother."

"No bother. I just had some work done on my Mustang. I'd like to drive it awhile to check it out." He gestured at a car in the next row that was old enough to be collectible.

"No, really, Zack, it's not necessary."

He held her car door while she belted up and started the engine.

"I don't intend to invite myself in," he said. "Just want to make sure you get home all right."

On the way, she tried to shake him. She made turns without signaling, drove slow enough to make any man seethe with impatience and changed lanes wherever there was traffic to block him. He managed to stick like glue even though it was a cloudy, moonless night. When she pulled into her parking slot on the basement level in the back of her building, he was right behind her. Her landlord would love the way Zack's front bumper kissed her back one as though he was trying to crowd into her slot.

"Lousy security in your building," he said, getting out and stretching lazily while she gathered her purse and locked the car.

"Not so bad that I'm not perfectly safe going up to my place alone. Good night, Zack."

"What does your landlord use here, thirty-watt bulbs?"

She started walking toward the door that went past the laundry room, then up two flights to her landing.

"Concrete steps and open iron handrails," he said, giving a litany of the building's shortcomings as he climbed behind her. "This place is a lawsuit waiting to happen."

"Bailey, go home." She turned to block his way.

"You probably think I followed you home for an overnight. Well, sweetheart, you are dead wrong. I just feel responsible for seeing you safely to your door."

"Fine." She ran up the remaining steps and stopped in front of her door, house key protruding between her fingers in the defensive way she'd read about in a woman's magazine.

"You are nervous about this place, but your chance of hurting an intruder with a key is about as good as knocking him over with a feather duster."

He was right, but the smirk on his face annoyed her to no end.

"I'm here. You've been chivalrous and all that. Thank you and good night." She unlocked her door.

"Good night," he said softly.

The way he said it made her turn and look at him. He was grinning, but not in his usual ironic, sardonic manner.

She felt she should say something instead of standing there letting him look at her in that puzzling way.

"I do appreciate your help in getting my grandfather off my case. He's obsessed with finding someone for me to marry," she said.

"And you're not ready?"

"Not yet. I have my career...." She didn't want to go there with the man who was turning "Do It Herself" into the parade-of-the-manly-chest fiasco.

"Think we convinced them?" He smiled broadly and made it hard to remember she hated him.

"I guess."

"Guess? I thought we were pretty convincing! I'll probably get a lecture about what a gentleman does and does not do in a public place."

"Your grandfather would have to admit he was spying on you."

"Then I guess he won't do that."

She stepped inside, and Zack followed.

"It was worth it to demonstrate to my grandfather how dangerous blind dates can be," she said with a light laugh.

"Ours was dangerous?"

"No, but..."

He was standing behind her, and she wasn't surprised when he circled her waist with his arms.

"The door." She had a comical vision of her two elderly neighbors lying on their bellies so they could spy on her through the crack under their door.

He released her to close it.

"I sort of thought you'd be on the other side of it," she said.

"I'll go if you like."

He rubbed her shoulders again. It felt better than sex, although she readily conceded she had yet to reach the pinnacle of success in that field.

"You're tense," he said.

"There's a strange man in my home. Why shouldn't I be tense?"

"We're hardly strangers. You tried to give me a milk bath in my bed."

"You've thrown my show into chaos with your burly muscles and too-tight jeans," she snapped without thinking.

"My jeans are too tight? They feel all right to me."

"Well, they don't look all right."

Why couldn't she keep her mouth shut? He provoked her like no man ever had.

"How did you happen to notice this alleged tightness?"

He was toying with her, and she was torn between sputtering and giggling.

"How about when you bend over. Or when you stick both hands in your pockets so the cloth is pulled tight over... Oh, never mind."

"You're observant." He was smirking. "I thought only men check for panty lines and speculate about hidden treasures."

She was backing up into the still-dark interior of her living room guided by the faint glow of the overhead fixture in the hallway.

"You really look nice tonight," Zack said.

"So do you. I never thought of how you might look in big-boy clothes."

They were buying time, she suspected.

Then his arms closed around her again. He wasn't play-acting now. Neither was she, and it was scary.

He kissed her until the skin around her lips burned and tingled, then their kisses deepened until the back of her neck was throbbing and her legs were wobbly.

Megan thought of protesting when he slowly slid the zipper on the back of her dress down to her waist, but she was too busy. He'd opened the top three buttons on his white dress shirt when he left his tie in the car. The thatch of dark hair that had escaped was silky against her chin, and she slowly unbuttoned his shirt some more to snuggle her cheek against his warm chest.

His hands were on her bare shoulders, caressing until she quivered.

There was something she should consider, she knew, but too much was going on. He unhooked her bra and took the weight of her breasts in his hands, teasing her nipples into hard, pulsating knobs.

"Touch me," he murmured, trailing his lips over her lids, down her cheek to her lips again, increasing the pressure of his fingers on her breasts until she was dizzy with pleasure.

He was erect and hard against the side of her thigh, and she had to struggle for a reason not to satisfy her curiosity. It had to be curiosity. She couldn't possibly want Zack to make love to her. It would complicate her life beyond belief. She wasn't a great actress. She couldn't endure doing another show with him if she knew how he looked naked. Her eyes would give her away. She might look at him *that way*.

And he'd be unbearable if he thought he could seduce her any time he liked. She wanted a real love affair someday, but not before she reached her career goals—to move to a bigger market and a better show.

Her dress had fallen to the floor, and Zack's calloused palm rasped slightly against the nylon of her panty hose.

"We shouldn't be doing this, should we?" she asked with a noticeable lack of conviction as his fingers caressed her thigh, then pressed insistently where she needed him.

"It's the dumbest thing I've done since Cole talked me into doing your show."

"We'll hate ourselves in the morning."

"Probably." His voice was low and husky.

She touched him through his trousers and wondered if he ached as much as she did.

"We don't even like each other." She was arguing with herself, not him.

"You're the most annoying female I've ever met."

"You're bossy, overbearing, rude, inconsiderate...."

"I'd rather roll naked in the snow than do your show."

"You've turned it into a male strip show for the bored and the brainless."

"Who do you think watches your shtick? Brain surgeons and corporate lawyers?"

"I used to have a good show!"

She wiggled away from the hand trying to roll down her panty hose and pushed at his chest for leverage to get to her feet. She didn't even remember sitting on the couch!

"This was a lousy idea," he growled, standing up.

"It certainly wasn't mine! You're the one with all the bright ideas."

He was buttoning his shirt and trying to stuff the tail under his waistband.

"You're a walking cold shower, Danbury."

"You weren't invited here!"

"No? If wiggling your butt all the way up the stairs wasn't an invitation, I've never seen one."

"Like I need a big macho man following me home!"

"You don't know how to let a man treat you well."

"I suppose you're an expert on what women want!"

"I damn well know you wanted this a few minutes ago!"

He ground her lips with a rough kiss that was more excitement than she could handle at the moment. She opened her mouth to tell him where to go—and he was gone.

9

She was suffering from an overdose of Zack Bailey, and the only antidote was a long heart-to-heart with her best friend, Andrea Byrne, whom she hadn't seen in forever. They already had plans for lunch on Sunday, the day after her bizarre blind date with Zack. When the phone rang a little before noon that day, she hoped Andrea wasn't canceling.

"This is me, live and in person," she said, expecting it to be her friend.

"Naw, must be a machine," a familiar male voice said. "The real Megan Danbury always snarls at me."

"Why are you calling, Zack?"

She wanted to talk about him, not to him.

"My grandfather was so impressed by our performance, he wants us to come to his place for dinner tonight."

"Did he admit to spying on us?"

"Marsh confess? No way. He claimed the two matchmakers just wanted to surprise us with a nice evening out. Didn't even bother denying they'd thought we needed a push."

"Well, tell him no, thank you. He's done enough manipulating...."

She picked up a pen and pad lying beside the phone and started making a list, something she always did when she was agitated.

"You're forgetting our deal," he reminded her. "I showed up at the Home Stop. Now it's your turn to come through for me."

"How do you expect to fool him? He'll expect a lovey-dovey couple. That is not us!"

She'd started listing all the reasons she couldn't stand him on the little pad. One page wasn't enough for all of them.

"Just smile and look pretty. It's not as hard as fending off a mob of shirt-grabbing souvenir hunters."

She added *sarcastic* to her list.

"I don't want to go."

"Neither do I. I'll pick you up at five-fifteen. He never gives up, so we might as well get it over with."

She'd just written *fantastic buns*. She blacked it out.

"Okay, but only because we made a deal. This is stupid, you know."

"Agreed." He hung up without a goodbye.

She ripped the list into tiny pieces and dropped them in the wastebasket.

Andrea was waiting at Olivia's Garden Café when Megan got there. The restaurant was busy, but most people came in larger groups on Sunday noon, so they got a table for two fairly quickly.

"This was a great idea," Andrea said when they were seated. "I've been dying to hear about the guy on your show. I watched the last tape four times. Where did you find him?"

Not you, too, Megan wanted to say, but instead she smiled weakly.

"Ed met him when Bailey Construction did some renovations for a friend. It was a few years ago."

"Does he look as good in person as he does on TV?"

Megan sighed and looked at her best friend since high

school. Andrea was six inches taller than she with dark brown hair and eyes, and in most ways they were as different as night and day. They'd never liked the same boys in high school.

She couldn't possibly tell Andrea how she felt about Zack when her friend was raving like one of his fans.

"What are you going to have?" Megan asked, picking up a menu.

What was there to say about Bailey, anyway? He was maddening, and she didn't want to feel the way she did about him. The *L* word was floating around in her head, but absolutely nothing could come of it. Look at the extreme measures he was taking to avoid matrimony. She'd be crazy to hope he'd ever commit himself.

She wasn't quite thirty—yet. Once she met her career goals, there would be plenty of time to find Mr. Right. He had to love kids and want a family of his own, which certainly eliminated Bailey.

"Earth to Megan. Have you tried the crab salad croissant?" Andrea asked.

"Sorry, no, I haven't. Sounds good, though."

She smiled at her friend and turned the conversation to less sensitive subjects. Much as she cherished her friendship with Andrea, Megan realized she wasn't ready to confide in her or anyone else about Zack. Instead she had to find a way to exorcise him from her system.

They lingered over lunch until Andrea had to leave to play tennis with her current not-too-serious boyfriend. The rest of the afternoon Megan tried to keep busy with little jobs around her apartment. Mostly she tried on clothes, trying to decide what a girlfriend of Zack's would wear to dinner at his grandfather's.

At five-fourteen she was dressed in black Capri pants with black flats and an off-the-shoulder ruffled blouse. She took a final look in the full-length mirror on the bedroom door. What was she thinking? She looked like a Swiss milkmaid!

The door buzzer sounded promptly at five-fifteen as she grabbed a knee-length muted blue T-shirt dress. She was still shimmying into it as she opened the door.

"New look?" he asked, tweaking the tag sticking out the front of her neckline.

She grimaced. The darn dress was on backward.

"Wait here!" she said.

"You can count on it."

This dress was too clingy for a command appearance at his grandfather's house. She stripped it off, tossed it on the bed with the milkmaid costume—something she never did—and settled on a flowery ivory sundress with wide straps and a hemline that fluttered just above her ankles.

"Ready?" he asked when she reappeared.

"I guess. Do you think it will rain before we get back? Maybe I should take an umbrella." She opened the door of her coat closet.

"Never mind. Let's get this over with," he grumbled.

He led her out to his vintage Mustang, the forest-green paint gleaming from a heavy wax job.

The car looked better than it sounded. She wasn't at all sure it would start, but the motor sputtered to life.

"We could take my car," she suggested.

"I just put seven hundred dollars under the hood, and it can darn well get us to Bloomfield Hills."

"Maybe you need gas," she suggested mildly when the car bulked and bumped its way up a ramp to the freeway.

"The gas gauge is goofy—another thing to fix," he complained. "I should have plenty left."

"Isn't this car a little old for city driving?"

"I love this car."

"Oh, dear."

They were losing speed, and Zack pulled onto the shoulder just as the motor conked out completely.

"Are you out of gas?"

"Don't see how I can be," he said none too happily. "I filled it up...."

"When?"

"Maybe two weeks ago," he admitted crossly.

"You should have stopped for gas!"

"I intended to, but you fussed around changing your clothes. Marsh is a bear about being late. I'll hike down the ramp. There's a service station not far from where we got on."

Big drops of rain splattered on the windshield. A semi roared past, making the car shake.

"First I'd better call Marsh and tell him we'll be late," he said unhappily, picking up his cell phone.

"There's nothing like a nice sprint in the rain," she said, looking at the heavy gray cloud cover over the city.

Heavy drops pelted the roof of the car, and another semi passed, practically sucking the Mustang into its wake.

"I'm not sitting here in this tin can while you walk all the way to a station," she said. "It's barely off the pavement."

Zack connected with his grandfather and ignored her protest. The rain got heavier as he talked, obscuring everything outside the windows.

He hung up the phone and tried the motor again, which, of course, only gave him a mechanical raspberry.

"If you have a better plan, I'd really like to hear it," she said.

"I'll call a tow truck." He reached across her knees

and opened the glove compartment. "I have an auto-club directory here."

"Have you ever thought of trading this for a car that runs?"

She was feeling really, really irritable. The windows were so fogged up she couldn't see the ravine on her side of the car, but she knew it was deep and muddy.

"No, I don't know what's wrong with it," Zack was saying into the cell phone, "but I'm sure we need a tow. Shouldn't be long," he said after he turned off the phone.

"Fine."

The car shook as another monster truck threw oily water against the exposed side of the Mustang.

She shivered. The rain was cooling the interior of the car, but darned if she'd mention how nice a warm arm around her shoulders would feel.

"What did your grandfather say?" she asked over the roar of another truck.

"Get a better car."

Wrong answer!

The windows were steamed, and she couldn't resist drawing a tictacktoe game on the windshield with the tip of her finger.

"X or O?" she asked.

"X."

He put his mark in the center square. There went any chance she had of winning. The game ended in a tie, and she wiped her wet finger on a tissue in her purse.

"Breath mint?" she asked, holding out a little plastic container.

"Will I need one?"

"I was only being polite." She dropped a couple of little candies onto his outstretched palm. "This isn't much of an entertainment center you have here."

"We could count trucks or bet on the water drops running down the windshield," he suggested with a crooked grin.

"Too exciting for me," she said dryly.

"What is your idea of fun?"

He touched her cheek with the back of one finger, trailing it under her chin to the other cheek.

"That tickles." She hunched her shoulders against the shiver that ran through them.

"No, it doesn't. This does."

He leaned close and nuzzled her ear, his warm breath making her giggle.

"Pretty dress." He fingered the gauzy material of her shoulder strap. "Worth the wait."

"How long before the tow truck gets here?" she asked, torn between wanting to distract him and wishing he would kiss her.

"Hard telling."

"Those trucks are making me nervous."

Another zoomed by, and she could imagine the car toppling down the ravine.

"Are you sure it's the trucks making you nervous?" He tickled the tip of her nose with his fingertip.

"What else?" She tried for levity, but it fell flat.

"I think you're afraid I'm going to kiss you."

"Are you?" She was embarrassed by a little spark of hope.

"Almost certainly."

He cupped her chin in one hand and ran a finger from one corner of her lips to the other, slightly parting them.

"The only question is when," he teased.

"Stop, Zack." She said the words but couldn't muster any real resistance.

"Not part of our deal, I know," he said so softly his

voice hummed in her ears. "But that which is not expressly forbidden is an implied privilege."

"Do you know what you just said?"

"No, I was hoping you would," he teased.

His lips were only a fraction of an inch from hers. She dropped her lids expectantly, but bright lights made her jerk them open.

"Tow truck," Zack said. "Stay here."

He got out on the highway side and sprinted to the cab of the rescue vehicle. Megan peered through the foggy windshield but couldn't see much except flashing yellow dome lights and red taillights.

Zack seemed to be out there forever, but it was probably only a few minutes. When he came back and opened the passenger door, his hair was plastered to his head and rain was streaming down his face.

"He'll tow the car to the service station. We'll have to hope I'm only out of gas. Come on."

She looked beyond him at the rain beating down on the muddy shoulder.

"We have to ride in the cab of the truck," he explained.

"I know that." Knowing was not doing. She couldn't have picked a worse dress for a deluge. "I should have brought my umbrella."

She thought longingly of her mock tiger-skin umbrella with jungle cats silhouetted around the edge.

"Wouldn't help. The rain's blowing too much. Let's go."

He grabbed her hand and pulled her out of the car, putting his hand between her and the top of the door frame so she wouldn't conk her head. Her foot landed on the ground with a splash, and they ran for the shelter of the tow truck. She was so glad to get inside, she almost ignored where Zack's hand lingered while boosting her up.

Almost! She'd add his wandering fingers to her long list of grievances when she recovered from his idea of a waiting-in-the-car-in-a-rainstorm game.

Their clothes looked as if they'd been pulled out of the washer before the spin cycle. Her hair was streaming even more than his, and her platform shoes squished when the truck let them off by a service island at the gas station. While Zack took care of pumping gas, she dashed inside to the ladies' room where she stared at a drowned rat in a murky mirror. Only she was the water-soaked rodent, and there was no way she could go to Marsh Bailey's house even if the Mustang could get them there.

She combed her hair until it stopped dripping and met Zack, who was coming in to pay.

"I'm soaked."

"No kidding?"

His knit top was so wet it was plastered to his torso like wallpaper. The way his wet khakis stuck to him made his usual tight jeans seem baggy.

"I can't possibly go to your grandfather's."

"I'll call him as soon as I pay for the gas, then take you home to change. By the way, the car started. I've got to get a new gas gauge."

"What wonderful foresight."

She stood with her back to a tall rack of chips and snacks, hoping her panties didn't show through the skirt clinging to her rear. She kept her arms crossed over her soaked front and watched Zack pay.

After she ran to the car, she needed wringing out again. Zack made his call. It was short and cryptic.

"He'll put our dinner on hold. After you change, we should be able to get there by the time they're having dessert," he said.

"Why not just cancel? You're soaked, too."

"I'll dry." He slicked back his hair, and water droplets ran down the back of his neck. "Or maybe you have a clothes dryer?" he asked hopefully. "Anyway, my mother is there, too, and Cole and Tess."

She wanted to cry. How could she meet his whole family under false pretenses? The rain had washed away the last of her self-confidence, and she wanted to go home and hide under the covers.

The rain was still coming down in droves when they pulled up close to her car in the shelter of her apartment's parking lot. She was shivering, and her air conditioner was still running when they went inside. She shut it off with Zack hovering right behind her.

Teeth chattering, she directed him to the bathroom while she peeled off her wet clothes in the bedroom.

She came out in her terry-cloth robe to find Zack, bath towel around his waist, tossing his pile of wet clothes into the apartment-size dryer she'd bought to save time waiting for the communal one in the basement. He'd toweled dry, and his chest hair stood up in curly little whorls. She tried not to look.

"I'm going to take a hot shower while your clothes dry," she said. "Help yourself to...whatever."

"Want company?"

She'd never heard two words with so much invitation in them.

Her mouth went dry. Her brain went on hiatus. Of course, she wanted him to join her, but it was such a bad, bad, bad idea.

"You know," he said, stepping so close she could see where every hair was rooted to his golden-bronze chest, "if we did what we're both thinking of doing, maybe we could get it out of the way and not be so stressed about it."

"I'm not thinking...."

That was true. She was all sensation with no sensible thoughts to put on the brakes.

"These aren't bedroom eyes?" He took her in his arms and lightly kissed her lids. "Aren't you just a tiny bit curious how we'd be together?"

"No! Anyway, I'm not prepared."

"Glove compartments are handy things. I found just what we need stuck in the auto-club directory."

"You drive around with..."

"They're vintage like the Mustang, but thanks to the miracle of foil..."

"I don't want to know. Anyway, it isn't something you get out of the way!"

"No, it's the natural thing when two people are attracted to each other."

"I'm not attracted to you!" It was her all-time biggest lie.

"I'm not suggesting you like me, only that you want me as much as I want you."

"In your dreams." She was shivering from her lips to her knees and trying not to let him see. "It's not my problem if you're..."

"It's crossed my mind we might be dynamite together away from the cameras."

He loosened the tie on her robe and let it hang from the loops on either side. She took a little half step toward him and let her treacherous heart direct her into his arms.

He put his hands under her robe, encircled her waist and drew her against him, soft breasts against firm chest.

They kissed until warmth flowed through her like steam heat, and she knew they had passed the point of no return.

"You need a warm shower," he whispered close to her ear.

"Yes."

"With me."

"Yes."

She needed him. He was as wrong for her as any man could be, but for once in her life, she was going to do something not on her list, not part of her agenda, not one of her goals.

She slipped her hand into Zack's and led him to the shower. To think she'd once regretted not having a tub instead of the roomy tiled stall.

He helped her out of the robe, and she couldn't quite believe she was standing in front of him with nothing on. The shock of her nakedness passed quickly, though, when he dropped the towel and stepped into the stall to turn on the water.

Her heart was going to shatter into a million zillion broken fragments if she did this. She loved him. It was terrible but true, terrible because he didn't even pretend to love her. But if she ever wanted to be with Zack, really with him, this moment might never come again.

She stepped under the cascade of warm water and into his arms, hardly noticing when he closed the door behind her.

He reached beyond her to the hanging rack of shampoo and soap and pressed the pump on her shower scrub until his hands were enveloped in suds. Knowing what he was going to do didn't make it any less pleasurable. He lathered her shoulders and throat and did each arm in turn with leisurely caresses, stopping to fill his hands with more bubbles.

"No," she said, giggling when he made soapy whirls on her breasts and tummy, then lathered her back and bottom until she felt slippery and silly and very, very sexy.

He was hard—oh, my, was he—and his breath came in rasps, but her pleasure was only beginning. He shampooed her hair, covering her eyes with one palm to protect them from the sudsy water streaming down her face, then knelt and lathered her legs. Picking up first one foot, then the other, he separated each toe and caressed while pleasure flowed through her.

"Your turn," he said with a sheepish grin, even more endearing because he looked goofy with happiness.

She'd never washed a man, never even thought of how to go about it. She loved running her fingers over the whorls in his ears and outlining the sometimes fierce line of his brows. Filling her hands with tendrils of his hair was so erotic she pressed against him, parted her thighs, then shut them tight against his male hardness.

He moaned and kissed her, then took and emptied the last of the nearly depleted bottle of shower scrub into her palm.

"You're nowhere near done," he said.

"I couldn't…"

She did, soaping in places her hand had never gone before. Was there anything as nice as round, firm, deeply cleft buns? She tickled his tailbone with a soapy nail and let the shower rinse away the lather.

"This is where I beg for mercy," he softly teased, reaching up and shutting off the water.

He found a towel on the rack and gently rubbed her dry, combing her long wet hair with his fingers. She vigorously rubbed his chest and back, then grew more shy and cautious until he impatiently took the towel and dried his legs.

"We still have to go to your grandfather's," she reluctantly reminded him.

He lifted her in his arms, cradling her against his chest for the few steps it took to reach her bed.

She had an instant of embarrassment at the array of discarded outfits on the bedspread, but he peeled it away, clothes and all, before lowering her to the bed.

The sheets were cool on her back, but when he hovered over her, she scarcely noticed.

"No second thoughts?" he asked softly.

Plenty! But she wanted him so badly it wasn't a choice anymore.

"You're always trying to tell me how to do things," she said. "This is your show—for now."

"Whatever you're expecting, darlin', I want you to be very, very happy."

"I'm ready...."

"You just think you are."

"Oh."

"Tell me what you like," he said, lowering his head to nuzzle her throat and breasts. "Or don't like."

She didn't have an agenda for something like this. She didn't have a clue how to answer him. As if she weren't speechless already, he took one nipple into his mouth and gently suckled while his hand explored the contours of her torso. Wherever he touched, she tingled, and when he parted her thighs, she covered his hand and pushed it harder against her.

He was strong in ways that had nothing to do with hard muscles. He kissed her inner elbow, the back of her wrist, the crease between her torso and thigh. He was breathing hard, but his lovemaking was leisurely even when she touched him, then stroked him with increasing urgency but some trepidation.

"Relax," he crooned, his lips as soothing as his words.

He moistened his finger on her tongue and slid it gently

into her, caressing until she throbbed and urgently guided him toward her.

She was afraid, not of Zack, not of what they were doing, but because she might disappoint him.

"Easy, easy," he murmured as if picking up on her apprehension. "You're wonderful, wonderful."

She opened her eyes and saw his face softened by passion, all the arrogance gone, so lovable she felt tears well in her eyes.

"Not yet, please not yet."

She didn't know whether he was talking to himself or her, but she was melting, clutching Zack's back to stay grounded.

He rose above her, his face a granite mask, plunged deep in a compelling rhythm and continued until she lost herself in the most amazing way.

"Oh, Megan!" He shuddered and held her close.

This was how it was supposed to be. She went limp and hugged him against her.

"That was so good," he said, softly kissing her swollen lips.

This was the first time she didn't hate him for being right.

"You are incredibly beautiful," he said.

Her hair was a damp tangle on the pillow, and if she was as flushed as she felt, she must be flamingo-pink from her forehead to the soles of her feet. If Zack noticed, it didn't seem to matter. She was so content nothing mattered but the man beside her.

"Come here," he said, pulling her into his arms again.

She snuggled closer.

"I like the second time best," he whispered close to her ear. "No hurrying and lots of cuddling."

Much later, when the room was the murky gray of dusk, he turned over on his tummy.

She was sitting cross-legged beside him, so happy she believed for the first time it was possible to levitate. How could this be? Why did she feel wonderful enough to float above the clouds? She'd met no goals and accomplished nothing. Zack hadn't committed himself to anything but a good time—a very, very good time. Yet she was sure she could soar to the ceiling and fly without wings.

"Bailey, are you going to sleep?" She switched on the lamp beside the bed and saw yellow eyes leering at her.

"What on earth?" She leaned over him. "A cat tattoo!"

"Panther," he lazily drawled. "And that is one dangerous feline, sweetheart."

"When did you have it done?"

She ran her finger over the dark head that would've seemed sinister if it hadn't been staring at her from his round, cute buttock.

"When I was young, foolish and more than a little drunk." He propped himself on one elbow and grinned sheepishly.

"Did it hurt?"

"Let's say it wasn't especially pleasant, not to mention lying bare ass up on a hard table while my buddies watched and commented wasn't a treat."

"I love it." She tweaked the inky beast's nose and laughed. "It's adorable."

"I did it just for you."

"You didn't even know me then."

"Do I know you now?"

He sprang up suddenly and toppled her down beside him, kissing her lightly and teasing her toes with his.

"Shouldn't you call your grandfather again?" she reluctantly asked.

"And say what?"

"Sorry?" she suggested mildly.

He looked at her bedside clock, the luminous letters showing just how late they were.

"After nine. Sounds like it's stopped raining."

"You can blame it on the car."

"Tell my grandfather I ran out of gas because the gauge isn't working in a car he's told me to get rid of dozens of times?"

"You could make up an excuse."

"Haven't I made up enough already?" He sounded soul weary, not physically tired from his recent exertions. "Marsh thinks we're serious. How long do you think we can pull this off? Life has gotten darn complicated lately."

"I'm still uncomfortable about not showing up. Your family…"

"Will get over it."

"Your grandfather has a right to be mad if you don't even call."

"His being mad is nothing new." He sat up and moved to the edge of the bed, his back to her. "If he knew we were doing this, he'd be elated."

"You won't tell him?" She couldn't imagine anything more embarrassing.

"It's something couples do," he said, walking to the window and looking out the side of the plastic-slatted blind. "Nothing to be ashamed of."

"But using it as an excuse to your grandfather!"

"Don't sound so upset. We had fun, didn't we?"

"Fun?" Suddenly, she felt incredibly let down.

"You don't need to worry. I won't give my grandfather

a blow by blow, much as I'd like to see him green with envy that I was with such a beautiful woman. Next time I hear from him—and it's sure to be soon—I'll mention we came back to your place because your dress was wet, and we got distracted. It will only confirm we're serious about each other.''

"Well, we won't get distracted again."

She said it as a fact, not an ultimatum. Zack hadn't wanted to go to his grandfather's, so he'd found something else to do. Why had she thought it was as special to him as it was to her? She felt humiliated by her earlier enthusiasm.

"I guess not," he agreed in a flat tone. "Think I'll go. My clothes should be dry."

"Yeah, dry."

"I'll see you Wednesday at the studio. What are we doing for next week's show? I haven't gotten my copy of the script yet."

"I don't remember," she lied, wanting him to leave— immediately.

She didn't even expect him to make the one obligatory after-sex phone call.

He walked out of the bedroom. The panther leered at her with evil yellow eyes, and she sat motionless until her apartment door closed after him.

10

MEGAN DIDN'T HAVE any of her usual enthusiasm when she went to work the morning after the night that shouldn't have been. Usually she liked Monday—a new beginning, a fresh start, a new list of things to accomplish. Not today.

Trouble was, she'd had the best encounter imaginable with the worst possible man. It would be funny if it didn't hurt so darn much. She never should have allowed herself to become involved with a man who thought marriage was a prison sentence. She wanted a forever relationship, one that would nourish a family. Zack was the exact opposite of the man she wanted.

"Megan, I've been waiting for you!"

Ed charged at her in the lobby of the station. She braced herself for bad news but not for the big bear hug that nearly knocked her off her feet.

"Have I got good news for you!" he said.

"What?"

"In my office."

He hadn't moved this fast since the University of Michigan clobbered Michigan State in his senior year.

"Shut the door," he said.

"What's up?" She couldn't help remembering some of his other brilliant ideas—bringing Bailey on the show, delivering flowers to the construction site...

"The Good Living Network is scouting the show Wednesday."

She looked at him blankly.

"They're sending a couple of people to watch the taping," he said.

"Why—how?"

"I sent them tapes of a couple of shows. You'll never be in a better position to move up. Local sponsors are clamoring to buy airtime on 'Do It Herself.' Mr. G. is thrilled, and our ratings have soared."

"You did that for me? What about your job?"

He shuffled uncomfortably. She'd caught him being nice.

"Hey, I would miss producing your show. We're a good team. But they'll find something else for me here now that I've produced a hit."

He grinned, and this time she hugged him.

"Georgia doesn't know how lucky she is."

"I'll tell her you said so. Now about today's episode…"

The Good Living Network was coming to see her show. She couldn't believe fulfilling her number one goal was a real possibility. She'd go over Wednesday's script and make sure every detail was perfect. Taking "Do It Herself" to a national cable network was a dream come true if it happened.

She went to her office and concentrated on the day's show, but she was too excited to stay focused. Maybe at last her career would go into high gear and she could think about her other plans—meeting and marrying Mr. Right and having children.

Unfortunately Bailey was hanging around in her head,

coloring everything she did and dulling her happiness at the prospect of going big-time.

She shouldn't waste time thinking about him. Sure, he was Mr. Too Sexy To Believe, but she wanted a guy who'd wake up beside her the rest of her life. Zack made it clear that wasn't him. He was willing—make that eager—to give away his share of a big company to avoid getting married. As a prospective husband, he ranked below a thrice-married loser with six kids and no job.

Julie came with program notes for the day's taping, and Megan forced herself to pay attention to the problems at hand. The intern was wearing a dark green shirt, which Megan hoped signified a slight lightening of Julie's tragic mood. She mentioned Brad about a dozen times, making Megan think she was over her crush and was now interested in her fellow intern.

Heck, if the Goth intern could recover, Megan could get over Bailey. He wasn't the only sexy hunk in the world, just the only one she loved.

Julie left, and Megan was headed toward her dressing room for makeup when she nearly collided with the person she least wanted to see.

"Zack, what are you doing here?"

"I need to talk to you."

He took her elbow and ushered her into the dressing room, closing the door behind them.

The little cubicle had never seemed smaller, and she didn't want any one-on-one with this man.

"I have to get ready for the taping," she said.

"You have plenty of time."

"Not for you, I don't."

"Don't worry." He raised both hands in a theatrical gesture that only annoyed her. "I won't touch you."

"You certainly won't."

She was backed against the dressing table and honest enough to know he wasn't the one she didn't trust.

"I'm sorry I left so…"

"Abruptly?"

"You were fantastic. Running off had nothing to do with you."

"I really don't want to talk about it."

"Anyway, I wondered if you'll marry me."

"What!"

"I put that badly. Would you consider pretending to get engaged?"

"Isn't that rushing it a bit?"

She knew this was only another ploy to hold off his grandfather, so why could she feel the pulse pounding in her throat?

"I guess it doesn't matter," she said, trying to sound matter-of-fact and uninvolved. "It's nothing but a big farce."

He shifted from one foot to the other. Was it possible Zack was uncomfortable? She'd never met anyone as much at home with who he was, but he was definitely fidgeting.

"Yesterday wasn't about fooling my grandfather," he replied, still sounding unsure of himself.

Or maybe he was using his dubious charm to con her deeper into this charade.

"Was he mad we missed dinner?"

"Yes and no."

"What does that mean?"

"About the dinner, no. But he isn't sure we're an item."

She knew it! Once again, all of this had to do with his stupid plan.

"He saw us at the restaurant."

"Yeah, but—well, I've had a few girlfriends in the past."

"A few?"

"A lot, okay?"

"I still don't see…"

"Just because he thinks we slept together doesn't mean he believes I'm going to set up permanent housekeeping with you."

"I understand," she said glumly. "Marsh doesn't doubt the sexual attraction, but he doesn't buy the commitment part."

"You make it sound pretty cold."

She didn't want to have this conversation.

"I have to get ready for the show. By the way, someone is coming from the Good Living Network Wednesday. Please try to behave."

"You don't understand about Marsh. He thinks you're too classy for me. He doesn't believe you even like me."

"Your grandfather is very perceptive."

"All I'm asking you to do is go to dinner at his house Friday evening. Meet my mom, charm the old boy. I have my fingers crossed Cole will be in the daddy business pretty soon. Believe me, Marsh wants a great-grandchild a whole lot more than he wants me to get married. Even a tentative engagement will keep him from bugging me about meeting his friends' granddaughters."

"What about your mother? Is it fair to let her think we're going to get married?"

"She'll get over losing a prospective daughter-in-law once there's a grandchild on the way."

"I'm glad I'm easily disposable."

He was dressed for work—scruffy boots, tight jeans and a black faded T-shirt. She ached to snuggle against him, but it wasn't going to happen, not ever.

"I'm sorry I started this," he said in a gruff voice, "but Marsh was driving me crazy. Since Cole got married, he won't give me breathing space. I've kept my part of the deal with the show, haven't I?"

She couldn't deny it even though he rarely did things her way. Her dilemma was she needed him for the Wednesday taping. She didn't have time to script a whole new show eliminating his part. Worse, the audience loved their on-air friction. The show might fall flat without him, and her chance of moving to a cable network would be lost.

"If I go along with you, will you cooperate on Wednesday's show?"

"I'll be on my best behavior," he said solemnly.

"No playing sick?"

"I'm not proud of that."

"No grandstanding?"

"What do you mean by that?"

"You know."

He didn't argue.

"You help me. I'll do all I can to impress the cable guys," he said.

"No! Don't impress them! Just follow the script. They're not here to scout you."

"There's not enough money in the world to get me to make a career in the glamorous world of TV." He sounded grim.

"All right, I'll marry you," she said, not trying to hide her skepticism.

"Great. Shake on it."

He held out his big hand, and she touched it lightly, pulling hers away before he could engulf it.

One more show, one more date, and she could seriously start getting him out of her system.

By FRIDAY Zack was pretty sure it would be safer to take a jungle cat from the Detroit Zoo to Marsh's house than spend the evening passing Megan off as the love of his life.

What the devil was love, anyway? He loved pro football, downhill skiing and good sex, not necessarily in that order. Megan had messed up his head so much in the past few weeks he'd rather fight with her than not see her for a day. If that was love, it was scary.

Cole called a few minutes before Zack had to leave.

"Sorry, we can't make it tonight," his brother said. "Tess isn't feeling so hot."

Zack chose to take that as a good sign. Pregnant women were notoriously unwell, weren't they?

"Any special reason?" he asked.

"Not sure yet."

"Well, sorry you won't be there."

"I think you've got a winner there," Cole said.

"Megan?"

"You could do a lot worse."

"Forget it. You're the marrying one in the family."

"I didn't think so until I fell for Tess."

That wasn't what Zack wanted to hear from his twin, but he couldn't expect much support from him. Marriage had changed Cole. He refused to acknowledge that Zack was their father's son, a man who should never risk hurting someone he cared about by marrying her. Especially not a woman who wanted stability and kids. For all he knew, he didn't have a paternal gene in his body.

HE PICKED HER UP fifteen minutes early with a full tank of gas. She was ready, and he couldn't fault her meet-the-family outfit. The dress was navy linen with big white buttons down the front, short but not too short. The little sleeves left most of her arms bare, and he liked that. She had gorgeous arms, not an ounce of loose flesh, and skin so smooth and flawless it hardly seemed real. Her legs were sleek and shapely in white hose that would make most women's look heavy.

"You look nice," he offered.

"Thank you."

There was frost in her attitude, and he could only hope she'd warm up by the time they got to Marsh's.

They talked about the weather as they drove to Bloomfield Hills, which was like not talking at all, as far as he was concerned.

As a kid he'd always been embarrassed when a friend saw the house where he lived for the first time. It had all the trappings of the good life—circular drive, Tudor facade, carefully manicured greenery, a garden with lacy iron furniture and an indoor domed pool with paneled walls that were removed to let fresh air circulate in the summer. It was as pretentious as his grandfather.

Megan didn't make a fuss over the place. In fact, she didn't seem to take much notice of it.

"Did your grandfather watch the show we taped Wednesday?" she asked as he stopped the car in the drive.

"'Fraid so."

"Great! He's more likely to believe I've hired a hit man to take you out than that I agreed to marry you."

"The audience loved that show," he said defensively.

"They loved seeing you staple the hem of my skirt."

"I've already apologized. It's not my fault you had me using such a cheap staple gun."

"You knew the Good Living Network people were watching. You were playing up to your dopey fans instead of paying attention to the job."

"I warned you not to get in the way when I was working."

"Well, you owe me a skirt. You shredded the hem getting the staple out."

"I could have done better if you'd taken it off." That was sure to rile her, but he didn't care.

"You're the only stripper on my show."

"Will you please stop complaining and act like you're in love with me?"

"If I could act that well, I'd set my sights on a movie career."

He walked around and opened the car door for her, knowing full well Marsh was probably watching from a front window.

"At least don't act like you hate me," he said. "I didn't purposely mess up your show."

Marsh answered the door with Zack's mother hovering a discreet distance away.

"This is Megan Danbury," Zack said.

"It's a pleasure to meet you, Megan. Your grandfather and I are teaming up for several seniors' tournaments this year."

"He does love his golf."

Zack gave her an A-plus for the smile, but then, Marsh had a way with women—or thought he did.

"Mom, this is Megan," he said, guiding her through the arched entryway to a huge living room crowded with period furniture and Marsh's glass, ceramic and art collections, which had the makings of a whole museum wing if the old man could find a taker.

Zack could count on his mother. She was gracious and natural at the same time, maybe the reason her sons weren't stuffed-shirt snobs like Marsh.

They followed the Bailey predinner ritual—sherry, small talk and a lecture on one of Marsh's current pet peeves. This evening the topic was unsafe toys. He was mad because a pull toy he'd designed had run into pre-production safety problems just as Sue had warned him it would. She was so good at her job, it was worth this charade to make sure she could keep it.

Dinner was the usual, as they were served Cornish hens with wild rice and a vegetable medley. Marsh's longtime cook was a doll, even allowing him to bully her into wearing a black dress and a frilly white apron to serve the meal. Everyone in the family knew she ruled the kitchen and controlled the old man's heart diet with an iron hand.

Sue carried the conversation, maybe to shield Megan from the grand inquisitor at the head of the long formal dining table. She and Megan really hit if off, but then, Sue adored Tess, too. Maybe she regretted not having a daughter. Zack and Cole had given her a hard time when they were younger, beginning with their rebellion against being catalog models for Bailey Baby Products. Nick was no angel, either, never mind that he was a half brother. They weren't exactly the best influences as older siblings.

Throughout the meal Zack threw in an occasional "darlin''' and ''sweetheart'' to demonstrate what a lovely-dovey couple they were. Megan tolerated it, but when he squeezed her knee under the table, she pried off his fingers and gave him an evil look.

He'd better drop the bombshell before she blew the plan.

''Megan and I have a surprise for you,'' he said with saccharine sweetness. ''She's consented to be my wife.''

Smile, dammit, Megan! It was the least she could do after he'd grinned like a trained chimp all the way through her big audition tape for those cable people. The skirt thing was her fault. The woman should know better than to distract a man who was holding a staple gun by bending over.

''Of course, it will have to be a long engagement,'' she said.

''Career is very important to Megan,'' he said. ''She had a national cable network looking at her in the last show.''

''Was stapling her skirt in the script?'' Marsh asked.

''Of course, it was,'' Megan lied.

Was she covering for him for a reason?

''I thought maybe you two were having a little spat on camera,'' Marsh said.

''That's our show-business persona,'' Zack said.

If Marsh bought that, he had some nice land to sell him—at the bottom of the Detroit River.

''Well, I couldn't be more pleasantly surprised,'' Marsh said, standing and walking to Megan.

He took her hand, gave it a squeeze and bent to plant a kiss on her cheek. He might not believe them, but apparently he'd decided to play along and see what happened.

Zack's mother sounded genuinely pleased. Zack felt rotten about deceiving her, but he had to humor Marsh until his share of the family stock was safely in Cole, Junior's—or Tess, Junior's—name. For years Marsh had threatened to sell controlling interest in Bailey Baby Products to strangers because none of his grandsons showed any interest whatsoever in the business. If he did, his mother's chances of remaining as CEO were slight. Zack was doing this for her even if she wouldn't approve of his mock engagement.

After a lot more chitchat and another round of hugging between everyone but him and Megan, the ordeal was over.

"Come on, sweetheart. It's time I get you all to myself," he murmured loudly enough to be overheard.

"Whatever you say, darling."

They were two steps outside the closed front door when she whipped out her cell phone.

"What are you doing?" He edged in close behind her in case Marsh was watching through the window.

"Calling for a ride, you low-down skunk. I know what you're up to. You're going to make me the bad guy. I'll have to dump you because my career is more important than my fiancé."

"That's one way to do it," he said cautiously, not willing to admit he'd been doing exactly that.

"How can I face a sweet person like your mom with that phony story?"

"You won't have to. I'll tell her when it's time."

"Why don't you just grow up and settle down?"

She was furiously pushing numbers. He grabbed the phone and turned it off.

"Give that back!"

"No, I'm taking you home. And don't worry, I'm not coming in."

"I wouldn't let you if you were the last man on earth."

She got her hand on the phone, but he didn't let go.

"You're not calling a cab."

"No, I'm calling a friend."

"A girlfriend?"

"It's none of your business."

He hated the idea that she could be calling a man. Somewhere along the way he'd gotten the impression she wasn't currently seeing anyone.

What he was thinking wasn't a good plan, but he couldn't come up with anything else. He scooped her up in his arms, taking her by surprise and allowing her to do a minimum amount of kicking and squirming.

"Put me down, you overbearing bully!"

"No way, and stop yelling. Do you want the neighbors to call the police?" he said, carrying her to the car.

"You're worried about your grandfather, not neighbors."

Trees and the gentle swell of the land blocked the nearest houses from sight, but he could practically feel Marsh's eyes through the opaque front window. He shut her up the only way he could—a long, hard kiss on her open mouth.

He let her slide to her feet beside the car while he opened the door, then he blocked the escape route, giving her no choice but to get inside.

He buckled her in and furiously ordered her to quiet down. Amazingly, she did. Maybe she was too mad to say another word.

The long, silent ride home seemed to confirm it.

He stopped on the street in front of her apartment building, not even bothering to drive around to the rear entrance she usually used.

"Good night," he said stiffly.

She didn't bother to respond.

This was going to be a very short engagement.

11

ZACK'S HEAD ACHED, and his throat was scratchy. His nose was stuffy, and his eyes had gray shadows under them. He had a genuine summer cold, not serious enough to keep him from going to work but the best excuse he'd had yet for not taping another show.

Unfortunately, Megan wouldn't buy it, and he couldn't blame her. The dumbest thing he'd done since they met was pretend to be sick—and get caught.

He showed up at the studio for yet another farcical guest appearance. Ed had called to be sure he would be there. The Good Living Network was taking a second look at Megan's show.

He must have been crazy to agree to do twelve stints.

He and Megan hadn't spoken since the dinner at Marsh's, his fault more than hers. He didn't know what to say about the whole fiasco, and they'd moved beyond recriminations and apologies.

There was more wrong with him than a head cold. He was so eager to see her, he forgot his usual preshow jitters.

"Zack, I have some people who'd like to meet you," Ed said, waylaying him in the reception area before he could find Megan.

"Where's Megan?"

"Around here somewhere. Come on."

The ex-jock could really move when he was motivated.

Zack followed him to the set, refusing to break into a trot to keep up.

"Here he is, folks," Ed said jovially, leading him to a pair of Good Living Network execs.

Zack shook hands with a skinny woman in a black suit and the head honcho, an Oklahoma good ol' boy in jeans who'd parlayed a single radio station into a broadcasting empire based in New York. They played good-guy, bad-girl with him, the boss glad-handing while his skeletal sidekick tried to pump him about how he liked working with Megan.

He said a lot of good things about her but didn't mention she sometimes drove him crazy with her lists and scripts and goals.

Where the devil was she?

"Better get to makeup," Ed said at last, releasing him from the cross fire of questions.

He was glad to escape the grilling.

"Hey, you look lousy today."

Julie the intern was doing his makeup today, obviously a learning experience for her.

"Hold still, I have to do something about your eyes," she ordered with the voice of newly received authority.

She smeared brownish makeup on his face while he impatiently watched the open doorway hoping to see Megan.

Ed had a surprise for him. He brought a bright blue T-shirt with the station logo while Zack was still sneezing from a blizzard of powder. Julie was nothing if not heavy-handed.

"Matching shirts for you and Megan," the producer said enthusiastically.

"I haven't worn a twin outfit since my brother and I

escaped the child-model business,'' he grumbled unhappily, but went off to put it on.

Megan looked a hell of a lot better than he did in the shirt. His was a size smaller than he liked, but hers was like a second skin worn with white jeans so tight she probably wasn't wearing panties under them. Bright lights, tight clothes and cameras rolling—the perfect combination to insure he'd really look like an idiot on this show.

"Hello, Zack," Megan said.

"How do you like being a twin?"

"It was *not* my idea, but I can't kill Ed in front of the Good Living execs. You look lousy. Maybe I should redo your makeup."

"Julie did a good job. I just have a summer cold."

"Yeah, and I have purple-spotted parrot pox."

She flounced to a decrepit old dresser with sagging drawers, broken knobs and loose veneer.

He looked from the piece of junk to the tools assembled on a nearby table. Zack had nixed using his own because they were more sophisticated than their audience was likely to own.

"What do we have here, a tornado survivor?" he asked, ambling over to Megan.

"Can you just for once approach a project without your negative attitude?"

"Okay, okay, whatever you say."

She was obviously nervous about having the New York execs in the audience again. He resolved to help her look good even though he was beginning to hate the idea of her show leaving Detroit.

It was what she wanted, and he could use it to explain why they weren't getting married. Still, it was a lousy move.

He walked around the junky dresser wanting to smash it to kindling with his fists. It had about as much potential as his phony engagement.

Megan gave her introduction, and he marveled at the way she put a positive spin on the project of the day.

"Hopeless, isn't it?" she asked as the camera went in for a close-up. "But you'll be amazed at how it will look with some easy repairs."

The white jeans were a mistake. She had the best rear end in the city, arguably the country. Who wanted to look at a heap of scrap lumber when she was walking around looking so cute? He felt light-headed.

"First we repair the drawers and add new knobs, then we'll be tackling the veneer," she said, sounding genuinely enthusiastic. "And here's everyone's favorite home repairman, Zack Bailey of Bailey Construction."

The thunderous applause made him feel like a fraud. If it weren't for Megan and his deal with her, he wouldn't waste thirty seconds on the wretched old dresser.

They had to work fast. She was promising more than was reasonable in one short episode, no matter how the final product was edited. The drawer went smoothly enough because it was nailed together, not dovetailed like fine old furniture.

"As you can see, the knobs are in bad shape," she said, introducing the next step. "Zack, how would you go about removing the old ones?"

He'd use an electric screwdriver, but the script called for a manual one. He got down on his knees to remove the one she'd indicated.

It stuck. He sat on the floor and strained to turn the corroded old screw from inside the front of the drawer while the camera hovered, watching him sweat.

"Zack's not up to full strength today." She joked to cover the delay.

He gave her a malevolent glance and dug at the wood next to the screw with the tip of the tool. It was mealy, confirming his low opinion of the dresser. He gouged some more and managed to extract the screw.

Megan gave him her hand and pulled him to his feet. Next she'd be patting his old gray head and recommending a rest home.

He got through the remainder of the show. No question, she'd looked a whole lot better than he did on this episode.

"Thanks, Zack," she said for his ears only.

"It's in my contract," he said morosely. "Good luck with the Happy Living people."

"Good Living."

"Won't Gunderdorf make you work out your contract here?" He felt a glimmer of hope.

"That's not how it works. If they want the show—if—they'll buy up my contract along with rights to the show. Gunderdorf will make out very nicely, plus he'll get the prestige of moving one of his shows to the national level."

"Well, if that's what you want, I hope things work out."

He stalked out of there, not even bothering to take off the ridiculous T-shirt.

BY THE END of the workweek Megan thought she'd have kittens before Gunderdorf's lawyers and the Good Living Network finished their negotiations. They wanted the show and they wanted her. The only issue was money, that and Zack's contract. They seemed to think he'd object to being written out and paid off. She knew he'd be delighted to get out of more appearances, but no one asked her. It was the oddest sensation she'd ever experienced, waiting for other people to determine the course her life would take.

The Good Living Network could put her at the pinnacle of her career. She could start concentrating on the other things she wanted—a loving husband and children. She couldn't allow herself to think about Zack. He didn't want a wife, and he didn't want her. She'd worked long and hard for this opportunity, but now that it was so close, she felt vaguely uneasy, not nearly as excited as she'd expected to be.

She was ready to go home for the day when Ed came to her office and shut the door behind her.

Was he there with bad news and didn't want anyone to overhear her reaction? She braced herself.

"It's a wrap," he said, grinning.

"They're buying the show?"

"Sure are. Joe will go over the terms with you Monday, but most you already know. You'll have to move to New York City, of course, and Zack doesn't figure into the new format."

"New format? I thought they liked my concept."

"They do, but the title is still up in the air. It will be their call. Lydia, your new executive producer, thought 'Do It Herself' is a little cutesy."

"Cutesy? What else didn't she like?"

"Well, she's enthusiastic about you. That's what counts. They have a soap opera actor who's auditioning for the role of your partner...."

"Partner? I don't want a co-host."

"Well, they'll work something out. They liked the way you and Zack bounce off each other, but it's a job for a professional actor."

She should feel elated. At last she'd be a personality on a national cable network. But what was this dull, hollow sensation in the pit of her stomach?

"Thanks for telling me, Ed."

"More good news. The whole gang here at the studio wants to say goodbye in style."

"I'm not leaving yet."

This was happening too fast. Maybe she wasn't as ready as she'd thought.

"You'll be out of here soon," Ed said. "The New York team doesn't waste time. Anyway, we're having a big party for you tomorrow night. Call it a celebration of your new job if you like. Even Mr. G. will be there. I'll get back to you on the time and place. Congratulations, little sis."

He kissed her forehead. Ed was usually as demonstrative as the Sphinx. She had to fight an unaccountable urge to weep.

"Thanks, Ed."

SATURDAY CAME too soon. Megan put on her little black party dress and drove herself to Roma's Ristorante, but she didn't feel ready to say goodbye to her co-workers. She was going to miss them all, even Brad who did everything in slow motion.

She made her way to the private room in the rear wondering how Ed had put together the celebration on such short notice. She'd be willing to bet Roma's would be getting a bargain rate on some airtime.

Everyone was there ahead of her. She walked into a room with streamers hanging from the ceiling and Mr. Gunderdorf, all five feet two inches of him, holding court by a portable bar. The Bulgarian chef was behind him trying to edge closer, and the dog man was nipping at his heels. Who would be the lucky one to get her time spot?

She made her way toward her boss, exchanging hugs along the way. Brad surprised her with a robust squeeze that was more than borderline cheeky. Mr. Gunderdorf rescued her.

"Megan, I'm very proud of you," he said warmly.

He might be short, but he was elegant in a dove-gray suit made by the Leonardo of Italian tailors. His carefully sculpted hair reminded her of someone—yes, Marsh Bailey. They both made growing old look good.

People continued enthusing over her opportunity, but she knew she'd be there for next week's show. She didn't feel ready for goodbyes yet.

The person she really wanted to talk to was nowhere in sight. She circulated, her eyes never straying from the door for long. Certainly Zack had been invited. Where was he?

The huge Italian buffet covered four big tables against the back wall. Her nephew, Jason, was first in line and was wrapping long strands of spaghetti noodles around his neck. Megan looked around for his keepers, but Ed was deep in conversation with Gunderdorf. Her grandfather was talking with a flame-haired woman she didn't recognize—maybe someone connected with the restaurant—and they looked too chummy to interrupt.

Georgia, slightly pudgy but still striking with blond hair upswept and a floor-length plum-colored dress, was having an animated conversation with the Bulgarian chef. She was trying to sell him on making her chocolate-marshmallow-cookie torte on his show, great publicity for her book if she ever finished it.

Megan had decided to tackle the kid with the spaghetti

necktie herself before he got creative with something hotter and messier when Zack walked up to her.

"Are you sure you want kids?" he asked, nodding at Jason, who was twirling another strand of spaghetti.

"Yes. Don't you?"

"Not in the foreseeable future. I don't think I'd be a very good father."

He'd make a wonderful father, but she couldn't tell him that.

"Aunt Megan! Look what I made!"

Jason, towheaded and dimpled like a kindergarten angel, was waving a spaghetti lariat, several strands of warm pasta mushed together.

"Come on," Zack said. "Let's find someplace private to talk."

He took her hand and pulled her down a back corridor with rest rooms and an emergency exit. Zack looked around and saw a pylon the custodian used when the floor was wet.

"Anyone in here?" he called into the women's room, then declared it unoccupied.

He dropped the pylon in front of the door, flipped over the wooden Women plaque hanging on a chain and pulled her into the rest room.

"You can't come in here."

"I just did."

"People will want to get in."

"There's another one in front."

He leaned against the door while Jason rattled the handle and called her name.

"Shush," Zack said, laying a finger across her lips.

She could hear the plastic pylon thudding in front of the door.

"Clever kid. Trying to use it like a pogo stick," Zack said.

There was a sudden silence, more ominous than Jason's noisy antics.

"I'm mad at you, Aunt Megan. I don't like you anymore."

She started to go after him, but Zack was still blocking the door.

"He'll get over it."

"I guess." She wanted to be with Zack, not baby-sit.

"We have to talk about our engagement," he said.

"Oh, that."

She feigned indifference, but her heart was doing crazy flip-flops.

"I couldn't be engaged to a nicer person," he said. "I'm really happy for you. You'll wow 'em in New York."

"I'm not so sure...."

"I've tried and tried to tell Marsh I'm not husband material. Just because Cole is high on being married doesn't mean it would work for me. I think deep down he always wanted that kind of permanence. I'm more realistic."

"That's a strange kind of realism."

She didn't want to hear more. Whatever he had to say, she was pretty sure it would hurt.

Someone pounded on the door he was holding shut.

"Go away!" he shouted.

"You can't hold the fort here much longer," she warned.

"I don't have that much more to say, just wish you luck. I'm too much like my birth father to offer anything else. He wasn't one to stick around, either."

She looked at the fancy pink sink and the coral tiles

surrounding it. This wasn't the kind of goodbye party she'd expected.

"I take it you're breaking our engagement," she said dryly.

"You're leaving me," he said grimly.

"What about your grandfather?"

"He'll have to understand. You're putting your career first and running off to New York. I'll be so brokenhearted I won't want anything to do with women—at least not until Tess has her baby. I just found out I'm going to be an uncle."

"Congratulations, but you're making me sound terrible! If I loved someone, and he loved me, I'd never leave."

He had the grace to look distressed, but it wasn't enough.

"What will your mother think? You're making me look shallow, self-centered…"

You're neither of those. Anyway, Mom is thrilled at the prospect of being a grandmother. She can handle a broken engagement."

"I hate being the bad guy!"

"You're not. Anyway, Marsh never entirely bought our act. He doesn't think you like me much."

"Well, he's right! I can't believe I wanted your advice."

"On what?"

She tried not to look at his one raised eyebrow or the way his eyes narrowed.

"It doesn't matter."

"No, tell me."

"Let me out of here."

"Not until you tell me what's worrying you."

He folded his arms across his chest and looked ready to block her way indefinitely.

"I've been mulling over the offer for my show. They're not giving me much control over it. Already they're auditioning a soap actor to be my partner. It's not going to be the same show."

"It's your big chance," he said reassuringly. "The better your ratings on the new network, the more say you'll have. It's natural to have some doubts about a big move like this."

He was so darn right, but this wasn't the response she longed to hear. The way she'd imagined it, he was supposed to admit he loved her and beg her to stay.

"I guess we should go to the buffet now," she said, instead of telling him how she really felt.

"I'm not staying for dinner," he said softly. "Tonight is all yours. I don't belong here—never did. You enjoy."

Yeah, enjoy.

How could she, when she was the least excited person in the room? She was going because there was no reason not to.

"Go. Have a good life," he said, touching her forehead with his lips.

"Is that all you have to say?"

Say you love me! Don't let me go! A little voice in her head was going bonkers.

"Don't forget how to install floating shelves."

He opened the door enough to slip out. She heard a clatter as he left.

He'd kicked the custodian's pylon down the corridor.

12

"WHAT DO YOU MEAN you're not going?" Ed bounded around his desk so fast his shoulder knocked a whole row of framed football photos into a crooked jumble.

"I'm not signing with the Good Living Network," Megan said. "They want a blonde who talks, not the person I am. I could be stuck doing anything they dream up—crocodile wrestling, home surgery, assault weapons for women. Their contract takes away my freedom."

She knew this was going to be Black Monday in the studio, and she really felt bad about Ed's disappointment. Her move up would've looked great on his résumé if he ever wanted to activate it.

"The lawyers will be here at eleven. It's all set," he insisted.

"No, I told Mr. Gunderdorf to cancel."

"How did he take it?"

"Pretty well, all things considered. He wants to keep 'Do It Herself' in the same time slot if Zack will still make occasional appearances."

"We're toast," Ed said glumly, pacing his tiny office and knocking another row of football stuff off-kilter. "Unless I can convince Bailey to—"

"No!"

"I'm sure we can come up with something if we put our heads together."

"Please, please, please, leave Zack to me," she pleaded.

"Well, if you think…"

"I definitely do. I'm sorry, Ed. You worked hard getting the opportunity for me. It was a wonderful party, too. I don't know how to thank you."

"No problem. It was Mr. G.'s treat. He thinks a lot of you."

"I hope this doesn't hurt your career. You're still stuck with 'Do It Herself.'"

"I have a few ideas about revamping the show. The title, for instance…"

"We'll talk," she promised, "but not now."

She started to leave, and Ed followed her to the corridor.

"You know," he said, lowering his voice to a husky whisper, "I was slated to be the Bulgarian's chef's fourth producer in five years. I'm glad to be back on your team."

"Thanks." She smiled. "But don't do anything about Zack. Promise!"

"Yeah, sure."

Two down, one to go. Gunderdorf and Ed had taken her decision better than she'd expected considering they would both lose money. Ed would have gotten a nice bonus as part of the compensation package, and she'd been surprised at the amount the Good Living Network had been willing to pay the station owner. But all they wanted was a talking head. She'd be a pawn in the ratings game with no creative control whatsoever. It wasn't what she wanted.

Telling Zack wouldn't be as easy as disappointing Ed and Gunderdorf, but at least she could throw away her lists and forget about goals. She loved Zack, and any future without him seemed bleak and purposeless. Maybe he would never marry her. She had to face the possibility that he didn't love her, but being with him wasn't an aspiration. It was a necessity. Her future and her happiness were in his hands.

Unfortunately he didn't know it, and he might not like it.

Megan took a deep breath. She had a lot of thinking to do.

ZACK KNEW he'd have to talk to Megan soon. She'd been leaving messages on his machine for two days, and every time he heard her voice he felt worse.

She was leaving. Even if he could stop her, he wouldn't. She deserved her chance on the national network.

He was in the company office going over a bid they were submitting on a school addition. Cole reached for the phone first and ignored Zack's negative signals. He wasn't ready to talk to Megan.

"Sure, he's right here, Megan," his treacherous twin said.

Cole handed over the phone with the goofy grin he'd been wearing since Tess confirmed the good news about the baby.

"Hi."

Zack listened, frowned, protested and listened some more.

"I can't believe that woman!" He slammed the receiver down so hard Cole raised his eyebrows. "She expects me to drop everything and rush to the studio to tape a show. I thought by now she'd be packed and out of town. Ed told me at the party they wouldn't need me this week."

"We can finish this after lunch," Cole said mildly.

"There's no reason I should go."

It was pure bluster, and he knew it. He'd go to the studio, but not because he still owed them some appearances. He wanted to see Megan, no matter how much it would hurt to say goodbye again.

He walked into her dressing room twenty-nine minutes later with a speeding ticket stuck in his back pocket.

"You could've given me more notice," he said, some of his anger dissolving when he saw her. "I didn't get a script this week. What's the show about today?"

"There's no show. They're using a rerun tomorrow."

"I drove like the devil was on my tail to get here. Got my first speeding ticket in years."

"You did that for me?"

"I did it so I could tell you I'm sick of television and I'm not on call for this lousy business anymore."

He turned to leave when something fluttered down on his head.

"What's this?" As if he didn't know.

Megan had thrown her silky blue blouse at him.

"Another performance?" he asked incredulously when he turned and saw her in a lacy lavender bra.

"I just want to talk to you. I've left enough messages to feel officially ignored."

"Well, this is some conversation starter."

He shut the door and pushed the handle to lock it. Whatever she had to say, he didn't want an audience.

"Do I have your full attention now?" she asked in a husky little voice as her miniskirt slid down her legs.

"What do you want?"

It was all he could do not to take her in his arms, but curiosity restrained him.

"I want you to do more shows. Not on a regular schedule. Just occasional guest appearances."

"I'm not going all the way to New York to make an idiot of myself."

He moved so close he could smell her flowery fragrance. She was beautiful and tempting, but vulnerable in a way that made his heart feel crowded in his chest.

"Not in New York," she said softly.

"You're doing more shows here before you go?"

"I'm staying here."

He moved closer and put his hand on her shoulder, looking into suspiciously moist blue eyes.

"But the opportunity—your goal…"

"I threw away all my lists."

"I thought I'd lost you," he whispered, hardly recognizing his own voice.

"How did you feel about that?"

"Miserable, rotten, more scared than I was the first time those cameras zeroed in on me."

He kissed her slowly, drawing out the exquisite pleasure of feeling connected to her.

"I have to tell you something," he murmured, lifting her onto the edge of the dressing table and ignoring a loud thud as something fell.

She wrapped her legs around his hips and pulled him closer.

"I want you," she moaned.

"You have me."

He bent his head to taste her lips, cupping her breasts and stroking the satiny fabric that held them. She caressed his face, his throat, his back with an urgency that matched his.

"I wish we could—here—now…" she murmured.

"We can."

"You don't have your auto-club guide, do you?"

"Does it matter?" he asked. "I would never put you at risk."

"You don't want children."

"It might not be so bad—if they didn't turn out like your nephew."

He slid his fingers under the elastic of her panties and leaned closer.

A loud knock startled them apart.

"Ignore it," he urged.

The pounding grew louder, more insistent.

"Megan!"

"It's Ed," she whispered. "He won't go away unless I answer. I'm busy right now," she called.

"I'll bet. I saw Bailey pull into the parking lot. But we've run into a glitch with today's show."

"We're using a rerun," she said loudly.

"We can't! They let Brad cover the reception desk while the regular girl was on vacation. He forgot about the rerun and gave out enough tickets to fill the Silver Dome. It's standing room only out there. I know Zack's still here. We have to tape a show. I've got the scripts here for the bookcase segment."

Megan looked at Zack with a sheepish little grin.

"Oh, let's do it," he said. "I've forgotten where we were anyway."

"I'll bet!" she slid off the dressing table into his arms and called to Ed on the other side of the door. "Okay, stall them while we get into makeup."

"No makeup for me!" Zack said, touching her breasts one more time for good luck.

"Okay, but I need a little."

He loved watching her hustle into her clothes and work makeup magic she didn't need to be the most beautiful woman he'd ever seen. When she was done, she sat him down and tried to comb his windblown hair.

"I give up. You're gorgeous," she said.

"Don't bend over in that skirt," he warned, "at least not for the audience."

"I'll wear the custodian's overalls if it will make you happy."

"I'm happy already—or I will be when this is over. Let's do it."

They rushed out, scanned their copies of the script and made sure the cue cards were in place. He had to hand it to Ed. The ex-jock could still move fast when he had to. There were enough planks, glass cubes, recycled bricks, plastic milk crates and assorted odds and ends to assemble temporary bookshelves for a whole college dorm.

"What do you do when you have more books than money and no place to keep them?" Megan began her introduction, a slight flush betraying what they'd been doing only minutes before.

They had a full house watching them. The projects were easy, and he was pretty sure they wouldn't take long enough to fill the time. That meant lots of questions from the audience, his least favorite part of the show.

Today it didn't matter. He had a plan of his own.

When the last demonstration was over, he stepped closer to the audience, trying to ignore the camera that was recording his every move.

"Usually we take questions from the audience at this time," he said, feeling the sweat trickling down his back. "Today I'm going to do the asking. Come here, Megan."

He knew she hated losing control of her show, but she came, puzzled but docile.

He had to do it fast or let stage fright get the best of him.

"Megan, I don't always follow the script. This time I don't need one. I want you to be my wife."

She opened her mouth, but no sound came out.

He took both her hands and looked into her sparkling eyes.

"Megan, will you marry me?"

The audience was so quiet the huge studio seemed deserted, but Megan was the only one he saw anyway.

"Yes, I think I will."

"You think?" He could feel his heart pounding. This was worse than his first time on her show.

"Yes, I will."

The audience gave a collective sigh, and pandemonium broke out.

"Zack, you're the last sexy bachelor in Detroit. What will we do if you get married?" a particularly loud fan yelled.

"Don't worry, darlin'. I've got a younger brother who's a whole lot cuter than me."

The audience surged forward, and Ed gamely went out to block. Zack grabbed Megan's hand, and they ran for the dressing room.

"I have to get back to work," he said, guessing the odds against quality time alone right now were about a zillion to one. "I'll call you tonight. We need to talk."

"Do we!"

He kissed her quickly and left through the back emergency exit.

MEGAN UNDERSTOOD when Zack couldn't come to see her that evening. One of his men got hurt on a job site, and Zack spent the better part of the night in the emergency room, then drove the worker home to the downriver community of Wyandotte.

On Thursday a big basket of flowers, a dozen varieties in shades of pink and deep rose with touches of white, was delivered just after she got home from work. She removed the card from a little envelope and smiled in spite of her disappointment that Zack hadn't sent them.

You'll like him better after you're married. I guarantee it. Welcome to the Bailey family. Affectionately, Marsh.

There was also a terse message on her answering machine. Zack couldn't get there that evening, either, something about an urgent trip out of town.

The man proposed and disappeared. He hadn't even said he loved her yet!

Was the on-air proposal just another stunt for his grandfather? She loved Zack so much it hurt. How could he ignore her like this when she was dying to see him?

Somehow she got through Friday. When she got home, her answering machine was blinking again. There was another terse message—"See you tonight."

She showered and put on a new yellow teddy and a short, silky robe with riotous tropical flowers in shades of orange, yellow and pink, a cool way to lounge on a hot summer night. Wearing it had nothing to do with Zack. Even if he did show up, she wasn't sure she'd let him in.

Was she fooling herself or what? When her doorbell sounded, she bounded to the door in three giant leaps, then counted to fifty so he wouldn't think she was eager.

"Hi."

He smiled, and she forgot everything she'd planned to say about men who proposed and vanished. Their eyes met, and she didn't even care that the door across the landing opened a few inches.

"Are you going to ask me in?"

She saw a wisp of white hair and an inquisitive blue eye peering out of her neighbor's apartment.

"I guess." She quickly closed the door behind him.

The first thing he did was walk to the laundry-basket-size arrangement of flowers that nearly covered the top of the end table beside her couch.

"Who sent the flowers?"

She'd lived to hear jealousy from Bailey.

"Your grandfather. How could you ask me to marry you, then drop out of sight? Was it an act for Marsh?"

"No, hell, no! I meant it, but I still don't understand why you're not taking the job."

"So where have you been?"

"In a minute." He tried to kiss her, but she turned her head.

"First things first," she insisted.

"Okay, why are you staying?"

She still hadn't heard the magic words, but now that Zack was here, she couldn't hold back the whole truth.

"Taking it would mean leaving you."

"I don't want you to sacrifice your career for me."

"New York isn't what I want. I have a life here."

"I see."

"How's the man who got hurt?"

"He'll draw disability for awhile, but it's nothing serious. I have to tell you where I went yesterday."

He put his arm around her shoulders and drew her down on the couch beside him. His voice made her uneasy, and she dreaded what he might say.

"I went to see my birth father. He lives in Ohio, just a couple of hours away."

"You've never met him before?"

"No, but Marsh fessed up when I insisted on knowing

where he is. My grandfather arranged an out-of-state job for him when he wanted to get rid of him. My mother was seventeen, and he wasn't much older. I guess a pay check was a lot better than taking on Marsh.''

''It must have been hard for you to see him for the first time.''

''I had to meet him to learn something about myself.'' He paused and took her hands in his. ''I've always thought I was tainted by bad blood, that a permanent relationship was contrary to my nature.''

Now she really was scared.

''Then Cole got married, and I fell in love.''

She inhaled deeply, not realizing she'd been holding her breath.

''I didn't find what I expected,'' he went on. ''He isn't an irresponsible failure. He's been married for over twenty-five years, has three kids and expects a second grandchild soon.''

''Did you like him?''

''That's a moot point. It's too late for us to have a father-son relationship. Anyway, I had a great stepdad. That wasn't the reason I went to see my birth father. I just had to see for myself that running out on Mom, Cole and me had nothing to do with the gene pool. He and my mother were both kids, too young to raise children. It doesn't excuse Marsh's high-handedness, but he was right about a teenager as a husband.''

''You waited so long to find him.''

She was in awe of what he'd done. It took a kind of courage that made stage fright seem trivial.

''I've never been in love before.''

He said it so softly she had to look at his face to be sure she'd heard it.

''I love you, Megan.''

"I love you, too!"

He scooped her up in his arms. She'd never again complain about being carried.

"Did you wear this for me?"

He laid her on the bed and hovered over her, untying her sash and nuzzling the lacy neckline of her teddy.

"There's a prize if you can figure out how to get it off," she said.

"Can I use my tool kit?"

"You won't need it."

She wiggled away and stood beside the bed, slowly tossing aside the bright tropical wrap. With bumps, grinds and giggles, she made short work of stripping off the teddy and kicking her mules across the room.

"I've imagined the end of your act a few times," he admitted.

"But have you imagined this?"

She came down beside him and slowly peeled up the red knit shirt he was wearing.

"Let me..." he said.

"Oh, no." She straddled his legs, her back toward him, trying to ignore the fingers playing along her spine.

His shoes had ties and were hard to pull off, but darned if even his toes weren't adorable under heavy white cotton socks.

"Now the hard part," she teased.

"You're driving me crazy."

He lifted his hips to help her free his khaki slacks.

He moaned when she deliberately fumbled with his navy briefs, reaching under them and finding the brush of silky hair.

"I want to produce *this* show," she said.

"Madame Producer, I'll do your show a thousand times if you'll keep doing that."

She giggled, tossed aside his underwear, then gasped with pleasure when she lowered herself.

"Now what do you think of home handicraft for girls?"

"I'm speechless."

So was she. Some things didn't require a script.

Later, when the room was dark and she was sure Zack would hold her forever because neither of them could move, Zack asked, "When will you marry me?"

"Is tomorrow too soon?"

"Don't you have to plan a wedding, make lists, et cetera, et cetera, et cetera?"

"Nope." She cuddled closer and wondered if anything on earth felt more glorious than lying in the arms of the man she loved.

"No lists, no plans, no goals?" he teased.

"One goal—marry the man I love and adore."

"I've got that covered," he whispered, drawing her closer still.

Brimming with passion and sensuality,
this collection offers two full-length
Harlequin Temptation novels.

Full Bloom

by *New York Times* bestselling author

JAYNE
ANN
KRENTZ

Emily Ravenscroft has had enough! It's time she took her life back,
out of the hands of her domineering family and Jacob Stone, the
troubleshooter they've always employed to get her out of hot water.
The new Emily—vibrant and willful—doesn't need Jacob to rescue
her. She needs him to love her, against all odds.

And

Compromising Positions

a brand-new story from bestselling author

VICKY LEWIS
THOMPSON

Look for it on sale September 2001.

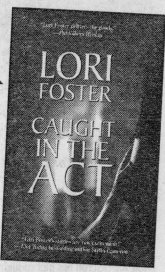

#1 *New York Times* Bestselling Author

NORA ROBERTS

**Will enchant readers with two
remarkable tales of timeless love.**

Coming in September 2001

TIME AND AGAIN

Two brothers from the future cross centuries to
find a love more powerful than time itself in the
arms of two beguiling sisters.

Available at your favorite retail outlet.

Silhouette®
Where love comes alive™

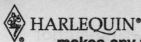